Abou...

After leaving her conv... studied the cello befor... embraced the emerging... as a programmer ende... daughters and bought a ... semi-rural community. She yearned to find a creative career from which she could earn money. When her sister suggested writing romances, it seemed like a good idea. She could do it at home, and it might even be fun! She never looked back.

Kim Lawrence was encouraged by her husband to write when the unsocial hours of nursing didn't look attractive! He told her she could do anything she set her mind to, so Kim tried her hand at writing. Always a keen Mills & Boon reader, it seemed natural for her to write a romance novel – now she can't imagine doing anything else. She is a keen gardener and cook and enjoys running on the beach with her Jack Russell. Kim lives in Wales.

When Canadian **Dani Collins** found romance novels in high school, she wondered how one trained for such an awesome job. She wrote for over two decades without publishing, but remained inspired by the romance message that if you hang in there you'll find a happy ending. In May of 2012, Harlequin Presents bought her manuscript in a two-book deal. She's since published more than forty books with Mills & Boon and is definitely living happily ever after.

Confessions

Confessions of the Maid

MIRANDA LEE

KIM LAWRENCE

DANI COLLINS

MILLS & BOON

First Published in Great Britain 2022
By Mills & Boon, an imprint of HarperCollins*Publishers*
1 London Bridge Street, London, SE1 9GF

www.harpercollins.co.uk

HarperCollins*Publishers*
1st Floor, Watermarque Building,
Ringsend Road, Dublin 4, Ireland

CONFESSIONS OF THE MAID © 2022 Harlequin Enterprises ULC.

Maid for the Untamed Billionaire © 2019 Miranda Lee
Maid for Montero © 2013 Kim Lawrence
The Maid's Spanish Secret © 2019 Dani Collins

ISBN: 978-0-263-31798-5

MIX
Paper | Supporting
responsible forestry
FSC™ C007454

This book is produced from independently certified FSC™ paper to ensure responsible forest management.

For more information visit: www.harpercollins.co.uk/green

Printed and Bound in Spain using 100% Renewable electricity at CPI Black Print, Barcelona

MAID FOR THE UNTAMED BILLIONAIRE

MIRANDA LEE

Dedicated to my sister, Wendy.
A lovely lady and my best friend.

PROLOGUE

JAKE NEEDED A HOUSEKEEPER.

But not the live-in kind. The last thing he wanted was someone underfoot all the time, picking up after him, forcing him to make conversation and invading his space. The reason Jake had bought a house a few years ago was to have his own space.

After spending weeks in hospital and then another month at the rehabilitation clinic, he'd wanted nothing more than to be by himself. So he'd turned down the offers to live with relatives and bought this place in East Balmain, calling it a thirtieth birthday present to himself.

He'd thought he could make do with a cleaner coming in three times a week. And he *had* managed—in a fashion, even in the beginning when he'd been pretty useless, his leg still not totally healed. He'd shopped online and sent his laundry out, a routine he'd continued even after he was fully better and back working.

But it had finally become tedious, seeing to all the other chores which owning and maintaining a house involved. He loathed having to wait for tradespeople, who didn't always turn up on time. Patience was not his strong suit.

Jake could well afford to pay someone to do everything for him. He'd already been a wealthy man before the success of his television show, so it had never been a matter of money. More of privacy.

Not that he had much privacy any more, his star having risen over the last couple of years, his every move recorded on social media and in the gossip rags.

But not at home. His home was his sanctuary, as well as his castle. So it was imperative that Jake find the right kind of housekeeper, a task which had proven to be much more difficult than he'd assumed, mostly because he simply hadn't *liked* any of the women he'd interviewed for the position.

It was silly, really, given he wouldn't have to have anything much to do with the woman on a personal basis. His brief to the various employment agencies was for his housekeeper to work only during the week, not at the weekends. She was to come in after he left for work every weekday morning, and be gone by the time he arrived home, which often wasn't until quite late. Producing and hosting *Australia at Noon* consumed every minute of every weekday from morning until late afternoon.

So it shouldn't really matter whether he liked his housekeeper or not.

But he couldn't stomach the thought of someone he didn't like in his personal space when he wasn't there.

The main problem was that every woman he'd interviewed so far had been a big fan of his show. Not a crime, admittedly. But irritating. They had all been way too gushy. And way too eager.

Jake was suspicious of eager, especially when it came to women. A flaw, he supposed, common with confirmed bachelors. Still, he kept picturing them putting things about their *wonderful* new job and their *wonderful* new boss on all the social media sites they would invariably be on, complete with photos.

The upshot was he hadn't hired any of them, and was instead waiting for another candidate to arrive, sent out by Housewives For Hire, a newish employment agency, the owner of which had fortuitously appeared on a segment of his show a few days ago.

Her agency promised to provide exactly the sort of employee he was looking for. Apparently, the women on their books were mostly housewives themselves, wanting to earn extra money whilst their children were at school.

He'd rung the lady who owned the agency the other night—her name was Barbara—explaining what kind of housekeeper he needed. He'd asked her to find him someone suitable, preferably a woman who didn't obsessively watch his show and think he was God's gift to women.

She'd promised to find him the right person.

So here he was, sitting in his study at five to two on a Saturday afternoon, waiting to interview Barbara's top recommendation, but thinking to himself he was possibly wasting his time again.

This woman Barbara was sending him was way too young for starters. Only twenty-six. And a widow no less. How on earth had that happened?

Barbara hadn't said and he hadn't liked to ask.

Jake sighed. A car accident, he supposed. Or an illness of some kind.

At least she didn't have children. Nothing sadder than a young widow trying to raise children alone. Nothing tougher, either.

This young woman—her name was Abby Jenkins—was apparently looking for work and wasn't qualified for much, her very short CV showing she had left high school at seventeen to work in a fish and chip shop till she'd married at twenty, shortly after which she'd left to become a stay-at-home housewife.

A strange choice for a modern young woman. Rather old-fashioned, in Jake's opinion. Made her sound a little odd. He didn't fancy employing odd.

But he would give her a chance. Everyone deserved a chance.

He heard a car pull up outside. A glance at his watch showed it was right on two. She was punctual at least.

Jake stood up and made his way from the study to the front door, arriving in time to unlock the deadbolt just as the doorbell rang. He took a deep breath and opened the door, not sure what to expect.

His breath caught at the sight of a very pretty blonde whose lovely green eyes were looking up at him with a decidedly worried expression. No, not worried. Nervous. The girl was terribly nervous, chewing at her bottom lip and clutching the strap of her black shoulder bag as if it were a lifeline.

He supposed it was only natural that she'd be nervous. Barbara had mentioned that this was the girl's first job interview for her agency. Possibly it was her first job interview ever.

Jake's eyes flicked over the rest of her appearance.

She was wearing dark blue jeans and a cream crocheted top, their snug fit showing a very good figure. Her honey-blonde hair was long and straight, pulled back into a low ponytail. She wasn't wearing make-up, not even lipstick. It pleased Jake that she hadn't dolled herself up like some of the other women he'd interviewed.

'Mr Sanderson?' she asked hesitantly.

Jake's eyebrows rose at the realisation that she didn't recognise him. Which meant she hadn't ever watched his show, or any of the documentaries he'd made over the years.

He didn't know whether to be happy or hurt, which was ironic.

Either way, it was still a positive factor. He definitely didn't want a housekeeper who was a fan.

'Yes, that's me,' he replied, willing now to overlook the fact that she was not only way too young but way too pretty. Jake reasoned that if he hired her, he wouldn't be around her on a daily basis so he wouldn't be in danger of being tempted by her very attractive package. Because, to be honest, it would be seriously hard to ignore those eyes. And that mouth.

Jake dragged his gaze away from it before his mind wandered into R-rated territory.

'And you must be Abby,' he said, smiling a little stiffly.

She smiled back. Not a big smile. A small one. But it showed lovely white teeth behind those luscious lips.

'Yes,' she said simply, then added in a rush, 'it's very good of you to give me an interview.'

'Barbara recommended you highly,' he said.

She seemed startled. 'She did?'

'Indeed, she did. Said she'd dropped in unexpectedly at your home before she signed you up and it was immaculate.'

A soft blush pinked her cheeks. Lord, but she was sweet as well as pretty. Jake liked pretty women, but he wasn't usually attracted to sweet.

Till now…

'I like to keep things nice and neat,' she said.

'Same here,' he said rather brusquely. 'Come in and we'll talk some more.'

'Oh. Right. Yes.' But she didn't move, her lovely eyes wide and unblinking.

Maybe he'd frightened her with his brusqueness. Jake could be very charming, when he chose to be. But he could also be intimidating.

Very charming was definitely not on. But intimidating was not nice either. Best stick to businesslike.

'Perhaps I should give you a tour of the house first,' Jake suggested matter-of-factly, stepping back and waving her inside. 'Show you what you'll be letting yourself in for. You might not want the job, even if I offer it to you.'

'I'm sure I will, Mr Sanderson,' she said and made her way past him into the hallway, where she stopped and stared down. 'Oh, what a lovely floor. I love polished wooden floors.'

'They're hard work to keep clean,' came Jake's blunt comment as he shut the front door behind her.

'I'm not afraid of hard work,' she said, turning to look up at him.

Jake admired the flash of feistiness in her eyes.

It came to him then that he liked this girl. Really *liked* her.

'Excellent,' he said, knowing that he had found his house-keeper at last.

And if it bothered Jake that he also found Abby very desirable, then he determined to ignore it. But he also determined to put things in place so that he would hardly ever see her.

Out of sight was out of mind, after all!

CHAPTER ONE

Twelve months later...

ABBY WAS HUMMING happily as she locked up her neat little weatherboard cottage and headed off to work. She never suffered from Monday-itis. She liked her job. Liked looking after Jake Sanderson's very beautiful house. And looking after Jake Sanderson himself, despite not liking *him* all that much.

Still, Abby would always be grateful to the man for hiring her when she had no current work experience or references.

Frankly, she still could not believe her luck at getting such a cushy position. Aside from the convenience of getting to work—East Balmain wasn't too long a drive from Seven Hills—she was her own boss since Jake was never there when she was. She could do as she pleased; have breaks whenever she wanted; work at her own pace.

Not that she was a slacker. Abby was somewhat of a perfectionist when it came to keeping house. You could eat food off the floors in her own home. And off Jake's by the time she left each day.

Admittedly, when she first arrived on Monday mornings, things could be on the extra messy side. Abby always knew when Jake had had company over the weekend, the kind who stayed the night and didn't bother to lift a finger to pick up dirty wine glasses or load the dishwasher or do anything other than whatever it was his playmates did. The man who'd been voted most popular television personality earlier this year was reputed never to be short of female company.

Abby's sister, Megan, who was addicted to Twitter and gossip magazines, kept Abby well informed about who her boss was currently dating. His latest squeeze was a newsreader from the same television channel that Jake's show aired on. Her name was Olivia, a stunning brunette with big brown eyes and a figure to die for. A smile to die for as well.

There had been a time when Abby would have felt jealous of that smile.

But not any more.

Abby stopped humming abruptly as her tongue ran over her top teeth, still amazed at how fantastic they felt. Her bottom teeth too.

Of course, porcelain veneers came at a huge cost. Abby still hadn't finished paying off the personal loan she'd taken out to have them done. But really, it had been a case of necessity rather than vanity.

'You need confidence to go back into the workforce after all this time, hon,' her sister had advised. 'Which means you need to do something about your teeth!'

And Megan had been so right. Imagine showing up for an interview with Jake Sanderson the way she'd been. She suffered from fluorosis, a condition which involved an excess of fluoride, caused perhaps by eating fluoride laced toothpaste as a child. She'd loved the taste. Her fluorosis had worsened over the years, the brown stains darkening, pitting her teeth, especially the top ones. Wayne had said she was beautiful the way she was. But Abby had never believed him. So finally, when there'd been no Wayne to object, she'd taken Megan's advice and gone to the dentist.

It had been the best thing she'd ever done, despite putting her into debt.

Not for much longer, though. Each week she saved every penny she could from her wages, not spending a cent on female fripperies like having her hair and nails done, or even clothes. She just made do with what she had. She also rarely ate out, or went out. If there were no further unexpected expenses—like having to pay for Timmy to have his tonsils out—she would be debt free by Christmas and able to finally start up her travel fund.

Abby had always wanted to see the world, dreams of one day travelling overseas sustaining her when she'd been an unhappy teenager. Okay, so those dreams had been replaced by other dreams when she'd married Wayne, her focus changing to creating a happy family life, the sort of family life that neither she nor Wayne had ever had.

But those dreams had failed to eventuate…

Abby swallowed hard for a few moments, pushing the awful memories aside and forcing herself to focus on dreams which were achievable. And which might make her forget. They did say time healed all wounds. Time, and hopefully travel.

Her dream holiday would encompass at least six months, seeing Europe, Asia and the Americas. There were so many places on her USA bucket list. Niagara Falls. The Grand Canyon. New York.

Which meant of course that one day she'd have to quit her job as Jake's housekeeper.

Megan thought she was crazy to contemplate giving up her cushy job to go tripping around the world.

But Abby didn't agree. She needed to have a dream which looked forward and not back. If she wanted to travel, then she would travel. And to hell with her job as Jake Sanderson's housekeeper. He'd survive without her, and she'd certainly survive without him.

Shortly before nine-thirty, Abby turned into the street which led to Jake's house. The road sloped gently down to the water, and the ferry terminal, most of the houses two-storey terraces which dated back to the early twentieth century. All of them had been renovated at some stage, Balmain being a very desirable address these days, a far cry from its working-class roots.

Jake's house had once been a large corner shop which

someone had bought and turned into a house, extending it up and out. Jake had bought it a few years ago. It had come fully furnished in the Balinese style and with everything else he wanted, including a no-lawn backyard, a lap pool with a relaxing water feature and an en suite guest bedroom downstairs.

Apparently, at the time of his purchase, he'd been suffering from some leg injury incurred whilst working overseas and hadn't been capable of climbing stairs for a while. He'd told her all this on the day he'd given her the job, when he'd shown her through the place and explained what he expected her to do. Frankly, he'd spoken to her more that day than in the subsequent twelve months.

Megan was always asking Abby questions about her *oh, so famous and handsome* bachelor boss, not quite believing her sister when Abby said she still knew next to nothing about him other than the basics, which was that he'd once been a famous documentary maker and was now an equally famous television show host. She had recently learnt that he had a favourite uncle named Craig who was a fairly famous foreign correspondent. Abby only knew this because the man himself had recently come to stay for a while after he'd suffered a skiing mishap.

Megan probably knew a lot more about Abby's boss since she avidly watched his programme every day. It was called *Australia at Noon*, a live one-and-a-half-hour programme which focused on celebrity interviews and current affairs, with a bit of variety thrown in—a tried and true formula whose success depended on the popularity of its host. Which Jake Sanderson was. *Very.*

Abby did turn his show on occasionally during her lunch break but found she wasn't as entranced by it—or by its handsome host—as her sister. She found it hard to match his charming television persona with the rather abrupt man who rarely said more than two words to her on the rare occasions their paths crossed.

Not that she cared, as long as he kept on employing her and paying her till her travel fund was full.

This last thought popped into Abby's mind shortly after she let herself into the house and saw what was written in capital letters on the whiteboard in the utility room, where her boss wrote down things he wanted her to do, or buy. He never texted her, seeming to prefer this rather impersonal method of communication.

Will be home around three.
Need to talk to you about something.
Jake

Abby's stomach flipped over, her immediate thought being that she'd done something wrong and he was going to fire her. But then common sense kicked in, Abby reasoning it might be nothing more important than his wanting to show her something which needed doing.

Yes, that was probably it. No need to panic.

But a sense of panic still hovered as time ticked slowly away that day. Meanwhile, Abby worked like a demon so that by the time three o'clock came around every room and surface in Jake's house was clean and shining. All the pictures and side tables had been dusted. The washing had been done and dried, the master bed remade with clean sheets and fresh towels hung in the main bathroom. Even the courtyard had been swept, and a few of the pavers scrubbed where some red wine had been spilled. She hadn't had a break, eating her lunch on the go.

At ten to three Abby removed her cleaning gloves and tidied her hair, brushing it before putting it back up into her usual ponytail. She always wore jeans and trainers to work, with a T-shirt in the warm weather and a sweater in the cold. Today's jeans were old and faded and a bit loose. Her black T-shirt was slightly too big for her as well. She'd lost weight lately, courtesy of her banning chocolate and ice cream from her diet.

Abby sighed at her reflection in the laundry mirror. She wished she looked better. She would have taken more trouble with her appearance this morning if she'd known she was going to have a meeting with her boss. But how could she have known? She hadn't seen him for weeks. Still, she really should go out and buy herself a few new things. Jeans and T-shirts didn't cost much at Kmart.

Three o'clock came and went without any sign of Jake. After ten minutes she wondered if she should text him. She did have his phone number but he'd made it clear from the start that she wasn't to bother him that way, except in an emergency.

Him being late was hardly an emergency. Still, if he hadn't arrived by three-thirty she would text him. Meanwhile, she hurried to the kitchen and put on the kettle.

CHAPTER TWO

JAKE STEPPED OUT onto the deck of the ferry and scooped in several deep breaths. His stomach was still tied up in knots. He'd done his best with his show today, but his mind hadn't been on the job. Not that he cared. Frankly, he wouldn't care if he never did another show. Andrew had stood in for him as host last Friday and the ratings were just fine. No one was indispensable in the entertainment game.

Jake contemplated letting Andrew take over for a week or two whilst he took a well-needed break. He'd jump at the chance, ambitious young buck that he was. Alternately, he might sell the show lock, stock and barrel and do something else with his life. Harvest Productions had been sniffing around for ages. If he could talk Sebastian into making him a half decent offer, he just might take him up on it.

Though maybe not…

Jake ran his fingers through his hair in total frustration. Damn it. He hadn't felt this indecisive in years. Of course he knew the reason. He just didn't like facing it. Sighing, he made his way over to the railing and stood there, staring out at the water.

Sydney Harbour on a clear calm day in spring was a sight to behold. But Jake wasn't in the mood for admiring his surroundings. Or even noticing them.

Closing his eyes, he surrendered to the grief which he'd had to put on hold today whilst he did the show, and which he'd been struggling to contain for several days.

Jake still could not believe that his uncle was actually dead. Not even the funeral last Friday had made it real. He could not picture Craig in that coffin. Could not conceive of the fact that he would never see the man again. Would not talk to him again. Or drink with him. Or anything at all with him.

Craig had been much more than an uncle to Jake. He'd been his mentor and his friend. His idol, too. Even as a boy, Jake had admired the way his uncle lived his life.

Craig hadn't gone down the traditional route, getting a nine-to-five job then marrying and having children. He'd become a foreign correspondent, travelling the world to all the wildly exotic and sometimes dangerous places which fired Jake's imagination. He'd also stayed single, explaining once to a teenage Jake that for him to marry would be cruel to the woman, and to any children they had because he would neglect them shamelessly.

There'd been women, of course. Lots of women. Beautiful, exciting women who'd graced the dashingly handsome Craig Sanderson's bed but who knew never to expect any more than his highly stimulating company.

Jake had decided long before he left university with his communications degree that that was the life for him. No way was he going to follow in his father's footsteps. Craig's only brother had married before he was twenty, when his even younger girlfriend fell pregnant, then worked himself to death—literally—to support his ever-increasing brood.

Jake couldn't think of anything worse. He could not recall his father—when he was alive—having any time to himself. Everything he'd done had been for his family.

When his dad died of a coronary at the age of forty-seven, Jake had been heartbroken but more determined than ever to embrace bachelorhood as well as a job which he loved and not one he was compelled to do just to pay the bills and put food on the table.

Jake had been true to his resolve. He'd spent his twenties making documentaries in far-flung corners of the world, earning a small fortune at the same time. He'd still be overseas, living that life, if a run-in with a group of rebels in war-torn Africa hadn't forced his life into a different direction.

Working in television was tame by comparison, but it had its moments. Jake couldn't really complain.

Admittedly, since he'd stopped flitting from country to country and city to city, Jake had given up one-night stands and fleeting flings in favour of longer relationships. If you could call a few months long, that was. His current girlfriend was a career-orientated and highly independent woman who was great company, great in bed and knew better than to pressure him for marriage or, God forbid, a baby. Olivia had assured him on their first date that she wouldn't get bitten by the biological clock bug like his last girlfriend. The only responsibility Jake wanted in life was paying his own personal bills.

Which was exactly the way things had been…till the solicitor for Craig's estate had dropped his bombshell at the wake.

Jake already knew he'd been left the bulk of his uncle's estate, Craig having given him a copy of his will for safe-keeping. What he hadn't known was that Craig had summoned his solicitor to his bedside a few days before his death and given him a letter for Jake, to be delivered after his funeral.

Jake pulled the letter out of his pocket, unfolded it and read it for the umpteenth time.

Dear Jake
Hope you aren't angry with me for not telling you about my illness, but there was nothing anyone could do and I do so hate pity. I had a good life, my only regret being that I didn't go out with more style. A bullet or a bomb would have been much more me.

But on to the reason for this letter. Jake, there's something I want you to do for me. Last July, when I stayed at your place after I bunged up my knee, I got to know your very nice housekeeper quite well. Abby was extra kind to me and went over and above the call of duty to make my stay both comfortable and enjoyable. And, no, nothing untoward happened between us. She's not that sort of girl.

Anyway, on to my request. I didn't want to add a codicil to my will. Too much trouble at this stage. Still, what I would like, Jake, is for you to buy Abby a new car to replace that appalling bomb she drives. Something small and stylish but with a long warranty.

I also want you to give her twenty-five thousand dollars out of your considerable inheritance to go towards her travel fund. Please insist that she not use it for any other purpose. Don't let her give it away to any of those free-loading relatives of hers.

I have every confidence that you will do this for me. You're a good man. And not a greedy one. Give Abby my love and tell her not to wait too long to see the world. Life is meant to be lived.

The same goes for you, my boy. I'll be watching over you from above.
Your Uncle Craig

Jake closed his eyes as he folded the letter, a huge lump having formed in his throat.

'Damn it, Craig,' he ground out, his heart squeezing tight with grief. 'You should have told me you were ill. I could have been there for you the way you always were for me. You shouldn't have had to die alone.'

And you should have just put a damned codicil in your will, came the added thought, grief finally giving way to exasperation.

It was impossible not to do what Craig asked, Jake accepted as he shoved the letter back in his pocket. But it annoyed him all the same.

It wasn't a question of money. He had plenty of money. It was the fact that fulfilling his uncle's deathbed wishes would force him into Abby's personal space—and company—something he'd been careful to avoid ever since he'd hired her.

Because let's face it, Jake, you fancy her even more now than ever.

But he could see no way out. He would just have to gird his loins and endure!

CHAPTER THREE

AT TWENTY PAST THREE Abby's boss finally showed up, looking slightly harassed but still very handsome in a smart grey
suit and a crisp white shirt which highlighted his dark hair,
olive complexion and deep blue eyes.

Even Abby had to admit that in the flesh her boss was
a hunk. But she'd never been blindly attracted to a man
on looks alone. Handsome is as handsome does, in her
opinion. What attracted her most in the opposite sex was
kindness and gentleness, qualities which Wayne had had
in spades.

'Sorry I'm late,' Jake said as he strode into the kitchen,
where Abby was making herself coffee. 'Damned ferry was
running late. Could I trouble you for some coffee? Black,
with no sugar,' he ordered as he slid on to one of the kitchen
stools, reefing off his tie at the same time.

Abby wanted to scream at him. Didn't he know how
stressed out she was? But she held her tongue and made
him the darned coffee.

'So what did you want to talk to me about?' she asked
as soon as she'd placed his mug in front of him. She stayed
standing on the other side of the breakfast bar, not daring
to pick up her own coffee yet for fear of spilling it.

His forehead bunched in a frown, which only added to
her discomfort.

'You're going to fire me, aren't you?' she blurted out.

His head shot up, his dark brows arching. 'What? No.
No, of course not! Good God, is that what you thought this
was about?'

She just shook her head at him. 'I didn't know what to
think.'

'Why on earth would I want to fire you? You are the best housekeeper a man could have. I'm sorry if you thought that.'

Abby found herself flushing at his compliment. And his apology. Relief swamped her as well. She didn't want to lose this job. Not for a good while yet.

'It's to do with Craig's will,' Jake said abruptly.

'Craig's *will*?' she repeated, feeling somewhat confused. 'Are you talking about your uncle Craig, the man who stayed here for a while during the winter?'

It had been back in July, she recalled, about four months ago.

'Yes. The thing is, Abby, he's left you something in his will.'

Abby just stared at Jake, shock joining her confusion. 'Are you saying that he's *dead*?'

'What? Oh. Yes. Yes, he died last week. Incurable cancer,' he finished up with a heavy sigh.

'But…but that's impossible! I mean, he was so *alive* not that long ago.'

'Tell me about it,' Jake said as he swept an agitated hand through his hair. 'It came as a shock to me as well. I gather he found out during an MRI for his busted knee about the cancer. But he never told anyone, not even me. And we were very close. I knew nothing about his illness till his solicitor rang and told me he'd passed away.'

Abby found it hard to understand what he was saying. 'You mean you weren't with him when he died?'

'No. No one was, other than the palliative care nurse. He'd booked himself into a hospice without telling anyone.'

'But that's terrible!' Abby declared heatedly, upset that anyone would choose to die like that.

Jake's shrug carried a weary resignation. 'It was what he wanted. I'm surprised you didn't hear about his death. It was all over the news at the weekend. He was quite famous.'

'I… I don't often watch the news.'

'I see.'

She wanted to ask him why he hadn't told her himself, but of course why would he? She wasn't a relative, or a friend. He wouldn't have known how much she'd enjoyed the time she'd spent with his uncle whilst he'd stayed here.

Craig had been a fascinating individual, highly intelligent, widely travelled and very well read. He'd been incredibly nice to her, showing an interest in her as a person and not just some kind of maid. The day before he'd left, he'd given her a list of ten books which he said everybody—especially young women—should read. She was still slowly working her way through them. They were the reason she didn't watch the news much any more, and why she hadn't seen the report of his death.

Tears flooded her eyes at the realisation that this very nice man was actually dead.

'He…he said he was going away to have a holiday.' Abby's voice caught at the memory.

'He told me the same thing,' Jake said.

'Instead he went away to die,' she choked out. 'Alone…'

Abby couldn't think of anything sadder than dying alone. It was the main thing which haunted her about Wayne's death. That he'd been all alone, out there in the ocean, with the storm raging around him and little chance of being rescued. Had he lost all hope in the end? Had despair engulfed him in the moments before he drowned?

Suddenly, a huge wave of grief overwhelmed her, emotional distress welling up in Abby till it could not be contained. Tears filled her eyes so quickly they spilled over and ran down her cheeks.

When a sob escaped her throat, Jake stared at her with a look of horror.

Embarrassment flooded in but there was no stopping her now. When more sobs racked her body, all Abby could do was bury her face in her hands. She simply couldn't bear to witness her boss watching her whilst she wept her heart out. No doubt she was making a fool of herself. No doubt he thought she was a typically sentimental female to cry over a man she hardly knew.

The feel of strong male arms suddenly pulling her into a comforting embrace shocked Abby rigid. She certainly hadn't expected a hug. Not from her very aloof boss. Unfortunately, his uncharacteristic kindness only made her weep all the more.

'There, there,' he said, patting her back as she clasped the lapels of his suit jacket and sobbed into his shirt. 'No need to cry. Craig had a good life, with no regrets. He wouldn't want you crying over him. Craig wasn't one for tears.'

Abby could hardly explain that it wasn't just Craig's death which had set her off, but the *way* he'd died. All alone.

Oh, God...

Abby was gritting her teeth and doing her best to pull herself together when Jake stopped patting her back and slid his arms right around her, holding her quite close. No doubt he was still just trying to comfort her but for some reason Abby no longer felt comforted. She felt very *dis*-comforted. Because she *liked* him hugging her like that. She liked it a lot. The urge to slide her own arms around his back was acute. She wanted to hug him back, wanted to bury herself in the solid warmth of his very male body and...and...

And what, Abby? Make an even bigger fool of yourself? For pity's sake, get a grip, girl.

Taking a deep gathering breath, Abby lurched backwards, releasing the lapels of Jake's jacket as she gulped down a sob of shame.

'I'm so sorry,' she choked out, her face flushing as she spun away from him and grabbed a handful of tissues from the box on the kitchen counter, not saying another word till she'd blown her nose and composed herself. She did note rather ruefully, however, that Jake didn't wait long to hurry back to the other side of the breakfast bar.

Her groan carried more shame. 'I've embarrassed you, I can see. It's just that… Oh, never mind.' Her fisted right hand came up to rub agitatedly at her mouth. For a moment she was tempted to confide in Jake about Wayne's tragic death. But only for a moment. Maybe, if he'd been any other kind of man she might have explained why she'd been so upset at the news of his uncle dying alone like that. But Jake didn't invite confidences. Why, he'd never even asked her how her husband had died!

Despite his hug just now, Jake didn't really care about her. She was just his employee, hired to look after his house. His housekeeper. A glorified cleaner, if truth be told.

Craig hadn't treated her like that. He'd been genuinely interested in her life. Not that she'd told Jake's uncle the total truth. Abby had become masterful at blotting out the really painful parts in her past. Talking about them wouldn't have achieved anything, anyway.

'The thing is,' she went on, compelled to make some excuse for her emotional display, 'I really liked your uncle a lot.'

'He must have liked you a lot too,' Jake replied.

'Well, yes,' she said slowly. 'He seemed to.'

'You haven't asked me what he left you,' Jake went on, his eyes on her.

'What? Oh… Some books, I suppose.'

Jake frowned at her. 'No, no books,' he said. 'Nothing as mundane as that.'

'Then what?' she asked, perplexed.

'To be honest, he didn't leave you anything directly. He left a letter for me with instructions of what he wants you to have.'

She blinked, then frowned. 'That sounds…weird.'

'Yes, I thought so too,' he agreed drily. 'But Craig was never a conventional man. Look, why don't we both drink our coffee before it gets cold? Then, afterwards, I'll fill you in on everything.'

When Jake picked up his coffee mug, Abby did likewise, sipping slowly and thoughtfully. A hot drink always calmed her. And brother, she needed calming after that crazy moment when she'd almost hugged her boss back.

'I would have liked to go to his funeral,' she said after a suitably calming minute or two. 'Was he buried or cremated?'

'Buried,' he said.

'Where?' she asked.

Jake's face looked grim as he put down his coffee. 'Rookwood Cemetery.'

She wasn't sure where that was. She didn't have a GPS in the ute and often got lost. 'I'd like to go and visit his grave some time. Pay my respects. Say a prayer or two. Would you take me?' she asked him before she could think better of it.

Jake's sigh suggested that was the last thing he wanted to do.

'Okay,' he said with a resigned shrug. 'But I can't go till next Saturday. In the meantime, wouldn't you like to hear about what Craig wanted me to give you?'

'Oh, yes. What is it?'

'Well, first of all he wants me to buy you a new car. Something small and stylish, with a decent warranty.'

Shock at this news was swiftly followed by confusion.

'But that doesn't seem right,' she said. 'As much as I would love a new car, why should he ask *you* to pay for such a thing?'

'It's basically Craig's money, Abby. He left most of his estate to me. Trust me when I say that my inheritance was considerable. So it's no hardship on me to spend a seriously small portion of it on you.'

'But why didn't he just leave some money to me in his will to buy my own car?'

'I have no idea. It might have been simpler all round if he'd done that. Apparently, he was worried that you might not spend it on yourself—that you might give it away to relatives.'

'Oh, dear,' she said, embarrassed. 'I suppose it's because I told him about paying for Timmy's operation.'

'No. He didn't mention anything specific. Who's Timmy?'

'My sister's little boy. She's a single mum and doesn't have any private health insurance. Timmy needed his tonsils out but would have had to wait eighteen months to have it done. She couldn't afford the operation so I paid for it to be done privately.'

'I see,' he said, his tone sceptical.

A degree of anger pushed aside Abby's embarrassment. 'Please don't think my sister's a user because she's not. She's doing the best she can under the circumstances. Megan didn't ask me to pay for Timmy's operation. That was *my* idea. She won't come and live with me, even though I said she wouldn't have to pay any rent. Your uncle got the wrong idea.'

'Possibly, but that's irrelevant now. I have no alternative but to follow through with Craig's dying wishes. He was most specific in his letter about what he wanted me to buy for you. A new car is the first cab off the rank. Then he wants me to give you twenty-five thousand dollars. For your travel fund, he said.'

Abby's mouth dropped open. 'Twenty-five thousand! But…but that's way too much. What will people think?'

'Who cares what they think?' came his arrogantly dismissive comment. 'And who are *they*?'

'My sister for starters. She'll think I've done something I shouldn't have with your uncle to get him to leave me all that money.'

'Really. Such as what?'

'You know what,' Abby shot back.

'True,' he said drily. 'In that case I suggest you don't tell her about your unexpected windfall.'

Abby gave a snorting laugh. 'Hard to hide a brand-new car.'

'True again. So what do you want me to do, Abby? Go against my uncle's wishes? Forget everything?'

She looked at him with pained eyes. 'I couldn't do that. I don't care so much about the new car, but I couldn't turn down the travel fund money. It's my dearest wish to go overseas and see the world. And I'd like to go before I get too old.'

Jake laughed. 'You're hardly ancient, Abby.'

'I might be by the time I save up twenty-five thousand dollars.'

He seemed startled by this statement. 'Do I pay you that poorly?'

'No. But I have a house and a lot of bills.' And the remainder of a debt for porcelain veneers.

Jake frowned. 'You have a mortgage?'

'No. My husband's life insurance paid that off. But I still have a lot of bills. Maintaining a house is expensive.'

'Tell me about it,' he said with the first hint of a smile that day. He really wasn't much of a smiler. Not with her, anyway. He smiled on television a lot though. Abby wished he would smile more. It really transformed his face from cardboard handsome into a likeable human being.

Unfortunately, his smile also did things to Abby which she was finding hard to process. Her stomach curled over and she found herself staring at his mouth and thinking totally unacceptable things. Like what would it be like to be kissed by him? And not just on her mouth.

Lord, but this wasn't like her. She didn't even enjoy sex that much, unlike her sister, who couldn't live without it. Sex with Wayne had been okay, but nothing to write home about. She'd done it whenever he wanted, more for him than herself, because she'd loved him so much. In her mind, making love was a natural part of loving. Of marriage. She'd never been into sex for sex's sake.

Why then was she looking at her boss and thinking that here was a man who just might change her mind on that subject?

Not that she'd ever have the chance to find out. Not only did he have a gorgeous girlfriend but he was totally off-limits. He was her boss, for heaven's sake! On top of that, he clearly didn't fancy her. A girl knew when a man fancied her and Jake definitely didn't.

Her eyes dropped from his to her near empty coffee cup.

'I'm still finding it hard to believe all this,' she said, glancing up again once she had her wayward thoughts under control. 'In one way it's like a dream come true. But I still can't get over your uncle dying like that. And all alone.'

'Indeed,' Jake said, that hint of a smile disappearing as quickly as it had come. 'I've been thinking,' he went on, his face very businesslike again. 'I'll put next Saturday aside so that I can take you to visit Craig's grave in the morning, then we'll go on and buy you a car afterwards. It's not far from Rookwood Cemetery out to the major dealerships at Parramatta. Do you trust me to pick out a car for you, or do you want to choose one yourself?'

'Well, I… I don't know,' she stammered, startled by how quickly he wanted to organise everything. 'I'm not much of a car buff. But if it's going to be mine I think I would like to look up a few possibilities on the internet.'

'It's a good idea to buy something that is cheap to repair,' he advised firmly. 'I would suggest you look at the Japanese cars. Or the Korean ones.'

'All right,' she agreed. He seemed to know what he was talking about, whereas she was pretty ignorant when it came to cars.

'And what bank account would you like the twenty-five thousand put into? The same one your salary goes into, or do you want to start up a special travel fund account?'

Abby was taken by surprise when her chin began to quiver. But really today had all been a bit much.

'Don't you dare start crying again,' he commanded.

Abby bit her bottom lip and blinked madly.

'Sorry,' she muttered through gritted teeth. 'I'm not usually a cry baby.' Which was true. Nowadays, Abby kept her emotions under tight control. There had been a time when she'd cried too much. And too often. But no longer.

Lifting her chin, she speared her boss with a dry-eyed and rather rebellious glare.

'Good,' Jake snapped, making Abby want to hit him. How on earth she could have been sexually attracted to this man—even for a moment—was beyond her.

'You should go home,' he went on in that same brusque manner. 'You look tired. Ring me when you've decided on the brand of car and we'll make arrangements for Saturday. You can tell me then what account you want the money put into.'

'All right. Bye then,' Abby went on rather sharply, gathering up her things and taking off before she could say or do something which might jeopardise her job. Or Craig's remarkable legacies.

She almost slammed the front door, just getting control of her temper in time. She did slam the door on the ute and accelerated off faster than her usual sedate speed. But she soon slowed down, telling herself not to be so silly. No point risking her life because her boss was a pain in the butt.

Think about your new car, she told herself. *And all that lovely money.*

Abby sighed. Yes, it was sad that Craig was dead, but life went on, as she very well knew. You had to search for the positives in life or you would go mad.

Another thought suddenly came to Abby which made her wince. How much of this was she going to tell Megan? As she'd said to Jake, you couldn't hide a new car. But perhaps it would be best if she didn't tell her sister about the money. It might make her jealous and, yes, suspicious.

Abby pulled a face at herself in the rear-view mirror. She hated lying to Megan but she just might have to. Oh, dear. Even when things took a turn for the better, life wasn't easy.

CHAPTER FOUR

'YOU HANDLED THAT WELL,' Jake growled as he pulled a bottle of red at random out of his wine rack. 'I love the way you kept her at a distance.'

Still, what could he do when she started crying like that? Common sense demanded he do nothing. But common decency insisted that he comfort her.

Big mistake.

The moment he'd taken her in his arms, all those good intentions of his dissolved in the face of a desire so strong it took every ounce of willpower not to pull her even closer than he had. He didn't want to pat her damned back. Or utter soothing words. He wanted to tip up her chin and kiss the tears from her lovely face.

Thank God he hadn't given in to that desire. Because she would not have surrendered to him as she did in his darkest dreams. She would have slapped him, then resigned as his housekeeper.

Abby didn't particularly like him. That, he knew.

Which should have been a relief, given his resolve never to act on his secret desire for her. Instead he felt peeved by her indifference. And jealous of her obvious affection for Craig. Which was all perverse, given his own decision not to have anything to do with her on a personal level, a decision which fate—courtesy of his uncle—had now blown out of the water. Next Saturday morning he would be *personally* escorting Abby to Craig's graveside, then afterwards he would be *personally* buying her a car.

That was all pretty personal, in his opinion.

But there was no way out, Jake accepted bleakly as he gazed down at the label of the bottle he'd pulled out and saw it was one of his favourites. A Shiraz from the Clare Valley. Good. Because he needed to get drunk. And he might as well do so on a favourite tipple rather than rubbish.

Not that he ever bought rubbish, he admitted as he poured himself his first glass. Long gone were the days when he drank rough red from casks. Hell, he hadn't done that since his university days. And yet they had been good days. Happy days. Carefree days.

Nothing like today, Jake thought ruefully as he lifted the glass to his lips for a deep swallow. Today would not go down as good. Or happy. Or carefree. Today was...what?

He wasn't sure how to describe it.

Dangerous came to mind. And not in a good way. Jake had enjoyed danger in his life at times. But this was a different kind of danger. This wasn't physical danger. This involved his emotions. Intense, uncontrollable emotions.

Jake didn't like intense, uncontrollable emotions. They made you do things which never ended well.

Jake carried the glass and the bottle out to his courtyard, where he placed the bottle on the small circular glass table he liked best then sat down in the chair next to it.

When his phone rang, he saw that it was Olivia.

He didn't want to talk to Olivia just now. He didn't want to talk to anyone. So he just turned off the phone and went back to drinking his wine.

CHAPTER FIVE

WITHIN SECONDS OF arriving home Abby rang Megan, not wanting to procrastinate over the call. Megan would only be even more suspicious if she waited too long to give her the good news.

'Hi there, kiddo,' Megan answered, a term of endearment which often led people to think Megan was the older sister. And whilst there wasn't much between them, Abby was actually older by fifteen months.

Abby had already decided that the best way to play this was to sound very happy about it. And she *was* happy. Just a bit wary about her sister's reaction.

'You'll never guess what's happened,' Abby said brightly as she dumped her bag on the floor and plonked herself into a nearby armchair.

'Something good by the sound of things.'

'Unbelievably good!' And she launched into an explanation of the day's events. As planned, she left out the part about the travel fund money and only mentioned the new car. Naturally, she didn't include the bit about her bursting into tears and Jake hugging her.

Megan exclaimed a shocked, 'No!' at the news about the new car, but thankfully didn't make any sarcastic crack about what Abby might have done with Jake's uncle to deserve such an incredibly generous gift. Things might have been different, however, if she'd mentioned the twenty-five thousand dollars as well. Though possibly not. Maybe Megan instinctively knew that Abby would never do anything sexual with a man she didn't love. Wayne had been her first and only lover because he was the first and only man she'd ever loved.

'Aren't you a lucky duck?' Megan said without a trace of jealousy in her voice. 'A brand-new car! And you don't even have to wait for probate to come through, since your hunky boss is buying you the car himself. This Saturday, you said?'

'Yes. This Saturday.'

'It's a wonderful gift. Especially when you hardly knew his uncle. But perhaps not so much if he was filthy rich. Was he filthy rich?'

'He must have been. Jake said he'd inherited heaps. That's why he doesn't mind forking out the money for me for a car.'

'Oh, right. Still, it's nice of him to do that. He's not legally obliged to, I would imagine.'

'Probably not, but he said he would never go against his uncle's deathbed wishes.'

'Did you see this letter his uncle left him?'

'Well, no, but why would he lie about something like that?'

'Maybe he fancies you.'

'Oh, don't be ridiculous! Why would he fancy someone like me when he has that gorgeous girlfriend? I've been thinking, Megan, since I'm getting a new car, would you like the ute? I know it's done a good few miles but it goes really well. Wayne put a new engine in it not long before he died.'

'Oh, I'd *love* it. Thanks, Abby.'

'Jake is going to take me to see his uncle's grave as well,' she blurted out before she could think better of it.

The silence at the other end of the line was telling.

'Oh, is he?' Megan said at long last in one of her knowing voices. 'And why is he doing that?'

'Because I asked him to,' Abby said, angry with herself. 'And, before you jump to conclusions, we're just dropping in at the cemetery on the way to the car yards at Parramatta. It's hardly out of his way. And you are so wrong about his fancying me.'

Megan laughed. 'We'll see, hon. We'll see.'

'Oh, for pity's sake.'

'You've always underestimated your looks, Abby. Even when your teeth were not great, you were gorgeous. Now that you've had them fixed, you're a knockout. And your figure is to die for.'

'Oh, go on with you!'

'No, I mean it. Your fantastic figure was one of the reasons Wayne was so possessive of you. And why he didn't want you to work after you were married. Because he didn't want other men lusting after you.'

Abby's first reaction was to hotly deny what Megan said. But in her heart of hearts she knew it was true. Wayne had been very possessive of her. Right from the start, he'd wanted her all to himself. Which had suited Abby fine. All she'd wanted back then was to be Wayne's wife, plus the mother of his children. She'd been only too happy to stop work and not have to face the world every day with her horrible teeth. Not so happy, however, as the years had passed and the nursery remained empty.

'That's probably the reason he wouldn't pay for you to get your teeth fixed,' Megan continued. 'Because he was afraid you'd be too beautiful and he'd lose you to another man.'

'That's ridiculous!' Abby protested. 'The reason I didn't get my teeth fixed back then was because it's very expensive and we had a huge mortgage. Besides, Wayne already loved me, even with my horrid teeth. As for being too beautiful, please don't make me laugh. Even if by some miracle I'd become the most beautiful woman in the world, I would never have left Wayne, no matter what. I loved him.'

'Did you, Abby? Or did you just love that he loved you with the kind of crazy obsession which can be oh, so flattering?'

'I did so love Wayne,' she insisted. 'Very much. We would have been happy together if we'd had children.'

Megan sighed. 'If you say so, Abby.'

'I do say so. Now, I do not wish to discuss Wayne

any more, thank you. I didn't realise how much you disliked him.'

'I didn't dislike him. I just didn't think he was good enough for you. You deserved someone better.'

Abby didn't know whether to feel flattered or frustrated. 'Such as who, Megan? Prince Charming?'

'Yeah, why not? And let me tell you something else, kiddo. If you bought some new clothes and put on some make-up occasionally, you would be so hot that every man you met would be drooling. And that includes your handsome hunk of a boss.'

Abby didn't like to tell Megan that she was being delusional—about Jake at least—so she just laughed.

'Yeah, you can laugh if you like. Just you wait and see. Speaking of your boss, did you happen to watch his show today?'

'Hardly. I was too busy cleaning his house.'

'He interviewed Maddie Hanks. You know, the latest Aussie actress who's made it big in Hollywood?'

'I know who you mean. She was in that biblical epic. Played a slave girl.'

'Yeah, that's the one. Well, she was flirting with Jake big time. And brother, she is stunning. He seemed very taken with her. Couldn't keep his eyes off her cleavage. Though I don't think her boobs are real. Anyway, I wouldn't mind betting they get together in the near future.'

Abby rolled her eyes. Truly, her sister was so addicted to gossip that she saw scandalous behaviour everywhere. 'Jake already has a gorgeous girlfriend,' she pointed out. 'That newsreader. Remember?'

'Huh! That won't stop him getting into Miss Hanks's pants.'

'He's not like that,' Abby said sharply.

'Oh, really? And how would you know, Miss I-Know-Nothing-Personal-About-My-Hunk-of-a-Boss? Did something else happen today that you didn't tell me about?'

'No,' she denied, blanking the hug out of her mind. 'Look, I'm not overly fond of the man, but he's not some sleazebag.'

'Wow. He's sure got you fooled. All men can be sleaze-bags if the right temptation comes along.'

Abby just shook her head. 'Truly, Megan, you are such a cynic when it comes to men.'

'I have good reason to be.'

This *was* true. Timmy's father hadn't been the first man in Megan's life to treat her badly. She'd met a few since becoming a single mother who'd wined and dined her till they got what they wanted before dumping her as cruelly as the cowardly creep who'd got her pregnant then disappeared once he discovered fatherhood was too much commitment for him.

'I hope you're going to make yourself presentable when your boss takes you out on Saturday,' Megan said.

'It's not a date, Megan.'

'You still want to look a bit nicer than you do when you clean his house.'

'I will do my best.'

'Good. Gosh, wait till Jan hears all this. She's going to be green with envy.'

Jan was Megan's next-door neighbour, a single mother like Megan. She was one of the reasons Megan wouldn't come to live with Abby, because she didn't want to leave her best friend. Abby wasn't overly keen on Jan, but she'd been a good friend to Megan and had a similar personality. Both were very easy-going but extremely untidy. Abby had been somewhat relieved when Megan knocked back her offer for her and Timmy to come live with her. Their messy lifestyle would have driven her mad within a week.

'Jan's sure to think I did something suspect with Jake's uncle,' Abby said drily.

'Nah. Now if it was *me*.'

Abby smiled. 'Come on, Megan, you're not as bad as you pretend to be.'

'Yeah, I am. Not everyone is as saint-like as you, sweetie. Though, to give you credit, being a goody-two-shoes got you somewhere this time. I dare say you waited on that rich old bastard hand and foot. You probably even baked him those delicious peanut butter cookies of yours.'

Abby fell silent with guilty embarrassment. She *had* made a fuss of Jake's uncle. But, at the time, it had been ages since her nurturing side had had an opportunity to flourish. Looking after Jake's house was a rather impersonal job. It had been so satisfying to bake cookies for a real man and, yes, watch him eat them with relish. She'd enjoyed it all immensely.

'You did, didn't you?' Megan said with laughter in her voice. 'No wonder he thought of you when he was dying. Those cookies of yours are super-yummy. Though way too fattening. I refuse to let you make me any more. Though Timmy wouldn't mind some, when you have your next baking session. I have to go and get the little devil himself now. He's been playing next door. Ring me tomorrow night. Gotta go. Love ya.'

'You too.'

After Abby clicked off her phone she just sat there, thinking about some of the things Megan had said about her marriage to Wayne. It was true that her husband had loved her more than she'd loved him. But she *had* loved him. Okay, not with a grand passion. Her feelings for Wayne had been based more on a deep friendship and eternal gratitude rather than the kind of wild sexual yearnings which some people obviously experienced.

Abby supposed she *had* been flattered by Wayne's fiercely possessive love. And his insatiable desire for her. After her second miscarriage, she'd wanted to take her doctor's advice to go on the Pill and give her body a rest. But no, Wayne had refused to countenance that idea, saying he didn't like to interfere with nature. He'd promised instead to abstain from sex for a while but, of course, that hadn't lasted for long. He'd never been able to control his desire for her and she'd never felt good about refusing him, mostly because she knew how much he seemed to need it.

Abby liked the kissing and cuddling part of lovemaking—she'd loved being wrapped in Wayne's strong arms— but she'd never felt any urgent need for the sex act itself, unlike Megan, who claimed she couldn't live without it. It had never really bothered Abby that she didn't come during lovemaking. It had bothered Wayne, however, so after a while she had just faked it.

She hadn't had to fake falling pregnant, however, and a few months after her second miscarriage she'd been pregnant again. But, once again, she'd miscarried at the three months stage. After that, she'd gone on the Pill without discussing it with Wayne, and she was still taking it long after her husband was gone, mainly because she'd discovered it saved her from premenstrual tension.

It felt good, Abby realised, to finally be in control of her body and, yes, her life. She'd been gutted by Wayne's tragic death, had taken months to get over it. But in the end she'd picked herself up and moved on.

Now, because of Craig's wonderful kindness and generosity, she would be able to move on some more. And Jake would find another housekeeper easily enough.

Thinking of Jake reminded Abby of what Megan had said about him, and about men in general. Abby had to admit that *her* view of the opposite sex was possibly narrower than her sister's. But she wasn't stupid. She was sure she would recognise a sleazebag when she came across one. And Jake Sanderson was no sleazebag.

But that was possibly the only good point of his character. Abby could see that he had a tendency towards arrogance and self-absorption. Neither was he into commitment, hence his never-ending parade of beautiful girlfriends. But that didn't mean he would be a cheater. She couldn't imagine him having sex with some flashy, fly-by-night actress whilst he was dating that truly gorgeous newsreader.

Abby would be utterly disgusted if she ever found out he *had* done something like that. Not that it was any of her business what her boss did in his private and personal life. Still, it bothered her a bit, thinking that he could be, right at this moment, meeting up with Maddie Hanks somewhere in the city then bringing her back to his place for the night.

It occurred to Abby that she would know within a minute of arriving at his house tomorrow morning if he'd had a new woman stay overnight. Abby knew his current girlfriend's smell because she recognised the perfume. It was a heavy musky scent which didn't wear off easily. During the last few weeks Abby had smelled that perfume every couple of days, and almost always on a Monday after the weekend.

But not *this* Monday morning, she suddenly realised. Which led her to wonder if maybe they'd split up. Maybe that was why he'd been giving Maddie Hanks the eye on his show today. Men like Jake didn't go without sex for long. Because they didn't have to. Women threw themselves at famous men in droves—beautiful, sexy, successful women who knew everything there was to know about lovemaking and never had to fake a thing.

A very rude word burst from Abby's lips as she stood up abruptly then marched into her immaculate little kitchen, where she snapped on the kettle then yanked open the freezer, which was full of frozen meals for one.

Still feeling decidedly disgruntled, she grabbed a chilli con carne and shoved it into the microwave to reheat, telling herself all the while that her boss's sex life was definitely none of her business.

'He can sleep with whomever he damned well likes,' she said in a tone quite uncharacteristic of her usual serene self. 'Just so long as he delivers everything he promised me today!'

CHAPTER SIX

JAKE LEFT IT until nine that evening to ring Olivia back, having learnt from experience that it was never wise to ring her before she'd been home for a while after work. After reading the news from six till seven, Olivia usually went for a de-stressing drink down near the quay before catching the Manly ferry home.

Her phone rang several times before she picked up.

'Well, hello, stranger,' she answered waspishly. 'Why didn't you answer when I rang you earlier?'

'I didn't feel like talking,' he said with blunt honesty.

'Are you upset with me for not going to your uncle's funeral?'

'No,' he told her with equal honesty. 'I didn't expect you to cancel your arrangements when they'd been organised weeks before Craig died.'

Olivia and five of her girlfriends had driven up to a resort in the Blue Mountains on the Friday for a hen party for one of the girls, who was getting married shortly.

'I was home by eight last night,' Olivia pointed out tartly. 'Why didn't you ring? I was waiting for your call. Or your text. Or something.'

Jake was totally taken aback. They didn't have the kind of relationship where they called and texted each other all the time. They were lovers, but not in love.

'You told me you were turning off your phone for the weekend,' he reminded her. 'Nothing stopped you ringing me when you got home last night.'

'I was tired.'

'More likely hungover.'

'Yes,' she admitted grudgingly. 'That, too. But you still could have contacted me this morning.'

'Come now, Olivia. You know I'm busy on weekday mornings, getting ready for my show.'

'Ah, yes. Your show,' she said in a tone which had a decided edge to it. 'I happened to watch your show today...'

'And?' he prompted when she didn't go on.

'I saw the way you were ogling that actress's boobs. You do know they're fake, don't you?'

Jake could not believe what he was hearing. He sincerely hoped it wasn't the sounds of jealousy. Because jealousy meant only one thing.

'I dare say it was the cameraman doing the ogling,' he said coldly. 'Not me.'

'That's not the way I saw it. Just remember that if you're dating me, Jake darling, you can look, but you can't touch anyone else.'

'Don't start getting possessive on me, Olivia,' he warned, his tone darkly ominous.

There was a short silence before she suddenly laughed. 'Of course not. I was only kidding. Any red-blooded man would have to be blind not to ogle Maddie Hanks's boobs. That's why they pay her so much to take off her clothes. So when am I going to see you next? I was thinking we could meet up somewhere in the city for dinner tomorrow night. Café Sydney, perhaps?'

Jake knew if he did that then Olivia would want to come back to his place for the night. And he simply didn't want to have sex with her. Truth be told, he'd been glad she'd gone away the previous weekend. After Craig's wretched funeral and wake he'd just wanted to be alone.

'I don't think so, Olivia,' he told her, trying not to sound as cold and hard as he suddenly felt towards her. But in his head he kept comparing her to Abby, who had cried in his arms over a man she hardly knew. And that was before she knew what he'd left her. Olivia might look all woman but she didn't have a soft or compassionate bone in her body. She could read the most tragic news and shed not a single tear.

'But why not?' Olivia demanded to know in the stroppy tone she adopted when things weren't going her way.

'I just don't feel like going out at the moment,' he replied wearily. 'I'm still down about Craig's death.'

'Then the best thing for you is to get out and about!'

'I said no, Olivia.'

'But I've missed you,' she went on, changing her tone to wheedling. 'Okay, how about I come to your place and we can get some food delivered?'

'Olivia, you're not hearing me. I don't feel like company at the moment. Please don't make a fuss. I'll ring you later in the week. We'll go out somewhere Saturday night.'

'Why not Friday night?'

'I've an early engagement Saturday morning.'

'Doing what?'

Jake sighed. He was an expert at picking up when his girlfriends started wanting more from him than what they'd agreed to. He sensed that something had changed over the weekend. Possibly something to do with this friend of hers getting married.

'Olivia, look, I...'

'Gosh, but don't you sound serious,' Olivia broke in, her voice light and teasing. 'I thought we promised each other never to get serious.'

'*You* were the one who was starting to sound serious,' Jake pointed out.

'Yes, I know. Silly me, getting all jealous about that actress. But you can't blame me, Jake. I'm competitive by nature and I just didn't like the way she looked at you. Like she was going to have you for supper.'

'Olivia, I have no intention of having anything further to do with Maddie Hanks. It was an interview. End of story.'

'Yes, of course. I'm sorry. Am I forgiven?'

What could he possibly say to that?

'Don't be angry with me, Jake,' she went on before he could find the right words.

'I'm not angry,' he said. Just dismayed.

'Excellent,' she said. 'Because I'm in desperate need of sex. And you, lover boy, are just the man to deliver.'

A week ago, before Craig's death, Jake would have laughed. He'd always liked Olivia's slightly bawdy nature, plus her sometimes insatiable sex drive. Why, then, did he feel so disgruntled over her reducing him to the role of stud? He should have been pleased. And relieved. This was all he wanted from a woman, wasn't it?

An image suddenly popped into his mind, of another woman—one with lovely big eyes wet with tears—one who would never say things like that.

'I'm sorry, Olivia,' he said. 'But I'm not in the mood for sex right now.'

Her silence showed how much his rejection shocked her. Jake knew in his heart that this was the beginning of the end. Olivia was not going to be happy, but it was better to break up whilst they were still friends.

'Maybe you should find someone else,' he suggested quietly, hoping she would get the message without his having to spell it out.

'Like you have, you mean,' she threw at him. 'Who do you think you're kidding, Jake? You're always in the mood for sex. There's someone else, isn't there?'

Jake swallowed half a glass of wine before answering. 'No, Olivia,' he told her rather wearily. 'There's no one else.' It wasn't really a lie, even if Abby's face kept popping into his mind.

'Then who are you spending next Saturday morning with?' she demanded to know.

'If you must know, I'm taking Abby car shopping,' he said, well aware that it would cause trouble. But he no longer cared. He wanted Olivia out of his life.

'Abby who?' she screeched.

'Abby Jenkins,' he told her quite calmly. 'My house-keeper. Craig left me instructions in his will to buy her a car.'

'But...but...why would he do that?'

'Apparently she was nice to him when he stayed here a while back.'

'Nice to him in what way?' she said nastily.

How predictable she was. 'In her usual sweet way, I would imagine. Abby is a sweet girl.'

'*Girl!* I thought you said your housekeeper was a widow.'

'She is. Her husband died young.'

'I see. So how old is she, if I might ask?'

'Twenty-seven.'

'You never told me she was that young,' Olivia said, her tone accusing.

'Well, I'm telling you now.'

'Is she attractive?' she snapped.

'Olivia, I don't like the way this conversation is going.'

'Just answer the bloody question.'

'Abby's a very attractive girl.'

'I'll just bet she is. I dare say you wouldn't hire any other kind. So how long have you been sleeping with her?'

'I am not sleeping with her,' Jake denied. 'I hardly ever talk to her.'

'I don't believe you.'

Jake remained silent as his temper rose. If he spoke now, he'd say something he'd regret.

'You're not fooling me, Jake. You are sleeping with your housekeeper and nothing you say will make me believe otherwise.'

'In that case, I think we should call it quits, don't you?'

'Absolutely,' she said, and cut him off without another word.

Jake sighed. He preferred his relationships to end a lit-tle more civilly, and a lot more classily. But sometimes it just wasn't possible. A pity, though. Olivia had suited his

lifestyle very well. Or she had, till Craig died and forced
Jake to face what he had been secretly wanting for a long
time: Abby.

No doubt Olivia would spread it around that she'd come
home from her weekend away to discover that Jake was
sleeping with his housekeeper. He could deny it, of course.
But he'd always found that denial fuelled rumours to greater
heights. It wasn't as though any of this would reach Abby's
ears. If he ignored the whispers around the channel—the
TV world had a gossip grapevine second to none—by next
week it would be yesterday's news.

Meanwhile, he had a week of shows to do and a difficult
Saturday to endure.

Shoving his phone into his pocket, he stood up and made
his way to the kitchen to make himself some supper before
retiring for the night. As he extracted two slices of raisin
bread from the freezer then popped them in the toaster, his
thoughts slid back to Olivia's accusation that he was sleeping with Abby.

He wished!

Okay, so he possibly could seduce Abby if he put his
mind to it. Jake knew he hadn't exactly been Prince Charming around her up till now. But seducing a woman like Abby
would be a double-edged sword. Because she was the kind
of woman men fell in love with—the kind of woman who
made men want to marry them. Maybe even have children
with them.

His mind boggled at this last thought!

Nope. Seducing Abby was one big no-no in Jake's head.

Now, if only he could convince his body to agree with
him…

The toast popped up but Jake didn't notice. He was remembering how Abby's breasts had felt pressed hard against
his chest. They were full and feminine and very soft. He
wondered what kind of nipples she had. Would they be small

and pink, or large and dusky? He didn't mind either way, as long as they were responsive.

Jake sucked in sharply once he realised where his thoughts were taking him.

'This is not good,' Jake muttered as he turned his attention to the rapidly cooling toast. He didn't want to be tempted to seduce Abby. It was a powerful temptation, though a dangerous one. Because, even if he managed to keep it to just an affair and not let his emotions get involved, Jake knew Abby didn't have the experience to handle an affair with a man like him. In the end, he would break her heart.

And it wasn't a hard-boiled heart like Olivia's. Abby's heart was soft and sweet. To risk breaking such a heart would be wicked. And Jake wasn't wicked. At the same time, he wasn't a saint. Best to keep physical contact with Abby to a minimum, came his firm lecture to himself. Be especially careful when you take her to that cemetery on Saturday, for starters. Whisk her away before she starts crying again. No more hugging. And not too much chit-chat.

Jake supposed he couldn't get out of helping her buy a new car, since she'd want to trade in that old ute and was sure to be taken advantage of by some slick salesman. But once he knew what kind of car she liked, he'd do a lot of the groundwork over the phone before Saturday then direct her straight to his chosen dealer, who would have her choice all registered and ready to go. That way there would be no dithering around. Before you could say Jack Robinson, she'd be driving off home in her new car, leaving him to watch her go with a clear conscience.

Humph! And who was he kidding? Jake suspected that by the end of Saturday his conscience—as well as his male hormones—would have been sorely tried. Hopefully, he would win the battle and not do anything stupid!

Crunching into a piece of cold raisin toast, he ripped off a large mouthful with a savagery which matched his mood.

Jake hadn't felt this frustrated since he'd been laid up in hospital with a useless leg.

Life as a confirmed bachelor, he decided, wasn't all it was cracked up to be!

CHAPTER SEVEN

AFTER AN UNCHARACTERISTICALLY restless night, Abby woke with butterflies in her stomach. She didn't want to care what Jake might have done with that actress the night before. She didn't want to rush into the master bedroom as soon as she arrived at his house this morning. She certainly didn't want to be compelled to inspect the bed for evidence of a female visitor the night before.

But Abby knew that was exactly what she was going to do.

There was no use pretending differently. Her curiosity had been aroused by Megan's insistence that Jake would not be able to resist Maddie Hanks. It was all she'd thought about the evening before. She'd tried to read. She was on to the last of the list of ten books Craig had given her, Daphne du Maurier's *Rebecca*, which she was thoroughly enjoying. But even that hadn't distracted her from thinking about what Jake might be up to. She'd tossed and turned until well after midnight.

Strangely, despite less sleep than usual, she didn't feel tired. Just annoyed. With herself. Even more so when she started dithering over what to wear to work.

'As if it matters what you look like,' she flung at herself, reaching for another pair of old jeans and an equally ancient T-shirt which had once been white and was now an unflattering shade of grey. 'He's not going to come home again while you're there today. Now stop all this nonsense about Jake Sanderson. Who he sleeps with is none of your business!'

Famous last words. For what did Abby do as soon as she let herself into his house? She dropped her bag in the hallway then dashed upstairs to the master bedroom, her heart going as fast as her feet.

It was a large room, dominated by a huge bed which could easily accommodate its long-limbed owner and whatever playmate—or playmates—he so desired.

Abby blinked.

Had Jake ever entertained more than one woman at a time in that bed?

It looked messy enough this morning to have hosted a whole harem in there last night. Maybe he'd had the newsreader *and* the actress.

With some trepidation Abby approached the bed. Gingerly, she picked up one corner of the snow-white duvet and threw it back off the end of the bed. That was followed by the top sheet, revealing nothing but a rather crumpled bottom sheet. No female perfume wafted up to her nostrils, the only smell being Jake's, which was a mixture of man and the sandalwood scent belonging to his aftershave.

Still not certain that he hadn't had company, Abby bolted into the en suite bathroom to see how many towels had been used since yesterday. Only two, she noted, flung carelessly over the bath as was Jake's habit. If he'd had someone to stay then she hadn't showered in here, or used a fresh towel.

Abby let out a deep sigh of satisfaction.

'I told you he's not a sleazebag, Megan,' she said aloud.

Feeling much better, Abby went downstairs, collected her bag from the hallstand and made her way to the kitchen. There, she put on the kettle before proceeding into the utility room to inspect Jake's whiteboard, which was empty. She'd returned to the kitchen and just poured herself some coffee when her phone rang, her heart jumping when she saw the identity of her caller.

'Hello,' she said, unable to hide the surprise in her voice. 'What's up?'

'Nothing's up,' her boss answered after a moment's hesitation. 'I just wondered if you'd decided what kind of car you wanted yet. And what colour.'

'I... I haven't got around to that yet. Sorry,' she added.

'No need to apologise. But could you decide by tomorrow? That way I can have it ready for you by Saturday. Perhaps give me two choices of colours though, to be on the safe side. White is always a good pick. It's cooler and holds its value better.'

'Yes, yes, I know you're right. But I rather like blue.'

He sighed. 'What colour blue?'

'Not pale blue. Or turquoise. A royal blue.'

'Right. A royal blue. I know the Hyundai i30 comes in a nice royal blue. One of my assistants on the show has one and she loves it. Look, check it out on the internet and give me a ring tonight with your decision. Also, work out what bank account you want your money put into.'

'Okay,' she said, thinking to herself that he really was in a hurry to have done with all this, a thought which was a bit of a downer. It came to Abby that, against all logic and common sense, she was beginning to have feelings for Jake which were not only unwise but pointless.

It was all Megan's fault, she decided irritably, for putting silly ideas in her head.

'Make sure you have your old car looking as good as you can on Saturday so you can get the best trade-in possible.'

'Oh, but I'm not going to trade in the ute,' she told him. 'I'm going to give it to my sister. She doesn't have a car.'

'Right,' he said slowly.

'Is that a problem?'

'No, no, I suppose not.'

His attitude once again betrayed a degree of annoyance. No doubt he would prefer to spend this Saturday doing anything but chauffeuring her around to cemeteries and car yards. But really, there was no other solution if he wanted this all done and dusted as quickly as possible.

'Okay,' he went on after a longish hesitation. 'Ring me

tonight and tell me if you're happy with that Hyundai and I'll get the ball rolling. But if they don't have any royal blues on the lot then it might have to be white.'

'That's all right. It doesn't really matter. What time should I ring?' She didn't want to ring him whilst he was out with his girlfriend. Or anyone else who would remain nameless.

'Any time after six. I'm not going out tonight.'

Why did she have to like the sound of that so much?

'Okay. Thanks, Jake. For everything.'

'No sweat. Bye.'

Abby just stood there for a while after they'd both clicked off, her head in a bit of a whirl. Pointless it might be, but she was definitely going to buy herself some new clothes before next Saturday. No way could she go car shopping with Jake looking anything but her best.

Thursday night was late-night shopping. Perhaps she would take Megan with her. Then again perhaps she wouldn't. Not only would her sister ask awkward questions about why she was buying new clothes all of a sudden, but Megan would also steer Abby into buying clothes which were to *her* taste, which meant tight and tarty.

Feminine pride demanded she look nice for Jake on Saturday, but not tarty.

No, she would go shopping by herself and buy a few mix and match things which weren't too expensive but which fitted properly and made her feel good. She might also indulge herself with a trip to the hairdresser. Get her hair trimmed and a treatment put in. Maybe have her nails done at the same time.

No, not her nails. That was going too far. She didn't want Jake to think she was trying to doll herself up for him. She just wanted to look as good as she could. She'd felt ashamed of herself yesterday in those daggy old clothes with her hair scraped back and not a scrap of make-up on. If she was really going to move on with her life, it was high time she started looking after herself.

She'd really let herself go since Wayne died. Abby vowed she would turn over a new leaf tonight by having a long relaxing bath and giving her whole body some well needed attention.

Once she had a firm plan of action, Abby got started on the house. On Tuesday afternoons she always popped down to the supermarket to restock Jake's cupboards and fridge. When she'd started this job, Jake had given her a long list of food items that he didn't like to run out of.

He occasionally cooked meals for himself, though not often. Abby suspected he ordered takeaway a fair bit. Mostly Asian food. She'd seen the many and varied brochures on top of his fridge, plus the empty cartons in the bin. Abby had never seen the signs of a proper dinner party, despite the house having a lovely dining room with a beautiful big table and eight chairs. He probably took people out to dinner instead. Or maybe his current girlfriend gave dinner parties for him at her place.

Abby was wondering if this Olivia was as good a cook as *she* was, when she pulled herself up with a jolt.

You have to stop this, Abby Jenkins, she lectured herself. *Jake Sanderson is your boss and that's all he'll ever be. There is no point thinking about him, or his sex life, or what his girlfriends do or don't do. It's just as well you'll be leaving this job soon and going overseas before the man becomes some kind of sick obsession. You're lonely, that's all. So go get that shopping done then get yourself home, and around seven ring Jake and, for pity's sake, just keep the conversation businesslike.*

She wished she hadn't asked him to take her to the cemetery to visit his uncle's grave but it was too late now. He'd think she was loopy if she kept changing her mind. She'd just have to be careful not to cry. Because she didn't want him hugging her again. Gracious, no. No more hugging!

By the time Abby arrived home, a degree of depression had taken hold, this sudden unexpected attraction towards Jake making her acutely aware of just how lonely her life was. Really, she had no close friends other than her sister. Most of her neighbours worked in the city and were gone all day. Then at the weekends their lives were taken up with their children and their houses. Occasionally she was invited to a barbecue, but not often.

There was only one neighbour she would classify as a friend, an elderly widow who'd been very kind to her when Wayne died, but who, unfortunately, was also a terrible gossip. Abby hadn't told Harriet that her boss was the celebrity host of *Australia at Noon*, knowing that if she let that little gem drop she would be bombarded with questions about Jake. She'd just said her boss was called Mr Sanderson—which was a common enough name—and was a bachelor businessman who worked long hours in the city and needed someone to look after the house for him. When Harriet assumed he was a middle-aged workaholic who was married to his job, Abby let her.

Abby had been relieved to see that her next-door neighbour Harriet's car wasn't in her driveway, which meant she was out and therefore wouldn't be dropping in for a cuppa as she sometimes did when Abby arrived home from work. Abby wasn't in the mood for gossip.

There was no doubt that life hadn't been very kind to her. Firstly there was her teeth, which had been a huge problem in her eyes but which her parents had dismissed as nothing. Probably because it would have cost money to fix and they'd spent all their spare cash on alcohol. Then, shortly after her father had been killed in a drunken pub brawl, her mother had also died, succumbing to too many sleeping tablets downed with too much gin.

The coroner had called it an accidental death as opposed to suicide, but what did it really matter in the end? There'd been no life insurance to consider.

Abby had only been seventeen at the time, just entering her last year in high school. It had been impossible to do well at her studies while living in a refuge. She'd left school in the end to work full-time at the local fish and chip shop, earning enough by working seven days a week to rent the small flat above the shop for herself and Megan. At twenty she'd married Wayne but she'd been unable to carry a baby full term.

That was the cruellest cut of all, even crueller, in a way, than Wayne's tragic drowning. Because, more than anything in the world, Abby wanted to have children, wanted to create a happy family, wanted to be the best mother in the world. Instead, she hadn't even had the chance.

When tears dripped from her nose into her tea, Abby shook her head quite violently, determined not to dwell on the past any more, or on anything negative.

'Time to run a bath and start looking after yourself, kiddo,' she said aloud, smiling at how much like Megan she sounded.

Her mood was still up when she picked up her phone to ring Jake at seven. Okay, so she found the man attractive. Most of the women in Australia did. There was no need to get into a twist over it. Nothing would come of it, and soon she'd be off overseas on the holiday of a lifetime.

Given all her common sense reasoning, it annoyed Abby that her hand still shook as she lifted her phone to her ear and waited for Jake to answer.

'Hi, Abby,' Jake answered in his usual businesslike voice. So why did the sound of it suddenly have her stomach curling over and her heart beating faster? 'Made up your mind about the car?'

In truth, Abby didn't really give a hoot about the make and model of the car. She was thrilled just to be getting a brand-new one. Not so thrilled that she was acting like some schoolgirl with a crush on her teacher.

'I like the look of that Hyundai you mentioned. And it doesn't have to be royal blue. A white one would be fine.'

'Good. I'll pick you up at ten on Saturday morning. Is that too early for you?'

'No, no. Ten will be fine.' She'd be ready at dawn if he wanted.

'See you Saturday morning.'

He was gone before she could say another word, leaving her with a dry mouth and the sure knowledge that the next few days were going to be the longest in her life.

CHAPTER EIGHT

BY FRIDAY JAKE found it difficult to concentrate on the preparations for his show. Or care. He hadn't been sleeping well and, quite frankly, doing this damned show every day was beginning to bore him silly.

There was no doubt now that he would sell it and do something else with his life, something more challenging, preferably overseas and well away from a certain girl who he couldn't get out of his mind. Instead of going over his notes for the show like he usually did, he kept thinking about tomorrow.

The door to his dressing room suddenly opened.

'Five minutes, Jake,' Kerrie said.

'Yeah, yeah, I'm ready.' Though he wasn't.

He did the show on autopilot that day, no one guessing that his mind was elsewhere. Or so he'd imagined. Afterwards, the director pulled him aside and asked him if there was anything wrong.

'No,' Jake said. 'Why?'

'A little birdie told me you've been having girl trouble.'

Jake smiled a wry smile. He'd known Olivia would become vicious and vengeful.

'Not me, Victor. I never have girl trouble.'

Victor didn't look convinced. 'Not telling, eh? Fair enough. But it's never wise to let your private life affect your professional life. The lights were on today, Jake, but nobody was home.'

Jake shrugged. 'Just a bit tired, that's all.'

'No sweat. No one else would have noticed. Only old eagle-eye here. But it might be an idea to get some shut-eye tonight. Man does not live by sex alone.'

Jake laughed drily. 'I wish.'

'So the rumours were right? Olivia's been dumped in favour of your sexy young housekeeper?'

Jake rolled his eyes. 'I didn't *dump* Olivia. We broke up because she jumped to the wrong conclusion about my housekeeper, who's a very nice, *sweet* girl and definitely *not* my lover.'

Again, Victor didn't look convinced.

When Jake's phone rang he stared at the identity of the caller, his emotions suddenly a-jangle. He hoped nothing had happened to prevent them getting together tomorrow. The truth was he couldn't wait to see her. 'I have to take this call,' he said sharply, then strode off down the corridor.

'Yes, Abby?' Jake said, an attack of anxiety making his stomach swirl. 'What is it?' He didn't mean to sound so abrupt but he was shocked by his nervous reaction to the possibility that he might not be seeing her the next day after all. 'I hope you're not going to change tomorrow's arrangements,' he snapped before he could stop himself.

'What? No, no. I just wanted to ask you if I could go home early today. I was going to do some late-night shopping last night but my sister wasn't well and she needed me to look after Timmy for her.'

Relief swamped Jake, as did remorse over his snapping at her like that.

'Of course you can go home early.'

'I've done everything I had to do.'

'I'm sure the place is perfect,' Jake said. 'It always is. What do you need to buy?' he added, hoping to redeem himself by showing an interest in her life for once.

'Just some new clothes so that I don't embarrass you tomorrow by looking like your cleaning lady. Even if I am,' she added with a sweet laugh.

'You are much more than my cleaning lady,' Jake said, the devil's voice whispering in his ear that he would like her to be a hell of a lot more. 'As I said the other day, you are the best housekeeper a man could have.'

Her sudden silence brought a tension to Jake which was wickedly sexual. Heat licked through his loins, giving him an inkling of how it would feel if she ever surrendered to him.

He had no idea what she was thinking but he hoped she might be softening towards him a little. Or was he just fantasising? Abby had been making him fantasise a lot lately, all of it rather R-rated. How many times this week had he pictured going home early and sweeping her up into his arms, kissing her senseless and having her then and there? His favourite fantasy scenario was to hoist her up on to the kitchen bench-top where he would spread her legs—she'd be somehow naked, of course—and sink into her as she wrapped her arms around his neck and urged him on and on. Then there was the polished floor scenario. And the one against the wall. In the lap pool. Across the dining table.

His raunchy fantasies were multiplying.

Deplorable, really.

And very dangerous.

Because they were oh, so exciting.

'So everything's still right for tomorrow?' he asked, his cool voice belying the heat in his body.

'What? Oh, yes…yes. I'll be ready. Ten o'clock, you said, didn't you?'

'Yes. Oh, and Abby, what account do you want the twenty-five thousand put into?'

'Just put it in the one my salary goes in.'

'Very well. I'll do that this afternoon.'

'I… I don't know what to say except thank you.'

'It's Craig you should be thanking.'

'I will, when I visit his grave tomorrow.'

'You do that. See you tomorrow then.'

'But you don't know my address.'

'Of course I do. It was on your CV, which is still in my computer. You haven't moved, have you?'

'No.'

'Then I'll see you at your place at ten on the dot. Have to go. Bye.'

Jake sighed heavily as he clicked off his phone.

It was always an intimate situation, driving a woman somewhere, especially in a car which had once been described by a motoring magazine as sex on wheels. Jake figured Abby had never seen his red Ferrari. During the week he kept it locked away in the garage. He always used the ferry to get to and from work, and took taxis if he was socialising in and around the city. The Ferrari was only brought out at weekends for drives either up or down the coast. Jake liked nothing better than to zoom along one of the freeways with the top down and a beautiful woman by his side, one who was as responsive as his car.

Jake suddenly recalled his thoughts the other day about Abby's breasts, and how responsive they might be. If he closed his eyes he could still feel how they had felt, pressed up against him.

He cursed and jumped to his feet. This was all getting beyond a joke. Anyone would think he didn't have any self-control. He needed to stop all this nonsense immediately and just act naturally with her. He would not, he resolved, do or say anything provocative or seductive or, God forbid, charming.

An affair with Abby was out of the question.

Still, as Jake headed out of the dressing room, he resolved not to tempt fate by putting the top down on the Ferrari on Saturday. Better to be safe than sorry.

CHAPTER NINE

For the umpteenth time that morning, Abby smiled at herself in her large bathroom mirror, which was, actually, the only mirror she had in her house. All those years of having horrible teeth had made her allergic to mirrors. She still wasn't entirely used to her new appearance. Still didn't smile as much as other people.

But Megan was right. Her face did look much better now that her teeth were lovely and even and white. Her face looked a lot better with some make-up on as well, and with her hair all shiny and blow-dried properly.

Deciding that she'd admired herself long enough, Abby returned to her bedroom, where she'd laid out all the clothes she'd bought after her trip to the hairdresser. Abby hadn't splurged out on too much—a couple of pairs of stretchy jeans and a few tops and T-shirts, all of them cheap but in fashion. She'd also bought a lightweight blazer, a pair of trendy sandals and a new handbag. Finally, she'd splurged on a delicate gold necklace which went with everything, along with some new make-up, nail polish and a small bottle of perfume.

All in all she'd only spent just over three hundred dollars, which she considered very reasonable. Really, you didn't have to spend a lot on clothes these days, and it was about time she made more of an effort with her appearance. With today promising to be warmer than yesterday, she selected the white jeans and a short-sleeved silky top that had a white background and little brown dots all over it. The slinky fabric hugged her curves and the scooped neckline was perfect for her new dainty gold chain.

A glance at the digital clock beside the bed made Abby

sigh. Only nine o'clock, excitement having got her up at the crack of dawn. She had a whole hour before Jake was due to arrive. That was, if he even arrived on time. People didn't seem to care about punctuality these days. She supposed it would take her a while to do her nails, but not an hour.

As the minutes ticked slowly away she became aware of her heart beating faster behind her ribs. Beside the excitement of a new car, she was nervous at the thought of being with Jake outside of a work environment. Would he think she looked pretty in her new clothes? Did she want him to think her pretty? Did she want him to…what?

Abby knew she was being foolish. He had a girlfriend. A gorgeous girlfriend. Why would he look at her twice? Why would she even want him to?

He's your boss, she reminded herself firmly. *And he's only doing all this because his uncle asked him to. He doesn't want to spend time with you. He doesn't want to buy you a new car or take you to a cemetery. Not really. He's honouring his beloved uncle's deathbed wishes. Get a grip, girl.*

The sight of a bright red sports car careering down her street was not a sight designed to make a girl get a grip.

Abby wasn't surprised when the sleek red car with the prancing horse logo on it slid into the kerb outside her house. For who else would drive a Ferrari but a man who'd been voted not only the most popular television personality but also Sydney's most eligible bachelor?

Megan kept her well informed about all aspects of her boss's professional and private life.

'Oh, *my*,' Abby murmured when Jake emerged from the driver's side, looking even sexier than his car, if that were possible. Up till now Abby had only ever seen her boss dressed in a business suit. Today, he was wearing a pair of chinos and a black polo shirt which hugged the contours of his upper body, showing off his naturally broad shoulders and nicely flat stomach. As he strode around the low-slung bonnet of the car, a lock of his dark brown hair fell across his forehead. Jake lifted his hand and impatiently combed it back with his fingers. The action brought Abby's attention to his face. It wasn't the face of a pretty boy but very handsome all the same, with a strong straight nose and a ruggedly squared jawline. His blue eyes—possibly his best feature—were hidden by a pair of expensive-looking sunglasses.

For a split second, Abby wondered what her neighbours would think when Jake walked up to her front door. It was a lovely spring day so quite a few of them were out in their gardens, mowing lawns and tending to their flowerbeds. Not that they would recognise him. He could be anyone in those glasses. Anyone handsome and very rich, that was.

Abby took a backwards step from the window when Jake stopped on the pavement to stare at her house, her hackles rising as he continued to stare at it for some time. What was he staring at? she wondered.

Abby wasn't in any way ashamed of her home. Okay, so it was small and old, built not long after the war. But it was nicely painted and neat, with well kept gardens, front and back. Inside, each of the rooms was equally well painted, the wooden floors shiny and polished. The furniture *was* on the cheap side but it had been bought new and looked quite stylish, like the clothes she was wearing.

He finally opened the gate and strode up the path to the small front porch, Abby using those few precious seconds to get a handle on her suddenly defensive mood.

It wasn't like her to be sensitive about criticism; it was a survival habit she'd acquired over her school years when her supposed friends had made bitchy comments about her teeth. But Abby suspected she would be very hurt if Jake made her feel small, especially today when she felt so good about herself. Hopefully, he wouldn't. He didn't seem an unkind person. But then, she didn't really know him all that well, did she?

The doorbell ringing made her heart jump, then race like mad. Lord, but she was getting herself into a right state. Gathering herself, Abby hurried to the front door, her head held high.

CHAPTER TEN

JAKE THOUGHT HE'D steeled himself sufficiently by the time he'd rung the doorbell, having given himself a firm lecture during the drive over. He'd told himself in no uncertain terms that he had to stop fantasising about what Abby might be like in bed and concentrate on the job his uncle had entrusted him with.

Craig certainly hadn't included seduction in his dying wishes.

Even after he'd arrived, Jake had lingered outside for another minute or so, harnessing all his willpower for the mental and physical battle he had ahead of him.

Jake thought he was well prepared until Abby opened the door.

His startled gaze raked over her from top to toe before returning to her face. He'd found her attractive before. Today she looked downright stunning, and so desirable it was criminal.

Thank goodness he was wearing sunglasses, the kind you couldn't see through.

What to say? Nothing personal. Nothing too complimentary. She might think he was coming on to her.

'Don't you look nice,' he said.

If only she hadn't smiled at him. Such a beautiful smile.

'I went on a bit of a shopping splurge last night,' she said a little sheepishly. 'I hope Craig would approve. I didn't spend too much.'

'I'm sure he wouldn't mind,' Jake said. But *he* did. That outfit she had on was extremely sexy, those tight white jeans contrasting with the silky top which skimmed her hips and left her full breasts oh, so accessible. In his mind's eye, Jake immediately saw himself pressed up behind her, their lower halves glued together whilst his hands slid up underneath, cupping her breasts. In his fantasy she moaned softly, her head tipping back against his shoulder. She moaned again when he unclipped her bra and took her erect nipples between his thumbs and forefingers and squeezed them.

Hard.

It was impossible to think such wickedly erotic thoughts and not have his body respond. Alarmed that Abby might notice, Jake did the only thing he could think of.

'Would you mind if I used your bathroom before we get going?' he asked with some urgency.

'It's the second door on the right,' Abby directed him.

Abby smiled as she watched Jake head for the bathroom, thrilled to pieces with his compliment on her appearance. And whilst she was flattered and pleased—she was a female after all—she was quite confident that Jake was not about to pounce on her the way Megan had said he might. She'd sent her sister pictures of her new clothes last night, and been subjected to renewed warnings over the male species and their lack of conscience and morals where pretty girls were concerned.

'Playboys like your Jake are the worst,' Megan had pointed out. 'They think they can't be resisted and, unfortunately, that's often true. Hard to resist a good-looking man with charm and money.'

When Abby argued that she'd never found Jake all that charming, Megan had just laughed.

'That's because you haven't been a target before. Once he gets a look at you in your new things he'll go into charm mode in no time flat. First will come the compliments, then the accidental touches, followed by flirtatious remarks, finishing up with a drinks or dinner invitation. You mark my words, kiddo.'

At this point, Abby had decided not to tell Megan that

she would be the one extending a dinner invitation. As a thank you gesture. Truly, sometimes it was best not to tell Megan things.

Still, she had to confess that she'd got a real buzz when he'd said how nice she looked.

Whilst Jake was in the bathroom, Abby collected her new bag from the lounge, then picked up the house keys from the hall table so she'd be ready to lock up when Jake was finished. She understood that he didn't want to waste the whole of his precious Saturday with her when he could be with his girlfriend. His attitude to this whole business had been one of impatience from the start.

Jake took his time, however, Abby's gaze travelling back to his car whilst she waited.

Now that was another thing she'd definitely not be telling Megan. Abby hadn't known till today what kind of car Jake drove so she would invent a nice safe sedan, if need be. She could just imagine what Megan would say if she found out her sister had spent Saturday afternoon swanning around in Jake's sexy red Ferrari.

By the time Jake left the bathroom he'd gathered himself, ready to face his tormentor with his body almost under control and his sunglasses firmly in place.

Jake wondered again what was making her so irresistible to him. Was it her relative innocence? Her lack of experience?

It wasn't just her beauty. He'd had lots of beautiful women in his life, and in his bed. No, it was something else. Something intangible. Something very sweet and very special.

It made him afraid for her.

He'd been right to be fearful, he decided as he watched Abby turn to lock up, her rear view as tasty as her front. He suppressed a groan and willed his own body to behave.

It ignored him and Jake swore at himself in his head.

'How long will it take to get to the cemetery?' she asked innocently as she turned back to face him.

'Not long,' he said a bit abruptly. 'I've also already contacted the dealership in Parramatta,' he went on, masking his inner torment behind his best businesslike voice. 'I spoke to a salesman there at length yesterday and they have a car on their lot which should suit you admirably. If you like it, you could drive it away today. It's all registered and ready to go.'

'Really?' She sounded pleased. 'What colour is it?'

'White. Sorry. No blue ones available. But really, it's the most sensible colour for our climate and city. Never gets too hot or looks too dirty.'

She laughed, bringing a sparkle to her eyes and some added colour to her cheeks. She was making things awfully hard for him.

And wasn't that an understatement? came the wry thought. Thank goodness he wasn't wearing tight jeans.

'I can't imagine me ever letting any car of mine get too dirty,' she said, 'especially a new one. Megan calls me a neat freak.'

'A good quality in a housekeeper,' he said through gritted teeth. And in a lover, came the pesky thought.

Jake liked his women well groomed. All over. Liked their clothes to be just so, especially their underwear. When he started wondering what Abby had on underneath that top and jeans he knew it was time to get this show on the road. 'Come on, let's get going.'

Quite automatically, he went to reach out and take her elbow, a habit he had when escorting a woman. He pulled his hand back just in time, instead waving her on ahead of him.

Damn, he thought wearily as he trudged after her. It was going to be a long morning.

CHAPTER ELEVEN

A VERY HAPPY Abby was striding along her front path towards the gate when Harriet, her elderly neighbour, suddenly popped her head up over the hedge which separated their two houses.

'Hello, dear,' she said. 'My, but don't you look extra nice today. Going somewhere special?' Her curious eyes zoomed from Abby to Jake to the Ferrari then back to Abby again.

Abby suppressed a sigh as she reluctantly ground to a halt and turned towards her neighbour. 'Just going car shopping,' she replied truthfully. 'Got a windfall from a long-lost uncle. My friend here's going to help me find the right one,' she said, casting a rueful glance over her shoulder at Jake. 'He's a car nut, as you can see. Can't stop and chat,' she hurried on, not wanting to have to get into awkward introductions.

'We're already running late,' she added, and headed for the Ferrari. 'Bye.'

'Drop in for a cuppa tomorrow,' Harriet called after her.

'Will do,' she called back.

Jake didn't say a word as he swiftly opened the passenger door for her. Neither did he help her, despite it not being the easiest car to get into. But Abby had always been an agile sort of girl, with long slender legs and sure hands, so by the time Jake closed the door and walked around to the driver's side she was all buckled up and ready to go, her new handbag settled in her lap.

'A car nut, am I?' Jake said wryly after he climbed in and gunned the engine.

Abby shrugged. 'I had to say something.'

'Will you really go in for a cuppa tomorrow?' he asked as he accelerated away.

'Probably,' Abby admitted. 'Harriet was very good to me when Wayne died. I wouldn't hurt her for the world. I just didn't want to have to introduce you.'

'Why's that?'

'Well, mostly because I don't want her to find out that you're the businessman I clean house for. She'd immediately think that there was something going on between us and, before I knew it, the whole street would think the same thing, which would be very embarrassing. Gosh, but this car is amazing,' she rattled on, happy to change the subject from their hypothetical affair. 'It must have cost you a small fortune.'

'There are more expensive cars but it wasn't cheap. I only drive it at weekends and when I'm on holiday.'

'It's not a convertible though, is it?'

'Actually, it is. The top retracts.'

'That's incredible!'

He said nothing for a few seconds, though he did glance over at her with a bit of a frown. But then he smiled a strange little smile as though he was secretly amused about something.

'I'll show you, if you like,' he said.

His offer startled her. 'Oh, no. No, please don't. Not today. My hair will get all messed up and it took me ages to do it.'

'Fair enough. Some other time then.' And he smiled another strange smile.

Abby could not envisage there would ever be such a time, which was a shame really. It would be wonderful whizzing along an open country road on a fine summer's day with the top down and her hair blowing in the breeze. Even better if she were driving.

She almost laughed. Imagine her driving a Ferrari. She wasn't a Ferrari kind of girl.

Jake was right. The cemetery wasn't far away but it was a depressing place. Abby didn't like the long rows of gravestones.

She hadn't buried Wayne. He'd been cremated with his ashes sprinkled in the ocean at his favourite fishing spot. Which was ironic given it was the sea which had killed him. But it was what he had once told her he wanted, if anything ever happened to him. Perhaps, however, he'd imagined being killed in a car accident, not what had actually happened.

'This way,' Jake said after they both climbed out. He set off at a brisk walk, not looking back to see if she was behind him. Which was so typical of her boss.

No charm yet, Megan, she said silently to her sister. One little compliment was as much as he could manage.

Abby followed Jake down a long row of well tended graves, some of which had fresh flowers in vases on them. She hadn't thought to bring flowers, her mind being on nothing but looking her very best this morning, a realisation which upset her a little. Stupid, Abby. Get your priorities straight!

Still, Jake might have thought it was overdoing things if she'd brought flowers.

He stopped suddenly in front of a freshly dug grave which was covered with a large green felt blanket topped with a huge arrangement of native flowers which didn't look at all bedraggled, although they had to have been there over a week.

'That's Craig's grave,' he pointed out, his rough voice betraying a depth of emotion which moved Abby.

Clearly, he had loved his uncle. A lot. Craig's death must have upset Jake terribly, his grief heightened by not having been able to be with the man when he'd died. It had been a cruel thing for his uncle to do. He'd probably thought he was being kind, and brave. But it had been selfish of him, really. Selfish and insensitive.

Abby opened her mouth to say something sympathetic, but when she looked up at Jake she found him staring down, not at his uncle's grave but at the grave on the left of it. The name on the gravestone was Clive Sanderson, beloved husband of Grace, much loved father of Roland, Peter, Jake, Sophie, Cleo and Fiona.

It didn't take a genius to realise this had to be Jake's father, the dates revealing he'd died at the age of forty-seven. How sad. What to say?

Nothing, Abby decided. She understood enough about her boss to know that he wouldn't want to talk about it. So she returned her attention to Craig's grave, closed her eyes and said a prayer of thanks to him, at the same time adding that he really should have told his family that he was dying.

But it was too late to change anything now, she accepted. Death was very final. It took no prisoners, as the saying went. When Abby felt tears prick at her eyes she blinked them away then looked over at Jake.

'I've said my thanks,' she said matter-of-factly. 'I think I'd like to go now.'

'Good,' he said, and stalked off in the direction of the car, not saying another word till they were both back in their seats. Only then did he speak.

'I'm sorry,' he apologised. 'I still can't get over his death.'

'Your uncle's, or your father's?' she asked gently.

'Ah. You saw.' He loosened his grip on the wheel and turned to face her. 'Both really. But Craig's is still very raw.'

'It gets easier with time,' was all she could offer. Though, down deep, Abby knew some deaths stayed with you for ever.

He sighed, leant back against the car seat, took off his sunglasses then glanced over at her. 'How did your husband die, Abby?'

'He drowned,' came her rather stark reply. But there was little point in not telling him the truth. 'He went out fishing in a small dinghy not suitable for the open sea. A storm came up and he was tipped into the water. He wasn't wearing a life belt. His body was washed up on Maroubra Beach a couple of days later.'

'You must have been devastated,' he said quietly, his eyes sad for her.

'I was.'

He nodded at the obvious sincerity in her statement. 'You are a lovely young woman,' he went on with a sigh. 'You'll find someone else eventually, get married again and have lots of equally lovely children.'

She laughed. She couldn't help it. 'I don't think so, Jake. I don't want to get married again.'

'You loved him that much?'

It was one thing to tell her boss the brutal truth about Wayne's death, but everything else was her own private business. She would not share it with him.

'It's not a question of love, Jake, but what I want to do with the rest of my life. I thought I wanted marriage and children when I was younger, but my priorities have changed. I want to travel whilst I'm still young. I want to see another side of life than just what's here in Australia. I want to see the world.'

He looked over at her for a long time. 'I see,' he said at last.

Probably not, she thought.

'We'd better get going again,' he went on gruffly. 'We have a car to buy.'

CHAPTER TWELVE

'OH, JAKE, I simply adore it!' Abby exclaimed when she climbed in behind the wheel of the sporty white hatchback. 'Thank you so much.'

Jake just smiled and let the salesman, Raoul, continue showing Abby all the features of her new car. After he'd run through everything, Raoul suggested Abby take it for a test spin round the block. Jake declined her invitation to accompany her, which in hindsight was not a good move, since Raoul was only too happy to go in his place. The salesman was about Abby's age, an immigrant from South America, tall, dark and handsome with a sexy accent and charm by the bucketload. Jake wished within seconds of them disappearing down the street that he'd gone with Abby.

He was damned if he did and damned if he didn't! When she'd confessed her wish to spurn marriage and see the world, he'd been momentarily overcome with joy that now he could seduce her and not feel guilty about it. But Jake knew in his heart of hearts that a girl like Abby would want marriage and children again one day. And then there was the unpalatable added fact that whilst she was grateful to him, she clearly wasn't at all enamoured with his character.

Was it too late to turn on the charm?

He rather suspected that it was.

Jake paced the car lot until Abby returned, doing his best to calm down whilst inside he was churning with regret and, yes, jealousy, an emotion he despised. But it was no use. He was jealous. As soon as the white hatchback turned into the driveway he strode towards it, anxiously searching for evidence that the couple inside were in any way attracted to each other.

Raoul, it seemed, was doing all the talking whilst Abby was just nodding. When Abby climbed out and smiled over at *him*, Jake was so relieved that he smiled back.

'So how was it?' he asked as she walked towards him.

'Brilliant!' she exclaimed. 'And so easy to drive.'

'It certainly is,' Raoul said on joining them. 'But then, you are also a very good driver, Abby.'

She smiled over at him.

Jake's gut tightened. He didn't want her smiling at other men, especially this one. What was the point in controlling his own desire for the girl if she fell into the clutches of some slick-talking salesman?

Jake decided it was time to go.

'You're happy with that particular car then, Abby?' he directed at her.

'Oh, yes. Very happy.'

'Then we'll take it,' he told Raoul. 'I presume I can pay for it with my credit card.'

'But of course, Mr Sanderson. Come with me into my office and I'll fix up everything for you.'

'Lucky you,' Raoul said when he finally handed over the registration papers and keys, 'to have such a generous employer as Mr Sanderson.'

'He's a wonderful boss,' Abby agreed.

Jake winced inside. He'd explained to Raoul on the phone yesterday that Abby was a valued employee of his and the car was her Christmas bonus. Jake had informed Abby of his little white lie just before they'd arrived at the dealership, but he'd forgotten that the male mind often thought the worst when it came to an attractive female. Clearly, Raoul had jumped to the conclusion that Abby was getting this car as payment for services rendered outside work hours. Fortunately, Abby didn't seem aware of this. He just hoped that he could get her out of here before she twigged to the situation.

'Thank you for your assistance,' Jake said, standing up and extending his hand over the desk.

The salesman stood up and took his hand. 'My pleasure, Mr Sanderson,' he returned in a rather unctuous manner.

'Now, if you have any trouble, Abby,' Raoul went on, smiling over at Abby, who had also risen to her feet, 'any trouble at all, you just ring me. Here's my card.'

Abby took it, of course. Which irked Jake considerably. Couldn't she see he just wanted to get into her pants? Surely she wasn't *that* naïve?

'If you have any trouble with your car, Abby,' Jake bit out as he walked her over to it, 'you ring me first, not that sleazebag.'

Abby lifted startled eyes to his. 'You think Raoul's a sleazebag?'

'Yes, I do.'

Takes one to know one, Jake, came the brutally honest thought.

Abby's face fell. 'And there I was, thinking he was just being extra nice. Because of you being famous, you know?'

Jake could see he'd upset her, which was the last thing he'd wanted to do. He'd loved seeing her so happy about the car.

'You could be right,' he said. 'Take no notice of me, Abby. I'm a cynical bastard at times.'

Abby frowned. 'No, you're probably right. Megan says I'm too trusting where men are concerned.' She glanced up at him and smiled. 'But I know a truly good one when I meet him. Which reminds me. I want to do something special for you, Jake, to thank you for everything.'

Jake tried not to let his mind trail over all the things he'd like her to do for him. But it went there all the same. She'd called him 'truly good', but he wasn't. Not at all.

He swallowed before he spoke, lest a thickened voice betray him. 'You don't have to do anything, Abby. It was my pleasure to follow through with Craig's wishes. He obviously liked and admired you a lot.'

She flushed prettily. 'Not as much as he liked and admired you. Look, I thought that perhaps I could cook you dinner one night. I know that's not much in the way of a thank you present, but I'm actually a very good cook.'

'I'm sure you are, Abby, but truly, it's not necessary.'

Her face fell again, which made him feel dreadful. After all, she didn't know the battle that was going on inside him. It was obvious she wanted to do this. A thought suddenly occurred which would hopefully save his sanity.

'Very well,' he agreed. 'Dinner it is. But not just for me,' he added. 'For my sister as well.'

Abby blinked her confusion. 'Your sister?'

'Yeah, my sister, Sophie. I promised to take her out to dinner next Friday night. She's the only one in my family who knows about Craig's letter and she was saying the other day that she'd love to meet you. We could kill two birds with one stone. What do you say, Abby? Would you mind cooking for her as well?'

'I wouldn't mind at all. But maybe your sister would mind.'

'Good heavens, no. She'd love it.'

'Well, if you're sure…'

'I'm very sure.'

'Your place or mine?'

Jake almost choked on the spot. 'What?'

'Do you want me to cook the dinner at my place or yours?'

What *had* he been thinking? About sex, of course. What else?

'I don't mind either way, Abby, but then I don't have a problem with neighbours. Perhaps we should have this dinner at my place?'

'Yes, I think that would be best.'

He looked at her and thought none of this was for the best. But Sophie's presence would at least stop him from doing something stupid—like piling on the charm and plying Abby with wine before carrying her up to bed and having his wicked way with her all night long.

'I presume you'll be okay to drive home alone in your new car,' he said. 'You won't be nervous, will you?'

'Maybe a little. But only because it's new. I really am a good driver. And the car has GPS. Even if it didn't, I know the roads around here like the back of my hand. I used to live out this way. The fish and chip shop I worked in for years is just around the corner.'

Jake was suddenly overwhelmed with curiosity about her life before coming to work for him, especially about her marriage and, yes, her drowned husband. The temptation to invite her to go for coffee with him somewhere was acute, but he resisted it.

Just.

'In that case I won't worry about you,' he said instead. 'Off you go then.'

Abby sighed. 'What a shame. I would have *loved* another ride in that gorgeous car of yours.'

Don't say a single word, his conscience insisted firmly.

Suddenly, Abby beamed up at him. 'But I'm going to enjoy driving my own gorgeous little car even more. Bye, Jake. And thanks again.'

'My pleasure,' he returned. And, despite everything else, it had been. How perverse was that?

He shook his head as he watched her drive off with surprising confidence, not hesitating before joining the traffic and changing lanes quite assertively. Naïve and vulnerable Abby might be in some ways, but in practical life skills she seemed experienced and assured.

Once again, he wondered about her life before she'd been widowed, and even before that. What kind of child had she been? What were her parents like? Had she been good at school? Possibly not, if she'd ended up working in a fish and chip shop. But she certainly wasn't dumb. When Raoul had been showing her all the features of the car, she'd been very quick on the uptake. She also claimed to be a good cook and Jake came to the conclusion that Abby would be good at anything she set her mind to.

Inevitably, his own mind shifted to other areas at which Abby might excel. She'd been married for quite a few years, after all. And she hadn't gone to work during all that time. Clearly, she'd been content to stay home and be the kind of old-fashioned housewife a lot of men craved, always being there when hubby came home. He could see her now, waiting on the man she loved hand and foot, giving him everything he desired, in bed and out. As much as Jake didn't want that kind of life—or wife—for himself, he could see its appeal. He could see Abby's appeal. He could feel it, right now. He didn't want to marry her, but he did want her.

'Damn and blast,' Jake growled to himself as he marched off to where he'd parked his own car. He virtually threw himself behind the wheel, slamming it with both fists in a burst of frustration unlike any he'd ever felt before.

When he eventually calmed down, he just sat there, thinking.

Jake decided he should never have broken up with Olivia. He wasn't the sort of man who liked to sleep alone for too long. And she would be a good distraction from Abby. But there was no going back now. And if he was honest he didn't really want to.

Maybe he should give Maddie Hanks a call. She was still in Sydney, he knew. Okay, so her charms were rather obvious but, on the plus side, she wasn't interested in becoming Mrs Jake Sanderson. She just wanted some fun and games whilst she was here. A man would have to be a fool to knock that back, especially one who was climbing the walls with frustration. She'd given him her number after the show and he'd politely put it in his phone, even though at the time he'd had no intention of acting on her none too subtle invitation.

But lots of water had gone under the bridge since then.

Jake pulled out his phone and brought up her number, his lips pursing as his finger hovered. Did he really want to go to bed with someone like that?

Jake could not believe it when he abruptly deleted Maddie Hanks's number and rang his sister instead.

Sophie answered quickly. 'Hi, Jake, darling. How are you bearing up? You know, I watched you yesterday on that silly show you do, and I thought you looked a bit down.'

'What do you mean, calling my show silly?'

'Perhaps silly is not the right word. Lightweight, then.'

'Still, hardly a compliment.' But she was right. It was lightweight. No wonder he was bored. He'd meant it to be a hard-hitting current affairs show when he'd conceived it, but it hadn't turned out that way.

'If the cap fits, wear it, Jake. Now, to what do I owe the pleasure of this call? You're not going to call off our dinner date next Friday, are you?'

'Not at all. But I have a favour to ask you…'

And he told her everything.

CHAPTER THIRTEEN

ABBY FELT SATISFIED as she surveyed the dinner table in Jake's formal dining room. She had copied the exquisite setting from one of her sister's magazines, having known straight away it would suit the polished wooden floors and white walls of Jake's dining room. She'd used Jake's cutlery and glassware, but she'd bought the snow-white tablecloth and white napkins, along with the red and black table mats and matching coasters from the magazine, which Abby had found in a city store.

Since Jake's dining table could seat eight she'd only set one end of it, with Jake at the head, his sister to his right and herself to his left. That way she was nearer the door and the kitchen. Abby had also bought a crystal candlestick as a centrepiece, which held one red candle. A vase of fresh flowers from her own garden sat on the carved wooden sideboard, along with a vanilla-scented candle which she hoped would mask any smell which might waft from the kitchen once she started cooking the prawns and scallops.

It had taken ages for Abby to settle on a menu for the dinner party. She didn't want to be dashing in and out to the kitchen all the time but, having been reassured by Jake over the phone that neither he nor Sophie were fussy eaters, she'd chosen a seafood platter entrée, rack of lamb for the main and a passionfruit-topped cheesecake which she'd cooked in advance and which she knew from experience tasted better after spending a day in the fridge. The various wines had come courtesy of recommendations from the man who owned her local wine shop.

A quick glance at her watch warned her that she only had twelve minutes before Jake and Sophie were due to arrive. Abby had told Jake over the phone that she didn't want him around whilst she was cooking, which hadn't seemed to bother him. Jake had said he'd go to his sister's place after work and they would drive to Balmain together.

Abby had had another reason for wanting Jake to be absent during her preparations for the evening. She'd wanted to surprise him with the table setting, not to mention the fact she was actually wearing a dress. When Jake had let slip that his sister was a professional stylist, Abby had gone shopping again, knowing instinctively that jeans were not the right sort of thing to wear for the dinner.

She did feel some guilt that she'd gone and bought some more clothes, but there was no denying the pleasure she got every time she looked at herself in the large mirror in Jake's hallway, which was what she was doing at this very moment, staring at herself and hoping Jake would like what he saw.

In one way, Abby wished it was just the two of them tonight. Though, really, that was all so much pie in the sky, hoping that he would suddenly fancy her the way Megan said he would. Abby knew how men acted when they fancied a woman and it certainly wasn't to organise a third person to be present when they could easily have been alone. On top of that, she wasn't at her best making conversation with strangers. And Jake's sister was a stranger.

No sooner had this wimpy thought entered Abby's head than it was banished.

'No more negative thoughts!' came her firm lecture as she stared at her reflection in the mirror and put on an assertive face. 'So you're a bit nervous about meeting Sophie. That's only natural. She's a professional stylist—a sophisticated career woman who's no doubt as good-looking as her brother. But you'll be fine. You look darned good yourself. And you're no dumb blonde. You're smart. You know you are. Jake's uncle thought so too.'

Whirling on her new high heels, Abby marched back into the kitchen determined to be more confident.

'You're not very talkative,' Sophie said after she parked her car outside Jake's place right on seven. 'If I didn't know you better, I'd think you were nervous.'

'Don't be ridiculous,' Jake snapped. 'I don't get nervous.' Which was true. He was, however, apprehensive about the evening ahead.

Despite having physically avoided Abby during the week, they'd talked a couple of times over the phone. Nothing personal, just Abby asking him about what foods he and his sister liked. But even her voice did wicked things to him. How was he going to cope with the real thing tonight? During one phone call he'd been so turned on, he'd been seriously tempted to tell her Sophie couldn't make it and it would just be the two of them.

If only Abby wasn't so darned sweet he might have done exactly that.

'Then what *is* your problem?' Sophie persisted as they walked up to the front door together. 'The girl said she didn't want to get married again. What's to stop you from dating her, if that's what you want?'

Jake threw his sister a convincingly exasperated look. 'Come on, sis. Abby only *thinks* she doesn't want marriage and children, but she'll change her mind about that eventually. Besides,' he added, 'she doesn't fancy me.'

Sophie laughed. 'Not only nervous but delusional. You've got it so bad your brain is addled. Of *course* she fancies you. That's why she offered to cook you dinner, you fool. You're not very good at reading between the lines, are you? And I thought you were a smart guy where women were concerned.'

'You don't understand,' Jake muttered as he inserted his key in the front door. 'I'm trying to do the right thing here.'

'Mmm... The road to hell is paved with good intentions, you know.'

'Yeah, I know. I'm already there.' And he pushed open the door.

'Something smells nice,' Sophie said on entering the hallway. 'Oh, look, it's a scented candle,' she added after peeking into the dining room. 'My, doesn't the table look lovely. Your Abby's gone to a *lot* of trouble.'

Jake heard the innuendo in Sophie's voice. 'Please don't start reading anything into this evening's dinner, sister dear. Abby has no romantic feelings for me whatsoever. She's just a very nice woman. This is gratitude, not lust.' *He* was the one in lust.

'Abby, we're here!' he called out as he took Sophie's arm and steered her down the hallway into the kitchen.

'My goodness!' he exclaimed. 'You're wearing a dress.' Or almost wearing one. His eyes clamped onto her cleavage and didn't budge.

Sophie winced at Jake's tone. Heavens, he made it sound as if wearing a dress was a crime.

Sophie watched the dismay on the girl's face quickly change to defiance.

'I am indeed,' she said as she came closer and twirled around for him to see her better.

Sophie tried not to smile at the look on her brother's face. Truly, the poor idiot was more than just smitten. If she didn't know him better, she might have thought he'd fallen in love. And she could see why.

Abby was one seriously attractive girl, with a delicately featured face with lovely greenish eyes, perfect skin and the most dazzling smile. There was nothing wrong with her figure either, which was most eye-catching, its hourglass shape shown to advantage in a floral wrap-around dress, the bodice crossing over her bust before tying into a bow on her left hip.

Of course, if Sophie had dressed her, she would have

chosen a block colour rather than floral, and the V neckline would have been much lower. Why have great boobs if you didn't flaunt them, especially when you were young?

But all that was beside the point. The point at this precise moment was the way her brother was acting. Which was totally unacceptable.

Sophie decided to step in and smooth things over till Jake could get control of his hormones.

'I'm Sophie,' she introduced herself brightly, coming forward to give Abby a brief hug and a kiss on the cheek. 'That's a fab dress you're wearing. You'll have to tell me where you bought it. Did Jake mention that I'm in the fashion industry?'

Abby knew she would never give Sophie *that* information. The little black dress Jake's sister had on screamed luxury designer whereas Abby's dress had been cheap as. But Sophie's kind compliments did make her feel better in the face of Jake's obvious disapproval. She did, however, feel somewhat comforted by the fact that Sophie wasn't drop dead gorgeous like her brother.

'Jake,' Sophie said sharply, 'stop glaring at Abby and tell her how lovely she looks.'

'She looks very nice,' he bit out. 'It was just a shock, that's all. I've never seen her in a dress before. How's the food going, Abby? I'm so hungry I could eat a horse.'

CHAPTER FOURTEEN

ABBY CONTROLLED HER temper with difficulty. 'Sorry. Horse isn't on the menu for tonight. You'll have to make do with lamb. Now, if you'd like to follow me into the dining room, I'll show you where you're both sitting.'

Jake winced when she swept past him with a hurt look cast his way. He knew he was behaving badly but he couldn't seem to find that much vaunted charm he was famous for. His social skills had completely deserted him in the face of a sexual attraction which was as cruel as it was powerful. Thank heavens he'd put his suit jacket back on before leaving Sophie's place. And thank heavens he would soon be sitting down.

Sophie came to his rescue, saying all the right things about the table setting, plus Abby's choice of wine. Jake finally opened his mouth to agree with his sister about the wine, which brought another cool look from Abby.

He fancied her even more when she was like this!

Jake tried not to stare when she poured Sophie some wine, but the action required her to bend forward, making the neckline of her dress gape a little. When she moved around to pour his wine, he kept his eyes firmly on the tablecloth. He knew his *thank you* sounded forced. He didn't want to thank her. He wanted to have sex with her, right here, on this table.

Jake sighed with relief when she left the room to cook the entree. Picking up his wine, he downed half the glass; he needed to do something to calm the storm raging within him, because if he didn't he might do something he'd bitterly regret in the morning.

'You've really got it bad, haven't you?' Sophie said quietly. 'You implied as much over the phone but seeing it is worth a thousand words.'

Jake glanced over at his sister, who was studying him over the rim of her glass with an intuitive gaze.

'I'll survive,' he returned before swallowing another large gulp of wine.

Sophie smiled knowingly. 'We'll see, Jake. Like I said before, your Abby's gone to a lot of trouble tonight.'

'She's not my Abby. She's still in love with her dead husband.'

'Maybe. But he's dead, Jake. And you're one handsome man.'

Jake sighed. 'Could we stop this conversation right now, please?'

Sophie did stop, but only because Abby entered the dining room carrying with her two plates which exuded the most delicious smell. When she placed his in front of him, Jake saw that it contained a mixture of prawns and scallops over which had been drizzled the source of that tantalising aroma.

'If this tastes as good as it looks,' he said, unable to restrain his admiration for her cooking, 'then we're in for an amazing treat.'

When Jake looked up and saw Abby's delighted face he was consumed with guilt over his earlier bad manners. He hadn't meant to hurt her.

'And, for what it's worth at this late stage,' he added, 'I think that dress you're wearing is stunning. If you ever wear it outside of this house, you'll be fighting the men off with sticks.'

CHAPTER FIFTEEN

ABBY SHOULD HAVE been thrilled with this last compliment. But she wasn't. And the reason was mortifying. Because it was *him* she wanted the chance to fight off, not other men.

Not that she would fight Jake off. Abby knew if he ever made the slightest pass at her, she would be a goner. But he wasn't about to do that, was he? For pity's sake, when was she going to get it through her silly female head that he was just her boss, plus the rather reluctant trustee of his uncle's dying wishes?

If she was brutally honest, it had always been painfully obvious that Jake hadn't wanted to do any of it. Not the car or the money. Or taking her to the grave. But he had, out of a sense of duty, and decency. She meant nothing to him on a personal basis. She was just the person who looked after his house who'd been lucky enough to score a generous legacy from his very kind and thoughtful uncle.

The hurt this realisation brought was very telling, reminding Abby of the various warnings Megan had given her about Jake. But Megan had been wrong. It wasn't Jake she had to worry about but her own silly self. Somewhere along the line she'd started caring about what he thought of her. Started caring for *him*. Which was a total waste of time.

It annoyed Abby that she'd turned into some kind of infatuated fool who fantasised about a man who was way out of her league. As a teenager she'd never had crushes on movie stars or rock stars, and she wasn't about to start now with a television star.

'I'll go get my entree,' she said, and hurried from the room, returning to find that her two guests had waited for her.

The dish was a success, as was the main course, judging by the many compliments she received, plus the evidence of empty plates. Hers weren't quite so empty, her appetite deserting her, as it did when she was emotionally upset over something. She tried not to look at Jake too much or too often, lest he see her feelings for him in her eyes. In the main, she looked at and talked to Sophie, who was quite the conversationalist, one of those women who liked to ask questions, mostly about Abby's likes and dislikes where fashion was concerned. During dessert, however, their conversation turned more personal.

'Jake told me about your husband's death,' Sophie said. 'How tragic for you. He must have been quite young. After all, you're only—what? Mid-twenties?'

'I'm twenty-seven. And, yes, Wayne was only twenty-five when he died. We were the same age.'

'How dreadful for you. And how long had you been married at the time?'

'Four years.'

Sophie's eyebrows arched. 'But no children?'

It was a question which used to cause Abby unbearable pain. It still hurt, but she'd grown to accept that she would never become a mother.

'We were trying,' she said. 'But it just didn't happen.' No way was she going to talk about her three miscarriages. That was way too private. And, yes, way too painful.

'Perhaps it was all for the best,' Sophie said, 'under the circumstances.'

'Perhaps,' Abby choked out.

Jake frowned, having picked up on the raw emotion vibrating in Abby's reply. He recalled he'd said something similar when he'd interviewed her. Suddenly, he saw that it was a tactless remark. He tried to catch Sophie's eye, but she was oblivious to his attempt to put a stop to her queries.

'So, Abby, Jake tells me you want to travel,' his sister continued in her usual blunt fashion.

'Yes. I do.'

'Alone? Or with a friend?'

'Sophie, for pity's sake,' Jake jumped in. 'Stop giving Abby the third degree.'

Sophie gave him a mock innocent look. 'I'm just talking. Okay, change of subject. Jake, how about letting me live in Craig's apartment for a while? Or are you going to sell it?'

'No,' Jake replied slowly. 'I'm not going to sell it. Not yet, anyway. Why do you want to stay there?'

Sophie sighed. 'My flatmate wants to move her boyfriend in and I can't stand him.'

'I see. Well, of course you can stay in Craig's place. I'll give you the keys before you leave.'

'I'll pay you rent,' she offered.

'I don't want any rent. Just pay the electricity bill when it comes in. And don't sublet it to anyone else.'

'I won't. I'm like you, Jake. I like my own space. I should never have shared a flat in the first place. I should have bought one. But I'm just too extravagant to save the deposit. All my money goes on clothes,' she directed at Abby. 'And hair,' she added, patting the chic red bob which flattered her square face.

Jake frowned. 'Craig left you enough for a deposit on a flat, I would have thought.'

'Yes, well, I know he did. But I have other plans for that money. Business plans. So, Abby, you do realise that my brother is going to be shattered when you leave him? He thinks you're the most incredible housekeeper. He never stops raving about you.'

'Really?'

'Really.'

'I'm sure he won't have any trouble finding someone else,' she said.

When her head turned his way, Jake had to use all of his willpower to douse the surge of desire which threatened to unravel him. But he was doomed to failure. He could not stop his eyes from dropping to her mouth, her extremely delicious mouth. How he wanted that mouth; how he wanted *her*!

Abby frowned. Why was Jake staring at her mouth like that? Perhaps she had some food on her lips. When she lifted her napkin from her lap to dab at them, he continued to stare, Abby glimpsing something in his glittering blue eyes which shocked her to the core. It was the way Wayne used to look at her when he wanted sex.

But what shocked Abby the most—aside from the fact that this was Jake lusting after her—was the intensity of her own physical response. Instantly her heart began to race, her belly and nipples tightening in a manner which was both perturbing and insidiously exciting. There was another tightening as well, deep inside her.

When an embarrassing heat threatened to turn her face and neck bright red, Abby quickly stood up.

'I'll go and put the coffee on,' she said, and fled the room.

'Well, well…' Sophie murmured. 'Those weren't the actions of a girl who doesn't fancy you. She's got the hots for you almost as much as you have for her.'

Jake didn't say a word, having been rendered speechless. Because if Sophie was right about Abby then nothing would stop him now. Not his conscience, or anything.

But maybe Sophie was wrong. Maybe Abby had seen the lust in his eyes just now and fled the room in panic.

'I have to get going soon,' Sophie said suddenly. 'I have an early start in the morning.'

Jake gave his sister a narrow-eyed look. 'Doing what?'

'Spending two hours in the gym working off the calories I've consumed tonight. Overweight stylists don't get much work, you know. And don't make a fuss. I'm leaving the path clear for you to finish the evening the way you've been living it in your head for hours. Not that I blame you. She's utterly gorgeous. But possibly a bit fragile after her husband's death. So be careful, Jake. Abby's not your usual type.'

'You think I don't know that?' he snapped. 'Why do you think I've been giving her a wide berth?'

Sophie tipped her head on one side. 'You really care about her, don't you?'

Did he? Jake supposed he did, otherwise he wouldn't have controlled himself this long. But the main reason for that control no longer existed and the dogs of desire he'd been trying to rein in had finally been let loose.

'Do me a favour, will you?' he said abruptly.

'Anything, within reason.'

'Go and tell Abby that you don't want coffee because you have to go home. Tell her you suffer from migraines and you can feel one coming on.'

Sophie shook her head at him as she stood up. 'I suppose there's a slim chance she might knock you back. But I doubt it,' she added laughingly, then went to do as he'd asked.

CHAPTER SIXTEEN

BY THE TIME Jake walked into the kitchen after seeing Sophie off, Abby had achieved a measure of control over her wayward body, mostly by busying herself clearing the table and stacking the dishwasher. Unfortunately, as soon as she glanced up at him, things started tipping out of control again.

If only he would stop looking at her like that!

Okay, so Megan had warned her that Jake might fancy her if she dolled herself up. But she hadn't really believed her. Until now.

For a long moment Abby just stood there next to the dishwasher, staring at Jake and thinking that if she let him seduce her—she could see in his eyes that was what he meant to do—she would be thrown into a world she was not equipped to handle. She wasn't like Megan. She'd never slept with a guy just for the sex. She'd never wanted to. That was what worried her the most. How much she wanted to sleep with Jake.

For pity's sake, at least be honest, she castigated herself. You don't want to do any *sleeping* with Jake. You want to have sex with him. But only after you've explored his naked body first, then kissed him all over. You want to do all the things you've read about but never experienced, or even wanted before.

When some shockingly wanton images filled her mind, panic wasn't far behind.

'I… I think I should go home,' she stammered, her cheeks burning with shame.

He shook his head then began walking slowly towards her, closing the dishwasher on the way.

'You can't,' he returned, his voice cool but his eyes still hot. 'You're over the limit.'

He was close now, close enough to reach out and touch her. He softly traced down her nose with one fingertip before slowly encircling her mouth. For a few fraught seconds, Abby held her breath, wide eyes clinging to his, pleading with him not to do this. Or that was what she thought her eyes were doing.

All Jake saw was the dilation of excitement. When her lips finally gasped apart, he smiled. It was a wicked smile, full of satisfaction and arrogance and erotic intent. He meant to have her tonight, and he knew she didn't want to say no.

'Abby, Abby...' he murmured, his voice husky. 'Do you have any idea how much I want you?'

Abby wondered dazedly if he said that to all his women. She had to admit that it was very effective. She shuddered when he pulled her into his arms, squeezing her eyes tightly shut as his head started to descend. The feel of his lips on hers brought a low moan from deep in her throat. When he stopped kissing her, her eyelids fluttered open to find his narrowed eyes scanning hers with concern.

'Tell me you want this too, Abby,' he said. 'Don't go along with me because of gratitude, or because you think you might lose your job if you don't.'

Such thoughts had never entered her head. Nothing much was entering her head at this moment. Nothing but the urgent desire for him to continue. Her lips remained parted as she struggled for breath, her body flushing with a heat which might have been embarrassing if it hadn't been so exciting.

'Tell me you want me to make love to you,' he repeated harshly. '*Say* it.'

Abby swallowed, then licked her lips in an effort to get some moisture into her mouth.

'Yes,' she croaked out.

'Yes, *what*?' he persisted.

'Yes, I... I want you to make love to me.'

He groaned then pulled her even tighter against him, his mouth crashing down on hers with a wild passion which surpassed anything she'd experienced in her marriage. Where Wayne had been gentle and tentative, Jake simply took, invading her mouth with his tongue whilst his hands roved hungrily up and down her spine, one slipping under her hair to capture the back of her neck whilst the other splayed over her bottom. She moaned at the feel of his erection pressing into the soft swell of her stomach, how hard it felt, and her insides contracted in anticipation. She wanted him, not gently, but roughly. Demandingly. She wanted him to fill her. She wanted to come with him inside her.

With a cry of naked need, Abby reefed her mouth from under his, her eyes wide and wild.

'What's wrong?' a stunned Jake asked her.

'Nothing. Everything. Oh, just don't stop, Jake. Please, I... I can't wait.'

Jake didn't need telling twice. He hoisted her up on to the stone counter, ignoring her startled gasp as he reached up under her skirt to remove her panties.

'Lie back,' he commanded as he drew her skirt up and eased her legs apart.

Abby's face flamed with a mad mixture of shame and arousal, sucking in sharply when she felt his hands slide up under her dress to take a firm grasp of her hips, gasping when he slid her forward so that she was right on the edge. She didn't dare look at him, keeping her dilated eyes firmly on the ceiling. But she could feel him, pushing against her hot wet flesh, searching for entry into her oh, so needy body. And then he was there, taking her breath away as yes, he filled her totally. Her head swam when he started up a powerful rhythm, each forward surge of his body bringing her both pleasure and even more frustration. She closed her eyes but nothing could shut out the sounds she started making, moans and pants. Just as she thought she could not bear another moment of such exquisite torment, Abby came, her flesh contracting around his with an electric pleasure that was as stunning as it was violent. Spasm followed spasm, evoking a raw cry from Jake. Then he came too, flooding her for an incredibly long time.

Jake shut his eyes as he wallowed in his glorious release, but it wasn't long before the heat of the moment cooled, and the reality of what he'd just done sunk in, along with the possible consequences.

Jake groaned at his stupidity. After all, the last thing he wanted to be confronted with was an unwanted pregnancy. Which was possible, given he hadn't used a condom.

He really didn't want children, even with a girl like Abby. He enjoyed being free to do as he pleased whenever he pleased. Even one child would put an end to that. Okay, so it was probably selfish of him, but better to be selfish than miserable. He wanted his uncle's lifestyle, not his father's.

When Jake finally opened his eyes, he encountered Abby staring up at him with glazed eyes. Her arms were flopped out wide in the form of a T, her breathing now slow and steady. He did note, however, that her lips remained softly parted as if they were waiting for him to kiss her some more.

He wished he could. But there was no getting away from what he had to do first.

With a sigh he scooped her up and held her close, his face buried into her hair. 'I'm so sorry, Abby,' he murmured with true regret in his voice.

She pulled back a little and blinked up at him. 'For what?'

'I didn't use a condom. But let me assure you,' he raced on when her eyes widened, 'that I'm no risk to you, health-wise. I've always practised safe sex. Till tonight, that is,' he confessed ruefully.

'It's all right, Jake,' she said. 'I can't get pregnant. I'm on the Pill.'

'You are?' He was genuinely surprised. Then relieved. Then curious.

'Don't think I'm not happy about that, but why?' he asked.

She shrugged. 'It gives me control over my body. I don't suffer PMT when I'm on the Pill.'

'So it's not just a birth control thing?'

'No. Though it's as well I am taking it, under the circumstances.'

'I'll say.'

A frown formed on her pretty forehead. 'Can I ask you why you didn't use a condom this time when you say you always practise safe sex?'

Jake didn't want to tell her the truth: that he'd been so crazy with desire for her for so long that stopping to put a condom on would have been impossible, even if he'd thought of it.

He produced a wry little smile as he wrapped her legs around his waist.

'Acute frustration,' he said instead. 'You can blame yourself. You looked so delicious in that dress that I've thought of nothing else but sex all night.'

'Oh…'

Gently, he cupped the back of her head and pulled it down against his chest. His hands stroked up and down her back as they had that day in this very kitchen. But this was hardly the same. Once again, she pulled back and lifted puzzled eyes to his.

'Is…is it always like that for your women?' she asked him.

Jake was somewhat taken aback. What exactly did she mean? Did his lovers always come? Did they come the way she'd just come? Like a woman who hadn't had a climax in years.

'Not always,' he said. 'Not all people click, sexually.'

She nodded at his answer. 'But we do. Click sexually, I mean.'

He smiled again. 'Very much so. We're going to have a great time together.'

'But…what about your girlfriend?' She needed to be sure he wasn't cheating with her.

'I broke up with Olivia some time ago.'

'I see,' she said thoughtfully. 'Yes, I see.'

Jake wasn't sure what she saw. He wasn't all that keen on the way women liked to analyse everything. He didn't want to have a post-mortem of why the sex between them was so good. He wanted to get back to some serious love-making. In bed next time. He just wanted Abby naked in his bed where he could make slow love to her for hours.

He didn't withdraw. He just scooped her up from the breakfast bar, holding her tightly as he headed for the stairs, their fused and very wet flesh reminding Jake once more that he hadn't used a condom. Walking up stairs while still inside her was doing things to him which should have been impossible, given he'd just had the most satisfying climax.

And wow it felt good. *She* felt good. Maybe he'd just forget the condoms for tonight. After all, they'd already done it once. Might as well be hanged for a sheep as a lamb, as they said. From tomorrow he'd go back to being super care-ful. Tonight, however, he would indulge himself to the full.

CHAPTER SEVENTEEN

ABBY HAD BEEN right about not wanting to actually *sleep* with Jake. She didn't. She couldn't. Every nerve-ending in her body was still electrified. *He'd* finally fallen asleep, however. It wasn't surprising after two hours of almost constant sexual activity. Abby had lost count of how many times she'd come, Jake showing her that a woman's capacity for orgasms far surpassed a man's, especially when said woman was being made love to by a man of his experience. He knew exactly where to touch. What to touch. How to touch.

Abby closed her eyes as she relived all that he'd done to her. First there had been that incredible episode on the kitchen counter. That had been amazing enough. But not as sensational as once they were both naked in bed together. After another incredible orgasm, just when she'd thought she couldn't bear any more, he'd carried her into the shower and revived her under some cool jets of water. After drying her off, he'd carried her back to bed, where some more kissing and caressing had soon had her trembling with desire again. His own flesh had been solidly re-aroused also, the size of him astonishing her at times. But always bringing her the most exquisite pleasure.

Such thinking sent Abby's eyes over to Jake, who was lying face down on the bed, sound asleep. She stared at his back, which had several red tracks where her nails had raked over his skin. She shook her head at the savagery of her passion for Jake. Not to mention her stupidity. What had possessed her to admit she was on the Pill? Her brain knew it was a risk to have sex without a condom, despite his reassurances. But her body hadn't cared. In truth, she would have let him continue even if she *hadn't* been on the

Pill. Which was insane! Just the thought of falling pregnant made her feel ill. She could not go there again. Not now. Not ever. It had hurt too much each time a baby had been wrenched from her body. More so because she'd wanted a child so much. Or she had, back then when she'd been married to Wayne. No way did she want Jake Sanderson's child. He didn't want a child, either. Or did he think he would simply pay her to have an abortion if the Pill failed and she got pregnant? Which it might. The Pill wasn't one hundred per cent safe.

A ghastly thought suddenly crossed her mind, propelling her from the bed. With a groan she hurried into the bathroom, where she wrapped a bath sheet around herself, intent on getting downstairs as quickly as possible to make sure she'd taken her Pill for the evening. Now that she thought about it, she couldn't actually remember taking it. *Oh, God!*

Abby didn't make it past the foot of the bed before Jake stirred.

'Abby?' came his slurred voice.

She froze as his right arm stretched out, feeling for her. Finding the bed empty, he rolled over and sat up.

'Where do you think you're going?' he asked.

'Downstairs,' she answered in an astonishingly calm voice. 'I… I have to check on something.'

He frowned. 'What?'

'I suddenly had this awful feeling I might have forgotten to take my Pill earlier. But if I have, please don't worry. I'll get the morning-after pill. I don't want to have a baby any more than you do. But from now we should use condoms. The Pill I take is a good one but no Pill is one hundred per cent safe.'

He nodded. 'Very true. Okay, from now on, we'll use condoms. After all, we don't want any unfortunate accidents, do we?'

Abby swallowed. 'No,' she said, thinking that surely fate wouldn't be that cruel to her. She always took her Pill around six-thirty. She glanced at the digital clock sitting on her side of the bed. Ten to one.

But she was getting ahead of herself, Abby realised. What she needed to do was get herself downstairs and check.

'I won't be long,' she said, and bolted for the door and the stairs, heading for the kitchen where she'd left her new bag on the counter-top next to the microwave. Ten seconds later she was almost sobbing with relief, as she saw the punched through dome where the day's Pill had sat. Thank heavens, she thought, though her heart was still racing. What she needed, she realised, was something to calm her down. Not coffee. Some wine perhaps.

A minute later, Abby hurried back up the stairs, carrying with her the bottle of dessert wine they'd hardly touched at dinner, along with two glasses. Hopefully, she didn't look as horrified at herself as she suddenly felt. In a matter of hours Jake had turned her into…what? A woman with needs— needs which this man could obviously satisfy.

The bed was empty when she entered the bedroom, Jake simultaneously walking back into the room from the bathroom. But where she had a towel wrapped modestly around her, he was stark naked.

Abby liked that she now felt free to ogle him. For he was a man worth ogling: magnificently built with broad shoulders, flat stomach, slim hips and long strong legs. His skin was naturally olive, his body hair dark but not overly abundant. It was thickest in the middle of his chest, arrowing down to his groin. Abby gazed at that part of him which she admired and desired the most. She hadn't kissed him there yet. But she wanted to.

'It's all right,' she said straight away. 'Pill all safely taken.'

'Fantastic. Now, why don't you dispense with that towel, wench?' he said as he climbed back on to the bed, sitting up with pillows stuffed behind his back.

'Can't,' Abby replied rather breathlessly. How easy it was for him to turn her on. 'My hands are full.'

'Then come closer and I'll do it for you,' he said, his smile quite wicked.

Her head spun as she approached his side of the bed, waiting there like a good little wench till he reached out and peeled the towel from her body. His gaze was hot and hungry as it travelled over her, lingering on her breasts till she could actually feel her erect nipples tingling with anticipation.

'Give the bottle to me,' he commanded.

She did so. He placed it on the bedside table.

'Now the glasses,' he added.

She handed them over and he filled each one halfway, handing one back to her.

'Drink,' he ordered, and she did, downing all of it.

He didn't drink any of his, putting the glass down next to the bottle. Abby stared when he dipped his finger in the chilled wine then reached out to dab it over her nearest nipple.

She gasped.

'You like that?' he asked throatily and she nodded, her tongue feeling thick in her throat.

'Come,' he said, taking the empty glass out of her hand and putting it down before drawing her back on to the bed. Not on her side, but on his, sitting her down first then tipping her back across his thighs.

When Abby stared up at him with stunned eyes, Jake knew then that she was as innocent as he'd always feared. Up until this point he hadn't been absolutely sure. The way she'd insisted on a quickie down on the kitchen counter hadn't smacked of innocence.

But it was obvious that no one had ever dabbed wine on her nipples before, let alone her clitoris. Her surprise delighted and excited him. He dabbed some wine on her other nipple before pulling her on to the bed so that he could bend his mouth to her very beautiful breasts. He loved the way she moaned when he sucked her nipples deep into his mouth. Loved the way she couldn't seem to stop him from doing whatever he wanted. He liked her lack of experience, but at the same time it worried him. If he wasn't careful she might fall in love with him, which was the last thing he wanted.

CHAPTER EIGHTEEN

ABBY LOVED THE feel of his mouth on her breast. Loved it when he lapped gently at her nipple. Loved it even more when he nipped it with his teeth. She groaned when his head lifted abruptly, not wanting him to stop.

'What's wrong?' she said when she saw his frown.

His intense gaze grew quite frustrated. 'I don't know why I'm going to say this but I am. You won't be silly and fall in love with me, will you, Abby?'

Abby could not have been more taken aback, her focus tonight having been all on her sexual feelings, not romantic ones. Still, once she thought about it, she could see that it would be easy for her to become seriously infatuated with Jake. But love? It was difficult to fall in love with a man who'd shown no interest in her till circumstance had thrown them into each other's company, coincidentally at the same time he'd broken up with his current girlfriend.

Abby wasn't a fool. She could see that his suddenly fancying her was very convenient to Jake, that was all. He wanted her, but only because she was there. And pretty enough to interest him. Wayne, however, had wanted her from the first moment he'd clapped eyes on her, stained teeth and all. Her husband might not have set her heart racing the way Jake could, but he'd been a man worth loving. Abby could never truly love a man who was only sexually attracted to her. That kind of man would never capture her heart and soul.

'I'm not interested in marriage and children,' he told her, cementing any possible doubts she might have about loving him.

'I know that, Jake,' she replied a little coolly. 'You don't have to spell it out for me. Your reputation precedes you. I'm not interested in marriage and children, either. I don't want anything from you but sex, so you don't have to worry.'

He blinked his surprise at her.

'It's true,' she said, nodding as she thought about what her sister would say to her.

You've discovered the pleasures of the flesh at last, hon. Enjoy it whilst it's on offer. Because a man like Jake will move on after a while.

Thinking of her sister's probable advice confirmed in Abby's mind what she was feeling for Jake. This was sex, not love.

'I assure you I won't fall in love with you.' In lust maybe, but never in love.

His laugh was dry. 'I guess I asked for that. But you don't have to sound so sure. That's not very flattering.'

'Sorry.'

He smiled wryly. 'No need to apologise. I appreciate honesty. Now, where was I?'

Before he could bend his mouth once more to her breast, Abby sat up. She no longer wanted him to do that. She wanted to do things to *him*.

'Jake,' she said sharply, her eyes a bit nervous as they met his.

He frowned again. 'What now?'

'Since you like honesty, can I be honest with you about something else?'

'Be my guest,' he said, leaning back against the pillows.

Abby swallowed then gathered her courage to get out what she wanted to say. 'The thing is, I've…um…only been with one man before you. My husband. I loved Wayne dearly but I…we…well, I don't think I clicked sexually with him the way I do with you. I've never come before, during sex. I mean I've come but not during actual intercourse. I've also never done some other things that I've read about and which I feel I…um…would like to do with you.'

It hadn't been easy admitting all that, especially with Jake's eyes on her all the while, mainly because she couldn't read his expression. Surely he couldn't be *pleased* with her confession. She would have thought he liked his women very experienced.

'I see,' he said rather cryptically. 'What kind of things?'

She tried not to blush. She couldn't imagine Jake liking women who blushed. Gritting her teeth, Abby resolved to continue telling him the truth without surrendering to silly schoolgirl nerves.

'Well, oral sex, for starters. That's one thing I'd like to do. But I want to do it properly. I was hoping you might show me how.'

CHAPTER NINETEEN

ABBY WOKE SLOWLY, awareness of her physical well-being seeping into her brain before she remembered whose bed she was in, plus everything she had done in it the night before.

'Oh,' she cried, sitting up abruptly in what proved to be a blessedly empty bed. Lord knew how she would have coped if Jake had been lying there beside her, bearing witness to her very fierce embarrassment.

What had seemed so natural—so *right*—last night, now seemed very wrong. And very decadent. It blew Abby's mind that she had told Jake she'd never come during sex before. As for her telling him she wanted him to teach her how to go down on him…

She might have sat there, castigating herself for ages if the man himself hadn't walked back into the room, holding two mugs of steaming coffee and smiling at her with genuine warmth in his eyes. He wasn't naked, thank heavens, though he was only wearing jeans, his chest still bare.

As was hers, she realised, snatching up the sheet to cover her breasts.

'Now, now,' Jake chided with dancing blue eyes as he approached her side of the bed. 'None of that false modesty this morning, thank you. I've already seen your beautiful breasts at close quarters. Not to mention the rest of your very lovely body.'

His compliments went some way to soothing her embarrassment, as did his totally natural manner. Abby realised that if she wanted to continue having sex with Jake—and she very definitely did—then she had to get her head around the way he expected his women to act. At the same time, she wasn't about to turn into some kind of exhibitionist.

'Well, that was last night,' she returned, keeping the sheet where it was. 'I don't like swanning around with no clothes on in the daytime.'

'How do you know?' he said, placing one of the mugs on the bedside table next to her. 'Maybe you should try it some time.'

Abby wondered if it had been a mistake telling him so much about her past sex life. It worried her that Jake might think he had a licence to do anything and everything with her.

He frowned at her as he sat down on her side of the bed. 'I have a feeling that you're suffering from a severe case of the morning afters.'

Abby shrugged, then carefully picked up the very hot mug with one hand whilst keeping the sheet in place with her other hand.

'Probably,' she admitted after taking a small sip.

'What's worrying you?'

She took another sip of coffee, mulling over what to say.

'I guess I just don't know how to act this morning,' she said at last. 'I mean…it's an awkward situation, with me being your housekeeper.'

'I think it's anything but awkward,' he said, smiling a wickedly sexy smile. 'It's very convenient that you're already here, in my house, every day.'

'I'm not going to be your secret mistress, Jake,' she warned him, despite suspecting that she would be whatever he wanted her to be. Provided he kept having sex with her.

'You can't be my secret mistress,' he said, the corners of his mouth twitching. 'I'm not married.'

She glowered up at him. 'Secret lover, then!'

'Okay,' he said. 'Fair enough. How about you just become my girlfriend? Nothing secretive. All above board. If you like, I'll tell the world on next Monday's show. Or, better still, I'll put it on Twitter this very day. *My gorgeous young housekeeper and I are now an item.*'

Abby looked horrified. 'Don't you dare!'

Jake's eyebrows lifted. 'Is there any reason why I shouldn't?'

'My sister is addicted to Twitter. *And* your show.'

Now his brows beetled together. 'You don't want your sister to know we're an item?'

'No!'

'Why not? Will she be shocked?'

Hardly, Abby thought, since Megan had warned her that this might happen.

Abby sighed. 'Probably not,' she admitted. 'But she'll go on and on about it. She'll want to know the ins and outs of everything, and I'm just not ready to answer all her questions at this stage.'

'So I'm to be *your* secret lover, am I?'

Only then did Abby realise that that was exactly what she wanted him to be. She simply wasn't ready to share this incredible experience with anyone else. She didn't want to risk spoiling anything. She didn't want a cynical Megan telling her not to expect their relationship to last. Not that it was a *relationship*. It was just sex.

'Would you mind?' she asked him, shocked by her own boldness.

Jake actually did mind. Quite a bit. He didn't like the thought that Abby wanted to treat him as a sexual object rather than a proper boyfriend. Which was ironic, considering that was what he'd done in reverse for years—treated women more as sexual objects rather than proper girlfriends.

But he could see no pluses in arguing with her just now.

'If that's what you want,' he said with a nonchalant shrug of his shoulders.

She stared at him. 'You're very easy-going, aren't you?'

'Very,' he lied, deciding this was the way to play the game for a while. Give her what she wanted. Though he had no intention of being her secret lover for long. That was not what *he* wanted. 'Now, how about I take you away somewhere for the weekend? In the Ferrari. You can do some of the driving,' he offered with a devilish grin.

'I'd love to,' she said excitedly. 'But won't you be recognised if we go anywhere in public together?'

'Maybe. Maybe not. Sunglasses and a baseball cap go a long way to disguising one's identity. But I'll certainly be recognised once I book us into a place for the night. The name on my credit card will give the game away. But *your* identity can be kept a secret. For a while. But only for a while, I suspect. The truth will out in the end, Abby. Your sister will find out eventually, even if you don't tell her. The media has long and very tenacious tentacles. So I would suggest that when we get back on Sunday evening, you give her a call.'

'We'll see,' she said, still not happy at the thought of telling Megan about them.

Abby couldn't deny she was flattered that Jake actually *wanted* her to be his girlfriend. But, if truth be told, she didn't feel adequate for such a role. She wasn't well educated, or well travelled. Hardly a woman of the world in the bedroom, either. Still, maybe that was what he liked about her, the way Max de Winter liked the heroine in *Rebecca*— because she was the total opposite of his dead but highly decadent wife. Maybe it was Abby's own ordinariness that appealed to Jake after having a string of over-achieving, super-glamorous girlfriends.

Of course, he wasn't about to propose, as the hero did in *Rebecca*. Aside from the fact that Jake was anti-marriage, men these days didn't have to marry to enjoy the pleasures of the flesh. Neither did women, Abby conceded, a highly erotic shiver running down her spine as she looked at Jake's beautiful male body. She could hardly wait to have it all to herself again. There was so much more she had to learn. So many more things she had yet to try.

'Keep looking at me like that, sweetheart,' Jake said drily, 'and we won't even get out of this house today.'

CHAPTER TWENTY

WHEN ABBY BLUSHED, Jake stood up abruptly before he gave in to temptation and made his last words come true. As exciting as sex with Abby was, he didn't want to confine their relationship to a strictly sexual one. He wanted her company out of the bedroom as well. He wanted to show her all the places she'd never been before. Wanted to share with her all the wonders the world had to offer.

This last thought jolted him a bit. He'd never travelled overseas with a female companion before. Nothing beyond a few days in some fancy South Seas resort, that was. But he wanted to with Abby. And he was done with that silly show of his. It actually annoyed him that he couldn't go anywhere these days without being recognised. He pretended he didn't mind to Abby but the truth was it irritated him to death.

So the decision was made. He would sell the show ASAP and do something more exciting and fulfilling with his life. But first things first.

'I'll go fix us both some breakfast while you get showered and dressed,' he said. 'Then we're heading north. Port Macquarie, maybe. That's a decent drive. Have you ever been there before?'

She shook her head. 'I've never been out of Sydney. No, that's not true. I went on a school excursion to Canberra once when I was twelve.'

'And what did you think of our capital?'

'Can't remember it much. I was only there for two days and I froze to death the whole time.'

'It's much nicer at this time of year. Would you like to go there instead?'

'I don't really mind where we go,' she said. 'You decide.'

'Canberra it is, then.'

'You'll have to take me home first,' Abby told him hurriedly. 'I'll need to change and get some more clothes. I only have the dress with me that I wore last night. And I'll have to get some overnight things.'

'Fair enough. We won't get waylaid by your next-door neighbour, will we?'

'Harriet doesn't get up till lunchtime on a Saturday.'

'We should be long gone by then. Now, hop to it, Abby. Patience is not one of my virtues.'

'What are your virtues?' she asked, her eyes sparkling with uncharacteristic mischief.

Jake shrugged. 'Not sure. Honesty, I suppose. And integrity. Now, no more chit-chat. Up!' he ordered as he strode purposefully from the room.

Abby sat there a few seconds longer, thinking that there was more to Jake's virtues than honesty and integrity. He was also generous and caring. She liked that he'd loved his uncle as much as he had. Liked the way he'd fulfilled his uncle's dying wishes, even though he'd obviously found her a nuisance at first.

Not so much a nuisance now, she thought, a rather naughty smile pulling at her lips.

'I can't hear the shower running!' Jake called up the stairs, his voice echoing in the quiet house.

'Just going now,' Abby called back, putting the mug down and throwing back the doona.

Abby never sang in the shower. But she did that day, feeling even happier than when she'd got her porcelain veneers. Nothing could compare with the delicious lightness of spirit which was surging through her veins at that moment. She could not recall ever feeling so exhilarated. Or so excited. It did cross her mind for a split second that she might be falling in love with Jake, but she immediately dismissed the idea as fanciful. She liked him very much. And lusted after him a lot. But that was the sum total of her feelings at this stage.

She did concede later, as she ate the fantastic breakfast Jake had cooked, that her feelings for him might deepen if he kept on spoiling her this way.

But she would not worry about that today. Today was to be devoted to having the kind of carefree fun she'd never had before. She might even get to drive a Ferrari. How incredible was that?

'You're quite a good cook,' Abby complimented him.

'I can do the basics like steak and salad, and bacon and eggs. But I could never cook anything like you did last night. That meal was marvellous, Abby.'

'It wasn't all that special,' she said, trying to be modest.

'I thought it was. And so did Sophie.'

'I liked your sister, Jake. You're very close, aren't you?'

'Yes. Much closer than my other siblings. Sophie are I are the loners in the family. The rest are all married with children.'

'Goodness. That must make for a big group at Christmas. Do they all live here in Sydney?'

'Yep. And you're right about Christmas. I've already hired a boat for a cruise on the harbour this year. No one's house can accommodate everyone, except when some of them go to the in-laws. Which apparently isn't happening this year. What about you, Abby? How many in your family?'

'Just me and Megan. And little Timmy, of course.'

'What about your parents?' Jake asked, curious about Abby's family now.

'They're dead. Dad got killed in a fight when I was seventeen. Mum died of an accidental overdose a few months later.'

Jake was taken aback by Abby's matter-of-fact relaying of what must have affected her badly at the time. 'That's very sad, Abby.'

'I suppose so. But truly, they were terrible parents. Always down at the pub. There was never enough money for me and Megan. All they loved was alcohol.'

Jake tried not to look too shocked at Abby's truly ghastly background. Poor thing. She'd had it really tough. No wonder she'd got married young. Probably wanted some man to look after her and love her. Which obviously this Wayne had before he'd died too.

Abby didn't like Jake's silence. No doubt he thought she came from a low-life family. He was probably regretting asking a girl like her to be his girlfriend. 'It's not a pretty story, is it?' she said, a bit defiantly.

'I admire the way you survived it with the lovely nature that you have,' he said gently.

Abby blinked rapidly as moisture suddenly pooled in her eyes.

'You're not going to cry, are you?' Jake asked, alarm in his voice.

Abby almost laughed. Clearly, he didn't like his girlfriends to cry. Which was perverse since she was sure every one of them cried buckets when he broke up with them. Which he always did. Eventually.

It was a sobering thought, and one which she vowed never to forget.

'No,' she said with creditable calm. 'I'm not going to cry. Now, why don't I clear up here whilst you go and get ready? Oh, and Jake…'

'Yes?'

'Um…don't forget to pack some condoms.'

Was he startled by her very practical request? Or annoyed?

Abby imagined that he didn't want to use condoms. Neither did she, if she were honest. But she refused to lose her head totally over Jake.

'How many should I pack?' he asked, his tone as provocative as his glittering blue eyes.

'How many do you have in the house?' she countered, constantly surprised at her boldness. Surprised but not displeased. Abby suspected she was going to like her new bolder self.

'Not sure,' Jake replied thoughtfully. 'There's one unopened box in the bathroom upstairs, as well as a few loose ones in the top drawers of both bedside tables. There's a couple more in the glovebox of my car and two more in my wallet. So a rough estimate would be about two dozen. How many do you think we might need?'

Abby kept a straight face with difficulty. The man was a wicked devil all right.

'Don't ask me,' she said, brilliantly po-faced. 'I only have last night to go by and that might have been a one-off for you. I would imagine a man can get it up quite a bit with a woman during their first night together. But after that, things might very well go downhill. It's not as though you're a teenager, Jake, or even in your twenties. Which reminds me, how old *are* you? Late thirties? Early forties?'

Jake glowered at her for a long moment before shaking his head then smiling a drily amused smile.

'You're teasing me, aren't you?'

'No more than you teased me.'

'Fair enough. And, since you asked, I'm thirty-four. Which makes me still in my prime. So watch yourself tonight. You might find yourself begging me to stop before I'm finished.'

Abby feigned a disappointed face. 'You mean I have to wait till tonight?'

Jake wagged a finger at her. 'I should call your bluff. But I won't. Now, let's get going.'

CHAPTER TWENTY-ONE

'YOU'RE RIGHT,' ABBY said, closing her eyes as she leant back, her hair flying free. 'Riding in this car with the top down is amazing. I would do this every day if I could.'

'Sorry. Weekend treat only. Next time we *will* head north to Port Macquarie.'

Abby opened her eyes as her head turned towards Jake. 'I wouldn't mind where I go,' she said. 'As long as it's in this gorgeous car.'

And as long as I'm with you.

'Great. Now, do you want to stop somewhere for lunch or just go straight to Canberra?'

'No,' Abby said straight away. 'I don't want to stop. Not unless you do. I'm not hungry at all. We can have something to eat when we get to Canberra.'

'A girl after my own heart,' he said with a warm smile thrown her way.

Abby's own heart twisted with his remark, because there was no point in her being after his heart. All Jake wanted from a woman was her body in bed, and her company when out of bed. He obviously liked having a steady girlfriend. Much more convenient for his lifestyle. What he didn't want was for his girlfriends to want more from him than he was prepared to give. Clearly, whenever a girlfriend started looking for more they were out of the door.

Abby realised she would only have herself to blame if she started wanting more. Forewarned was forearmed.

To give Jake credit, he'd been honest with her about his intentions. Or lack of them. She recalled he'd listed honesty as one of his virtues. Integrity as well. Which meant he wouldn't have lied to her about not being a risk to her health when he didn't use a condom.

Thinking of condoms brought Abby's mind back to the incredible climaxes she'd had with Jake last night. She hadn't known till then that such pleasure existed. Whenever Megan raved on about how much she enjoyed sex—how much she actually *needed* it at times—Abby had thought her some kind of nymphomaniac. Now, she appreciated where her sister was coming from. Abby felt sure that by tonight she would very definitely be needing sex with Jake. Already she could feel herself responding to just the thought of being with him, desire invading her body from her curling toes right up to her spinning head. Waiting till tonight was almost beyond bearing. But she *would* wait. No way was she going to humiliate herself by throwing herself at him any earlier.

Abby turned her head just enough so that she could at least have the pleasure of looking at him.

He was wearing stonewashed grey jeans and a white polo top, along with sunglasses and a black baseball cap which did, thankfully, make him more difficult to identify as Jake Sanderson, famed television host and one of Sydney's most recognisable personalities.

Abby didn't want to share him with his adoring public today. Or any other day, for that matter. She couldn't think of anything worse than having strangers come up to them all the time, asking Jake for his autograph. She certainly didn't like the thought of people looking at *her* and wondering what on earth Jake was doing with such a nobody.

Not that she wasn't attractive, especially now that she was dressing better and wearing make-up. Jake, however, was the type of man who dated movie stars and supermodels, or at the very least glamorous newsreaders who were instantly recognisable. They were also women who didn't wear clothes from bargain basement stores. When she'd put on the same outfit this morning that she'd worn when Jake had taken her car shopping last week, Abby had been happy enough with the way she looked. She'd thought— possibly mistakenly—that her tight white pants and spotty top looked quite classy and not cheap. But maybe she'd been deluding herself.

Abby jerked her head round to stare out of the passenger window, not liking that she was suddenly losing confidence in herself. I *do* look good, she told herself firmly. Stop with the worrying.

But the worries continued. Not with her appearance but with what Megan would say when she rang her sister on Sunday night and confessed all. As much as she would like to keep Jake as her secret lover, she could see he wasn't going to allow that to happen.

No doubt Megan would say 'I told you so' in the most irritatingly smug way. She wouldn't be shocked. Well, not about the sex part. She would, however, be shocked that Jake wanted her to be his girlfriend. Abby could just imagine Megan's reaction to that. It would be pure cynicism.

Abby wasn't looking forward to that conversation one little bit. She wanted to enjoy her time with Jake. The last thing she needed was her cynical sister telling her it was only a temporary role. For heaven's sake, she already knew that. She might not be a genius, but she wasn't stupid. Okay, so it was inevitable that one day she would get her marching orders. Abby resolved that she would face that moment when it came. Meanwhile, she aimed to live for the moment. Wasn't that what those lifestyle gurus were always advocating? Not to worry about the past or the future but to seize the moment. Well, at the moment she was in this gorgeous car with a gorgeous man and she wasn't going to let anybody or anything spoil things for her.

Famous last words, Abby thought, and heaved a huge sigh.

'Would you like me to put on some music?' Jake offered, perhaps thinking that her sigh meant she was bored.

'No, thanks,' she replied with a quick smile his way. 'I just want to relax and enjoy the scenery.' Plus try very hard to just live in the moment.

'Actually, the scenery's not that good. That's the trouble with motorways. They bypass the interesting bits.'

'I don't really care about the scenery. I'm just enjoying the ride. And the company,' she added smilingly.

CHAPTER TWENTY-TWO

ME TOO, JAKE THOUGHT, confirming his earlier idea about taking Abby overseas with him. Not that he would mention it to her just yet. It was too soon. Not for him. For her.

'Would you mind if I asked you something?' he said.

'That depends, I guess, on what it is.'

'Nothing too personal. While I was waiting for you at your place this morning, I saw a big pile of books on your coffee table in the living room. I couldn't help noticing that they included some of my uncle's favourite novels, which reminded me that you asked me if he'd left you books in his will. Am I right in presuming he gave you those books?'

'Actually, no, he didn't. But he did give me a list of books which he said any self-respecting female should read. I bought them myself from a secondhand book shop.'

'I see. And have you read them all yet?'

'I'm on the last one now. *Rebecca*.'

'And which ones are your favourites?'

'Goodness, that's a hard question. I liked them all. But I guess not equally. I'd already read three of them at school. *Pride and Prejudice* and *Wuthering Heights* and *Jane Eyre*. Oh, and I've seen about three movie versions of *Great Expectations*, so I knew what was going to happen, which half spoils a story, doesn't it? Though I can see now how brilliantly written they all were. Difficult to pick out just one. Hmm… I adored *Shōgun*. What a fantastic story with a fantastic hero! *The Fountainhead* was riveting stuff too, though the main characters were a bit OTT, in my opinion.'

'I couldn't agree more,' Jake said. 'What did you think of *To Kill a Mockingbird*?'

'Oh, that was a wonderful story. It made me cry buckets. So did *Anna Karenina*. That poor sad lady.'

'So you don't have an all-time favourite?'

'Not really. Though it might be *Rebecca*, as long as it finishes well.'

'What part are you up to?'

'She's about to come down the stairs dressed in that same outfit Rebecca wore, and I just *know* Max is not going to be very happy.'

Jake had to smile. 'You can say that again. Actually, you've quite a bit more to go. And a few more surprises to come.'

'Don't you dare tell me anything!'

'Obviously you haven't seen the movie version.'

'No. I didn't know there was one.'

'Yes, it was made in nineteen forty, only two years after the book was published. Alfred Hitchcock directed it. Laurence Olivier played Max and Joan Fontaine was the unnamed heroine. I'll get a copy for you after you've finished the book.'

Her face carried a touching mixture of disbelief and excitement. 'Would you really?'

'Of course.'

'But where would you get a copy from?'

'You can get just about everything over the internet these days.'

Happiness radiated from her truly lovely green eyes. 'Would you watch it with me?'

'It would be my pleasure. It's a great film. Craig loved it, though not as much as the book.'

'Your uncle was an incredibly well-read man, wasn't he?'

'Yes. And he read books right across the spectrum from literary works to popular fiction. He was the same with music. He absolutely adored the classical composers, but he loved all music, from Country and Western to rock and even rap. There wasn't a snobbish bone in his body.'

'You loved him a lot, didn't you?'

Jake's heart squeezed tight in his chest. He scooped in a deep breath then let it out slowly. 'I'm still angry with him for not telling me he was terminally ill.'

Abby nodded. 'You're right. He should have told you.'

Jake shrugged, not wanting to spoil their weekend together by talking about sad things. Thinking of Craig, however, had reminded Jake of what his uncle had told him in that last letter, about living life to the full. Suddenly, he didn't want to wait to take Abby overseas with him. Time to seize the day!

'Do you have a passport, Abby?' he asked.

'What?'

'A passport. Do you have a passport?'

'No. Why?'

'You're going to need one when we go to Hawaii in January.'

She blinked over at him. 'Are you serious? You want me to go to Hawaii with you?'

'Not just Hawaii. I also want to take you to mainland America. California first, and possibly Vegas, then later over to New York. After New York, we'll go on to Europe, but only after the weather turns kinder. Europe in the winter is not for a girl who's never been out of Australia.'

'But…but…don't you have to be here in Sydney to do your show?'

'No. I don't want to do it any more. I'm going to sell it. I have a buyer who's been after the show for ages. You're going to love Europe, Abby,' he swept on, feeling the excitement already building. 'And Asia. Especially Japan.'

When he glanced over at her, she was shaking her head at him, her expression troubled. 'Maybe by January you won't want to take me anywhere.'

Jake could not have been more startled. 'And why would that be?'

'You might grow bored with me.'

He smiled over at her. 'I find that highly unlikely. What's the matter, Abby? Don't you want to go?'

'Yes,' she said after a heart-stopping space of time. 'Of course I do. It's just that...'

'Just that what?'

'What if you grow bored with me when we're overseas? You won't dump me in some strange city, will you?'

Jake was so shocked he almost ran off the road. As it was, he hit the shoulder, sending gravel spurting out behind them.

'Hell, Abby, what kind of man do you think I am?' he threw at her once he'd righted the car. 'I would never do anything like that. And I won't grow bored with you. Where on earth is all this talk of boredom coming from?'

'According to Megan your girlfriends don't last very long.'

Jake rolled his eyes, inwardly cursing the tabloids for reporting every time one of his relationships broke up, even the ones that never really got off the ground. They made him sound like a playboy of the worst kind. He realised Abby would take some convincing that he wasn't that bad.

'Firstly, let me say that it's not always me who ends the relationships. The women I've dated always claim they don't want marriage, but in the end they do. That's a deal breaker for me, Abby. You sounded very sure last night when you said you didn't want to get married again and I believed you. Was I right to believe you?'

'Absolutely,' she said with a little shudder.

Jake still couldn't make up his mind whether her aversion to marrying again was because she'd loved her husband too much to contemplate marriage to another man, or because her dead husband had done something to turn her off the institution.

He decided to find out.

'But why *is* that, Abby?' he asked. 'What happened to turn you off the idea of remarrying?'

CHAPTER TWENTY-THREE

ABBY STIFFENED. SHE hadn't expected their conversation to take this path. She hadn't expected Jake to offer to take her overseas, either. She certainly hadn't expected him to ask her to explain why she didn't want to get married again.

Clearly, she would have to tell him something, or he might rescind his offer. The thought of travelling to all those exciting places with Jake was way too tempting. But what to say? Not the truth, that was for sure. Just when she was getting desperate, Abby remembered something she'd recently read.

'If you must know, my reason is like what Scarlet told Rhett in *Gone with the Wind*, when he asked her to marry him.'

Jake frowned. 'Sorry. I can't remember what she said. Enlighten me.'

'She said she didn't *like* being married.'

'Ah, yes, I remember now. But Abby, that reason was about her not enjoying sex. Maybe you didn't enjoy sex with your husband but you sure as hell enjoy it with me.'

Which means, Jake thought, that she might change her mind at some future date and want to marry him.

'No, no, you've got the wrong end of the stick,' Abby said firmly before he could explore that rather worrying thought. 'It's not the sex part of marriage that disappointed me. Not really. I quite liked sex with Wayne, even if I didn't come the way I do with you. What I didn't like was my loss of independence, plus my total loss of freedom. In the beginning, I thought I wanted to be an old-fashioned housewife, but the truth is I was just running away from life because I had no self-esteem. I thought I would be happy staying at home twenty-four-seven and being a good little wife and mother. Wayne was a very nice man and he loved me to death, bad teeth and all. But in the end I wasn't happy.'

Which was a huge understatement, Abby thought as she swallowed the lump in her throat then gritted her teeth so she wouldn't cry.

'I'm glad now that we didn't have children,' she lied. 'Once I got over my grief I decided I had to get out there and get myself a job. But first I had to get my teeth fixed or I simply wouldn't have the confidence to go for an interview. Not that I was all that confident when I first showed up at your house,' she added with a rueful little laugh.

'You were a bit nervous,' Jake admitted.

'I was surprised when you gave me the job. Surprised and grateful. It did wonders for my self-esteem. But it was meeting your uncle, Jake, which changed me the most, not just on the outside but on the inside. He made me see myself as an intelligent woman with a lot of potential. He made me braver. It was wonderful of him to give me a new car and some travel money, but his legacy is much more than that. The old Abby would never have dared go to bed with you last night or come away with you this weekend, let alone contemplate going overseas with you. The new more adventurous Abby, however, simply can't say no. I want to do all the things I've never done before—to go places I've never been before. I want to be carefree, not committed. I want to have fun. Is that terribly selfish of me?'

'Hardly, since it's the credo I live by. Why do you think I don't want marriage and children? During my growing up years I witnessed two ways of life with my father and my uncle. When my father died at forty-seven, a worn-out shell of a man, I knew which one I would choose. I was only a teenager when I made a conscious decision to live the life of a bachelor and I've been very happy doing that.'

Up till now, came a sudden and rather perturbing thought.

He eased off the accelerator as he brought his attention back to the road.

'If ever there was a car designed to corrupt it's this little baby,' he said ruefully.

'Same as its owner then,' Abby quipped.

Jake's eyebrows shot upwards. 'You think I've corrupted you?'

Abby smiled. 'Don't sound so shocked, Jake. Of course you've corrupted me. And I dare say you haven't finished yet. But not to worry, I'm enjoying every single moment.'

Their eyes locked, Abby finding it difficult to maintain her saucy attitude in the face of Jake's intense gaze. She could talk big all she liked but underneath her bold facade the old Abby still lurked. Even the new Abby had trouble accepting the strength of Jake's sexual interest in her. She was glad when his eyes swung back on to the road.

'No more talk now,' he said abruptly. 'I have to concentrate or I really will lose my licence.'

Abby didn't mind not talking. That way she could get back to living in the moment. She certainly didn't want to discuss her marriage any more, because inevitably it made her remember her miscarriages and the pain associated with them.

Maybe Wayne's death was a blessing in disguise, Abby decided. Because she knew she could not bear to ever lose another baby. That was why she didn't want to marry again. That was why she couldn't. But of course she could never tell Jake that. He would think she was emotionally damaged. Which, admittedly, she was. She'd always wanted children—wanted to give them the kind of secure and loving upbringing which she'd never had.

Failing to fulfil this most basic human need had been devastating for her. Her last miscarriage had nearly broken her, as had Wayne's tragic death. She'd been dreadfully depressed for months. But eventually she'd begun to recover, finding a resilience and a courage which surprised her.

Signing up with the Housewives For Hire agency had just been the first step in her plan to embrace a different life than that of marriage and children. As soon as she'd got her job with Jake, she'd begun putting that plan in action by saving every cent she could. Even if Jake's wonderful uncle hadn't left her all that money in his will, she would eventually have saved up enough to travel. In the meantime, she would have done a course to help her with her finances. Something in hospitality. A barista course perhaps, and a bar course. There was always work for an attractive girl in pubs and cafés.

And she *was* attractive, Abby conceded, as she smiled at herself in the side mirror of the car. Attractive enough for Jake to consider her girlfriend material. In truth, he seemed well and truly smitten now, enough to consider taking her away on a grand tour with him. Her mind still boggled a bit at that one. Obviously, he genuinely enjoyed her company. It came to Abby that Jake was somewhat jaded with life at the moment, hence his desire to sell his television show and travel overseas. And who better to go with but a female companion for whom he currently had the hots and who would be oh, so impressed by all the places he took her? Which, no doubt, she would be. No use pretending she wouldn't.

But how long before her lack of worldly experience and serious lack of education wasn't quite so appealing? Would it irk him when he couldn't have the same kind of intellectual conversations which he'd had with his very clever uncle and that last newsreader girlfriend who probably had a degree in journalism or communication or whatever degree newsreaders had to have? Female newsreaders weren't just pretty faces these days. They were also smart. Super smart.

Abby realised all of a sudden that silence wasn't good for her. It led to too much negative thinking. She'd come a long way lately in feeling good about herself and she didn't aim to go backwards.

After glancing around, Abby was surprised to realise

she actually recognised where she was. On the long avenue which led to the centre of Canberra. She felt sure that soon they would go over a bridge and then past lots of famous buildings before ending up in front of a grassy hill on which stood the houses of parliament—both old and new.

'I remember more of this than I thought I did,' she said as they approached the bridge which crossed Lake Burley Griffin, named after the man who'd designed the city of Canberra. Abby recalled vaguely that he was an American architect who had won some sort of competition to have the honour, but she didn't say so in case she was wrong.

'Well, the layout of Canberra is very memorable,' Jake remarked. 'And quite beautiful.'

'Yes, it is,' Abby said as she gazed at the expanse of lovely blue water they were crossing. 'It was a marvellous idea to put a lake in the middle of the city.'

'Did you know you can go for a balloon ride over the city?'

'No, I didn't. But no, thank you. A balloon ride would scare the life out of me.'

'You only live once, Abby.'

'I'd still prefer to keep my feet on the ground, thank you very much.'

He threw her a questioning glance. 'Does that attitude apply to planes as well? Because, if it does, it's going to be a slow boat ride around the world next year.'

'No. I'm prepared to fly, but only on a very reliable airline, one with an impeccable record for safety.'

Jake smiled. 'I wouldn't dream of letting you fly any other way. You're too precious to me for that. Now, I think we'll whip into this car park over here. It's only a short walk to the National Gallery, where there is a very nice café.'

Less than one minute later, Jake had zapped into an empty space in the underground car park, a dumbstruck Abby still not having recovered from his remark about her being too precious to him. She wondered if he really meant it or if he said that kind of thing to all his girlfriends. Whatever, it had done things to her insides which were perturbing. She didn't want to fall in love with Jake, but it seemed a futile wish if just a few words could send her into such a whirl.

'Don't do that,' he said when she went to open her own door. 'Let me do it for you.'

He jumped out from behind the wheel and strode round the bonnet of the Ferrari with a few long strides, opening the passenger door with a masterful flourish and holding out his hand to her.

Abby almost told him that he didn't have to play the gentleman with her. He hadn't done this when he'd taken her car shopping. Or at any other time today. Though she hadn't exactly given him the opportunity, had she? This morning she'd driven her own car home, with Jake following in the Ferrari. Then, after she'd changed outfits, she'd hurried out of the house and practically dived into the passenger seat before any of the neighbours saw her. Jake had rolled his eyes at her at the time but she hadn't twigged to why.

'Do you treat all your girlfriends like this?' she asked him as she placed her hand in his.

His fingers closed tightly around hers as he helped her out of the low-slung seat. 'Only when the woman deserves it. Which you do, my lovely Abby. You deserve the best of everything.'

'Wow,' she said. 'But really, Jake, you don't have to overdo the compliments. Trust me when I say I'm already a sure thing tonight.'

He laughed, then pulled her into his arms. 'Goodness, but I adore you!'

Abby stared up into his glittering blue eyes and thought that maybe he did. For the moment. But the moment was all that she could rely on. History invariably repeated itself and Jake's history with women was not good.

Abby pushed aside this painful thought, telling herself

firmly that she wasn't going to worry about the future. She was going to live for the moment. And this moment felt quite wonderful.

'As much as I would like you to kiss me right now,' she said, 'I am in desperate need of the ladies' room. And then something to eat.'

CHAPTER TWENTY-FOUR

As JAKE TOOK the last swallow of his coffee he began wondering how best to spend the afternoon. He had no intention of arriving at the hotel he'd booked till after five, well aware that he wouldn't be able to keep his hands off Abby once they were alone. He didn't want this weekend to be nothing but a sex-fest. He wanted to *show* Abby that he enjoyed her company out of bed as well as in. Hopefully, that would allay her fears that he would quickly get bored with her.

'Did you visit this place when you came down with your school?' he asked. 'Not this café. The National Gallery itself.'

'No, I don't think so. We weren't here all that long. Only two days. We drove down one morning and had lunch in a park somewhere. Then in the afternoon we visited both parliament houses. Then they drove us out to a kind of tourist park for the night. The next day they brought us back in here to visit a science centre. Can't remember what it was called. It started with a Q.'

'Questacon,' he said. 'It's not far from here. I went there once. Great place.'

Abby rolled her eyes. 'For you maybe. I found it boring.'

'Well, you won't find the National Gallery boring. The art in here is fabulous. Not just paintings either, but sculptures as well.'

Abby looked a bit worried. 'I don't know all that much about art.'

'That's probably better then. You won't have any preconceived ideas. Promise me you won't say you like something just because it's in here, okay? Some of the purchases have been very controversial over the years. Have you ever heard of *Blue Poles*?'

'It rings a vague bell,' she replied, frowning.

'It's a very famous painting by an American artist, Jackson Pollock. It was bought by this gallery in 1972 for one point three million. They had to get special permission from the Prime Minister at the time to spend that much money. Caused a massive stir. Still, it's reputed to be worth up to twenty million now so I guess it was a good investment after all. Come on. I'll take you to see it,' he said, standing up and reaching for her hand.

'It's huge!' was Abby's first comment when she stood in front of the painting, which measured approximately two by five metres.

'It certainly is.'

'The artist must have had to stand on a ladder to paint the top bits.'

'Actually, he did it whilst it was lying flat on the floor. But that's all beside the point. Do you *like* it?'

Abby scrunched up her face as she stepped back and stared at it for a long moment. 'I can't make up my mind if it's brilliant or an Emperor's New Clothes piece of rubbish.'

Jake had to smile. Only Abby would dare to question what was considered to be Jackson Pollock's best work.

'No, no, I take that back,' she said after a few more seconds of narrow-eyed scrutiny. 'It's definitely one of those paintings that grows on you. But you could hardly hang it in your living room, could you?'

'True,' Jake said, trying not to laugh. But she was such a delight. And so natural, her opinions untainted by the one-eyed opinions of art critics and pseudo intellectuals.

'I certainly wouldn't pay twenty million for it,' she added.

'Me neither,' a male voice said from just behind them.

Jake recognised that voice. Instantly.

He spun round. 'Tony Green, you old devil! Fancy running into you here.'

Abby was astonished when Jake enfolded a tall, skinny, darkly bearded man in a big bear hug.

'I thought you weren't ever coming back to Australia,' Jake added as the man hugged him back. When at last they pulled apart they both had boyish grins on their happy faces.

'Neither were you, if I recall,' the bearded man said. 'Till a bullet changed your mind.'

Abby sucked in sharply at this news, but Jake just shrugged. 'I was about ready to come home, Tony. I'd had enough. Now, before we go and have a drink together and catch up on old times, I think I should make some introductions.' He turned back to Abby and took her by the hand again. 'Abby, this is Tony Green, the most fearless cameraman money can buy. But also just a tad dangerous to work with.'

Tony laughed. '*You* ought to talk. This man's a maniac. I told him he was crazy to go into that particular village that day, but he wouldn't take any notice. Said he'd come to help rescue some girls who'd been kidnapped by a gang of rebels and he was going to free them, come hell or high water. He just wouldn't listen to reason. And guess what? The girls did get rescued but our boy here almost lost his life in the process.'

'Goodness!' Abby exclaimed. 'I had no idea…'

Tony grinned. 'Modest as well as brave. That's our Jake. But also stubborn. Once Jake makes his mind up to do something, nothing will change his mind. But then you probably already know that, since I gather you two are an item.'

'We are,' Jake said, giving Abby's hand a squeeze. 'And I'll have you know I'm not a maniac any longer.'

'Possibly true. I couldn't believe it when I got back to Australia last month and saw you hosting that chat show. I mean, that's not you, mate.'

'It suited me at the time, Tony. And it's my own production. But I've decided to sell it before Christmas. Abby and

I are going on a world tour together next year. *Not* to the places *we* went to. To the nice places.'

'Wow. So you two are pretty serious about each other then?'

'You could say that,' Jake replied, and gave Abby's hand another squeeze.

'You *have* changed. Look, as much as I'd like to get a drink and catch up on old times, I can't. I'm meeting someone up at Parliament House in about fifteen minutes. I just popped in here to fill in time till she gets off work.'

'Someone special?' Jake asked.

'Very. We met over the internet. She's the reason I came back to Australia.'

'I see. Well, I hope it works out for you.'

'You too. We should stay in touch.'

'I'm on Facebook,' Jake told him.

'Me too. Have to go, mate. It's been great seeing you again.'

They hugged once more and Tony was gone.

'Well,' said Jake with a sigh, 'fancy that. I honestly never expected to see him again.'

There was so much Abby wanted to ask Jake, the many questions in her head underlining how much she didn't know about him and the job he used to do. But right now, here in this gallery, with people milling around, didn't seem the right place to have such a conversation.

'I don't really want to walk around looking at art, Jake,' she said truthfully. 'Can't we just go to that hotel you booked? Or is it too early?'

Their eyes met, the desire which they'd both put on hold earlier flaring between them.

'And you accused me of corrupting you,' he murmured wryly, then glanced at his watch. 'It's only half past two. Check-in time isn't till three. But I suppose I could call them and play the celebrity card.'

He played the celebrity card, Abby wishing for a few

excruciating minutes in Reception that he hadn't. The behaviour of the attractive brunette behind the desk was more
than embarrassing. She gushed all over Jake, half flirting
with him whilst totally ignoring Abby's presence. By the
time Jake steered Abby over to the bank of lifts in the corner, she wasn't sure who she felt sorrier for, herself or Jake.

She sighed as they entered a blessedly empty lift.

'Yes, I know,' he said ruefully. 'But it won't be like that
when we're booking into hotels overseas. Over there, I'll
be a nobody.'

'I suspect you'll always get special treatment from female staff, Jake,' Abby said a bit tartly. 'You're way too
handsome for your own good.'

He smiled at her. 'That's the pot calling the kettle black.
I haven't forgotten the way dear old Raoul came on to you,
beautiful.'

Abby blinked up at him. 'Are you saying you were jealous of Raoul?'

'Painfully so.'

'Good,' she said, and he laughed.

'I like it when you get stroppy with me. And when you're
jealous.'

The lift doors opened on the tenth floor, Jake wasting no
time steering Abby along the corridor to their room. Their
overnight bags were waiting for them inside, as was a bottle of chilled champagne and a fruit basket, courtesy of the
management. The room was what was called superior, with
views over the lake, a separate sitting area, a king-sized bed
and a spa bath.

Although impressed, Abby wasn't all that interested in
any of it. All she wanted by then was for Jake to take her
in his arms and kiss her.

'Care for a glass of champagne?' he asked her as he lifted
the bottle out of the ice bucket and set about opening it.

Abby winced. How did you tell a man that all you wanted
was him?

He glanced over at her then and laughed. 'You should see the look on your face.'

Now she blushed.

'I take it you don't want the champagne just yet,' he said as he walked slowly across the room to where she was standing beside the bed.

'Do you?' she asked him.

'The only thing I want at the moment, my darling girl,' he said, 'is you.'

He undressed her quickly, without so much as a kiss, not stopping till she was totally naked. Then he left her standing there like that whilst he undressed, his eyes on her all the while. Her own gaze was hot and hungry as she watched him strip off, her need intense before he'd even laid a finger on her. She closed her eyes when he scooped her up and laid her on the bed, gasping when he started stroking her body, first her breasts then her stomach, her thighs, her calves.

'No, no…' she moaned when he spread her legs and used his mouth on her.

But protesting was useless and she splintered apart under his tongue within seconds. Her climax hadn't abated when he rolled her over on to her stomach and started stroking her again. Her back this time, then her buttocks. And between. She writhed beneath his knowing hands, and his wickedly probing fingers. In no time her desire for release became desperate again. Her legs moved invitingly apart, her hips moving restlessly in a circular fashion.

'Not that way, my darling,' he growled, and flipped her back over. 'Not this time. I want to see your eyes when you come. Just give me a sec.'

She groaned at the time he took to don the condom, crying out when he entered her at last, penetrating her with a forceful surge which filled her to the hilt. His own eyes, she noted, were wildly glittering, his breathing ragged. He groaned when she wrapped her legs high around his back, pressing her hips hard up against his.

'Hell on earth, woman,' he ground out. 'Be still or I'll come.'

'I want you to come,' she told him in a wickedly wanton voice as she moved her hips in a slow sensual circle, squeezing him at the same time.

A decidedly crude four-letter word punched from his throat.

Abby didn't swear much herself, but somehow, today, at this moment, it turned her on. 'Yes,' she said with a low moan. 'That's what I want, too. Just do it, Jake. I don't care if I come or not.'

'Bloody hell,' he muttered, then started to move, the veins in his throat standing out as he set up a steady rhythm.

Abby was touched by his efforts to last, but she would have none of it, certain that she would come if he came. She kept squeezing him mercilessly, and rotating her hips, watching with increasing frustration as he tried desperately to maintain control. Desperate herself now, she removed her hands from where they'd been gripping the sheet on either side of her, clamping them onto his buttocks and digging her nails in as she pulled him even deeper into her.

It was the final straw for Jake, tipping him over the edge with a speed and power which Abby found thrilling. He didn't watch her come because his eyes were shut at the time. But come she did, exulting in the way her body matched his, spasm for spasm. They shuddered together for ages till finally they were done, Jake rolling from her and collapsing on to the bed, still gasping and panting. Abby just lay where she was, a very deep languor seeping through her sated body as her breathing calmed and her muscles relaxed. She didn't want to go to sleep, but her mind had other ideas. Five minutes later she was out like a light.

CHAPTER TWENTY-FIVE

JAKE WAS BEYOND words for some considerable time. Frankly, he was somewhat stunned at how he'd lost control of the lovemaking. There he'd been, thinking he would show Abby this weekend what a great lover he was and bingo, he'd come with the speed of a randy teenager. For a girl of limited experience, she seemed to know exactly what to do to drive a man wild.

Jake sighed. So much for not wanting this weekend to be a sex-fest. Suddenly, that was all he could think about. His head turned to where Abby was lying on the bed, her naked body splayed out in the most provocative pose. Unfortunately, she was also sound asleep. But that didn't stop Jake from looking.

Naked, Abby had the sort of body a man could look at for hours, with its delicious combination of slenderness and curves. Her breasts were just the right size. Full but not heavy, her nipples surprisingly large and yes, very responsive. Not pink, they were a dusky brown colour which made them stand out from her rather pale skin. Jake's stomach tightened at the urge to roll over right now and suck them. But he didn't. Though he would, after he'd been to the bathroom. She didn't need to sleep for long. Hell, it was only mid-afternoon. She could sleep later tonight, after he'd run out of steam. And condoms.

Climbing off the bed, Jake walked into the bathroom to attend to the condom. He wished he didn't have to use them.

'I really don't want to take *any* chances, Jake,' she'd reiterated at breakfast today. 'I went through a few nasty moments there last night when I thought I'd forgotten to take my Pill.'

It would have given him more than a *few* nasty moments if she'd become pregnant, Jake accepted. Which meant he would just have to keep on using condoms.

Not that it really mattered. Safe sex was a way of life for him. Still, perhaps after they'd been together for a while, she might tell him not to bother with the condoms any more. He trusted her to take the Pill every day. After all, she seemed just as paranoid about falling pregnant as he was. Meanwhile, he still had almost a dozen condoms left for this weekend, which seemed overly ambitious...but then he walked back into the bedroom and saw that Abby had rolled over and curled up into a foetal position.

Just looking at Abby's peachy bottom started doing things to him which would have been impossible a few minutes earlier.

Jake climbed back on to the bed with a rueful smile on his face.

'Abby, darling,' he crooned, running a single finger up and down her spine. 'You can't go to sleep yet. It's only four o'clock.'

'Go away,' she mumbled. 'Tired.'

Jake smiled as he rose and went back into the bathroom, where he poured some of the provided bath salts into the spa bath he'd noted earlier. After that, he turned on the water, adjusted the temperature, then went to collect the champagne and the fruit basket, the bath fortunately having ledges large enough in each corner to accommodate the ice bucket and two glasses. Once the water was at the right height, he switched off the taps, hid a couple of condoms amongst the fruit then joined Abby on the bed, this time bending his lips to her shoulder.

'Jake calling Abby,' he murmured between kisses. 'Do you hear me, Abby?'

Her eyes fluttered open as her head turned and gazed up at him with heavy lids. 'You can't possibly want to do it again this soon,' she said sleepily.

'Not right away,' he said. 'I've run us a spa bath. There's room enough for two.'

She blinked, then sat up abruptly, her messy hair falling across her forehead and one eye. 'But I haven't... I've never...'

'What happened to the girl who told me she wanted to experience everything?' he said as he gently pushed her hair back from her eyes. 'Trust me, okay?'

She rolled her eyes at this.

'I've taken some refreshments in there for us to enjoy,' he went on. 'I thought you might be hungry. We can eat and talk at the same time.'

'You want to talk? I thought you wanted sex.'

'Not until you wake up properly.'

Jake kept a straight face as he said this.

But, perversely, Abby took him at his word.

'So what are we going to talk about?' she said even before she'd lowered herself into the warm water.

'Whatever you'd like to talk about,' he replied, temporarily settling back into the opposite end of the bath. 'But first I'll pour us both some champagne.'

Abby wondered as she watched Jake pour the bubbly just how often he'd done this. She wasn't jealous, but she did rather envy his know-how. Did he have any idea how awkward she felt at the moment? How...ignorant?

Not a total fool, however. He hadn't brought her in here to talk. And whilst she did want him to make love to her some more in whatever exotic ways he wanted, there *was* something she wanted to talk to him about whilst she had the chance.

'That man in the gallery, Jake,' she said as he handed her a glass of champagne. 'Tony,' she added after taking a sip.

'What about him?' Jake asked.

'He said you were shot. And I was wondering where.' She hadn't seen any scars on him.

'Africa. Sierra Leone.'

'No, no, I mean where on your body.'

He laughed. 'Here,' he said, and showed her a scar on his inner thigh which was more towards the back than the front. No wonder she hadn't seen it.

'Heavens. You were very lucky.'

'Sure was. A couple of inches either way and I would have lost the family jewels.'

'Which would have been a dreadful shame.'

'My feelings exactly.'

'Still, it was very brave of you to do what you did that day.'

'More stupid than brave.'

'I don't agree. So I suppose that was when you stopped making documentaries?'

'Yep. I had to come home to get proper medical treatment. Then, once I was home, I decided I'd had enough of traipsing around the world. Craig said I'd get tired of it one day and he was right.'

'Then why do you want to go back overseas?'

'Travelling as a tourist is very different from what I was doing, Abby. Have you seen any of the documentaries I made?'

'No.'

'Then don't. They're grim viewing.'

'Then why did you make them?'

He shrugged. 'Initially, I thought it would be great fun, following Craig around and filming the places he went and the things he witnessed. But after a few years I found myself becoming emotionally involved in the injustices I saw. I naively thought that if the problems of the Third World were shoved in the face of the Western World, they might do something to solve at least some of those problems. That was when I became a crusader. But I was deluding myself. People liked watching my more hard-hitting documentaries. I made a lot of money out of them. But they didn't inspire much action. There's still war and poverty and abuse of the worst kind. Nothing ever changes.'

'But you tried,' Abby said gently. 'All you can do is try, Jake.'

'You *are* sweet,' he said. 'But could we possibly change the subject?'

Abby was touched by his sensitivity. Clearly, he wasn't as selfish and self-centred as he liked to pretend. But then, she'd already known that, hadn't she, even before she'd heard the good things Tony had said about him. Look at the way he'd followed through with his uncle's legacy to her, even though he hadn't wanted to at first.

A thought suddenly occurred to her.

'Were you telling the truth when you said you were jealous of Raoul?'

'Jealous? I wanted to tear him limb from limb.'

'But why? I mean…we weren't an item then.'

'Maybe not. But I already wanted you like crazy.'

She shook her head from side to side. 'I find that hard to believe.'

'Oh, Abby, Abby, you gorgeous thing, you.' He sighed and shook his head back at her. 'You don't understand men very well, do you? Now, drink up your champers, sweet thing. I have an urge to have my wicked way with you. All chit-chat is to cease as of this moment. That is, except for words like, *Yes, Jake. Please, Jake. Don't stop, Jake.*'

She couldn't help it. She laughed.

'Don't you dare laugh at me, you cheeky minx.'

She smiled instead and said, 'Yes, Jake.'

CHAPTER TWENTY-SIX

It was light when Abby came to consciousness, turning over on to her back and stretching before glancing over at the sleeping male form next to her in the bed. Jake was lying on his side, his back to her, his breathing deep and heavy.

She smiled in memory of Jake's reluctance to let her go to sleep, even when it was obvious he'd exhausted himself making love to her. The only time they'd stopped was first at six-thirty so she could take her Pill and then when he'd ordered room service around eight, a huge seafood platter which they'd devoured together in record time before getting back to devouring each other.

Abby picked up her phone from the bedside table and checked the time, surprised to find that it was after nine. They'd finally gone to sleep around two, so both of them had had a good seven hours of sleep. Still, no need to wake Jake yet, she decided, rising quietly and going to the bathroom. Closing the door behind her, she turned on the light and took a good look at herself in the large mirror.

Not only was her hair a total mess—she really should have put it up before that last shower—but she had faint bruises on her breasts.

'Goodness, Abby,' she said, sounding slightly shocked. 'You look like a woman who's been well and truly ravaged.'

'And didn't you just love it,' she answered herself in a low sexy voice which wasn't at all shocked.

The new Abby realised there was no point in pretending. Given she was unlikely ever to come across a lover like Jake again, she aimed to take full advantage of his erotic skills—plus his gorgeous male body—whilst she had the chance. If she had to have her heart broken by him at some stage in the future, then she was going to enjoy herself in the meantime.

Though how long that meantime lasted was anybody's idea, she accepted with an inevitable lurching of her silly female heart. Okay, so he'd asked her to go overseas with him next year. And he *had* sounded as if he meant it. But that could just have been a wild impulse on his part. He could change his mind tomorrow. Or next week. Or next month. It was only mid November. All she could rely on was today. The present. This moment.

'That's it, kiddo,' she told herself firmly. 'Live for the moment. Now, go wake up old sleepyhead.'

With her body buzzing from wicked resolve, Abby returned to the bedroom and climbed in under the sheet next to a still unconscious Jake. She didn't hesitate, snuggling up to him with her naked front pressed up against his back, her left hand free to travel at will over his body, much the same way as he had done to her in the bath. He stirred slightly the moment her fingers brushed over his nipples, but shot awake with a raw gasp when her hand moved further south.

'You have a beautiful penis,' she murmured. 'Nice and long. And so silky up here.'

He made a strangled sound as she ran her thumb pad over the engorged tip.

'You like that, don't you?' she crooned, another echo of what he'd said to her when he'd teased her at length in the water. 'But you'd rather I do this with my tongue, wouldn't you?'

When he swore she laughed. 'No, not this time, Jake. This time you're going to let me have *my* wicked way with *you.*'

It surprised Abby how in control she felt, her own needs firmly in check as she set about making *him* lose control. She loved it when he called out her name as he came, blown away by the satisfaction she felt as his whole body shook.

But alongside the satisfaction lay the certainty that she

would not feel this way with any other man. The realisation hit suddenly that she loved Jake—loved him in the way she should have loved Wayne, but hadn't. The thought sent tears into her eyes, tears of guilt and regret and true sadness.

The old Abby might have fallen apart at that moment. The new Abby was a far tougher creature. She told herself firmly that she'd gone into this affair with her eyes open and it was a little late to start becoming maudlin. So she gathered her emotions, blinked away the tears and lifted her head.

It was impossible not to look at him. Impossible to stop her emotions suddenly getting the better of her. How awful it was to love someone the way she loved Jake without being able to tell him.

Jake was taken aback when he saw she was on the verge of tears.

'Abby! Darling! What is it? What's wrong?'

'Oh, God,' she cried, then burst into tears.

Stricken with remorse over he knew not what, Jake cuddled her close, searching his mind at the same time for the reason behind her tears.

'Tell me what's wrong,' he said as he cradled her face and rained kisses all over it.

She made a choking sound, closing her eyes at the same time.

'You wanted to do that, didn't you? I didn't ask you. You *wanted* to. And I loved it. Truly I did.'

Still, she said nothing, just buried her face into his shoulder and wept.

'Please don't cry, my darling.'

She opened her still wet eyes then and just stared at him. 'Don't call me that,' she blurted out. 'I'm not your darling.'

Jake didn't know how to respond. Had her husband called her his darling? Was that it?

'What do you want me to call you?'

She closed her eyes again as she shook her head. 'Oh, God. I'm so stupid.'

Jake sighed. He wished he knew what was going on in her head. But he'd never been good at reading women's minds. Females could be complex creatures. Maybe she was hormonal. Maybe her period was due. All he knew was that he hated seeing her upset, her tears calling to something deep inside himself which was impossible to control. His heart actually ached with the need to make her feel better.

'Abby... I hate seeing you like this. I wish you'd tell me what's wrong. I want to be your friend as well as your lover. I want you to feel that you can tell me anything.'

He waited and finally, when she opened her eyes, her expression was calmer. Or was it resigned?

'It's not you,' she said. 'It's me. You haven't done anything wrong. I love what kind of lover you are. I've had more fun with you this weekend than I've had in years.'

Jake pulled a face. Now she made it sound as if he was shallow. Yet he felt anything but shallow when he was making love to her. Perhaps because that was exactly what it was. Making love. Not just having sex. Jake could no longer pretend that he wasn't becoming seriously involved with Abby. He'd avoiding falling in love in the past because he didn't want marriage and children. What Jake hadn't realised was that true love could not be avoided. It just happened. If truth be told, he'd been half in love with Abby from the moment he'd hugged her that awful day, long before she'd stormed past his conscience less than two days ago. Now he was well and truly head over heels.

But of course he couldn't tell her any of that. Not yet. She didn't want him to love her. Not at the moment. Perhaps one day, when the time was right, when he was sure that she returned his feelings, he would declare his love and they would find a way to spend their lives together. Not marriage. Though perhaps a child eventually, if that was what she ever wanted. Jake still wasn't thrilled with the idea of becoming a father but one child might be manageable.

'So why were you crying just now?' he asked.

Abby shrugged. 'This will sound silly but I was feeling guilty that I couldn't give my husband the pleasure that I obviously give you. Wayne deserved better than a wife who didn't really love him.'

'You did love him, Abby,' he reassured her. 'I know you. You wouldn't have married him if you hadn't loved him. Maybe it wasn't a mad passion but it was love all the same. It wasn't your fault that the physical chemistry between you wasn't right. It wasn't his fault, either. But that's all in the past, Abby. You can't change what happened in your marriage and it's a waste of time to beat yourself up over it.'

'You're right,' she said, nodding. 'I can't change anything that's already happened. All we have is the present. I decided earlier today that I want to live in the moment from now on. That's what you do, isn't it?'

'To a degree,' he replied carefully. 'I do make some plans for the future when required.'

'You mean like when going overseas.'

'That's a good example. You can't just show up at the airport and take the first available flight. You need to do things first.'

'Like get a passport,' she said, her eyes looking marginally happier.

'Indeed,' he said, smiling.

'I'll get straight on to that first thing next week. And I might do some more clothes shopping at some stage. I don't want you ever feeling ashamed of me.'

Jake was truly taken aback. 'I would never be ashamed of you.' But it did occur to him that women thought differently to men on matters of fashion.

'You should go clothes shopping with Sophie. She would know exactly what you need. I tell you what; I'll ring and ask her to take you.'

'Oh, no, don't do that. I can't afford the sort of clothes your sister would show me.'

'Yes, you can. I'll give her my credit card. It doesn't have a limit.'

'I can't let you do that!' she exclaimed.

'Why not?'

'Because…because…'

'I'm a very rich man, Abby. I want to do this for you. Please don't say no.'

'I shouldn't let you.'

'Don't be silly. I'll ring her and tell her you need a new wardrobe to cover every occasion. Now, no more objections. I insist. And another thing, you have to ring your sister tonight and tell her about us.'

Abby groaned. 'I really don't want to, Jake.'

'And I don't want to keep on being your secret lover,' he growled. 'I certainly don't intend to spend every date with you wearing sunglasses and a baseball cap. The world is going to find out about us sooner or later, Abby, and there's nothing you can do about that.'

'I know,' she said with a sigh. 'But at least we have today before that happens.'

'Don't you believe it. That receptionist last night was probably on Instagram and Twitter within seconds of our booking in. You can't keep anything a secret these days, not if you're in the public eye. You just have to not care what people think or say. People that don't matter, that is. Family is different.'

'Are you going to tell your family about me?'

Jake smiled. 'I won't have to. Sophie will. But, speaking of family, I want you to join us for our harbour cruise on Christmas Day.'

Dismay filled Abby's face. 'I'm sorry, Jake, but I can't do that. I've already invited Megan and Timmy to spend Christmas Day with me and I would never disappoint them.'

'I see,' he said, thinking he should have known. Olivia

would have dumped her family like a shot if he'd asked her to be with him on Christmas Day. But Abby was not Olivia. She was unique. A woman in a million. 'Well, there's no reason why they can't both come on the harbour cruise with all of us,' he said. 'There'll be plenty of room, and plenty of food. And lots of other kids for Timmy to play with.'

'That's incredibly generous of you, Jake, but I'm not sure Megan will want to come.'

'Why's that? Is she shy?'

Abby laughed. 'Not exactly.'

'Look, when you ring her tonight, just ask her.'

'What if she says no?'

'Then I'll ring her and ask her myself. I've been told I can be very persuasive, when I want to be.'

Abby's expression was pained. 'As long as you don't flirt with her. If you do that, I won't be too happy. She already thinks you're God's gift to women.'

'In that case persuade her to come yourself. Because I don't intend to be without you on Christmas Day. I also want to show you off to my whole family, and that way we can do it all in one go. Far better than having to trot you around to everyone one at a time.'

'You won't tell them about my background, will you? And my teeth!'

'Sorry, sweetheart, they'll already know everything about you by then. Sophie is not renowned for keeping her mouth shut. And why wouldn't you want them to know about your teeth? They look fabulous!'

'I wasn't referring to my new teeth but my old ones.'

'There's nothing shameful about having had problem teeth.'

'Pardon me if I don't think so,' Abby said, rolling away from him on to the bed, her body language indicating she wasn't happy.

'Okay,' he said nonchalantly.

'What?' Stormy green eyes shot his way.

'I'll pardon you. For about ten seconds. You're the one who said you wanted to move on with your life. Well, the first thing for you to do is not be oversensitive about your past. I want to tell my family all about you because I'm serious about you, Abby. I don't want you for a fling. Okay, I might not want marriage but I want you in my life. If you must know, I was attracted to you from the first moment I saw you.'

'You *were*?'

'I certainly was. But I thought you were the sort of woman who would want marriage and children so I kept my distance. Regardless of what you think of me, I am not a compulsive womaniser. I would never target a woman who was emotionally vulnerable, which I thought you were, being a widow. But on Friday night you confirmed that you didn't want to get married again. After that, I decided to hell with resisting temptation any longer. I wanted you like mad by then and decided I was going to have you.'

Only then did Jake realise Abby was looking pole-axed by his confession. He wasn't sure if that meant she was pleased, or sceptical.

'That was why I was jealous of Raoul,' he went on. 'Now, no more of this nonsense. And no more regrets about the past. You're living for the moment, are you not? And the moment calls for two activities. Breakfast first. I don't know about you but I'm starving. Then once we're dressed, fed and out of here I'm going to do something really amazing.'

'And what's that?'

'I'm going to let you drive my car.'

CHAPTER TWENTY-SEVEN

'I CAN'T BELIEVE IT,' Megan said for the umpteenth time since Abby had called her that Sunday night.

Abby sighed. 'I don't know why you keep saying that. You were the one who warned me Jake might come on to me if I smartened myself up.'

'It's not that I don't believe he fancies you; it's all the sex! I always thought you were frigid.'

'Well, I'm obviously not.'

'Obviously. At least, not with lover boy. But then, he's had a lot of practice seducing women.'

'Jake did not seduce me, Megan. I was with him all the way.'

'Honestly?'

'Honestly.'

'Wow.'

'He's asked me to go overseas with him next year.'

'You have to be kidding me.'

'I kid you not. I'm applying for my passport this week. Apparently, it takes a few weeks to get it.'

'This is insane, Abby. You do know that, don't you? I mean…it won't last. Men like Jake…they don't do for ever.'

'I'm well aware of that, Megan. He was nothing if not brutally honest with me on that score. No marriage and no children. But he claims he does want a relationship with me, not just a fling. So I am going to go overseas with him and nothing you say is going to stop me.'

'Oh, God, you've fallen in love with the bastard, haven't you?'

Abby sighed again. 'Jake is not a bastard, Megan. He's a very nice man. A gentleman, in fact. And yes, I've fallen in love with him. But not to worry. I've already come to terms with my feelings. I know I'm going to be hurt at some time in the future but I've decided not to worry about the future for a while. Or the past. I'm living for the here and now. Jake likes me. A lot. And he wants me. A lot. I won't give that up just because it might end badly one day.'

'I've never heard you talk like this, Abby. You sound so sure. And so mature.'

'I've grown up a bit since Wayne died.'

'He wasn't right for you,' Megan said gently, bringing a lump to Abby's throat.

'I can see that now,' Abby agreed. 'I talked with Jake about my marriage and he said I had to let it go. That it was past history.'

'He's right. But surely you didn't tell Jake everything, did you? I mean I know how you hate talking about your miscarriages.'

Abby's heart immediately squeezed tight in her chest. 'No, I didn't tell him about them. He thinks we were trying for a baby but it just didn't happen. It was more my relationship with Wayne I talked about. I told Jake I didn't want to get married again.'

'When did you say that?'

'I'm not sure. Some time recently. It might have been the day he took me car shopping.'

'After which he decided it was safe to seduce you,' came Megan's dry remark.

Abby rolled her eyes. 'Whatever.' Abby hadn't told Megan about Jake's declaration that he'd had the hots for her from the day he hired her. Mostly because Megan was too cynical to believe that. But, surprisingly, Abby did. For she could find no reason for Jake to lie to her. Not that it would change the ultimate outcome of their relationship. It gave Abby a real thrill to think she'd captured his interest but he'd cared enough about her emotional well-being not to pursue her at the time.

'I bet you'd marry Jake in a shot if he asked you to.'

'He isn't going to, Megan. He has, however, asked me to spend Christmas Day with him and his extended family on a harbour cruise.'

'Wow. He must be pretty serious about you then, if he wants you to meet his mum and dad.'

'He's only got a mum. His dad's dead. But he also has two brothers and three sisters, four of whom are married with children.'

'Good grief, I hope it's a big boat.'

'Very big, he said. Which is why you and Timmy are invited as well.'

'What? You're kidding! This is just so out there. I'm going on a harbour cruise with Jake Sanderson and his family? Golly, I'll have to go on a diet straight away. And buy something new to wear.'

'Speaking of new clothes, I'm going clothes shopping with Jake's sister some time this week. Jake insisted on buying me a whole new wardrobe.'

'Seriously? A whole new wardrobe?'

'Yes. And before you make any smart cracks about me being a kept woman, how about I get her to pick out something for you at the same time? I know your size and she'll choose something really stylish, since she's a stylist.'

Megan laughed. 'You're worried I'm going to turn up in something cheap and trashy, aren't you?'

'Not at all!' Abby exclaimed.

'You're such a bad liar. But not bad at keeping secrets, it turns out. There I was, trying to ring you all weekend and getting really mad, thinking that you'd accidentally turned off your phone. And now I find out that you did it on purpose so that you and your boss could bonk away like a pair of bloody rabbits.'

'You have such a delicate turn of phrase.'

'Gee, Abby. Ever since you started reading all those fancy books you seem different.'

'Different? How?'

'Oh, you know. Like you had some toffee-nosed education. Don't forget your roots, girl. You're a Westie and there's nothing you can do to change that.'

'I'm not trying to change that. I know exactly where I came from. But there's nothing wrong with trying to better myself. Even if my affair with Jake hadn't happened, I would have been going to night school next year, as well as saving up to travel all by myself.'

'But Jake has happened, so now you'll drop all those plans. Just don't forget that when *he* drops *you* you're going to lose your job as well. Have you thought of that?'

'It's crossed my mind. But like I said, I'm not going to worry about the future too much, Megan. I'm going to live for the moment.'

'That's because you're madly in love at the moment.'

'You can't talk me out of this, Megan. Now, I'm getting off this phone and going to bed. I've had a very tiring weekend.'

'Yeah, so I heard. I still can't believe it. Did you two do anything else this weekend except have wild sex?'

'I never said it was wild.'

'Yeah, right. Pull the other leg. I'll bet lover boy did more to you in one weekend than Wayne did in five frigging years.'

'You could be right there.'

'Ooh, do tell!'

'Absolutely not. I'm off to bed. Goodnight, Megan.'

Abby shook her head as she terminated the call then turned off her phone. She didn't have a landline so her sister and her curiosity would have to wait. Megan might want her to give a blow-by-blow account of her various sexual escapades but Abby was not that kind of girl. She was a very private person. And so was Jake, in his own way. She could see he didn't overly like his celebrity status any more than she did.

Abby got herself ready for bed, since she actually was *very* tired. Which was just as well. She didn't want to lie in bed and start overthinking everything. There was a time for deep and meaningful thinking, and it wasn't now. Now was the time for sleep.

Abby was settling herself down into sleep mode when all of a sudden she remembered that Jake had asked her to call him and tell her how things went with Megan. Sitting up in bed abruptly, she reached for her phone, instantly energised by the thought of talking to Jake. He answered on the second ring.

'I was beginning to think you weren't going to call me,' he said.

'I'm sorry, Jake. I forgot.'

'That's not very flattering, I must say. A couple of hours out of my sight and you forget me.'

Abby knew he wasn't really angry. She could hear the teasing note in his voice. 'You're not going to be one of those boyfriends, are you?' she teased back.

'And what kind is that?'

'The obsessive kind.'

'That depends on whether you're going to be one of those girlfriends.'

'And what kind is that?'

'The ones who drive men insane because they don't ring when they say they're going to.'

'I said I was sorry.'

'You also said you forgot.'

'I dare say you're not used to being forgotten.'

'Not often. But all this is beside the point. Did you tell your sister about us?'

'Yes.'

'And?'

'She wasn't shocked that we're sleeping together, but she's worried that I'm going to lose my job when we eventually break up.'

'Who says we'll eventually break up?'

'It seems likely, given your history with women.'

'I'm not as fickle as the tabloids make out.'

'I know that. But, in any case, I'm not worried. I can always get another job, provided you give me a good reference.'

'I'm not sure I like that sister of yours. She sounds like trouble.'

'She's only looking after my best interests.'

'And I'm not?'

'Don't go getting all huffy, Jake. Why do you think I didn't want to ring her? But you insisted. Sometimes she rattles me with her cynicism but this time I didn't take notice of anything she said, which rather pleased me. I want to be with you, Jake, and nothing that Megan or anyone else says is going to change my mind.'

'You've no idea how glad I am to hear that. Because I want to be with you too. And not for just a few weeks, or a few months. I have a feeling this relationship might go the whole nine yards.'

Abby sucked in sharply. 'And what does that mean?'

'Now, don't *you* go getting all huffy. I'm not talking marriage. But I am talking about living together, as of tomorrow.'

'Tomorrow?'

'Too soon for you?'

Abby tried not to lose her head. She might be madly in love with Jake but she wasn't about to let him run every aspect of her life.

'A little,' she said. 'How about we wait till after Christmas?'

'But that's over five weeks away!'

'That's hardly a lifetime.'

'So you're knocking me back.'

'I'd like us to just date for a while before taking such a big step.'

'But you've already agreed to go away with me next year,' Jake argued.

'Yes, but that's just a holiday, not real life.'

'Not real life,' he echoed, clearly taken aback.

'Jake, could we not get into this right now? I'm tired and I want to go to sleep. We can talk about this tomorrow.'

Jake could not believe that Abby was giving him the brush-off. He hadn't been on the receiving end of that before. He almost blurted out that he loved her but he held his tongue just in time.

'Fair enough,' he said. ''Till tomorrow then. Goodnight.'

'Goodnight, Jake. And thank you again, for such a wonderful weekend.'

Jake kept the dead phone clamped to his ear for ages whilst he tried to work out exactly what he was feeling. Frustration, mainly. Not sexual frustration—frustration that for the first time in his life he wanted more from a relationship than the woman did. Not only did he want Abby to move in with him, he wanted her to love him the way he loved her. But she didn't want to fall in love. She wanted fun and games, with a fancy holiday overseas thrown in for good measure.

'Not real life,' he growled when he finally threw his phone down. He'd show her real life. He'd take her to places in Asia and Africa where real life meant crippling poverty and appalling cruelty, with no hope for the future.

But no sooner had these vengeful thoughts entered his head than Jake realised he would never do anything so contemptible. Abby deserved better than to be on the receiving end of that kind of behaviour. She deserved the very best this world had to offer. He would take her to large vibrant cities like London and Paris, Tokyo and New York. And then there were the magnificent rivers. He'd take her cruising down the Seine, and the Rhine, and the Danube. Maybe even the Nile, if Egypt got its act together.

Jake's good humour returned as he thought about their trip next year. It would be incredible. The trip of a lifetime, for both of them. And who knew, by the time they returned Abby might care about him enough to move in with him permanently. She might even love him.

He wasn't that unlovable, was he?

CHAPTER TWENTY-EIGHT

ABBY HAD ALWAYS liked Jake's house, sometimes fantasising in her head as she'd cleaned it that if she ever had a spare couple of million dollars she would buy herself such a house. She loved the white walls and the polished wooden floors, the high ceilings and the unfussy furniture. She especially loved the sparkling white kitchen and bathrooms.

But as she cleaned Jake's house that Monday morning it wasn't buying such a house she began fantasising about, but living here. Which of course was no longer a wild fantasy but a fact, *if* she changed her mind and moved in, the way Jake wanted her to.

She was tempted. She wouldn't have been human if she wasn't tempted. But as much as Abby had resolved to live in the moment, common sense demanded she not ignore what would happen if she gave in to Jake's suggestion. Before she knew it she would stop being a Housewife For Hire, but a housewife for real. She'd start thinking of this house as her home and Jake her de facto husband. She'd start cooking for him and caring for him and, yes, loving him with all her heart and soul. Inevitably, the day would come when she'd blurt out how much she loved him.

And that would be the beginning of the end.

Far better, she decided as she worked her way steadily through the upstairs rooms, that she stay strong and not do what Jake wanted. Except in the bedroom, that was. She was not foolish enough to think she wouldn't do whatever he wanted there. Already, she missed his lovemaking, waking this morning with a wave of desire so powerful that it had taken all of her willpower not to ring him on the spot and beg him to come home early from work.

Fortunately, she'd got a grip in time and plunged herself into the shower instead. But her heart had leapt when her phone rang as she exited the bathroom.

It was Jake.

'Hi,' he'd said in that lovely voice of his. 'Sleep well?'

'Like the dead. And you?'

'So-so. I would have slept better if you'd been with me. Which brings me to the point of this early morning call. I understand that you don't want to live with me twenty-four-seven, but most girlfriends sleep over occasionally.'

Abby resisted telling him that she *had* noticed that.

'I probably will,' she'd said carefully. 'But only after we've been out on a date.'

'I see. In that case I'll just have to ask you out every night.'

'I wouldn't want to go out every night, Jake. I do have other things I have to do, and a sister I like to visit.'

'Fair enough. What about tonight?'

She'd wanted to say yes. Desperately so. Abby knew, however, that she had to maintain some control over this relationship or she'd be lost for ever.

'I don't think so, Jake. I noticed this morning that my place needs some attention. If I don't water the garden soon, all my plants will die. We haven't had rain for ages.'

'The weather forecast predicts a storm this afternoon,' he'd pointed out, his voice on the stormy side itself.

'I never listen to weather forecasts.'

'Don't you watch morning television?'

'I don't watch much television these days.' She used to watch it non-stop when she was a stay-at-home wife with no children and nothing much to do. She still watched the occasional movie but on the whole Abby now preferred to read.

'Have you ever watched my show?'

'Once or twice.'

'And?'

'You're very good at what you do.'

'Sophie thinks it's lightweight. And it is. Which is also why it's so popular, and why I'm going to get oodles of money for it.'

'You're definitely going to sell?'

'I've already put the sale in motion. It will take a couple of weeks to finalise things, though. Meanwhile, I have to do the show and keep the ratings up.'

'Right. Maybe I'll watch it today. Tell you what I think of your performance.'

Jake laughed. 'While I've got you on the phone, Sophie is going to ring you today. I told her all about me wanting her to help you with your new wardrobe and she wants to line up a date.'

Abby sighed. 'Do I really have to buy a whole new wardrobe?'

'Why can't you be like other women, Abby? Most of them would be over the moon at getting a whole new wardrobe, especially one chosen by one of Sydney's top stylists.'

'I guess I would like it better if I could pay for it myself. I have the money. Twenty-five thousand dollars, remember?'

'That's not for clothes. That's for travel. Not that I expect you to pay for anything when you're with me. Think of that money as your emergency fund. For later in your life. Or for when you tire of me and want to go your own way.'

Abby knew she would never get tired of Jake. She loved the man. But she could hardly say so. 'If you insist.'

'I insist. I'll be home early so don't rush off till I get there. I have a surprise for you.'

'What kind of surprise?'

'If I told you that then it wouldn't be a surprise.'

'You're a terrible tease, Jake Sanderson.'

'Takes one to know one. See you around about three.'

It wasn't even close to three, Abby thought as she started cleaning Jake's kitchen later that morning. It was only eleven-thirty. But already her body was humming with anticipation. Not just because of his promised surprise but because she wanted to see him, wanted to kiss him, wanted to make love to him, and vice versa.

In the end, she turned on the television at noon and watched his show, just so that she could feast her eyes on his handsome face and those sexy blue eyes. After it was over, she could hardly remember the content, her mind filling with images of what they'd done together over the weekend and what they might do in the future. No, not the future. Today. This afternoon. As soon as he got home. She could not wait till they went on some stupid date; her need was too strong for that.

Abby was feverishly cleaning the kitchen counter tops when her phone rang again. But it wasn't Jake. It was his sister, Sophie, who was in a rush and quickly told Abby when and where to meet her the following day before apologising and then dashing off before Abby could object to anything.

Like sister like brother, she thought.

By five to three that afternoon, Abby was in quite a state, her body at war with her mind. To throw herself at Jake as soon as he walked in the door would undo all the groundwork she'd laid down to keep some control over her life. But oh, how she wanted him.

The sound of his key in the front door brought a cry to her lips followed by an abrupt stiffening of her spine. *Be strong, Abby! And, above all, be cool.*

He strode into the kitchen, still dressed in the superb suit he'd worn on his show.

'Hi there,' she said, her smile feeling a tad forced. 'Want me to put on some coffee for you?'

'Not particularly,' he replied as he swept across the kitchen and pulled her into his arms.

'Coffee is the last thing on my mind at the moment,' he ground out as his head descended.

'Could I tempt you into sleeping over tonight?' Jake asked when his mouth finally lifted from hers, his hands remaining clamped over her shoulders. 'After I take you out to dinner, of course.'

Abby took a couple of seconds to get her head together, which wasn't easy considering it was totally scrambled.

'I can't stay the whole night,' she said with dismay in her voice. 'Your sister rang and she's arranged to take me shopping all day tomorrow. Which means I have to go home some time tonight and do all sorts of girl things so that I look my best.'

'Fair enough,' Jake said, then kissed her some more.

'What about my surprise?' she asked when he finally gave her a breather.

Jake smiled. 'I almost forgot about that. Look, it's nothing sparkly or expensive. I suspect you don't want to be that kind of girlfriend. It's just a fun present.' And out of his suit pocket he brought a packet of condoms, each one with a different fruit flavour. 'I thought, since we have to use condoms, then we should at least make things interesting.'

Abby had to smile. 'Where on earth did you buy them? Over the internet?'

'Nope. I did a segment on condoms one day on my show and these were given to me as samples. I've had them in a drawer in my dressing room for months.'

Abby liked that he hadn't used them on any of his other girlfriends. 'Such interesting flavours,' she said as she read the list on the packet. 'I like the sound of pineapple and coconut. And, of course, passion fruit. Blood orange sounds dangerous.'

'In that case, we'll try that one first,' he said as he shoved the condom packet in his pocket then bent to scoop her up into his arms.

'Come on,' he said. 'Let's go have some fun.'

CHAPTER TWENTY-NINE

'NO, NOT THAT one,' Sophie said when Abby came out of the dressing room in a black and white spotted dress that she herself had chosen. 'It makes you look too busty. When a girl is as well endowed as you, Abby, she should never wear dresses which come right up to the neck. You should mainly stick to lower necklines, not to mention block colours. You can get away with some patterned materials but only if the design is delicate and not overpowering. That dress you wore last Friday night looked good on you because the pattern wasn't too big, or bright. And the dress had a V neckline, if you recall.'

Abby sighed. 'There's a lot more to choosing the right wardrobe than I ever imagined. It's also very tiring.' They'd been at it all day, only stopping for a light lunch. Admittedly, they'd bought heaps, Sophie waving aside any protest from Abby, claiming she'd been given instructions from Jake that there was to be no expense spared. Abby was to have a full wardrobe suitable for travelling, and which catered for every occasion and season.

Abby had stopped looking at the price tags after a while, but she knew the clothes had to be costing a small fortune, Sophie taking her into several expensive-looking boutiques as well as those floors in the big city department stores which carried the designer ranges. Jake's sister got special treatment everywhere she went, the sales people obviously knowing her well. They didn't even have to carry their purchases around, the various shops agreeing to deliver everything they bought—free of charge.

Whilst Abby felt somewhat overwhelmed by the experience, she suspected she could quickly get used to being treated with such consideration and deference. She could also get used to wearing the kind of clothes which fitted perfectly and looked fantastic. Ignoring any qualms that she was fast becoming a kept woman, Abby resolved to enjoy the experience. After all, Jake could afford it; Sophie told her over coffee just how much he'd inherited from his uncle. Not that she'd sounded jealous. Apparently, Sophie had received a substantial cash legacy, as had all her brothers and sisters; her mother as well.

'Come on,' she said to Abby. 'Get that dress off and we'll call it quits for today. Tomorrow I'll take you shopping for shoes and handbags and underwear.'

'Underwear?' Abby exclaimed.

'Got to have the right underwear, Abby. It can make all the difference to the way a garment looks. Same with the shoes. And then, of course, there's the jewellery.'

'No,' Abby protested at last. 'No jewellery.'

'But…'

'No buts. And no jewellery. I've gone along with this wardrobe business because I don't want to embarrass Jake by not being dressed correctly. But I am his girlfriend, Sophie, not his mistress. So I'd like to keep the underwear and the accessories to a minimum, if you don't mind. I'm not broke. Once I know what I should be buying I can get some of these things myself. I appreciate your help, I really do. But enough is enough!'

'Wow. You can be really forceful when you want to be.'

Abby realised with some surprise that that was true. But forcefulness was a fairly recent trait.

'I've had to learn to be forceful with Jake,' she said. 'He's way too used to getting his own way with women.'

Sophie grinned. 'You could be right there.'

'Did he tell you he asked me to move in with him?'

'No!' Sophie exclaimed, stunned. 'Now that's a first.'

'Oh, dear. Maybe I shouldn't have mentioned it.'

'Why not? Am I right in presuming you said no?'

'Yes, I did. For now, at least.'

'Good for you. Make the devil wait.'

'He might not ask me again,' Abby said with a frown.

Sophie smiled. 'I think he will. Now, why don't you put on those sexy blue jeans you had on earlier? I'll find you a white shirt to go with them, and some little black pumps. Then we'll go down to Café Sydney for some drinks before dinner. I'll text Jake to meet us there instead of going home.'

'No, please don't do that,' Abby said straight away. 'I got a text from Jake earlier today saying that he has a meeting with the man who's buying his show and he's sure to have to take him to dinner. Look, I honestly think I should just go home. I'm wrecked. I wouldn't mind a coffee first, though.'

She didn't want to tell Sophie that she could feel a headache coming on. She really needed to sit down for a while and take a couple of painkillers before it developed into a migraine.

Unfortunately, by the time they got out of the department store and into a café, Abby was seeing circles in front of her eyes. Fortunately, the table they were shown to had a bottle of water already on the table with two clean glasses. Abby poured herself a glass immediately then dived into the inner zipped section of her handbag where she kept her painkillers. It was also where she always put her Pills if she was going to be away from home in the evening, like last Friday night.

The sight of her strip of Pills made Abby catch her breath. There was one more than there should have been. *What on earth...?*

Instantly alarmed, she checked the strip again.

'What's the matter?' Sophie asked. 'What have you lost?'

Abby groaned. She hadn't lost anything, except perhaps her mind. For she knew immediately what must have happened. She'd forgotten to take the Pill on the night of the dinner party, just the way she'd feared. And then in the panic of the moment she had miscounted.

Her head spun at the thought of all the unsafe sex she'd had that same night. Just the *possibility* that she might have fallen pregnant sent her stomach swirling and her breathing haywire.

'Abby, what's wrong?' Sophie asked, alarmed.

'I think I'm going to be sick,' she choked out, leaping up and rushing for the Ladies, where she dry retched into the toilet. Afraid that she was going to faint, she sank down on to the tiled toilet floor, pale-faced and panting.

Sophie didn't know what to do. Abby looked dreadful. It reminded her of how her father had looked when he'd had his heart attack. Though surely Abby was too young to have a heart attack.

'Do you have any pains in your chest?' she asked frantically.

When Abby nodded, Sophie didn't hesitate. She called for an ambulance. Ten minutes later, paramedics were checking Abby over, taking her blood pressure and asking her questions. In the end, they declared that she wasn't having a heart attack but a panic attack, which sometimes had similar symptoms to a coronary. They administered a sedative, both for her nausea and her nerves, then suggested Sophie take her straight home. Before they left, one of the paramedics quietly told Sophie to encourage her friend to see a therapist to discover the cause of such a severe panic attack.

Within no time they were in a taxi heading for Balmain, Sophie overriding Abby's request to go to her own home, saying that she wasn't taking her anywhere she would be alone. Then she rang Jake and explained the situation. Not that she could really *explain* the situation.

'A *panic* attack?' Jake exclaimed, sounding both shocked and puzzled. 'What in hell happened to give her a panic attack?'

'Honestly, Jake, I don't know. She was looking for something in her handbag when she suddenly went a ghastly colour. Then she bolted for the Ladies. Look, I suggest you make your excuses and catch a ferry home. I dare say we'll be at your place before you are, even though this is the long way around. I'll put Abby to bed in the downstairs guest room. She's almost asleep now. The ambulance guys gave her something to calm her down.'

'I wish I knew what upset her in the first place.'

'Me too. We'll put our heads together when you get home.'

'I'm on my way.'

'Good.' She clicked off then dropped her phone in her own handbag.

'You shouldn't have called him,' Abby mumbled from where she was half sitting, half lying in the corner of the back seat.

'Are you kidding me? Jake would have had my guts for garters if I hadn't. He loves you, Abby,' Sophie said, not because Jake had confessed as much to her but because she knew her brother better than anyone. No way would he have asked Abby to live with him if he didn't love her.

Abby shook her head from side to side. 'No, he doesn't.'

'Oh, yes, he does,' Sophie insisted, wondering if this was part of Abby's problem—the fact that Jake was asking a lot of her without telling her that he loved her. She would have to speak to him about that.

'But let's not worry about that right now,' Sophie went on, and gently pulled Abby over towards her, putting an arm around her shoulders and cradling her head against her chest. 'All you need to do at the moment is rest.'

When a deeply emotional shudder rippled through Abby's body, Sophie wanted to weep. She wasn't the most empathetic of people, but there was something about Abby which touched her. Sophie could see that she'd touched Jake too, more than anyone else ever had. She had no doubt that he loved her. Of course, it was highly possible her anti-commitment bachelor brother didn't know that he'd fallen in love at long last. Maybe she should tell him. As soon as he got home—*before* he went in to talk to Abby.

His blue eyes stormed at her across the kitchen. 'You're not telling me anything I don't already know, Sophie. I realised over the weekend that I was in love with her.'

'Then why haven't you told her?'

'Perhaps because she doesn't want *any* man to love her at the moment, Miss Smarty-Pants. You heard what she said last Friday night. She doesn't want to get married again. If you don't mind, I would like to go in and talk to Abby and see if I can find out what upset her.'

'She might be asleep,' Sophie called after him as he strode from the room.

She wasn't. She was just lying there in the bed, on her back, her hands crossed over her chest, her eyes fixed on the ceiling. Jake watched her from the doorway for a long moment, his heart going out to her, his ego troubled by the thought that he might not be able to fix whatever it was that had distressed her so much. When he finally walked into the room, she turned her head to look at him, her face bleak but worryingly blank.

'Sophie shouldn't have interrupted your meeting,' she said in a dull voice. 'Or brought me here. I would have preferred to go home but she insisted and I was too weak to argue with her.'

Jake sat down on the side of the bed and picked up one of Abby's hands. It was alarmingly cold.

'She did the right thing,' he said as he gently rubbed her hand with both of his. 'You had a nasty turn, from what I've been told. A severe panic attack, according to the paramedics.'

'Yes,' was all Abby said before she turned her eyes away to stare up at the ceiling again.

Jake hated seeing her like this. So sad. *Too* sad.

'Do you know what caused it?' he asked softly.

'Oh, yes,' she said with a strange sigh.

Jake's hands stilled on her. 'What?'

'The Pill in my handbag,' she answered, still without looking at him. 'I miscounted, which means I didn't take my Pill last Friday night after all. Which also means that I could be pregnant.'

Jake tried to make sense of her rather confused confession but failed, so he just cut to the chase, which was that it *was* possible she'd fallen pregnant last Friday night since they'd had heaps of unsafe sex. He could understand that this would upset her, but not to the extent of having a panic attack. He was definitely missing a piece of the puzzle here.

'You'd have to be unlucky to fall pregnant on one slip-up, Abby,' he pointed out.

She laughed. A short dry laugh which worried the life out of him.

'That's me,' she said. 'Unlucky. Especially when it comes to babies.'

He recalled her saying that she'd tried for a baby during her marriage but it hadn't happened. Which should have reassured her, in a way. Obviously, she didn't fall pregnant easily.

'It's not the end of the world if you did have a baby, is it?'

Again that odd laugh.

'You don't *have* to have a baby these days, Abby,' Jake continued gently. 'Terminations are legal and not dangerous.' Yet even as the words came out of his mouth Jake knew he wouldn't want her to terminate *their* baby. It shocked Jake to discover that he wasn't unhappy with the idea of Abby having his child.

Not Abby, though. She obviously found the idea devastating.

Her eyes flashed his way, eyes full of sudden fury and hurt. 'I should have known that was what you'd suggest. But you don't have to worry about arranging a termination for me, Jake. I'm the original baby terminator. Put a baby in me and it's lucky to last three months. Do you know what it's like to lose three babies, Jake? No, how could you? You don't want children, anyway. But I did. Once upon a time. More than anything I wanted to make my own family where the mummy and daddy truly loved each other as well as their children. Wayne did, too. He'd been a foster child, did I mention that? My parents were pretty rotten but his were even worse. Oh, God,' she sobbed, her hands lifting to cover her face. 'I failed him on all counts, didn't I?'

When Jake saw the tears seeping out from under her fingers he felt like weeping himself. But at least he now knew why she'd had that panic attack. Abby was suffering from a type of Post Traumatic Stress Disorder, something he'd become acquainted with after several years of filming in war-torn countries. When he'd started not sleeping, then having flashbacks of the various horrors he'd witnessed, he'd gone to a doctor who'd diagnosed his problem and suggested he go home and do something less stressful. Of course he'd dismissed the doctor's diagnosis as rubbish and kept on filming the world's atrocities till one day a bullet had forced him to come home.

During his recovery he'd read up on PTSD and finally agreed he had been suffering from the condition. Apparently there were only so many rotten things you could see and experience before it affected your well-being. He imagined that for a woman who desperately wanted children even one miscarriage would be distressing. Three definitely qualified as traumatic! Where once Abby had longed to fall pregnant, now just the possibility of falling pregnant set off old hurts which were so full of pain and loss and grief that her whole nervous system had gone berserk.

Unfortunately, Jake didn't think she was in a fit state right now to listen to that kind of logic. What she needed at this moment was kindness and compassion.

'Abby…darling,' he said, holding both her hands tightly as he searched for the right words to say. 'I'm sure Wayne never thought of you as a failure. He obviously loved you very much. And if I know you, I'm sure you were very loving to him in return. As far as your miscarriages are concerned, things like that happen sometimes. One of my sisters-in-law had a couple of miscarriages before she carried a baby full term. There's no reason why this baby—if there is a baby—won't survive, and be born happy and healthy.'

'No, no,' Abby sobbed. 'It won't survive. And I won't be happy. Oh, God, you don't understand.'

'I understand more than you realise. You're crossing your bridges before you come to them, Abby. Why don't we wait and see if you are pregnant? I'll take you to the doctor tomorrow to have a test done. They've made great strides with pregnancy tests these days. They can tell if you are or not even after a few days.'

She snatched her hands away and looked at him then, her expression strangely wary. 'How come you know that?'

'Not for the reason you think. I did a segment on the subject on my show.'

'Oh…'

'And if you are pregnant, then I want you to know that I will stand by you, no matter what you decide to do. I promise I'll be there for you, Abby. Always.'

She stared at him, her eyes still sceptical. Which he supposed was better than sad.

'You won't want to take a pregnant lady overseas with you,' she said.

Jake smiled. 'How do you know?'

'I know.'

'Why don't we just wait and see what the doctor says?'

Abby groaned. 'I really don't want to be pregnant, Jake.'

Not with my baby, Jake thought with some dismay. The temptation to tell her he loved her was acute, but it still didn't feel like the right time.

'Why don't you close your eyes and go to sleep? Then

later, when you're feeling better, I'll cook you something
for dinner.'

Her chin began to quiver.

'No more tears now,' he said, his voice thick with emotion. 'Everything will be all right, just you wait and see.'

When he returned to the kitchen Sophie was there, looking anxious.

'Did you find out what upset her?'

Jake nodded. 'I'll just get us a drink and then I'll tell you
the whole wretched story.'

'Oh, the poor love,' Sophie said once she knew everything. 'No wonder she had a panic attack. So what are you
going to do, Jake? I mean, if she *is* pregnant.'

'That rather depends on Abby, don't you think?'

'Would you marry her?'

'In a heartbeat.'

'Did you tell her that?'

'No.'

'Why not?'

'Because I honestly don't think it's what she wants. Not
right now.'

'You could be right. There again, you could be wrong.'

Jake rolled his eyes. 'Thanks for the vote of confidence.'

'Sorry. But there are no certainties in life, Jake. Or guar-
antees. Sometimes you just have to take a risk.'

'That's very good advice,' Jake said thoughtfully, deciding then and there that as soon as the time was right, he
would tell Abby that he loved her.

CHAPTER THIRTY

ABBY WAS UNABLE to get an appointment with her doctor until four o'clock the following Friday. Jake had wanted to take her to *his* doctor but Abby had insisted on her own, a very nice female doctor who was both understanding and kind.

In the meantime, Jake had tried to get her to stay at his place but she'd refused, saying she'd prefer to go home after work each day. He'd rung her several times, insisting that he go to the doctor with her. But Abby had refused this as well. She wanted to be alone when she heard the news. She didn't want him to confuse her any more. Bad enough that she was already half wishing that she *was* pregnant. Which was crazy. But it was hard to think straight when you were as deeply in love as she was with Jake.

'Abby Jenkins?' her doctor called out from across the waiting room.

Abby tried to smile as she rose from the chair. But there were no smiles left in her. 'Coming,' she said.

Jake drove into the surgery car park and parked next to Abby's car, having determined to be there for Abby as he'd said he would. He didn't go against her wishes and go inside, but no way was he going to let her leave this appointment without his love and support.

The wait felt interminable. He put some music on to distract his escalating tension, but it didn't work, his stomach doing a somersault when he finally spotted Abby emerging from the building shortly before five.

He was out of his car like a shot, his eyes searching her

face for signs of distress as she walked towards him, not finding any comfort in her frown.

'What are you doing here?' she demanded to know straight away. 'I told you not to come.'

'Sorry,' he said straight away. 'I simply had to. So what did the doctor say? Did he do one of the new tests?'

'She's a she and yes, she did a very new test, and no, I'm not pregnant.'

Jake didn't know if he was disappointed or not, though, of course, his main concern was how Abby felt.

'Well, that's good news, isn't it?' he said.

'Yes,' Abby bit out. 'Good news.'

Why, then, he wondered, didn't she *sound* happier?

'I see,' he said, wishing he knew what was going on in her head. 'So what are you going to do now?'

Her sigh was heavy. 'Go home, I suppose.'

'Don't do that. I'd like to take you somewhere for dinner.'

'To celebrate, you mean,' she said with a decided edge in her voice.

'In a way…' Jake thought of the diamond engagement ring he had in his pocket and which he hoped would convince Abby of his feelings for her.

Just then, some more people emerged from the surgery. When a woman started staring at him and pointing, Jake decided it was time for a quick getaway.

'Hop in, Abby,' he said quickly as he reefed open his passenger door. 'Before that woman gets on Twitter and the paparazzi arrive.'

'But what about my car?' she asked even as she did as she was told.

'We'll come back and get it later.' He quickly exited the car park and zoomed up the road.

Abby suddenly bursting into tears brought a groan to his lips, and a swift end to his idea of a romantic dinner. 'Oh, Abby. Darling. Please don't cry. Look, I'll take you home.'

'Yes, please,' she choked out, obviously doing her best to stop crying. But it was no use. The waterworks were open and she kept on weeping.

Jake took her not to her home, but to his. By the time they arrived she'd stopped crying but was looking totally worn out. He parked out front and led her inside, where he offered her either coffee or a glass of wine. She opted for the latter, sliding up on to one of the kitchen stools whilst he did the honours with a bottle of chilled Sauvignon Blanc.

'Can I ask you something, Jake?' she said when he'd poured two generous glasses.

'Of course.'

'What would you have done if the test had come back positive?'

He hesitated, though not for long. 'I was going to ask you to marry me.'

Her silence did not augur well. When Jake glanced over at her, she was staring at him with shock in her eyes.

'You don't mean that,' she said at last, sounding shaken. 'You don't do marriage and you definitely don't do children. You made that quite clear. You said it was a deal-breaker for you.'

'That was before,' he said.

'Before what?' she demanded, sounding angry now.

'Before I fell in love with you. Actually, I was going to ask you to marry me today, whether you were pregnant or not.'

She shook her head from side to side, her eyes disbelieving.

'But that's crazy, Jake. You're not thinking straight.'

'I had a feeling that might be your reaction,' he said. 'So I thought I had better have backup.'

'A backup?'

'Yep. A backup.'

Jake put down the bottle of wine, his whole body tensing up as he faced a startled Abby, though he tried not to show it.

'Sophie said you were averse to me buying you jewellery but I gather that was because you didn't want me treating you like a mistress. So I bought the one piece of jewellery which would never be given to a mistress.'

When he brought a small black box out of his pocket and flipped it open, revealing a diamond engagement ring set in yellow gold, Abby stared down at it, then up at him.

'Oh, my God,' she choked out. 'It…it's lovely, Jake. And so are you. I'm touched. Really I am. But I… I can't.'

Dismay made his heart turn over. 'Are you saying that you don't love me?'

The loving look in her eyes was some comfort. 'Of course I love you. Surely you must know that. But I can't marry you. Because marriage means children to me. And I just can't go there again. Not yet. Maybe not ever.'

Jake did his best to hide his hurt and disappointment.

'Can't we just stay as we are, Jake?' she pleaded. 'You know you don't really want marriage, anyway.'

Actually, I don't know any such thing, Jake thought, a great lump filling his throat. After Craig died, he'd realised that his way of life wasn't as great as he'd thought it was. Who wanted to die alone, with no one at their bedside, holding their hand and telling them that they were loved?

Abby's hands clasped the sides of her face, a face full of escalating panic.

'Oh, God, if only you could understand…'

When she looked as if she was about to burst into tears again, Jake knew she was thinking about the babies she had lost. It must have been truly terrible for her. He could see that. He could also see that he had rushed her with his proposal. She wasn't ready to face that kind of commitment.

But one day she would be. And when she was he would be right there by her side.

Slipping the ring box back into his pocket, he smiled over at her. 'It's all right, Abby,' he said gently. 'We'll do what you want and just go on as we are. But could you at least move in with me?'

She lifted adoring eyes to his. 'Oh. Yes. I'd love to.'

CHAPTER THIRTY-ONE

Twelve months later...

'IT WILL BE so good to see Megan and Timmy again,' Abby
said excitedly as the plane started its descent into Mascot.
'And your family too.'

'We'll see them all on Christmas Day,' Jake told her. 'I
booked the same boat we had last year.'

'Did you? You didn't tell me that.' Which surprised Abby.
Because she and Jake told each other everything. During
the last year, their love for each other had deepened to a true
love. It wasn't just lust, as Abby had once feared. Travelling
together, living together, twenty-four-seven had been marvellous. She'd loved every minute of it. Paris in the summer
had been magnificent, even if she had picked up a tummy
bug. But honestly, she was glad to be home.

'I wanted to surprise you,' Jake went on. 'I have another
surprise for you as well.'

'What?'

'Tomorrow morning you have an appointment with one
of Sydney's top fertility experts.'

Abby sucked in sharply, her stomach tightening as well.
'You...you shouldn't have done that without talking to me
first.'

'Abby,' Jake said gently but firmly, 'it's time.'

And it was. He was right. During the last year, Jake had
convinced Abby that he really would like to marry her. And
one or two children would be all right by him. And whilst
she'd remained on the Pill they had stopped using condoms.
But there wasn't a single day that she forgot to take that Pill;
she'd programmed her phone with a reminder.

The trouble was, Abby was still afraid. Afraid of hoping and wanting and having her dreams dashed one more time.

'If all else fails,' Jake said, 'we can adopt.'

Her eyes widened. 'Are you sure?'

'Absolutely. There are a lot of wretched orphans in this world who would love a wonderful woman like you as their mother.'

Abby's heart melted with love for this man. 'That's the nicest thing you've ever said to me.'

Jake smiled. 'So when we get home can I drag out that engagement ring which is still sitting in a drawer somewhere?'

'Oh, God, I still feel awful about that ring. Have you forgiven me for turning down your proposal that day?'

'There's nothing to forgive. You were right to turn me down. It was too soon. But it's not too soon now, Abby. It's time for us to face the future together.'

Jake watched Abby fiddling with her ring as they waited for their turn with the doctor. She was terribly nervous. But then so was Jake. He knew how much having children meant to Abby. He'd seen the look in her eyes every time they'd come across a happy family during their overseas travels. Becoming a father still wasn't an all-consuming dream of his but anything that made Abby happy would make him happy.

The door to the doctor's office opened and Dr Gard walked out. She was about fifty, tall and slim with a plain but kind face.

'Mr and Mrs Sanderson?' she asked, whereupon Abby threw Jake a wry smile.

They traipsed after the doctor into her rooms, where she waved them to two chairs in front of her desk. Clearly, she often saw couples together.

Jake listened to Abby bravely tell her whole medical history, even though her voice was shaking. The doctor listened intently, throwing in a question every now and then.

'I think, Abby,' she said at last, 'that I should examine you. Would you mind?'

Of course she didn't mind and was taken behind a curtain for what felt like an eternity to Jake. Finally, the two women emerged with the doctor's expression a rather puzzled one.

'Well,' she said once they were both seated again, 'I have to confess that this doesn't happen to me very often.'

'What?' Jake asked immediately, sensing that it wasn't all bad news.

Her eyes were directed at Abby. 'You said you were on the Pill?'

'Yes,' Abby replied.

'And you've been having regular periods?'

Abby flushed. 'Well, not exactly. We've been travelling and I've been skipping the white pills so that I didn't have to worry about periods.'

'I see,' the doctor said with a smile. 'Well, Abby, I am happy to inform you that you're actually pregnant.'

'Pregnant!' Abby gasped whilst Jake held his breath. His head was whirling.

'Yes. About four months, by the feel of your uterus. We'll know for sure when you have an ultrasound. I'll organise one for you straight away.'

Both Abby and Jake were in shock as they were taken into another room for the ultrasound. But underneath the shock lay the hope of happiness. If the doctor was right, then Abby was already past the three-month danger time, which was further than she'd ever got before.

Jake held her hand whilst the doctor moved the instrument over Abby's gelled-up stomach, which did indeed have a small baby bump. She'd complained only the other day that she'd put on weight, blaming all the restaurant food they'd been eating. But it hadn't been that. It had been a baby. *His* baby.

Jake's heart turned over as he stared at the screen and saw the outline of a living, breathing human being.

'A little more than four months, I would say,' the doctor told them. 'Do you want to know the sex?'

'Yes, please,' they both chorused.

'It's a girl. Small but beautifully formed.'

'Oh,' Abby said through her tears.

Jake lifted her hand to his lips. 'Just like her mother,' he said, his heart so full of love for this woman, and his child, he was almost in tears himself. He vowed then and there that he would be the best husband and father. Just like his own dad, who he saw now might not have had wealth, but had been rich with love.

'You…you think I'll be all right then?' Abby tentatively asked the doctor.

The woman smiled down at her. 'I'm sure you'll be fine. After all, you have a very good doctor. Don't you worry, dear. I'll look after you.'

EPILOGUE

THE DOCTOR WAS as good as her word. Jake and Abby's daughter went full term. She came into the world a very beautiful baby with a soft crown of fair hair, big blue eyes and the prettiest little face. The birth was a natural one but with enough drugs to make sure Abby wasn't in too much pain.

After the birth, Abby could not stop looking at her daughter, and cuddling her. Jake hardly got a look in. Not that he minded. He knew how much having this baby meant to Abby. Finally, after she'd had her fill, she handed the bundle over for him to hold.

Parental love squeezed Jake's heart as he rocked his daughter to and fro.

'Paris,' he murmured. It was the name they'd chosen once they worked out that that was where she'd been conceived, the doctor explaining that the gastric bug Abby had caught had probably rendered the Pill ineffective for a few days.

'Well, Mrs Sanderson,' he said with the fatuous smile of a besotted father, 'you've produced a real beauty here.'

'She is lovely, isn't she?'

'She's the spitting image of her mother.'

'Do you think so?'

He did, and so did everyone else who came in to visit them. Sometimes, there were so many people in Abby's room that the nurses would complain about the noise. The maternity ward breathed a sigh of relief when Jake took Abby and Paris home.

Sophie and Megan were asked to be godparents at the baby's christening three weeks later, both of them receiving very generous gifts from the happy parents. Abby gave an over-the-moon Megan her old house and Jake presented Sophie with the deed to Craig's apartment.

The following Christmas was an especially joyful one. Jake hired the same boat for another harbour cruise, amazed at how much he enjoyed the family gathering, perhaps because he could show off his very beautiful daughter. Abby revelled in everyone's compliments plus the knowledge that, at last, her dream of creating her own happy family had finally come true. Already she was planning a second baby, and Jake was happy to oblige. Truly, for a man who'd once claimed not to want marriage and children, he'd proved to be a wonderful husband and father.

'She was a big hit, wasn't she?' Jake said that night as they stood next to Paris's pretty pink cot and stared down at her sleeping form.

When he slipped a tender arm around Abby's waist, she leant her head against his and sighed. 'It was a wonderful Christmas Day. Even better than last year.'

Jake had to agree. Though last year's Christmas had been pretty special. It had been, after all, their wedding day as well. Which reminded him.

'I have a surprise present for you,' he said. And he produced another ring box, which contained an emerald and diamond eternity ring.

'Oh, Jake,' Abby choked out as he slipped it on her finger. 'It's beautiful.'

'Not as beautiful as you, my darling.'

'You say the loveliest things to me.'

'That's because I love you.'

'I'm still not sure why, but I'm glad that you do.'

Jake bent his head and kissed her. He could think of a thousand reasons why he loved Abby, not the least that she was the bravest, kindest, most genuine person he'd ever met. He thanked his uncle every day for the legacy which had set him on a path that showed him marriage and children need not be a grind; they could be a joy. He'd never been happier than during the last year. Of course, he was lucky that he didn't have to work if he didn't want to. But Jake knew he would not enjoy being idle for long. He was already thinking of creating a series of documentaries called the *Honeymoon Show*, highlighting places to go for a honeymoon, a feel-good show full of happy people who actually loved each other.

Now that would be different…

When Abby gave a small moan of desire, his head lifted.

'Time for bed, I think, my love.' And, taking Abby's hand in his, he walked off with her into the future.

* * * * *

MAID FOR
MONTERO

KIM LAWRENCE

CHAPTER ONE

SOME MEN IN Isandro's position would have whined about press intrusion. He didn't. He considered he had little to complain about in life, and he knew it was perfectly possible, even for someone whose financial empire drew the sort of global media attention that his did, to have a private life.

Of course, if his taste had run to falling out of nightclubs in the small hours or the routine attendance of film premieres with scantily clad models, it might have been more difficult, but neither pastime held any appeal for him.

He viewed security as a necessary evil, a side effect of success—like midges in the Highlands—but he was hardly a recluse who lived his life behind ten-feet-high walls.

If he had had a family to consider, possibly he might have seen potential danger lurking around every corner, but he didn't. He only had an ex-wife, with whom he exchanged Christmas cards these days rather than insults, and a father he had very little contact with. Given that he was confident in his ability to look after himself, Isandro was not alarmed when the electronic gates that guarded the entrance to his English estate—which did actually have ten-feet-high walls—did not swing open as he approached, for they were already open.

Slowing his car, he swept the area with narrow-eyed, irritated speculation. While he didn't automatically assume this suggested anything dark and sinister, it did suggest a carelessness that he did not expect from those who worked for him.

The groove between his dark, strongly defined brows and his level of irritation deepened as his glance lighted on a brightly coloured bunch of balloons attached to an overhanging branch that looked incongruous beside the discreetly tasteful sign that simply read 'Ravenwood House: Private'.

He had owned Ravenwood for three years, and in that time on the admittedly rare occasions he had visited he had never found cause for complaint, which was nothing less than expected. He employed the best, be they corporate executives or gardening staff, paid them extremely well and expected them to earn their salary.

It was not a complicated formula but one that he found worked, and if it didn't... He was not a man renowned for patience or sentimentality in his professional or personal life. If those in his employ didn't perform to the high standards he expected and deliver the goods they did not remain in his employ.

He opened the window, reached out and caught hold of the string dangling from the balloons. As he tugged two popped on the branches and the rest rose into the air, embracing their freedom. Following their merry progress with his eyes, he frowned before he pulled his head back in. He was not ready to read anything significant into the open gates or the balloons, but there had been a recent staff change, and the housekeeper did play a pivotal role at Ravenwood.

The previous postholder had not only been efficient, but had combined excellent man-management skills with the ability to blend into the background. She had never been obtrusive.

Under her watch he could not imagine open gates, invisible security or balloons. It was always possible none was connected with the new housekeeper, and he kept an open mind on the subject, innocent until proved guilty. No one could say that he wasn't scrupulously fair, and he made allowances for human error.

What he couldn't live with was incompetence.

He was prepared at this point to believe that the new housekeeper was as perfect as his personal assistant, who had interviewed the candidates, had indicated. He trusted Tom's judgement, as the younger man had always shown it to be excellent and it had been his efforts and diplomacy that had gone a long way to soothing local ill will when Isandro had bought the hall.

Three years ago the local community had greeted the change of ownership of the local estate with deep suspicion bordering on hostility. The family that had given the house and the village their name had contributed nothing tangible to the local economy in decades, and the previous owner spent more time falling out of nightclubs and entering rehab clinics than repairing the roof or earning money to do so—so the locals' blind loyalty to them seemed perverse to Isandro.

With Tom's help he had addressed the situation with his usual pragmatism. He did not wish to be best friends with his neighbours, but neither did he want the inconvenience of being at war with them. The initial stream of complaints had faded to a trickle and visits from officials with clipboards from conservation and heritage groups that had halted work on the house and grounds had lessened and eventually vanished. He made a point of employing only local artisans and firms on the restoration work and made a donation that had put a new roof on the leaking church.

He considered the situation resolved.

Of all the houses he owned, this was the one where Isandro felt as close to relaxed as he ever did. It was beautiful and he enjoyed beauty. He invited none but his closest friends, and even then rarely. He never drove through the gates without feeling he was shedding the pressures of work.

He anticipated the next few days of rare relaxation, his wide sensual mouth twitching into a half-smile as he drove slowly through the pillared entrance. A moment later he was reversing.

The balloons snagged in the branch could have been accidental; this was not. Bizarrely tucked in beside one classical pillar was an upturned packing case.

With a mixture of growing incredulity and irritation, Isandro read the handwritten sign propped on it that informed him the eggs were free range and cost one pound per half dozen. There was no sign of the eggs mentioned, just a jar that was stuffed with coins and several notes suggesting trade had been brisk—the area had an unusual level of honesty.

Long brown fingers beat out an aggravated tattoo on the steering wheel. He had driven halfway down the long horsechestnut-lined driveway and was trying to rediscover his mellow mood when the noise hit him—a mixture of music, laughter, dogs barking and loud voices.

'What now...?'

Angular jaw set, he swore and floored the accelerator. A moment later he hit the brake, bringing the vehicle to a screaming halt on the top of the rise that gave him the first view of the delightful Palladian mansion considered by those in the know to be an architectural gem set in a parkland setting complete with lake, folly and beautifully tended formal gardens.

The manicured west lawn, where on occasion he watched invited guests play a game of croquet—and where he had spent the journey from the airport picturing himself enjoying the silence and solitude, sipping some brandy and perhaps catching up on some reading after the month of intense negotiations—was barely visible beneath the massive marquee, several smaller satellite tents, makeshift stage, cluster of stalls and what appeared to be a small…yes, it was a funfair of sorts, he realised as he identified the giant teacups slowly spinning to the strains of an early Tom Jones number, the volume so loud even at this distance to vibrate in his chest.

Staring in unwilling fascination at the surreal spectacle, he started like someone waking from a nightmare as a voice over the loudhailer system announced the winner of the best behaved pet competition to be Herb—a result that, judging from the volume of the cheers and clapping, was popular.

Isandro swore loudly and at length in several languages.

The person responsible for this outrage would not be around to regret this invasion and misuse of his trust for long. For that matter he might sack the bunch of them because while this might have been the brain child of one person—presumably the new housekeeper—the rest of his staff must have sat back and let it happen, including his highly paid so-called professional security team.

Great! So much for leaving stress behind. His resentment levels rose as he mentally said goodbye to his much-needed, greatly anticipated break... So what if after a couple of days he'd get bored with the inactivity and grow restless? The point was he wouldn't have the option of being bored now.

The feeling he had wandered into some sort of alternative universe intensified as a balloon that had presumably followed him up the drive floated past his head. It snagged on a branch and popped—the sound breaking Isandro free of his teeth-clenched scrutiny of the disaster scene.

His dark eyes as warm as ice chips, he reversed with a screech of rubber back to the intersection in the drive and took the secondary road that led directly to the stable block at the rear of the house, which seemed blessedly free of the insanity taking place elsewhere on his property.

Entering the house via the orangery, he snapped grapes from the vine that grew in coils across the roof as he went. He made his way to his study, not encountering a soul to demand an explanation of or vent his simmering anger on. When he reached the inner sanctum, however, he did discover someone: a small child he had never seen before, who was almost hidden by his desk as she spun around in his swivel chair.

The child saw him and grabbed the desk to slow herself, leaving a neat imprint of sticky finger marks on the antique wood. His lips twisted in a grimace of distaste. He had few friends with children and his exposure to them had been limited to brief appearances at baptisms bearing appropriate gifts. None had reached this child's age yet... Five? Six? he speculated, studying the grubby freckled face.

'Hello. Are you looking for the toilets?'

The question was so unexpected that for a moment Isandro did not respond.

'No, I am not.' Was it normal for a child to be this self-possessed? She definitely didn't seem even slightly fazed to see him.

'Oh.' Hands on his antique desk, she began to twist in the seat from side to side. 'The lady was but the other man was looking for Zoe. Are you looking for Zoe, too? I can do fifty spins and not be sick. I could probably do more if I wanted to.'

Glancing at the Aubusson carpet underfoot, he cautiously caught the back of the chair before she could put her boast to the test. 'I'm sure you could.'

'You picked grapes.' The kid stared at the grapes he had carelessly plucked from the vine as he had walked through the orangery. 'You're not meant to do that,' she said, shaking her head. 'You'll be in big trouble, and maybe even go to jail.' The thought seemed to please her.

'Thanks for the warning. Want some?' She seemed so at home he almost began to wonder if the place had been invaded by squatters and nobody had seen fit to mention it to him!

'Can't. You're a stranger. And they're sour.'

'Georgie!'

Isandro's head lifted at the sound of the musical voice with just a hint of attractive huskiness.

'I'm in here!' The kid bellowed back into his right ear, making him wince.

A moment later a figure appeared in the doorway. The body that matched the voice was not a let-down—anything but! Tall, slim, dark-haired with the sort of figure that filled out the faded denim jeans she wore to perfection. His immediate impression was of sinuous supple grace and an earthy sexuality that hit him with the force of a hammer between the eyes. Though the main physical response to her appearance was somewhat lower than eye level.

Isandro's aggravation levels reduced by several notches as he studied this new arrival, who didn't just have a great body but a vivid, expressive face he found himself wanting to look at. Stare at.

She possessed the most extraordinary eyes—electric blue that tilted slightly at the corners—and a mouth that made any man looking at it think of how it would feel to taste those plush pink lips… Isandro exhaled and reined in his galloping imagination. He had a healthy libido but he prided himself on his ability to control it.

'Georgie, you shouldn't be in here. I've told you. Oh…!' Zoe stopped halfway through the open doorway of the study. Her blue eyes flew wide as she sucked in a tiny shocked breath, registering the presence of the tall figure who was towering over her niece.

The strange reluctance she felt to enter the room was strong, but not as strong as her protective instincts, so, with a cautious smile pasted in place, Zoe stepped forward.

There had been many occasions in her adult life when she had been accused of being too trusting, too inclined to assume the best of others, but since Zoe had acquired responsibility for her seven-year-old twin niece and nephew she had developed a new caution that bordered, she suspected, on paranoia, at least when it came to the safety of her youthful charges.

Under the pleasant smile, her newly awoken protective instincts were on full alert. She moved towards the man whom she had not seen outside. And she would

have noticed him, because despite the casual clothes—
expensive casual—he definitely wouldn't have blended
in with the carefree and relaxed people milling around
outside.

She doubted that face did relaxed or carefree.

Without taking her eyes off the incredibly handsome
stranger any more than you'd take your eyes off a stray
wolf—and the analogy was not inappropriate, as he had
the entire lean, hungry look going on—she held out her
hand to her niece.

'Come here, Georgina,' she said in a tone meant to
convey a sense of urgency without overly alarming her
niece. Not that the latter would be likely—Georgie was
friendly to a fault and she had no sense of danger whatsoever. Real parents probably knew how to make their
kids sensibly cautious without scaring them witless and
giving them umpteen issues later in life…but Zoe wasn't
a real parent and most of the time she felt like a pretty
sorry substitute for not one but two brilliant parents.

She took a deep breath and fought her way clear of
the oppressive weight of emotions that continued to hit
her when she wasn't expecting it. There wasn't time to
feel angry at fate or the drunk driver whose carelessness
had taken away the twins' parents. There was barely
time to comb her hair some days!

'I'm sorry. I hope Georgina wasn't bothering you.'
It was more polite than 'what the hell are you doing in
here?' but in her experience it was always better to try
a smile before you brought out the big stick.

Though it would take a very big stick indeed or even
a small army to make this intruder leave if he didn't
take the hint, she thought, sliding a peek at him under
her lashes and looking away quickly. The heat climbed
into her smooth cheeks as she realised her scrutiny was

being returned, though there was nothing remotely sur-
reptitious or apologetic about the way his dark eyes were
wandering over her.

She flicked her plait back in a businesslike manner
over her shoulder and, raising a brief cool hand to her
cheeks, she wished that her protective instincts were
the only reason she could feel the heavy, frantic beat
of her heart in every inch of her body.

She'd never come across a man who exuded such a
raw, sheer maleness before and it was deeply weird, not
in a pleasant way, to find her indiscriminate hormones
reacting independently to the aura he projected. She
pressed her hand protectively to her stomach, which
was quivering the way it did when she found herself
in any situation that involved high places and the possibility of falling.

Logic suggested he was no danger to Georgie, just
another visitor to the Fun Day who'd got lost or was just
plain nosy but…the fact that she was the person whose
job it was to protect the twins from everything bad in
the world meant that Zoe was taking no chances.

'Now, Georgie, please.'

With a show of reluctance and a big sigh the copper-
headed little girl responded finally to the note of com-
mand and slid out of the chair. But Isandro wasn't
watching. His eyes were trained on the sliver of pale,
toned midriff that was on show. The tantalising flash
of flesh vanished as the woman's hand closed over the
child's. Drawing her in, she bent to speak, saying something to the kid that made her nod before running out
of the door.

Isandro watched as the young woman straightened
up, throwing the fat plait of glossy dark hair over her

shoulder again, exposing the firm curve of her jaw and
the long elegant line of her pale throat.

The recognition that his response to her had been primal, out of his control, produced a frown that faded as
he put the situation in perspective. Just because he had
experienced an unexpectedly strong physical response
did not mean he couldn't control it... Since his failed
marriage he had never been in any form of relationship
that he couldn't walk away from, and he never would.

She straightened up. 'Sorry about that.'

Now the child was gone some of the tension seemed
to have left her slender shoulders, though a degree of
caution remained in the blue eyes that studied him now
with an undisguised curiosity mingled with a critical
quality he was not accustomed to seeing when a woman
looked at him.

Isandro's smile held a hint of self mockery... If she
had not been beautiful would he have chosen to be
amused...?

His appreciation of beauty was not restricted to ar-
chitecture. He put this woman somewhere in her early
twenties, young enough at least to wear no make-up and
look good. Her clear skin was flawless, pale tinged with
the lightest of roses in her smooth, rounded cheeks. She
was not just sexy, she was beautiful.

Not in the classical sense perhaps, and absolutely
nothing like the sort of woman he normally found attractive. For starters he dated women who worked hard
at and took pride in their appearance. This woman's
grooming left a lot to be desired, but her oval face with
wide-set, slanting blue eyes, delicate carved cheekbones
and wide, full lips had an arresting quality that combined sexiness with a sense of vulnerability.

Vulnerability was another thing he avoided in women.

Needy was just too time-consuming, and time was a precious commodity.

His response simply proved that sexual attraction was not an exact science. Her look was not even smart casual, more scruffy casual. Despite his unflattering assessment of her style he was conscious of a heaviness in his groin by the time his eyes had made the journey up the length of her lusciously long, denim-clad legs. Tall and slender but with feminine curves that the oversized white shirt she wore did not hide, she really did have a delicious body—and she would scrub up well, he decided, picturing her in something silky and insubstantial, and then in nothing at all.

He found his mood mellowing some more. The day might not be a total washout after all. He found himself more attracted to her than he had to a woman in months… It was possible that part of the appeal was she was not his type, not a samey clone. That and the clear-eyed stare, plus the extraordinarily sexy mouth, and the fact he felt confident that he could slide his fingers into her hair and not come away with a handful of hair extensions. Now that had been a real mood killer!

What had the kid called her…?

Not Mum, and she wasn't wearing a ring, but that didn't mean anything, so he remained cautious.

There were enough complications in life without inviting them, so Isandro kept his love life simple. He didn't do long-term relationships and was upfront about it, and even so he had never had to work hard to get a woman into his bed.

Married women, single parents, women who wanted commitment were not conducive to simplicity, so he ruled them out. He had learnt from his mistakes, and an expensive divorce that had lost him both a wife and a best friend provided a steep learning curve. Quite frankly there was no point in inviting problems when there were any number of attractive unattached women who did not come with baggage.

He could fight for a prize when it was required, but it was not his style to fantasise over the unattainable. He had no problem walking away from temptation, however attractively packaged, so he was surprised to recognise that in this instance it was a struggle to adopt his normal take-it-or-leave-it attitude.

Now that her niece was safely away from strangers she should have been able to relax slightly, but Zoe discovered she wasn't.

Obviously she had registered the fact he was not ugly the moment she entered the room, but she hadn't noticed the ludicrously long eyelashes, the jet-black, deep set heavy-lidded eyes they framed, or the incredible sculpted structure of his patrician features. Each strong angle and plane of his face was perfect.

He was her idea of a fallen angel—fatally beautiful and seductively dangerous—supposing angels were six-five and wore designer black from head to toe.

He smiled. It was usually possible to tell when a woman felt a reciprocal tug of attraction, and in this case it definitely was… She either wasn't attempting to hide her reaction or she didn't know how, not that she was trying to flirt with him, which was actually refreshing. Even a perfect vintage could become pedestrian if a man drank it for breakfast, lunch and dinner; he enjoyed flirtation to a point, but once you knew the moves of the modern mating ritual it could on occasion become painfully predictable.

A sense of expectation buzzing through his veins,

he bit into the grapes. They were sour, as predicted, but he smiled.

The flash of white teeth and the intensity of the stranger's hard dark eyes sent a shiver through Zoe's body unravelling like a silken ribbon of desire. It was a relief when she finally discovered a flaw, which should have made him less attractive but had quite the reverse effect. The imperfection was relatively minor—a scar, a thin white line that began to the right of one eye and traced the curve of one chiselled cheekbone.

Zoe swallowed and plucked at the neckline of her shirt as the palpable silence in the room stretched. Her tingling awareness of him was so strong that there was a delay for several seconds before her body responded to the desperate commands of her brain. She was close to applauding with sheer relief when she managed to gather up the shreds of her self-control and lower her gaze.

'I'm afraid you shouldn't be here, either.' She pitched her tone at friendly but firm, it came out as breathy. Nonetheless, she was happy—breathy was a big step up from open-mouthed drooling!

Isandro's gaze lifted from the logo plastered across the T-shirt she was wearing—not that he had read a word of the inscription, but mingled in with the mental image of him peeling the shirt over her head an astonishing idea had occurred to him, making the pleasurable picture fuzz and fade.

Surely not… She couldn't be…could she?

Had Tom lost his mind?

If she was, he definitely had!

Or had his normally super-reliable assistant been thinking with a different part of his anatomy when he appointed this woman to the post of housekeeper?

No, she couldn't be, he decided, clinging to his mental image of the perfect housekeeper—a woman of a certain age with an immovable iron-grey helmet of hair and a brisk manner. He didn't expect the new housekeeper to possess all the attributes of her predecessor but this woman—girl!—couldn't be…?

'This part of the house isn't open to the public, actually,' she admitted, softening the gentle remonstrance with a smile.

Madre di Dios, she was! Tom actually had lost his mind.

'None of it is but people keep wandering…' She heard the sharp note of anxiety that had crept into her own voice and closed her mouth, shaking her head as she smiled brightly and concluded in her best 'fasten your seat belt' tone, 'So if you'd like to follow me…?'

The irony of being asked to leave his own study was not lost on Isandro, but instead of putting this person in her place he found himself considering the question.

Would he like to follow her…? Yes, up the sweeping staircase and into his bedroom, which was not possible as he didn't date employees. It was a no-exception rule. But he was about to sack her, which would make her not his employee…?

Maybe Tom had been having similar thoughts when he had decided this woman fulfilled the brief of experienced and efficient. Maybe she possessed both these qualities in the bedroom? Maybe his assistant already knew…?

The possibility that his assistant had given his girlfriend a job she was patently unsuited to because of her skills in the bedroom sent a rush of rage through Isandro.

Was he mad because Tom had broken the rules, or

mad that Tom had broken them before Isandro had got the chance?

Responding to the voice in his head with a heavy frown that drew his dark brows into a single disapproving line over the bridge of his nose, Isandro gave a frustrated grunt of tension.

When the tall, unsmiling stranger with his film-star looks and smoky eyes didn't react to her invitation to leave, Zoe felt the panic she had been struggling to keep at bay all day surface before she ruthlessly subdued it.

She could panic when this day was over, even though right now it felt as if it never would be.

How could anything that had started so innocently become this monster? she asked herself despairingly.

The answer was quite simple: she'd lost the ability to say no... She'd agreed to so many things she'd forgotten or more likely blocked half of them; by this point if the Red Arrows did a fly past she wouldn't have been surprised.

CHAPTER TWO

IT WAS A total nightmare. In the past five days, she had lied more—by omission, which amounted to the same thing—than she had done in her entire life!

It was that first lie that had kicked it off and started the snowball effect, but the snowball was now the size of an apartment block.

It had seemed so innocent and she had been so desperate to help when poor Chloe, her dead sister's best friend—Chloe who always put on a brave face—had broken down in tears after inviting Zoe to a coffee morning.

'Who am I kidding? A coffee morning!' She shook her head in teary disgust. 'Do you know how much Hannah's operation costs?'

Zoe shook her head, guessing that such groundbreaking medical care in the States did not come cheap.

'And that's without the cost of travel to America. And time's running out, Zoe, while I'm organising coffee mornings and treasure. Baking isn't going to get Hannah to that hospital—it'll take a miracle!' she sobbed. 'In three months' time the disease might have progressed too far and the treatment might not work… They might not even agree to try and she'll be stuck in a wheelchair for life!'

Her heart bleeding for the other woman, Zoe hugged her, feeling utterly helpless.

'This isn't you, Chloe. You're a fighter. You're tired, that's all.' And small wonder. God knew when she had had a break; she commuted almost daily for Hannah's hospital appointments. 'Everyone's behind you, so involve us! We all want to help.'

She shook her head, wishing she had more than platitudes to offer the other woman. Then it came—the inspired idea—and she didn't pause to think it through, just blurted it out.

'Have your coffee morning at the hall. You know what people are like—they'll come just to have a nosy. We could put up some trestle tables in the garden and I'm sure Mrs Whittaker would bake some of her scones.' She knew that the entire community were gagging to see the changes made by the enigmatic new owner of the hall almost as much as they were gagging to see the man himself!

'Really?' Chloe had taken the tissue Zoe offered and dried her eyes. 'Won't Mr Montero mind? I wouldn't want to get you in trouble. I know when we asked if we could use the cricket pavilion for the charity match we got the thumbs down, though he did provide a nice shiny new cup for the winners,' she conceded with a sniff.

Wasn't hindsight grand? Of course it was easy now to recognise that this had been the moment to admit she'd have to run it past him, but she hadn't and neither had she run it past him afterwards because she knew what the reply would be. Chloe had been right: her new employer did not want to continue any old traditions or start any new ones of his own. He wanted, as Tom had explained, to keep the village the other side of the ten-foot wall.

'Not that he's not a great guy,' the loyal assistant had assured Zoe when he saw her expression. 'He's just private and he doesn't like getting personally involved. He's very generous, does heaps of stuff you don't hear about, but any charitable donations he makes are through the Montero Trust.'

The Montero Trust was apparently involved itself in such diverse projects as adult literacy programmes and providing clean water to remote Third World villages. It seemed worthy, but a solution loaded with red tape, and Chloe needed help *now*; she didn't have time to be at the bottom of a pile of worthy causes.

'Let me worry about that.'

And she'd been worrying ever since, but her reward had been Chloe's smile. She thought about that smile every time she got a fresh attack of guilt, which was often.

What had Tom said at her interview? 'He'll expect you to work without supervision, show initiative.' She suspected that today might be classed as too much initiative, but it wasn't as if the man would ever know. And his standing in the local community had been massively raised without any effort on his part. It was a win/win... or lose/lose for her if he found out!

No matter how hard she tried to rationalise what she'd done, Zoe knew that she had overstepped her authority big time and, as she was still working her trial period, if her actions were discovered the 'inspiration' could well lose her her job!

Her job...which meant her home and a roof over the twins' heads.

Small wonder she'd not had a decent night's sleep for the past week. And that was even before it had all got horribly out of hand. For some reason, once she had started saying yes she couldn't stop! Everyone had been so enthusiastic and generous, contributing their time and talents, that it had seemed churlish to be the one dissenting voice. The tipping point was probably the bouncy castle. After that Zoe had stopped even trying!

The only thing she could do today was stay on top of things and make damned sure that the grounds were returned to pristine condition once the day was over. She had an army of volunteers lined up for the task.

But right now what she had to do was get rid of this man—not as easy as it sounded because he made no effort to move as she stood back to let him pass—then check nobody else had wandered into the house.

'If you were looking for the toilets, go past the tombola and the refreshment tent and follow your nose.' In his case the nose, narrow and aquiline, was just as impressive as the rest of him. As she made a conscious effort not to stare their glances connected, only briefly but long enough to make all her deep stomach muscles contract viciously.

Seriously shaken by the extent of her physical response to this man, she huffed out a tiny breath from between her clenched teeth to steady her nerves and focused on a point over his left shoulder.

'You can't miss it.'

He still didn't take the hint. Instead he set his broad shoulders against the panelled wall and looked around the room.

'You have a beautiful home.'

Zoe folded her arms, hugging tight to hide her involuntary shiver. He had the sexiest voice she had ever heard and the faint accent only added another fascinating layer to it.

'No, yes...I mean it isn't mine.' It crossed her mind

that he was being sarcastic. 'As I'm sure you can tell,' she murmured, flashing him an ironic grimace before extending a trainer-clad foot and laughing.

His hooded stare made a slow sweeping survey from her extended foot to her face. 'I try not to judge by appearances,' he drawled.

Her eyes narrowed. 'That's not always easy.'

Like now it was hard not to judge this man by the faint sneer and the innate air of superiority he exuded. She supposed arrogance was natural for someone who looked in the mirror each morning and saw that face looking back…and his body, from what she could see, was not exactly going to give the owner any major insecurities! Her gaze moved down the lean, hard length of his long body. Not only did he look fit in every sense of the word, he was supremely elegant in an unstudied, casual sort of way.

Her smooth cheeks highlighted by a rose tinge, she brought her lashes down in a protective sweep. If there was a time to be caught mentally undressing a stranger, this was not it.

'Actually I just work here…' The sweep of her hand encompassed the elegant room with its warm panelled walls and antiques. 'It is beautiful, though, isn't it?' A cross between a museum and a very expensive interior designer's heaven, the place, in her view, lacked a lived-in-look. There were no discarded newspapers, open books or sweaters draped over the backs of chairs, no sign at all that anyone lived there—it was just too perfect.

But then essentially no one did live here. It amazed her that anyone could own such a beautiful place and barely spend any time here at all.

The staff had been more than happy to fill her in

on the many houses owned by their elusive boss, and the many cars and private jets... Isandro Montero obviously liked to buy things whether he needed them or not. Zoe had always suspected that people who needed status symbols were secretly insecure. Mind you, having a bank account that hovered constantly just above the red made a person feel insecure too. Zoe knew all about that sort of insecurity!

His mobile ebony brows lifted in response to the information. 'So the owner has allowed his home to be used for this...event?'

Zoe felt her cheeks heat.

'How generous and trusting.'

If he had been trying he couldn't have said anything that made her feel more terribly guilty. Her eyes fell. 'He's very community minded.'

If he could hear me now, she thought, swallowing a bubble of hysteria as she imagined the expression on the face of the billionaire who didn't want to rub shoulders with the locals.

Her blue eyes slid to the wall lined with valuable books. Did he spend his time here reading the first editions on the shelves or were they, like the cricket pavilion, just for show...part of the entire perfect English Country Home?

What was the point in restoring a cricket pavilion if you never intended to use it? What was the point in buying books you were never going to read?

'The house is out of bounds today.'

He did not comment on the information. He was staring with what seemed to her far too much interest at a painting on the wall.

She went pale as for the first time she realised how vulnerable the house was. If he could just walk in here, how easy it would have been for someone to wander in—still was, and…not just someone! Her blue eyes suspicious, she turned to look at the tall stranger who continued to stare at the painting. God, she had been so sidetracked by physical awareness of him that it hadn't even crossed her mind that his presence here might not be accidental!

'There is an excellent security system in place, and security guards.'

He heard the nervousness in her voice, saw the sudden alarmed dilation of her pupils and smiled slowly, without feeling any sympathy. Well might she be worried, he thought grimly. The odds were that some of his valuables were even now in the pockets of light-fingered visitors. His security team would be lucky to come out of this with jobs.

'So I couldn't just pick up…' He made a show of looking around the room, then reached out and picked up a gilt-framed miniature from its stand. It was one of a pair he had outbid a Russian oligarch for six months earlier. He did not begrudge the inflated price, as he liked the sense of continuity—the miniatures were coming back to where they had been painted. 'This?'

The casual action made her tummy muscles flip. When she had first arrived she had literally tiptoed around the place, seriously intimidated by the value of the treasures it housed and scared witless of damaging anything. Though she had relaxed a bit now, seeing this valuable item treated so casually was alarming.

She gave a nervous laugh and thought, Calm down—no genuine thief would be this obvious…would they?

'No, you couldn't…' She sucked in an alarmed breath and fought the impractical urge to rush forward and snatch it from him. She didn't have a hope in hell of taking anything away from six feet five inches of solid muscle. She looked at his chest and swallowed, her tummy giving a nervous quiver as she pressed a hand to her middle where butterflies continued to flutter wildly.

'Is it genuine?' he asked, holding the delicate gilt frame between his thumb and forefinger.

'A clever copy,' she lied, nervousness making her voice high pitched. 'All the valuable stuff is locked away in the bank.' I wish!

'So that's why you're not concerned about stray visitors putting a souvenir in their pocket and walking out.'

Zoe swallowed as she watched the miniature vanish into the pocket of his well-cut jeans, but was able to maintain an air of amused calm as she returned his wolfish grin with a shaky smile of bravado and shook her head. What did it say about her that even at a moment like this she had noticed how rather incredible his muscular thighs were?

'We're not actively encouraging it, but if anyone's tempted we have a very strong security presence.' She saw no need to explain that this presence was at the moment helping out with directing people in and out of the parking areas. She felt extra bad about that because she had pretty shamelessly taken advantage of the absence of the head of the security team to persuade his deputy to relax the rules. She had used every weapon, including moral blackmail and some mild but effective eyelash fluttering.

'So I would be stopped before I left the building...?'

Even though she positioned herself strategically in the doorway, Zoe was well aware that he would find her no obstacle to escape if he wanted. Though she was not sure he wanted to—he seemed just as happy taunting her as making good his escape.

Zoe placed her hands on her hips, lifted her chin to a don't-mess-with-me angle and resisted the temptation to return an 'over my dead body' response. He might decide to take it too literally. Instead she said calmly, 'Definitely not. I'll have to ask you to return the miniature. It's very valuable.'

'Yes, it was quite a find.' The blue eyes he held blinked and a small furrow appeared between her dark feathery brows. He experienced a stab of guilt. She was obviously scared stiff and he did not enjoy scaring women even if on this occasion she deserved it.

'Find?'

He tilted his head in acknowledgement of her bewildered echo. 'The lady here was considered a great beauty of the day, but she was trade—the daughter of a wealthy mill owner. The marriage caused quite a scandal when Percy there brought her home.' He glanced at the twin of the portrait he held still sitting in its stand. 'It turns out that old Percy started a trend in the family, though I'm afraid the other heiresses that subsequent male heirs married were not always so easy on the eye as Henrietta here.' He studied the painting, taking a moment's pleasure from the masterful brush strokes and eye for detail shown by the artist. 'He really caught her… Such a sensual mouth, don't you think? Personally I think this is better than the Reynolds on the staircase.'

His eyes were trained, not on the portrait in his hand as he spoke, but her own mouth. The effect of the dark-eyed stare was mesmerising. Zoe didn't respond, mainly because she could barely breathe past the hammering of her heart against her ribcage, let alone speculate on how he knew so much about the history of the house and family.

'Maybe they were in love?' Her voice sounded as though it were coming from a long way away.

He laughed. The throaty sound shivered across the surface of her skin, raising a rash of goosebumps. 'A romantic.'

The amused mockery in his voice made Zoe prickle with antagonism. What was she doing discussing love with a possible art thief? Was he? He certainly seemed to know more than she did about the artwork in the house.

'Actually, no, I'm not.' Her chin lifted. 'But if I was I wouldn't be ashamed of it. Now, Mr... I have things I need to attend to. If I could ask you to—'

'Shame is a very personal thing,' he mused, cutting across her. 'I wonder if Percy was ashamed of his heiress? You call it love, but I call it symbiosis.'

She compressed her lips. 'I wasn't calling it anything. I was simply not discounting the possibility.'

He tilted his dark head in acknowledgement of her interruption. 'Well, there is no doubt that she had money and he had social position, the ability to guarantee her acceptance into society, though maybe looking at that mouth there might have been other factors involved?'

He levelled his obsidian gaze on Zoe.

'Do you not think she has a sensual mouth?'

Now there was a case of pot calling kettle, she thought, dragging her gaze from the firm sculpted outline of his own mouth.

'I'm no expert on sensuality.'

'I'm sure you are being modest.' He arched a satiric brow and the speculation in his smoky stare sent a rush of embarrassed heat over her body. 'Well, I shall continue to think that our Henrietta was a woman of passions...and that perhaps Percy was a lucky man? We will, I suppose, never know. What we do know is that when there were no more rich social-climbing heiresses, the family sold off treasures and land until finally there was nothing left. There is a certain sense of continuity in seeing this pair back where they started.'

'That's very interesting but...' She stopped, the colour fading from her face. His manner, his accent, the fact he displayed no sign of discomfort being caught in the house... Of course he had acted as though he owned the place, because he did!

How could she have been so stupid? Because he wasn't what she had been expecting, of course—if she'd walked into a room and found a short, balding man using expensive tailoring to hide an affluent middle-aged spread she would immediately have considered the possibility that she was looking at her employer.

She squeezed her eyes shut. Small wonder the stable girl who had shown the double-page spread to her in the society magazine had looked at her oddly when she'd responded to the Welsh girl's enthusiastic, 'Isn't he utterly unbelievably lush?' with a polite but surprised response that he wasn't really her type. He hadn't been the man in the photo handing out the cup at the polo tournament—he'd been the one receiving it!

She had left the stables that morning reflecting sadly on the number of people who saw a man's bank balance before anything else. If the stout, balding man handing over the cup to the Latin-looking polo captain had not had the odd billion in the bank pretty Nia wouldn't have looked twice, and there she was acting as if he were some sort of centrefold pin-up.

My God, he was the centrefold!

Struggling to accept the evidence of her own eyes

and lose the invented image in her head, she watched the polo-playing captain put the portrait back in its place.

I just knew this job was too good to be true.

CHAPTER THREE

'MY NAME IS Zoe Grace.' She lifted her chin and clung to a shaky façade of calm. 'I'm your new housekeeper, Mr Montero. I'm sorry, we weren't expecting you,' she apologised stiffly.

'So I was looking for Zoe after all.' He met her confused blue stare before his glance fell to the hand extended to him and, ignoring it, he continued in the same conversational tone. 'I think you'll find you're my ex-housekeeper. You may have managed to con Tom…'

Zoe's shock at the calculated insult was followed swiftly by anger that she couldn't check. 'I didn't con anyone!'

'Then I can only assume you're sleeping with him because I can't think of any other reason why Tom would employ someone so stupendously unsuited to this or, as far as I can see, any other position of trust. And before you waste your time fluttering your eyelashes at me I have to tell you I'm not Tom. I enjoy a good body and—' he paused, his eyes making a cynical sweep of her face before he delivered a crushing assessment '—passably pretty face, but when it comes to staff I prefer to keep the lines firmly drawn. It cuts down on confusion and time-consuming, messy litigation.'

Zoe hated him before he was halfway through the scathing tirade.

Dismay widened her blue eyes. He was already turning away. In the grip of panic she surged after him, catching hold of his arm. 'You can't sack me!'

He arched a brow and looked down at her hand.

Zoe let it go, biting down on her full under lip as she backed away, shaking her head.

'I mean, you can, obviously you can, but don't...' She swallowed and bit her lip. Unable to meet his eyes, she lifted her chin, a note of sheer desperation creeping into her voice as she added huskily, 'Please.'

There were times when a person had to swallow her pride and this was one of those occasions.

Of course, if it had been just her she would have told him where to stuff his awful job. In fact if there had been just herself to consider she wouldn't be doing the job to begin with.

But there was more than herself to consider now.

Even if she could get some sort of job locally that would enable the twins to continue going to their school—they'd had enough disruption in their lives without being snatched away from everything that was familiar—Zoe couldn't have afforded the rent on a property within the catchment area. As for buying—she would have been laughed out of any bank.

The property prices were inflated in the village because of the number of affluent parents eager to move into the area due to the success of the local state school. Laura and Dan had frequently joked that they were sitting on a fortune, but their lovely little thatched cottage had been taken by her brother-in-law's creditors along with everything else they had.

Though his expression did not soften, Isandro did after a short pause turn and face her.

'I need this job, Mr Montero,' she said, wringing her white hands in anxiety at the prospect of being jobless and homeless.

His expression held no hint of sympathy as he read the earnest appeal in her blue eyes.

'Perhaps you should have thought of that before you turned my home into a circus. Unless this is all someone else's fault...?'

Zoe didn't even consider passing the buck. She lifted her chin and thought, You got yourself into this, Zoe, now get yourself out—crawl, grovel, whatever it takes. 'No, this was all me.'

'And you're not even sharing the profits of this little enterprise...?'

Anger made Zoe momentarily forget her determination to grovel. 'Are you calling me a...?' She lowered her gaze and added quietly, 'I'm not making money from this. Nobody is!'

He arched a sceptical brow. 'No...?'

'All the money goes to a good cause a—'

He lifted an imperative hand. 'Please spare me the sob stories. I have heard them all before. And as for appealing to my community spirit, don't waste your breath. I don't have any.'

Or a heart, either, Zoe thought, trying to keep her growing sense of desperation and panic under control.

She bit her lip. 'I know I overstepped my authority but I didn't see how a coffee morning could do much harm.'

His ebony brows hit his hairline. 'A coffee morning?'

She flushed and lowered her gaze. 'I know, I know... things got out of hand. It's just they were so enthusiastic and—' she lifted her eyes in appeal to his '—it was such a good cause that it was hard to say no.'

A flash of irritation crossed his lean features. If this woman expected he would react to a combination of emotional blackmail and big blue eyes she was in for a disappointment. 'It is always a good cause,' he drawled carelessly.

Zoe had to bite her lip to stop herself reacting to his contempt.

She bowed her head. If he wanted humble, fine, she could do that… She had to do that. 'We weren't expecting you.'

'How inconsiderate of me to arrive unannounced.' The sarcasm brought a flush to her cheeks. 'I admit I'm curious—what part of your designated role as someone responsible for the smooth running of this establishment did you think you were providing when you decided to turn my home into a cheap sideshow?'

'I thought…well, actually…I've already said it did get a bit out of hand, but it's not as if you are ever here.'

'So this is a case of while the cat's away. You have a novel way of pleading your cause, Miss Grace.'

'I need this job.' It went against every instinct to beg but what choice did she have? Speaking her mind was a luxury she could no longer afford. 'I really need this job. If you give me a chance to prove myself you won't regret it.'

His lifted his magnificent shoulders in a shrug. 'Like I said, you should have thought about that.' He studied her white face and felt an unexpected flicker of something he refused to recognise as sympathy as he could almost taste her desperation. 'Have you actually got any experience of being a housekeeper?'

She was too stressed to give anything but an honest answer. 'No.'

'I think it might be better if I do not enquire too far into the reason my assistant saw fit to offer you this job.'

'He knew I needed it.'

Her reply drew a hard, incredulous laugh from him. Actually, he had some sympathy for his assistant. If her performance at interview had been half as good as the one she was delivering now, he would not have been surprised if the man had offered her more than a job.

He would be having words with Tom.

'If when I take an inventory there are any valuables missing you will be hearing from me. Other than that I shall expect you to have vacated your flat by the morning.'

Zoe gave a wild little laugh. Short of falling to her knees, which might give him a kick but would obviously not change his mind, what was she meant to do? She had no skills, nothing to sell... The sheer hopelessness of her situation rushed in on her like a black choking cloud.

Falling back on the charity of friends was her only option, and that was only temporary.

She made one final attempt.

'Please, Mr Montero.'

His mouth thinned in distaste. 'Your tears are very touching, but wasted on me.'

She looked at him with tear-filled eyes. There was no longer anything to lose by telling him what she really thought. 'You're a monster!'

He shrugged. Being considered a monster was to his way of thinking infinitely preferable to being a sucker.

Zoe lifted her chin and, head high, walked towards the door, feeling the honeysuckle-scented breeze blow-

ing through the open window stroke her cheek as she
walked past him.

She was so blinded by the tears she fought to hold
back that she almost collided with the vicar who was
entering the room.

'Oops!' he said, placing both his hands on her shoulders to steady her. 'Zoe, dear, we were looking for you.'
In the act of turning to include in this comment the
woman who stood beside him with the child in a wheelchair he saw Isandro and paused, his good-natured face
breaking into a beaming smile as he recognised him
before surging forward.

'Mr Montero, I can't tell you how grateful we are...
all of us.'

Isandro, who had met the man on one previous occasion, acknowledged the gushing gratitude with a tilt
of his head. 'The work is finished on the new roof?'

'New roof? Oh, yes, that's marvellous but I am talking about today. This totally splendid turnout. It warms
the heart to see the entire community pulling together.'

He didn't have a heart to warm, Zoe thought as she
saw the hateful billionaire tip his dark head and hide his
confusion behind an impassive mask of hauteur. Actually it wasn't a mask; it was probably just him. Cold,
cruel, vindictive, positively hateful!

'Mr Montero, oh, thank you... Hannah, this is Mr
Montero, darling. Come and say thank you.'

Startled to find himself being hugged by a tearful
woman, Isandro stood rigid in the embrace, his arms
stiff at his side. Oblivious to the recipient's discomfort,
Chloe sobbed into his broad chest and told him he was
marvellous.

Zoe took a small degree of comfort from the discomfort etched on the Spaniard's handsome face. She'd

have preferred a job and a roof over her head but it was something.

When Hannah propelled her wheelchair over, her little face wreathed in smiles, and informed the startled billionaire that he could have a puppy from the next litter, his expression almost made her smile…though that might have been hysteria.

'Bella is the smartest dog, even though she was the runt, and everyone wanted her last puppies, though this time we think the father might be… Well, that's all right, you've plenty of room here and you look like a dog person.'

At a loss for once in his life, the dog person swallowed and wondered if the entire community here were off their heads.

Chloe still bubbling, her face alight, stopped her daughter's chair before it hit the desk. 'You two made this happen…' She took Zoe's hand and then that of the man she considered benefactor and pressed them palm to palm before sealing them between her own.

Standing there with a frozen smile on her face, Zoe had to fight the urge to tear her hand free. The only comfort she found in the situation was that he had to be hating this as much as she was.

'We made the target, so you won't have to shave your head!'

Zoe, forgetting for a moment her own situation, smiled happily, without noticing the expression on the tall Spaniard's face as he watched her light up with pleasure.

'Oh, Chloe, that's marvellous! Is there enough for John to come with you?'

'Not quite,' the older woman conceded. 'But he wouldn't be able to take that much time off work anyway. And we'll have so much to tell Daddy when we come home, won't we, Hannah?' She released the two hands she held and ducked down to her daughter, leaving Zoe standing there with her fingers curled around the long brown fingers of Isandro Montero.

While Chloe was kissing her daughter, and the vicar was taking off his glasses to study one of the paintings on the wall, Zoe took the opportunity to wrench her hand free and sling a poisonous look up at his face.

'Oh, Zoe, you've worked so hard. How will we ever be able to thank you? And don't you worry—we'll be here bright and early to clear away.' She stretched up to kiss Zoe's cheek. 'I wanted you to know first. Now I think we should go and tell everyone else...Vicar?'

'Yes, indeed. Mr Montero, you have a very impressive art collection here...amazing...' He wrung the younger man's hand with enthusiasm before following Chloe from the room. Zoe, who had tacked on behind them, was stopped by the sound of her name.

'Miss Grace, if I could have a moment...?'

Half inclined to carry on walking but knowing if she did the likelihood would be that the story would come out, Zoe paused and turned back, promising Chloe she would catch up. She knew it was inevitable that her friend would feel in part responsible for her sacking, but she saw no need to cast a cloud over this happy moment for the family who had not had a lot to be happy about recently.

She held herself rigid as he walked past her and closed the door.

'So?'

She shrugged and matched his tone. 'What?'

'Would you like to tell me what that was all about?'

Now he wants to know. 'I was trying to explain.'

Isandro's jaw tightened. He was furious to have been put in the position of being treated like some sort of hero and not having a clue why, and his anger was aimed at the person he held responsible for it.

'Well, explain now.'

'The fund-raiser was for Hannah.'

'The child in the wheelchair?'

Zoe nodded. 'Hannah had surgery for a spinal tumour. It was successful, they got all the tumour, but the pressure on the spinal cord caused damage and she can't walk. The doctors can't do anything, but Chloe, her mum, found a hospital in Boston that might be able to help. The treatment is experimental but so far the results have been really good.'

'And all this today was for that cause?'

She nodded.

His dark brows drew together in a straight line above his hawkish nose. 'Why on earth did you not tell me this straight away?'

She stared at him, staggered he could ask the question with a straight face... Priceless—the man was incredible. 'Possibly because you didn't give me a chance?'

Before he could respond there was a tap on the door and Chloe poked her head into the room.

'I almost forgot—we're having a party tomorrow at our house. Please come, Mr Montero.'

'Isandro.'

'Isandro,' she said, smiling. 'I'm sure Zoe will drive you if you want a drink,' Zoe was mortified to hear her friend suggest warmly. 'Her being the teetotaller she is.'

Zoe tensed, dreading the man would respond with a crushing refusal to the invitation, but to her surprise he simply nodded and said, 'Most kind of you.'

'Great—we'll see you both at seven.'

The door closed. 'Don't worry, I'll make your excuses. I'm assuming that as you know I'm not some sort of con artist you'll allow me to work my notice. I'm not asking for myself, but the children—'

Frowning, he cut across her. 'They all seem to be under the impression that I gave the go-ahead for this... this...'

'Fund-raising Fun Day.'

'Fun?'

'It started out as a coffee morning and then it just...'

He produced the sarcastic smile that made her want to stick a pin in him.

She clenched her teeth. 'Got out of hand.'

'It would seem you have a problem saying no.' He looked at her mouth and imagined her saying yes to a lot of things...yes and please. 'Did it not occur to you to tell me what this was about?'

She lifted her chin in response to his daunting disapproval and countered, 'Did it not occur to you to tell me who you were?'

The retort drew a frown. 'You have placed me in an impossible situation,' he brooded darkly.

Logic told him his hands were tied.

Sack her now and he would go from being the hero of the hour to the villain in a breath, and while he did not care overly for his standing in the local community, what bothered him was the press getting a sniff and running with it.

With the Fitzgerald deal in the balance the timing was as bad as it could be and this was the sort of story that the tabloids loved. The wheelchair-bound child, the rich landowner... He could see the headlines now, closely followed by the deal he had spent the last six months pulling together going down the drain along with all the jobs it would bring.

As tempting as it was to let the dismissal stand— every instinct he had was telling him she was nothing but trouble—Isandro knew the more sensible alternative was letting her stay. He had no doubt whatever that he would not have long to wait before she provided him with ample legitimate reasons to dismiss her.

An image of the pale freckled face flashed into his head. 'The child could not be treated in this country?'

Zoe smiled—the day had done some good. 'No, the surgery is ground-breaking.'

'And shaving your head?' He directed a curious glance at her glossy head, the light shining from the window highlighting natural-looking glossy chestnut streaks in the rich brown. 'A joke?'

Zoe lifted a self-conscious hand and flicked her plait over shoulder. 'Not really. Chloe has bad days sometimes and to make her laugh I said if the day didn't raise the money she needed I'd shave off my hair to raise more.'

'No!' The strength of his spontaneous rebuttal startled Isandro as much as it appeared to the owner of the hair.

She blinked, startled. 'Pardon?'

'It would not be appropriate for my housekeeper to go around with a shaved head.'

For a moment Zoe stared at him, her hope soaring despite the voice in her head that counselled caution. 'Housekeeper. Does that mean…?'

'I will be back tomorrow and I expect—' He broke off as a great roar went up from outside. 'I will expect things to be back to normal.'

'So you're not sacking me?' Zoe lowered her gaze, appalled to find her eyes filling with weak tears of relief.

'I will give you a trial period.' He gave her a month.

'You won't regret it.'

He probably would. 'The child…?' He touched the back of the chair she had been spinning around in. 'The one with the ginger hair.'

'Auburn. That was Georgie…Georgina.'

'She is…?' he prompted impatiently. It was like getting blood out of a stone.

'My niece.' She beamed happily. He could look down his aristocratic nose at her as much as he liked—she was no longer homeless, jobless and virtually destitute.

'She is staying long?'

'She lives with me and her twin brother, Harry.' In her head she could hear Laura on the phone when the scan had revealed she was carrying twins… One of each, Zoe, how lucky are we?

In the act of opening a diary on his desk, he stopped, his hands flat on the desk as he lifted his head. 'You have two children living here? No, that is not acceptable. You will have to make other arrangements.'

Zoe stared at him, breathing deeply to distract herself from the rush of anger. 'Arrangements? What,' she asked, 'did you have in mind?'

His eyes narrowed at the edge of sarcasm in her voice. 'I know nothing about children.'

'Except that you have no room in your twenty-bedroom house for two small ones.'

'So you're suggesting you move into my home.' He arched a sardonic brow and watched her flush. 'Or perhaps you already have?' It struck him that this might not be so far from the truth—the child had looked very comfortable in his chair.

Zoe flushed and bit her lip. 'Of course not.'

'So you would agree that the accommodation that comes with the job is not suitable.'

'It's fine.' It was free and in the catchment area of the twins' school, which made it not just fine but incredible!

His dark eyes sealed to hers as in interrogation mode he ran a hand across his jaw, shadowed with a day's growth of stubble. 'Correct me if I'm wrong...'

Oh, sure, I bet that happens a lot, she thought, struggling to keep her placid, perfect housekeeper smile pasted in place. She could see him now surrounded by little yes men falling over themselves to tell him how wonderful he was.

'But I was under the impression that the housekeeper's apartment had one bedroom?'

'A very big bedroom, and it has a perfectly comfortable sofa bed in the living room.'

'You sleep on a sofa bed?'

He could not have looked more appalled had she just announced she dossed down on a park bench or in a shop doorway.

'The arrangement works very well.' She smiled brightly in the face of his undisguised scepticism. If he was looking for an excuse to give her the push, she wasn't going to give him any. 'I'm always up before the twins, and they are in bed before me.' It wasn't a room of her own that kept Zoe awake at night, it was balancing her budget.

'In other words it is a perfect arrangement.'

Zoe pretended not to recognise the dry sarcasm. 'Not perfect,' she conceded calmly. 'But a workable compromise.' Like he knew a lot about compromise, she thought, but, smothering the prickle of antagonism, she continued serenely, 'And if you're thinking that the twins have a negative impact on my work, actually the reverse is true.'

'Indeed?'

'Having a family and responsibilities makes me ultra-reliable.' And totally lacking in pride, suggested the scornful voice in her head.

'You mean you need this job so you'll bite back the insult hovering even now on the tip of your tongue.' His hooded dark eyes slid to the soft full outline of her quite spectacularly sexy lips.

The words hovering on the tip of Zoe's tongue involved telling him to stop staring at her mouth.

She found herself thinking with nostalgia of the days when her temporary cash shortages had been dealt with by not buying the pair of shoes she'd been drooling over, or cutting back on the number of coffees she bought in a week. Things were no longer so simple. She was still reeling over the cost of new school uniforms for the twins, who had both shot up the previous term.

'You are speaking as if this arrangement is permanent. I assumed the children were spending their holiday with you.'

And I could have let him continue assuming that— the man is here so rarely he wouldn't have known the difference—but no, I had to go open my big mouth.

'No. They are my sister's children.' She swallowed. She didn't discuss the details of the accident that had killed her sister and her husband or mention the underage drunk driver going the wrong way on the motorway who had been responsible for the simple fact that she was afraid if she did she would start shouting. 'She and her husband died. I'm the children's guardian.'

'I am sorry.'

She nodded, not trusting herself to speak.

According to the grief counsellor anger was normal… It would pass, she said. There might be a time when she would stop being angry, but six months after that terrible day Zoe could not imagine a time when she would come to terms with it, stop wanting to beat her bare fists against a brick wall at the sheer terrible waste.

'You are very young to have such responsibilities.'

'That's relative, isn't it?' Only last week Zoe had watched a programme that followed a week in the life of children who were the main carers for their disabled parents. It had made her feel ashamed—compared to them she had it easy.

'Surely there is someone more suitable who could take care of these children?' He scanned her up and down and shook his head.

'My sister was my only family and Dan didn't have any family. It's me or social services.' She'd do what it took to stop that happening. The children would enjoy the sort of childhood she'd had… It was far too short as it was.

Zoe closed her eyes, remembering Laura's face the day she met Dan, and swallowed, concentrating on the anger, not the pain, as the same old question followed—why? Why Laura of all people in the world? Why did it have to be her?

He eyed her beautiful face cynically. 'I am assuming that housekeeping was not a career choice for you.'

Zoe moistened her lips, trying to decide what the right answer to this question was. In the end she kept it simple and honest.

'I never really knew what I wanted to do with my life.'

There had never seemed any hurry to make up her

mind. She liked to travel; she liked new experiences and meeting new people.

Well, now it was her turn to step up to the mark and, yes, she would beg and be tearfully grateful to this awful man. She would grovel if necessary, even if it killed her. She would do whatever it took to keep her family together.

She gave a quietly confident smile. 'But I never give any less than a hundred per cent, and I'll do whatever it takes to keep this job… Anything,' she added fiercely.

'Anything…?'

Something in the way he said it made her feel less secure, but she wouldn't back down—she couldn't. She nodded.

'Absolutely.'

Expression impassive, he brushed an invisible speck off his dark top with long brown fingers.

'"Anything" covers a lot of territory so if you're offering sexual favours I should tell you I normally get it for free.'

Zoe's hands curled into tight fists at her sides as she breathed through the energising rush of anger. He was taunting her, but he knew full well she couldn't respond and in her book that made the man a bully. She rubbed the hand that tingled to slap the expression of amused disdain off his smug, impossibly handsome face, and tilted her chin to an enquiring angle.

But would she…?

She pushed away the question and willed herself not to blush, unwilling to give him the satisfaction of seeing her squirm. At least she was safe from any unwanted attentions—the man was obviously too much of a snob to consider sleeping with the help.

But if he did?

Her body reacted to the unspoken question and Zoe had no more chance of halting the visceral chain re-action than she did stopping her fingers jerking back from a hot object.

Taking a deep breath, she brought her lashes down in a protective sweep and wrapped her arms across her middle in a hugging gesture, glad that she was wearing a loose-fitting top. She was saved the added embarrassment of having her shamefully engorged nipples on view, but it didn't stop her being painfully conscious of the chafing discomfort of her bra or the heavy liquid ache low in her pelvis.

Closing down this internal dialogue as her temperature rose, Zoe managed to break contact with his disturbing steely stare and lifted her shoulders in a tiny shrug.

'Jokes aside, I can promise you I shall be totally professional.'

He arched a brow and didn't look convinced by her claim. She felt panic trickle down her spine and thought, God, please don't let him change his mind.

'You won't be sorry.' Her fingernails gouged crescents into the soft flesh of her palms as she held her breath awaiting his response, feeling like a prisoner in the dock waiting to hear his sentence read out.

His tall figure framed in the doorway, Isandro turned. He already was regretting it.

'I am sorry for your loss, but I have to tell you I do not allow sentiment to sway my judgement, so do not expect any special favours here.'

Just how well would his judgement withstand the pressure of great legs and a stupendous mouth?

Her smile was cold and proud. 'I won't expect any.'

'We'll see. I judge by results, not promises.' Or lips,

he thought as his gaze made an unscheduled traverse of the lush pink curve of her wide mouth before he could think better of it.

'I never had any complaints.' The unintentional innuendo after his previous comment brought a flush to her cheeks. 'In any of the jobs I've had,' she added hastily.

'That cannot be many. How old are you?'

'Twenty-two, and actually—' She lifted a hand, about to list the jobs she had done, and dropped it again, not wanting to give the impression that she didn't have staying power. As it happened, it was too late, as his next disturbingly perceptive remark revealed.

'What is the longest time you have remained in one job?'

Outwardly cool, inwardly thinking, Why, oh, why can I never keep my big mouth shut? she furrowed her smooth brow. 'Is that relevant?'

'It is if you walk after a week.'

'I have done a number of jobs, it's true, but who hasn't in this job market?' As if he knows such a lot about this job market. He may employ a lot of people in his various empires, but to him they are statistics on a chart. 'I've never left anyone in the lurch. I'm totally reliable.'

'But you don't like to stay in one place long? You have no staying power?'

'I have…' She forced her lips into a smile and bit back a retort even though it choked her to do so. 'Please don't judge me on first impressions. I have responsibilities now that I did not have previously.'

'We'll see.' He flicked his wrist and glanced at his watch. 'My chef will be here later. You will make the arrangements.'

She nodded and produced a smile that oozed professional confidence. 'Of course.' She wrinkled her nose. 'What arrangements would they be?'

Unable to decide if she was joking, he regarded her with an expression of stern disapproval. 'This is not a work experience position, Miss Grace.'

'Of course not, Mr Monster...Montero.' Thrown into confusion by the horrifying Freudian slip, she almost fell over in her haste to get to the door before him to open it.

'I do not require grovelling. I require efficiency.'

She tipped her head meekly. 'Of course.' What he required, in her opinion, was taking down a peg or several hundred. She just hoped she was around to watch when it happened.

Passing through the door, Isandro revised his month estimate. She wouldn't last a week. If she had mouths to feed that was not his problem—he was not a charity.

CHAPTER FOUR

IF HE FOUND so much as a curtain fold out of place she'd eat her rather grubby trainers, Zoe decided, doing a final survey of the room.

The army of volunteers had cleared away any sign of yesterday's festivities in the grounds. The word had got around that the boss had put in an unexpected appearance the previous day and the staff had really gone the extra mile on the house. The rest of the rooms were equally pristine, about as lived-in as your average museum, but presumably cosy was not what he wanted.

Thinking the word 'cosy' in the same thought as Isandro Montero made her lips quirk, but not for long. She had spent a really awful night reliving yesterday's encounter, by turns breaking out in cold sweats when she thought of how close she'd come to losing the roof over their heads and seething with resentment that she'd had to crawl to keep it.

The couple of times she had managed to drift off she hadn't been able to escape the awful man who held their fate in his elegant, over-privileged hands. Shivering, she pushed her fingers into her hair and shook her head. Typical. She normally forgot the contents of her dreams the moment she woke up. But the dark erotic images from last night remained disturbingly fresh, as did the lingering shivery feeling in the pit of her stomach that did not diminish with each subsequent flashback.

Get a grip, Zoe, she told herself. The man only comes here once in a blue moon, so grit your teeth and give him no opportunity to criticise.

'You don't have to like him.' And you definitely don't have to dream about him, she added silently as she rubbed a suggestion of a smudge off the surface of a mirrored bureau door with the sleeve of her sweater.

Catching sight of herself, she gave a horrified gasp. The house and grounds looked terrific but she didn't!

Rushing out into the square marble-floored hallway, dominated by the graceful curving staircase that rose to the second floor and the glass dome above that flooded the space with light, Zoe couldn't help glancing nervously at the big front door, her heart beating fast in reaction to the image in her head of it opening to reveal the master of the house. A shiver travelled the length of her spine before she shook her head, laughing.

Master?

'Really, Zoe!' She shook her head again, ignoring the fact her laugh this time had a breathless sound to it. Living with all this history was making her thoughts turn positively feudal, she decided, exiting through the door that led into a long winding inner hallway and in turn to the sturdy door that led outside into the quadrangle of outbuildings at the rear of the building.

She headed across the cobbled yard, past the rows of stone troughs filled with artistically arranged tumbling summer flowers, and up the stone steps that led to the flat above what had once been a coach house but now housed what was by all accounts an impressive collection of vintage sports cars.

Inside the flat she closed the door and leaned against

it, relieved that he hadn't put in an appearance while she was looking like a scarecrow. Walking across to the fitted cupboard that housed her clothes, she grimaced at her reflection in the full-length mirror inside the door. Not exactly the image of cool efficiency she was determined to exemplify.

Stripping down to her bra and pants, she folded her jeans. When the space was limited neatness was essential but fortunately she didn't have many clothes, which made her choice of a suitable outfit pretty easy. Padding through the living room and through the twins' bedroom into the en-suite, she popped her dusty top in the linen basket, then pinned her hair up before she stepped into the shower. Though she would have liked to wash her hair, it took an age to dry and she was short of time.

Fifteen minutes later, wearing a crisp white blouse, a pair of narrow-legged tailored black trousers and with her hair in a fat plait down her back, she slid her feet into a pair of sensible black leather loafers. She gave herself a critical once-over, bending at the knee to see the top of her head in the angled mirror. Resisting the temptation to jazz up the sombre outfit with a pink scarf dotted with orange roses, she slid a pair of gold hoops into her ears. The sound of them jingling brought a smile to her lips as she lifted her head, more confidence in her stride as she headed across the courtyard. She was determined to make up for the disastrous first impression she had made; she could do it.

She had to do it.

Her smile faded slightly as she approached the building, tensing as she heard a car in the distance, but the vehicle that drove through the arch was a delivery van from the local butcher's. She started breathing again, delivering the silent advice, Cool it, Zoe, before she paused to thank one of the gardeners for donating a box full of the vegetables from the kitchen garden to the raffle the previous day, and admiring the magnificent lavender tumbling from a group of barrels.

'The smell always makes me think of summer and at night it fills the flat,' she told him, adding warmly, 'The flowers you cut for the house were marvellous.' She had spent a pleasant half-hour filling bowls in several of the rooms with the fragrant summer blooms.

He tilted his head in acknowledgement and looked pleased with the compliment. 'The other one here before you sent up to London for fancy arrangements every week. I told her it was a criminal waste.'

'I'm sure they were very beautiful.' The gardener might approve, but Zoe suddenly felt less secure about her amateur attempts to add a touch of colour to the house; they were hardly professional.

Resisting the impulse to run back to the house and remove all the flowers, which in her mind were fast becoming tasteless and ugly displays of amateurism, she chatted a little longer to the man before she finally excused herself.

In the end she couldn't bring herself to dump the freshly cut flowers, deciding as a compromise not to volunteer the information she was responsible—unless directly asked, which seemed unlikely. She walked around the place a final time to double-check everything, leaving it until the last possible moment before she jumped in her car and set off to pick up the twins from school.

For all she knew Isandro Montero might not arrive until midnight; he might be a total no-show—if she was very lucky.

The narrow country lane that led to the village was

in theory a short cut, but Zoe got stuck behind a tractor, and the children were already waiting at the gate when she arrived, chatting to Chloe and Hannah.

'I'm sorry I'm late!' she exclaimed.

'You're not late,' Chloe soothed. 'They only just got out.' She took in Zoe's outfit and her brows lifted. 'Wow, you look very...'

'Weird,' supplied Georgie bluntly.

'Very sexy librarian,' Chloe corrected.

'Are librarians sexy?' Harry asked.

Chloe exchanged a look with Zoe, who suppressed a smile and said, 'In the car, you two.' Adding, 'Do you want a lift, Chloe?'

The older woman shook her head. 'No, I'm picking up some glasses for tonight from Sara on my way back.'

'I hope you all have a great night, I wish I could come but...' She lifted her slender shoulders in a regretful shrug; her babysitting arrangements had fallen through that morning.

'You can... I know, just call me fairy godmother. You know how John's mum is having Hannah? Well, she's offered to have your two as well. John will pick up the twins on his way home and he'll fetch them back in the morning.'

'Oh, Chloe, that's really kind but I couldn't impose...'

'It's not imposing. Maud offered and they'll have a great time, you know they will.'

'Yes, but—'

'Yes but nothing, Cinders, you're going to the ball and don't forget the invite includes your utterly gorgeous boss... I tell you, if I was a few years younger I'd give you a bit of competition there.'

Zoe struggled to smile at the joke. 'He's not here, I'm afraid.' She felt a guilty tug as her friend's face fell.

'I thought he was due back today. John's going to be so disappointed—he wanted to thank him personally and return his hospitality. Half the people there only came because they wanted to take a look at the hall.'

Zoe's unease increased. Short of admitting that the hospitality they wanted to return had not been given freely, she had no way of preventing the decision to treat the new lord of the manor as a community-minded philanthropist.

'He was...is...due today,' she admitted. 'But when I left he hadn't arrived.'

'But he might do.'

'Anything's possible,' Zoe admitted, but the thought of Isandro coming to a party where the glasses were borrowed and the food was provided by guests! Possible but not very likely, thank goodness!

'Well, promise you'll remind him if he does turn up? Tell him that we'd love to see him and he seemed very keen to come. He's obviously making an effort to be part of the community.'

Zoe didn't have the heart to shatter this illusion and explain that the man had only said yes to cut the scene short and get rid of them as quickly as possible.

'If he does I will,' Zoe promised, imagining with horror the admittedly unlikely scenario of Isandro putting in an appearance at the party. Him spending the entire evening with his lips curled contemptuously would suck the joy out of any occasion and Zoe wanted to save her friends that. On a less unselfish note she wanted to save herself from spending her precious off-duty time with a man who made her skin prickle with antagonism even before he opened his mouth and said something

vile and unpleasant. The fact that half the vile things
he said were actually the truth was neither here nor…
Losing track of her train of thought, she shook her head
slightly to banish the image of the lips that combined
overt sensuality with an underlying hint of cruelty.

She was getting fixated on the man's mouth when
it was the things that came out if it that she ought to
worry about.

'John will be by around six to pick up the twins.'

Isandro did not get involved in other people's lives.
His charitable donations to selected good causes were
made anonymously, and he never responded to any form
of moral blackmail or sentimental sob stories, but the
story of the little girl and her 'last chance to walk' trip
to America continued to play in his mind.

Admit it, Isandro, the kid got to you.

This perceived weakness was responsible for putting the indent between his sable brows. His father had
been a sentimental man, a kind, trusting man who was
moved by the suffering of others. A man who taught
his son the importance of charity, and led by example.

And where had that got him?

Universally liked and admired certainly—but at the
end he had been a broken and disillusioned man.

Isandro had been forced to stand by helplessly and
watch while the woman his father had married and her
daughter had systematically robbed the family business,
stealing not just from his father but from major clients.
He had no intention of emulating his parent, had no
room for sentimentality in his life, expected the worst
from others and was rarely disappointed.

Experience had taught him that everyone had an
angle and the most innocent of faces could hide a devi-

ous heart, like his stepmother and her daughter. Forced to brake hard to avoid a cat that shot across the road out of nowhere, he shook his head, banishing the thoughts of the pair of con artists who had with clinical efficiency isolated his father, alienating him not just from trusted friends and colleagues but his family, ensuring that when Isandro had passed on the concerns expressed by senior staff it had been treated as jealous spite.

Isandro would never be the man his father had been; he'd make sure of that. The possibility that his name was synonymous with cold and heartless was to his way of thinking infinitely preferable to being considered a mug.

A faint smile flickered across his face. According to the lovely Zara he was both cold and heartless among other things. She had lost it big time and reverted to her native Russian, a language Isandro had only a smattering of, so some of the choicer insults had been lost on him, before she swept majestically out of the restaurant on her designer heels.

He exhaled, feeling a fleeting spasm of regret. The woman looked magnificent even when she was spitting fury, and the sex had been excellent.

Great sex had been about the only thing they had going for them, and it had been pretty much the perfect relationship while Zara's demands had stayed in the bedroom, but recently… He shook his head. He was not into post-mortems but if he'd lived last night again he might not have replied so honestly when Zara had pouted and asked, 'Have you listened to a word I've been saying all night?'

If he'd contented himself with an honest, no frills 'no' he might have cajoled her out of her sulks and things might not have escalated so noisily, but he hadn't.

He'd irritably gone into more detail, rather unwisely revealing that he had minimal interest in shoes, the latest way to remove a skin blemish, or minor royals.

To Zara's frigid, 'I'm so sorry if I'm keeping you awake,' he had responded with an inflammatory:

'Barely.'

Zara's wrathful intake of breath had caused heads to turn and half the room had heard her hissing, 'Do you want to split up?'

The ensuing scene could have been avoided. His error of judgement had been assuming she expected to hear him say yes.

He still wasn't sure why he'd said it. It wasn't as if Zara had ever been anything but shallow, but that had never been a problem. In fact it had always suited him. It wasn't her fault that her beauty budget for a month could have paid for a disabled child's medical treatment.

Dios, but the child had really got to him, he thought, seeing not the child's face but the disapproval and contempt etched on the beautiful face of his new housekeeper.

There were no balloons along the driveway, just a peacock who sauntered across the road at a leisurely pace, forcing him to wait, then one of the team of gardeners at the wheel of a lawnmower on the now empty lawn as he drove past. Superficially at least everything was back to normal.

It wasn't until he drove into the courtyard that he realised how hard he had been searching for a legitimate cause for complaint. Frowning as much at the flash of insight as at the beat-up Transit van parked beside one of the estate Land Rovers, he opened the door and peeled out of the low-slung sports car he was driving.

He had taken a couple of steps across the cobbles

when he saw a denim-clad bearded figure he assumed was the driver of the eyesore vehicle, who up to that point had been concealed from Isandro by his van.

He wasn't alone. He held in his arms a tall slender figure. Isandro stopped dead at the sight. The woman wrapped in the circle of another man's arms had her face hidden from him but the slim body was that of his housekeeper.

Anger flooded into his body, the speed and strength of the flood of emotion leaching the colour from the sculpted bones of his strong features. For the space of several heartbeats his ability to think was obliterated by pure fury as he stood with his hands clenched into fists at his sides.

As the woman emerged from the embrace, pulling away from the man's chest, he kept hold of her upper arms, saying something that made her laugh before jumping into the van and closing the door behind him with a bang.

It was the musical sound of her laughter and not the reverberating sound of the door being slammed that shook him from his fugue.

Isandro inhaled and loosened his clenched fingers. His temper had been a problem when he was a boy but he was no longer a boy—he was a man who was known for his control and objectivity.

And he had objectively wanted to drag that guy off her. It wasn't an overreaction, but a perfectly legitimate response to having his trust abused. This wasn't about a public kiss—though you had to wonder at the woman's taste. The point was this was not only his home, it was her workplace. This little scene represented a total lack of professionalism. He had given her a second chance, hoping that she would blow it, and she had not disappointed.

Feeling more comfortable having a satisfactory explanation for his moment of visceral rage, he began to walk towards her, the sound of his footsteps drowned out by the van's engine as it vanished through the arch. He knew for a fact that he did not do jealousy, especially when the woman concerned was his employee. A jealous man would not have been amused rather than angry when his lover of the moment had been caught on camera by the paparazzi being as friendly as a person could be in public without being arrested.

Waving as John's van drove away, Zoe held up her hand even after the van had vanished. Then taking a deep sustaining breath, she dropped it and turned around to face the figure she had been aware of in the periphery of her vision as John had given her a goodbye hug.

Before reaching him, her gaze swept over the low-slung powerful car parked the opposite side of the courtyard. It was a monster, low, silver and sleek. She hadn't heard it arrive but then the noise of the running engine of John's van had presumably drowned out the sound of the Spanish billionaire's arrival. It had been the prickling of the hairs on the nape of her neck that had alerted her to the presence of the tall dynamic figure as she stood there saying goodbye to John.

If she'd acknowledged him then she'd have had no choice but to introduce him to John, which was something she wanted to avoid if possible.

She had promised Chloe she'd ask him about tonight and she would. This way she could sugar-coat his response—that it would be no was a given, that he wouldn't go out of his way to frame his refusal nicely was an equally safe bet.

'Good evening. I hope you had a good journey—'

He cut across her, launching without preamble into blighting speech. 'I do not find the sight of my house-keeper with her tongue down the throat of a tradesman a particularly edifying sight. In the future I would be grateful if you kept your love life or what passes for it behind closed doors and on your own time the next time you fancy a bit of rough.'

For a second she was too startled, as much by the icy delivery as his interpretation of a simple goodbye hug, to respond to this ludicrous accusation. But when she did her voice shook with the effort to control her response. She took a deep breath and closed off her fu-rious train of thought, tipping her head in an attitude she hoped suggested humility while she badly wanted to slap the look of smug contempt off his face.

'I'll keep that in mind when I feel the urge to force myself on some passing tradesman.' Focusing her thoughts on the price of school sports kits helped her stay calm as she levelled a clear blue gaze at his dark lean face and finished her thought. 'Though actually, for the record, on this occasion I was simply hugging a friend goodbye.' Like it's any of your business, you sanctimonious creep. 'You're right, he is a tradesman, but not rough at all,' she added, unable to keep the note of shaky indignation out of her voice. 'John is sweet.' She lifted her chin. 'And not the sort of man who judges people by appearances or what they do for a living.'

Politely framed or not, it was impossible to miss the fact he was being called a snob. For a moment Isandro was too astonished to be angry. For a long time in his life now there had been no one who would presume to tell him if he was out of line.

The moment passed and astonishment gave way to anger that caused the muscles along his angular jaw to tighten and quiver. 'I do not care what the man does for a living!'

She arched a feathery brow and said politely, 'Of course not.'

Isandro clenched his teeth, seriously tempted to give her her marching orders and to hell with the consequences, then he recalled the delicacy of the deal on the negotiating table and the outcome was by no means a given. Any hint of scandal now would make the old family firm walk away from the table.

'What I care about is the man conducting his sex life on my doorstep!'

She stared, her blue eyes widening to their widest before narrowing into angry sparkling slits. He made it sound as if he'd discovered her having an orgy! What she couldn't understand was how could anyone have seen anything sordid in a perfectly innocent hug?

He was madder than he had been when she had given him cause. His reaction to her using his house to raise funds without his permission had been clinical, but there was nothing at all clinical about his reaction to her imagined sin now.

'The next time get a room.' The snarled suggestion triggered a free-fall avalanche of images that made him lose his thread.

'Get a room? John is married!'

His nostrils flared. 'All the more reason, I would have thought, to show a little more circumspection,' he declared austerely.

'I would not have an affair with a married man!' She

took a deep breath. It really hurt to have to explain herself to this man but what choice did she have? 'What you witnessed, Mr Montero, was simply a goodbye hug between friends,' she told him stiffly. 'That was John, Chloe's husband. You remember Chloe?'

Taking his silence to be a yes, she explained further. 'He was picking up the twins. They're staying with his mother tonight. She's babysitting, because John and Chloe are having a party...you remember?'

He remembered.

'I saw—'

'You saw nothing, because there was nothing to see.'

His mind replayed the image that had caused him to jump to conclusions and he realised he had not seen anything beyond two people close. His expression froze, his discomfiture revealing itself in the faintest deepening of colour along the slashing angles of his sybaritic cheekbones. Isandro cleared his throat. Embarrassment was a foreign sensation and one he did not enjoy.

He stopped his jaw tightening. 'I apologise. I made a mistake.'

Zoe fought a smile. Clearly every syllable of his apology had hurt. 'Apology accepted. I left your mail on your desk. I wasn't sure if you wanted it forwarded. If you let me know what time is convenient I'll let the maid know when she can clean your study. Oh, and shall I let your chef know what time you'll want dinner, sir?' She took a breath and thought, Wow, I'm good.

His brows lifted. 'I assumed that we would be dining out.'

Zoe shook her head, losing control of her 'perfect housekeeper' smile. 'Dining?'

'What time did your friend say—seven?'

She gave a little laugh, her face clearing. 'The party! Oh, goodness, you don't have to come.'

'Then the invitation is not genuine?'

'Yes, it's genuine—Chloe and John are very genuine people. I just thought that under the circumstances...'

He arched a questioning brow. 'Circumstances?'

This deliberate display of obtuseness brought her full lips together in a pursing line of annoyance. 'They are going to want to thank you, and I'd assumed that you'd find that embarrassing.'

Of course her analysis was dead on, but it turned out his reluctance to attend this party was not as strong as his enthusiasm to not follow the script she clearly wanted him to.

Where women were concerned Isandro did not consider himself complacent, but neither did he anticipate rejection. It was his male pride responding, rather than common sense, as he bared his white teeth in a smile that did not reach his dark eyes and framed his silky response.

'It is always pleasant when people are grateful.' Some women would be grateful to be offered the chance of sharing an evening with him. 'You will find I'm not easily embarrassed.'

Zoe struggled to hide her dismay. 'Does that mean you want to come?'

While he knew it was illogical to put himself through what would be an uncomfortable and almost certainly boring evening, the dismay in her voice that she didn't have either the skill or the good manners to disguise hardened his stubborn resolve to attend the damned party with her at his side—and she'd damned well enjoy it! he thought.

'It's not a matter of want. I gave my word.'

She struggled to read the expression on his lean sardonic face and faltered. 'They'd understand if you...'

'What time will you pick me up?'

Zoe's heart sank to her boots and she shook her head, feigning incomprehension.

Isandro smiled. She was a very bad actress—an actress with the most incredible mouth he had ever seen.

'Was that not the arrangement—you take me...?' he asked, utilising his much more polished acting skills. 'Of course, I can arrange a driver if you have other plans.'

Her only plan at that moment was to retreat to her little flat and bang her head on a brick wall! Inevitably he would be a back-seat driver. The sinking sensation in the pit of her stomach as she thought of being forced to share such a small space with him raised goosebumps over her body, but she cheered herself with the mental image of his elegant length folded into the not at all elegant confines of her Beetle that had seen better days. She squared her slender shoulders and ran her tongue across the surface of her dry lips.

Time to accept the inevitable and make the best of the situation. She was still mystified why he would want to come. Perhaps he just enjoyed having people tell him what a great guy he was, she thought scornfully, but the reality was it was going to happen so she'd better stop fighting it and make the best of the situation. It was one evening of her life, and she was probably worrying unnecessarily—his social skills were probably not nearly as bad as she feared.

'No, that's fine. I thought I'd leave around seven, if that suits you?'

He lifted his shoulders in a fluid shrug. 'I will be waiting.'

Her brave smile tipped his emotions over into amusement tinged with determination. He had always found it hard to resist a challenge. By the time this evening was over he would have Miss Zoe Grace eating out of his hand.

CHAPTER FIVE

GIVEN THE LIMITED storage space in the flat it was lucky Zoe didn't have a lot of clothes. Those that didn't fit into the cupboard in the hallway she kept in a case under the twins' bed.

On her knees she dragged it into the middle of the room, then sat back on her heels and went through the contents. The choice did not take long as she only possessed two half-decent summer dresses. After a few moments of narrow-eyed contemplation, she chose the maxi, mainly because it had fewer creases. Putting it on a hanger she hung it over the bathroom door and turned on the shower, hoping the steam from it would smooth out the few there were in the light chiffon fabric that she was a bit nervous about pressing because she still hadn't got around to replacing her iron with its dodgy thermostat.

Fifteen minutes later, some light make-up applied, her hair loosened from the plait and brushed into silky submission in waves that almost reached her waist, she switched off the water in the bathroom and was pleased to see that it had worked—the creases had virtually all fallen out of the misty blue fabric.

Slipping it over her head, she adjusted the shoe spaghetti straps and stooped down to get a glimpse of herself in the mirror. She hardly recognised the grave young woman who looked back at her, and allowed herself a complacent smile. When was the last time she'd dressed up? So long ago she couldn't remember. It was a shame that on this occasion she had that terrible man along for the ride.

With any luck he would get bored and leave early.

Hugging this comforting thought to herself, she walked across the courtyard back to the big house and found him waiting outside the porticoed entrance.

The sound of the fountain drowned out the noise her heels made on the cobbles, so she was able to study him unobserved for a few moments. He was wearing an open-necked shirt and dark tailored trousers. She was admiring the way he looked, hard not to, and reflecting that it was a shame that someone who had everything physically should be so lacking in the personality department when he turned suddenly, startling her enough to make her fall off the strappy wedge she was wearing.

He was at her side supplying a steadying hand to her elbow with startling speed. Flustered, she lifted her face to his, the pupils of her dramatic cornflower-blue eyes dilating as they connected with his dark ebony burnished stare.

She caught her breath sharply as a shimmy of sensation that slid down her spine made her shiver. The man had a sexual charisma that really was off the scale!

'I'm not used to the heels.' She pulled and his hand fell away from her elbow. 'I'm afraid my car's not very…' Her voice faded as she picked her way with more care now across the cobbles.

Isandro had been pierced by an arrow of sheer lust the moment he had seen her walking towards him. Walking behind her gave him the opportunity to admire her delicious bottom and the long elegant line of her seemingly endless legs, revealed rather than hidden by the long skirt that clung and flowed as she walked.

'The seat belt's a bit...' She took the football he held and with a grimace slung it into the back seat on top of the motley collection of toys and turned the ignition. 'It takes a few times before it... Sometimes...'

'Will you stop apologising?' He nodded towards the back seat. 'Your nephew plays football?' He spoke not out of any genuine interest but a desire to stop himself asking her if she had a boyfriend. It wouldn't make a difference—she worked for him and some rules he did not break. Still, there was no rule against looking.

'Harry?' Zoe laughed and shook her head. 'No, Harry hates sport. The ball is Georgie's. Harry is... quieter.' A man like Isandro Montero would never understand a sensitive boy like Harry. Her brow furrowed. Harry was a worry; he was such an easy child that he tended to be overlooked.

She glanced towards her passenger, and her lips twitched at the thought of anyone overlooking the scorchingly handsome Spaniard. It should have been laughable to see him squashed into her Beetle, but Zoe was unable to raise even a smile. The fact they were virtually rubbing shoulders made her feel a lot less comfortable than he appeared to be.

Being in this sort of enclosed space with him made Zoe want to crawl out of her own skin.

'It's not far.' Thank God for small mercies.

'I will sit back and admire the scenery,' he said, studying her profile. He had thought she would scrub up well and he had been proved right—she was stunning.

A few minutes later she crunched the gears and

winced as she drew up outside the local convenience store.

'Your friends live here?'

'No, they live the other side of the village. I need to stop to get a bottle of wine.'

'I thought you didn't drink.'

'I don't, but other people do,' she said shortly without looking at him.

'You should have said. There's plenty of wine in the cellar.' Good wine was always a sound inflation-proof investment.

A small choking sound left her lips as she thought of the vintage stuff stacked in the hall's cellar being served from borrowed glasses and drunk by people who in her hostess's case preferred her wine mixed with lemonade.

'Don't worry about it. I'll get this.'

Inside the store she snatched two of the second-cheapest bottles off the shelves and took them to the checkout.

'Nice stuff this, so they say,' the man at the till approved, putting the bottles into a bag for her while she dug into her purse. It became embarrassingly clear pretty quickly that she was short of cash to pay and her plastic was at home in the drawer, which had seemed the safest way to avoid temptation while she adjusted to her new straitened circumstances.

'Sorry, it'll have to be the Spanish one—do you mind if I change them? Fifty pence short, I'm afraid.' She nodded towards the stacked coins.

'No problem, it's very nice too, love.'

Her hand had closed around the bottles on the counter when a big hand covered it. 'Let me get those.'

Looking from the warm hand covering her own to the face of the tall, sleek, exclusive-looking man who had moved to stand beside her, Zoe shook her head, struggling to recover her composure and painfully aware of the tingling pain in her peaked and aching nipples. She was shamed and embarrassed by her weakness.

'No, really, I'm fine. I'm going to have the Spanish one…wine, that is…' she corrected and promptly felt like a total idiot.

'I hate to be disloyal, but take it from a Spaniard—that is not wine,' he told her with a shudder.

'It's not a wine snob sort of party.'

He was prepared to swallow the insult, but not the wine on the shelf. 'No, I insist, the least I can do since you are being my taxi,' he said, taking his wallet from his pocket and handing over the money.

Short of having a fight right there in the shop, Zoe had no choice but to accept the offer with as much grace as possible.

With his hand on the small of her back he guided her out of the shop and back towards the car. She didn't enjoy the light physical contact—actually any contact at all with this man made her feel uncomfortable—but she could tell that the natural courtesy came as second nature to him.

He held the door open for her, then went around to the other side of the car. The entire vehicle shook as she slammed the door closed. 'Do you not drink out of choice or because you have a drink problem?'

Her lips tightened. Was the man worried that his new housekeeper was an alcoholic? 'Neither, sir.' She emphasised the title before adding factually, 'I simply can't metabolise alcohol. I get drunk on the smell.'

'I rather think it might be more appropriate if you do not call me sir tonight.'

She shrugged and steered her car past the others parked along one side of the narrow lane. 'Is that an order, Mr Montero?'

'If you like, and try Isandro. It is my name. Relax,' he recommended. 'This is a party. I will not cramp your style...'

'It's not that sort of party and be careful there's a...' She stopped and hid a smile, adding as he surveyed his muddy shoe, 'A bit of a ditch that side.'

Zoe had been concerned for her friends' feelings, but slowly let down her guard as she realised that, far from looking down his nose at her friends, he was charming them. She could relax and enjoy herself; why not? Against all her expectations he was not being aloof or even icily polite. From the moment they had arrived and he had been swept away by Chloe, who had wanted to show him off, he had given the appearance of enjoying himself.

Watching Isandro talk easily with John and the local vet—who, according to Chloe, had not worn low-cut blouses before her divorce—it was Zoe who found herself feeling like an outsider. She felt her resentment rise as the red-headed divorcee threw back her head and laughed throatily at something Isandro had said, giving him an excellent view of her cleavage. Zoe's teeth clenched—and he looked, of course; he was a man!

How predictable. Shaking her head in a combination of contempt and cynical amusement, she felt embarrassed for the woman who was being so obvious. And he wasn't doing anything to discourage her, she thought. Her eyes narrowed as the woman's hand came to rest on his arm and stayed there, her long nails showing as flashes of scarlet as they curved over his biceps.

Zoe couldn't decide if the woman was pathetic or predatory...and whether she herself was embarrassed or envious.

Ignoring the laughable possibility that she wanted to touch Isandro, she directed her stubbornly critical glance over his strong, arrogant profile, pushing away the image of moving her hands over the hard muscular contours of his body, waiting for the hot hormone rush that tinged her cheek with pink to recede.

This was insane, she told herself. How could the man be all the way over the other side of the room and still manage to jangle every nerve ending in her body? His masculinity really was totally overwhelming. She sipped her drink, wishing that there were something stronger than fruit juice in it—though maybe not; the last thing she needed was her social restraints vanishing. Zoe had not exaggerated when she explained her reaction to alcohol; she had learnt after a couple of deeply embarrassing experiences that she and booze were not a good combination.

Common sense told her this was about hormones. She'd just have to accept it as an uncomfortable fact, like a pollen allergy, and deal with it. No point whatsoever in overanalysing the primitive physical response he had awoken in her, and it didn't really matter if this was all about timing or that he had been the catalyst for kicking her dormant hormones into life. She would treat it as an inconvenience rather than a disaster. There were always coping mechanisms and for the rare occasions there weren't, you avoided the problem. Like her body's inability to cope with alcohol—she didn't touch it; she wasn't going to touch Isandro. Simple.

What would be a disaster or at least an unwanted distraction would be to think too much about the primitive hunger she sensed was somewhere inside her. She should acknowledge it and forget about it. She was human; she had rotten taste in men. But she must not go there.

The vet, on the other hand, had clearly no such qualms about going where God knew how many women had been before, Zoe thought, her lips moving in a grimace of distaste as the older woman and her curves moved in closer. She had all but trapped him in the corner now...not that he showed any inclination to escape.

Her lips were still tightened in a cynical sneer of superiority when, without warning, Isandro turned his head slowly as though sensing her scrutiny. His dark eyes sought and connected with hers across the room. It was as if he possessed some radar that told him exactly where she was standing...where she was staring.

Their eyes locked, and for a long, heart-thudding moment Zoe could feel her own pulse over every inch of her skin, the vibrations reaching her tingling fingertips. She stopped breathing. Her stomach muscles quivered; her legs felt weak and oddly heavy; her knees literally shook.

The contact might have lasted moments or an hour, she didn't have a clue, but by the time she managed to bring her lashes down in a protective fan her insides had dissolved. Her throat was dry as she raised her empty glass to her lips and struggled to regain some semblance of self-control.

She closed her eyes, her lashes brushing her cheeks. As she willed her body to relax they shot open at the sound of her name.

'Sorry, I was miles away. How are you?' she asked Chloe's elderly aunt who was lowering her bulk into a chair.

'I can't complain, but of course I do. Thank you, dear,' she added as Zoe retrieved her stick that had fallen to the floor. 'Unless you want your man going home with someone else I'd get over there, Zoe.'

Blushing, Zoe followed the direction of the old lady's sharp-eyed stare to where Isandro stood, looking like the personification of a predatory male. And the hunter was still being hunted, she saw, her mouth twisting as she watched the redhead lean into him and stroke his sleeve. 'I'm his taxi, not his date. He's my boss.'

'In my day it was most girls' dream to marry their boss. I did—not, of course, that George ever looked like that.' She saw Zoe's expression and gave a chuckle, adding, 'I'm old, child, not blind.'

'And I'm not thinking of getting married.'

If she ever did it would not be to a man like Isandro Montero, she thought, summoning a mental picture of a man who would treat her as an equal, a man who would love the twins as much as she did. Her brow furrowed as her employer's face superimposed itself over her mental image, causing her eyes to drift across the room to where…he was no longer standing, and neither was the voluptuous vet.

Maybe she wouldn't have to put up with his aggravating company on the return journey…?

'Very wise. Of course, in my day it was different. You couldn't have sex outside marriage…if you were a nice girl, that is. We didn't have your freedom.'

'Actually, I don't believe in casual sex. Not for me anyway.'

Zoe was wondering why she felt the totally uncharacteristic need to discuss her feelings on the subject, when she realised that the old lady was not looking at her, but past her.

Her stomach quivered; she knew without turning who was standing there. Had he heard what she'd said?

His expression told her nothing.

'I was wondering if you are ready to go home?'

'I thought you'd already left.'

'What gave you that idea?'

'You make friends very easily.' The moment the remark left her lips she regretted it. She glanced guiltily over her shoulder to where a distinctive throaty laugh placed the vet. The woman had by all accounts been dumped by her husband of fifteen years for a younger model. Who only knew what insecurities her flirtatious behaviour masked?

Zoe felt a stab of shame. The woman was vulnerable and needed sympathy, not catty remarks behind her back. She actually deserved admiration—she had come out fighting after being kicked in the teeth.

'Actually, I don't.'

The comment brought her attention back to the tall Spaniard. It was clear he had not been canvassing the sympathy vote, simply stating a fact.

'I think you've made a few today.' Not a single person she had spoken to had had a bad word to say about him, and several had told her how lucky she was to be working for him.

Frankly, all the rave reviews were beginning to grate. People were so superficial they didn't look past the handsome face, perfect body and incredible smile. How many people but her had noticed him empty his glass of wine into the pot plant? Possibly the ones who hadn't taken their eyes off him all night? No, they acted as if he'd done them a favour by deigning to show up.

Zoe had been forced to bite her tongue on several occasions. She'd hoped he'd behave well and not upset anyone but she hadn't bargained on him turning the entire community into his devoted fans, who wouldn't believe that the man had sacked her within two minutes of setting eyes on her, that he was still looking for an excuse. Oh, yeah, he really was a great guy!

Friendship required trust. Isandro did not consider his inability to trust easily a character flaw; rather he valued his true friends all the more because he knew how rare they were.

His eyes brushed her face and he was struck again by the directness of her blue stare. 'I have many acquaintances, but few friends.'

And you're not even an acquaintance, Zoe. You're an employee. The taxi driver, not the date. 'I suppose it's difficult to tell if someone loves you or your bank balance.'

'I do not require love.' His brows lifted. 'Or are you talking about sex?'

'Sex?'

By some horrid twist of fate her yelped echo coincided with a lull in the conversation.

Oh, let me die now, Zoe thought as everyone turned to look at her.

'Strange how that always happens.'

'Not to me, it doesn't.' She struggled to see him as gaffe prone. 'If you'll excuse me, I see...' She made a vague gesture and headed across the room, accepting a few good-natured teasing comments as she went.

'What I need,' she muttered, 'is to cool down.'

'God, yes, it's warm in here, isn't it? Try one of these.' Once again her comment had reached more than its target audience—herself.

She looked at the tall glass that clinked with ice in

her hand, and opened her mouth to ask the person with the tray what it was, but he was gone.

Walking out through the open French windows, she sniffed it warily before picking out a floating strawberry to taste. The overwhelming flavour over and above the fruit was pineapple. It seemed innocuous enough, and a tentative sip reinforced this analysis. Satisfied it was one of the delicious mocktails that Chloe had made, she took a swallow.

She passed a group of men chatting, then wandered out onto the steep sloped lawn shaded by a row of tall oak trees in the field beyond. She sat down on the stump of a recently felled tree and swallowed some more of the fruit concoction. It was actually so delicious it made you wonder why people bothered with alcohol.

Tipping her head back to look at the starry sky, she thought that a person really should stop occasionally and just enjoy being alive. Lie on the grass and feel the earth…and why not?

Lying flat on her back, staring up at the stars, she began to hum a little tune softly to herself before she closed her eyes. Did she drift off?

'I can't, I really can't take this…' She half lifted her head at the sound of John's voice. Why was he ignoring her? She let out a small giggle and thought, Because he can't see me! I'm lying down.

'Yes, you can. Just think how much better it will be for Chloe and Hannah if they have you there to support them.'

This deeper voice with the sexy accent—she recognised that, too!

John and Isandro.

'I don't know what to say.' There was the sound of

crinkling paper and a gasp. 'Hell, that's too much…
no…I couldn't.'

'All tax-deductible. The only thing is that I'd prefer
this was private between you and Chloe and me. I'm
not comfortable with…'

'Understood. We won't forget this.'

Zoe lay there turning the conversation over in her
head. It took her foggy brain a little while to process
what she had overheard, but when she did tears of emotion sprang to her eyes. Isandro had just given John the
money he needed to join his family in Boston—and
more than enough, by the sound of it.

'That is so, so incredibly lovely!'

Isandro turned in time to see a figure rise from the
mist, hovering over the grass at ground level like some
sort of spectral vision.

'Zoe, what were you—?' The glorious goddess-like
figure flew towards him like a heat-seeking missile.
Madre di Dios, she was plastered!

'I heard everything, and I think you're w…won…
marvellous,' she declared earnestly.

'I think you should sit down.'

'I will, but first…' Standing on her tiptoes, she
reached up and took his face between her hands. 'You're
a very beautiful man and I've been mean to you, very
very very mean. I'm so ashamed! But that's all over.
You're a hero.' She leaned in closer, her soft breasts
crushing against the barrier of his chest as she fitted
her mouth to his.

The warm, soft mouth that pressed against his tasted
of booze. Standing rigid, his hands wide, he knew if he
touched that body, drunk or not, he would not be able
to stop himself having her right there on the grass. He

somehow managed to resist the blandishments of those luscious lips.

The effort brought a sheen of sweat to his skin and a great deal of pain to his groin, but he held out. Though the throaty little mewling sound of complaint she made in her throat when he didn't respond almost broke him.

'I think…I think I might sit down.' Clutching her head, and without warning, she sank gracefully to the grass and sat there cross-legged.

Isandro sighed and picked up the almost empty glass he saw there. He dipped his finger in the contents and licked it. A lot of fruit juices and vodka. Not a lot, but it was there.

Behind him he heard Chloe and John approach.

'Is that Zoe?'

'Hi, guys…yes, it's Zoe,' Zoe said, waving her hand. 'Chloe, you musht give me the recipe for that mocktail.'

'Oh, God!' Chloe gasped.

'He's not a monster, Chloe, he's a hero—did you know that? A real-life hero. He doesn't like me, though…sad.'

Isandro handed John the glass. 'It's pretty innocuous.'

'It doesn't matter. It's a metabolic thing with Zoe— she couldn't have known. What are we going to do with her? We've got a full house tonight, not even a spare sofa.'

Isandro saw them both looking at him.

Isandro, who never did anything he did not want to, heard himself say, 'I'll take her home. Don't worry, I've not been drinking.'

Once they got her in the car she immediately went to sleep curled up like a kitten, her mouth slightly open.

'Will she remember when she sobers up?'

'Oh, yes,' said Chloe, a wave of sadness crossing her face. 'Or that's what Laura always said.'

Isandro nodded. He was pleased with the reply. It only seemed fair that she would remember, because he surely would. It was hard to forget the extremely painful cost of being a hero; he was pretty sure that the resulting frustration would cost him a night's sleep.

Zoe continued to sleep like a baby all the way back to the hall, which was good because he wasn't sure his response would be quite so noble if she made another attempt to jump him.

When he opened the passenger door the cool night air woke her. He was amazed and relieved that she had recovered enough to make it up the stone steps to the flat without any assistance from him, but he followed behind just in case.

'You'll be all right?'

She looked at him blearily. 'I think there was something in my drink.'

'Vodka.'

'Oh, God! I thought it… Sorry…' She had no idea what she was apologising for, but it seemed safe to assume that there was something. 'Goodnight, Mr Montero.'

Isandro watched the door close. He was quite pleased with his demotion back to monster. Monsters were not obliged to behave with honour—they could take what they wanted.

CHAPTER SIX

ROBBED OF HIS early morning ride after discovering his horse had pulled a shoe, Isandro returned to the house, leaving the stallion in the capable hands of his groom. An hour on a cross-trainer in the gym did not really touch his frustration levels.

Heading downstairs after his shower, he reached the galleried landing when he almost fell over her.

'What the hell are you doing?' If she appeared at all this morning he had imagined she would be nursing a hangover, not on her knees singing to herself.

Seemingly oblivious to his presence, she continued to bang the hand-held vacuum into a crevice under a console table, still humming along to the music playing in her ears. Her singing voice was totally flat but her behind was not. Isandro, who had opened his mouth to deliver his demand again, closed it as she reached further forward, the action causing her delightful bottom to tighten against the pair of jeans she was wearing.

Lust hit him like a hammer blow to the chest. Beside his sensual mouth a nerve quivered, beating out an erratic tattoo as in his head he saw himself dropping down beside her, tipping her onto her back... His chest lifted as he sucked in a deep breath and swore through gritted teeth. He had never experienced this degree of blind, relentless lust before. Not even in his teens had he felt so obsessed.

He swore under his breath and bellowed, 'What the hell are you doing?'

One hand on the floor to steady herself, Zoe turned her head, a questioning furrow in her smooth brow. She saw Isandro and her half-smile faded with a speed that under other circumstances he might have found amusing.

'It is always nice when people are glad to see me,' he muttered under his breath.

'Pardon…' Zoe lowered her voice, murmuring a self-conscious, 'Sorry.' She pulled the earphones out of her ears and looked up at the figure who towered over her. 'I didn't see you there.' She stopped herself from asking whether there was anything she could do for him, afraid that he might tell her—and even more afraid that she might deliver his request.

She was probably worrying over nothing. Last night he hadn't even kissed her back.

It was the ultimate humiliation. She had offered herself up on a platter and he had said no, thank you, and she remembered every mortifying, cringeworthy detail. It had been about three a.m. when she'd sat bolt upright in bed and it had all come rushing back to her.

Unable to resist the masochistic compulsion to relive the scene over and over, by this morning she didn't see how she could face him. And now it felt just as awful as she had imagined.

Should she mention last night? Wait for him to? Or should she pretend it never happened?

'I said what the hell are you doing?'

'I'm vacuuming the carpet.' She held out the hand-held vacuum she was using to reach the crevices, flicking the switch into the on position to demonstrate as she got up from her knees.

'I can see what you're doing.' He reached over and flicked the switch off. 'What I want to know is why?'

'Susie couldn't come in this morning.'

'That does not answer my question, and who the hell is Susie?'

'Susie is one of the cleaning staff. She lives in the village.'

He folded his arms across his chest and looked unimpressed by her explanation. 'Will you stop waving that thing at me?'

Zoe lowered the vacuum, but lifted her free hand to shade her eyes from the shaft of strong morning sun that shone in from the tall floor-length window behind Isandro, framing his tall figure in a golden haze of light. As if he needed any help to look as though he'd just stepped down from Mount Olympus! It was like a massive conspiracy to turn her into some sex-starved bimbo.

'You're really not a morning person, are you?'

A gleam flashed in his dark eyes. 'I've never had any complaints.'

It took a few seconds, but when the penny dropped her face flamed. She brought down her lashes in a protective sweep to shield her eyes. Head down, she swept off the scarf she had tied over her hair. Ruffling it with her hand as it slipped down her back, she struggled to maintain a professional attitude given the reel of lurid images now playing in her head.

Isandro felt the hunger flare, his body hardening as he watched the river of glossy silk settle down her narrow back. The sexy little black outfit was gone and she was back in jeans, complete with a tear in one knee and belt loops he could have hooked his fingers into and jerked her… The effort to suppress his lustful imagination drew a short harsh rasp from his throat.

'This still doesn't tell me why I find you down on your hands and knees like some…'

Her head lifted; her blue eyes shone with anger. 'Servant?' she bit back. 'Maybe because I am.'

'You are the housekeeper.'

She shrugged, not sure why he was making such a big thing of this. It wasn't as if the workings of a vacuum cleaner were alien to her. 'Call it multitasking…'

'I call it inappropriate. What sort of first impression would it give if I had walked in with a group of important guests and the first thing they see is the housekeeper down on her knees?' He shook his head.

'You didn't walk in with…'

Isandro's expression made her wish she had held her tongue.

'It is totally inappropriate to your position here.'

'What was I meant to do? Drag poor Susie in with her abscessed tooth? Her mother says the poor girl is in agony.'

'You were meant to delegate.' It amazed him that she had not grasped this basic precept.

'I don't like telling people what to do.' Zoe found it was easier and less stressful to do things herself.

'Delegation is part of your job. Scrubbing floors is not.'

His coldness hit her like a slap in the face. 'I wasn't…' She bit her tongue and bowed her head.

The show of humility did not fool Isandro for one second. He knew full well it was an act. She was about as humble as a battle cruiser.

'Part of your job is also learning the difference between showing sympathy and being a soft touch.'

Zoe's head lifted at the suggestion. 'I'm not a soft touch!' she protested indignantly.

'People take advantage of you.' His annoyance that she was either unable or unwilling to see this was etched on his hard features.

'You didn't!' She closed her eyes and lifted a hand to her head, let her chin fall to her chest and thought, Please let me die now. 'Sorry. I didn't mean to say that. It just sort of slipped out.'

'Not because I did not want to, if that is what is bothering you. Did you get any sleep?' The violet smudges under her eyes showed up clear against her translucent skin, as did the handful of freckles across the bridge of her nose.

She nodded. 'And I woke with a bit of a headache.'

His mobile lips twitched. 'Called a hangover.'

Zoe shuddered as she got to her feet. 'I can't imagine why people drink.'

'Not everyone has your zero tolerance. For some people it's their drug of choice, and it's legal.'

'What's yours, or don't you need one? Sorry…I keep forgetting… Can I take your order for dinner, sir?'

'You can't go from trying to kiss my face off to calling me sir. Neither are what I expect of my housekeeper. I will settle for a happy medium.'

The mortified colour rushed to her cheeks as she pressed her teeth into her full lower lip. 'I am sorry for last night. I really am. But what you did for Chloe and John, that was…very kind.'

His features froze. 'That stays within these walls. Is that understood?'

Before she could reply to this terse warning, the front door swung open and the twins rushed in. At least Georgie rushed. Harry walked with his nose in a book.

'No, not here. I've told you, the flat—'

'We know. You forgot to put the key under the mat.' Georgie looked at Isandro and grinned. 'We have to keep out of your way.' She wrinkled her nose. 'Don't you like kids?'

'It depends on the kid.' He strolled across to the boy, a skinny child with strawberry-blond hair. 'You're Harry.'

Harry nodded.

'Run along, children.' She pulled the key fob out of her pocket and tossed it to Georgie. 'I've left you some sandwiches for eleven. I'll be over at lunchtime.'

'What's that you're reading?' Isandro looked at the title on the spine. 'You like the stars?'

Of course he did. Skinny, undersized boys with books and no friends always did. Isandro knew because he had been one himself. In his case he had grown twelve inches at sixteen and gone from being the despised wimp to the jock that everybody wanted to know.

Harry nodded, his face suffused with pink.

'On the wall on my desk I have a photo of the Horsehead nebula. Have you seen it?'

'We're not allowed in the house. Especially your office.' So Harry was not a rule-breaker. 'I like looking at the night sky, but I want to be an astrophysicist when I grow up.'

Zoe blinked. This was news to her.

'Cool,' Isandro said.

'Run along, children.' She was both pleased and relieved when they both did as she asked—with Georgie, you never knew.

'You, too,' Isandro said when they had left. 'Ring the agency first and get a replacement for…whatever her name is.'

'Susie.'

'Then take the rest of the day off. I'm off to London.'

She assumed when he left that they would not see him for some time. She had understood that this was the norm. But over the next few weeks he kept arriving unexpectedly, sometimes spending a night, sometimes not even that long.

At first mystified by his behaviour, she realised that he was hoping to catch her out, though it did seem a lot of trouble to go to. Never knowing when he would turn up made it difficult to relax…and though trying to catch her out made sense, it didn't explain the occasion he brought Harry a book full of photos of galaxies and nebulae.

The little boy looked forward to his visits…but was he the only one? Why would anyone look forward to a visit from someone who blew hot and cold? Who was cold and remote one moment and relaxed and friendly the next?

As they approached the crossroad Alex slowed for a red light. Isandro shut down the tablet and looked through the window, dragging a hand through his dark hair. He had planned to spend the weekend in London, but at the last moment had decided to drive down to Ravenwood, reasoning he could spend the weekend reading the report without distractions. Sure, no distractions at all, mocked the voice in his head.

'Is that…?'

Pushing away the thought, Isandro followed the direction of his driver's nod. 'Yes, it is, Alex,' he confirmed.

'Are they alone?'

Isandro, who had been looking for that glossy dark head attached to a body he had spent some time thinking about, nodded. All right, not just some time—a lot of time. He was finding it pretty much impossible to think about anything but his housekeeper, who did not know the meaning of 'unobtrusive'.

'It looks like it.'

Which in itself was strange. While Zoe Grace might not be about to win any prizes for her housekeeping skills, when it came to her youthful charges she took the role extremely seriously. He could not imagine her allowing the twins to wander around town unaccompanied.

'Shall I pull over?'

Isandro nodded and unclipped his seat belt as the car drew to a halt on a double yellow. When he reached the twins they were still on the pavement. They appeared to be arguing—and more significantly there was still no sign of their aunt.

It was Harry who saw him first. Seeing the relief on his freckled face, Isandro experienced an emotional tightening in his chest.

Isandro controlled his strong inclination to hug him, aware that the boy had already measured him up as an unlikely male role model. It would be nothing short of cruel to allow the boy to become reliant and then fade out of his life.

Instead he gave the boy a manly pat on his painfully skinny shoulder. The kid could do a lot better than him for a father substitute. Did his aunt's determination to sacrifice her own needs for her charges extend to her choice of partner? Would she choose the 'good father' material over a good lover? The woman was probably determined to be a martyr. She'd probably end up alone

or with some boring loser whom she deemed solid and
responsible.

'We've lost Aunty Zoe. Actually, we ran away and
now we're lost, too.'

For which Isandro correctly read his sister had run
and he had followed. There was no doubting who the
dominant and reckless twin in this equation was.

'We're not lost,' his sister interrupted. 'And if you
hadn't made me come back…'

'It was stealing!'

'It was not stealing. We were bringing it back, and
that's borrowing, isn't it?' she appealed to Isandro for
support.

'Borrowing without permission is stealing. And
running away from your aunt is… Have you any idea
how worried she will be?' An image of a terrified Zoe
flashed into his head and he hardened his heart against
their stricken expressions. 'She will be frantic!'

The twins exchanged worried glances.

'We didn't think,' Georgie admitted.

Isandro steeled himself against the quiver in her
voice and struggled to maintain his stern expression
as he ushered them towards the car. The sniff was too
much for the ruthless captain of industry to withstand.

'Don't worry,' he soothed. 'I'll ring your aunt and
let her know—'

'You can't,' they said in unison.

He shook his head. 'Why can't I?'

'Her phone wasn't charged. It died on her when Aunt
Chloe was talking.'

He exhaled. If he had been in Zoe's position—which
was unlikely, because not only would he not have let
his phone battery run down, he certainly wouldn't have

taken on responsibility for this pair of demons—he would now be retracing his footsteps.

The demons regarded him with the expressions that said they had total faith that he would come up with a solution.

'Right, then, where were you when you ran away, and where were you before that?'

The terrible clawing panic in her stomach when she had turned to tell the twins to get a wriggle or the car would be clamped would stay with Zoe for ever. When she found them she would never let them out of her sight again…always supposing she didn't throttle them.

She jogged along the pavements, retracing her footsteps, stopping occasionally to ask people if they had seen two children, oblivious to the stares that followed her progress. She kept telling herself over and over like a mantra, Tomorrow this will just be a memory. I'll laugh about it with Chloe.

Tomorrow seemed a hell of a long way away, though, and Chloe was still in Boston!

By the time Zoe had worked her way to the boat-hire booth her heart was thudding so hard she felt as if it would crack her ribs. She was only kept going by the strong conviction that had gradually taken hold that the twins were out there on the river.

It was so obvious. Why hadn't she smelt a rat when the wilful youngster who would never take no for an answer had not argued or even tried to cajole when she'd refused to take them out in a kayak. Now of course it made sense. Georgie hadn't suddenly become malleable, she'd simply cut out the arguing, and she'd dragged Harry with her.

The ticket booth was closed, but before a frantic Zoe

could think of what to do next a boy came around the corner carrying a padlock and a large bunch of keys. He removed the earphones from his ears when he saw her.

'Sorry, we're closed.'

'I'm looking for my niece and nephew,' she said before he could put the earphones back in. 'They're seven years old. I think they might have gone out in one of your kayaks.' The effort to stay calm and not sound like an unbalanced lunatic made her voice shake, but she was pretty proud of her effort.

'Sorry, we're closed.'

She watched, her pent-up fear tipping over into rage, as he began to insert the earphones.

Her eyes narrowed, she stepped forward and snatched them out, drawing a yelp from the boy. 'My niece and nephew—they wanted to go out in a kayak. Have you seen them?' she yelled, fighting the impulse to shake the information from the stupid boy who was backing away from her.

'I don't know what your problem is, miss, but the public are not allowed here. There's a sign. It's health and safety.' He pointed to a no-entry sign on the wall of the booth.

Give me strength! 'I've been trying to tell you what the problem is. I'm looking for two children, a boy and girl. So high...' She held her palm at the appropriate height. 'They wanted to go out...' She closed her eyes, seeing Georgie's expression when she had refused their request. God, but she really should have seen this coming. 'I think they might be out there.' She swallowed as her eyes moved to the horizon where the grey water of the river met the darker grey sky. 'In one of your canoes.'

'No children allowed in the kayaks without a responsible adult. Besides, we're closing early—there's a storm coming.' His phone rang and he wandered away with it pressed to his ear.

When Zoe took the situation into her own hands the youth was close enough for her to hear him say, 'No way...outside the pub at five.' But not close enough, thanks to a tree, for him to see her wade into the shallow water and push out a stray canoe that had not yet been dragged onto the artificial beach.

She'd been kayaking before, she reminded herself as she managed on the third try to clamber into the swaying boat. Of course on that occasion Laura had been paddling, and she'd been only five years old, but this was a detail. How hard could it be?

Five minutes later Zoe had gone several hundred yards. But she had no idea whether she was heading in the right direction. She didn't have the faintest idea where they were! She was acting on intuition, but wasn't that another name for blind panic?

She squared her shoulders and dipped her oar into the water. She had to stay positive.

The obvious sensible thing to do would have been to go to the police...so why was she just realising that now when she was literally up the creek? Then the rain started.

The downpour was of biblical flood proportions. Within two minutes she was drenched. Her hair plastered against her skull; the water streamed down her face, making it hard to see. More worrying than her wet clothes was the water sloshing around in the bottom of the canoe.

Trying to see past the rain that was now being driven horizontally by a gale-force wind into her face, she recalled the weather man's prediction of light showers and laughed.

The hysterical sound was whipped away by the wind, which was again blowing her in the wrong direction. Head bent, she paddled hard but, despite the fact her arms felt as though they were falling off, she made no headway. She put oar down for a moment to ease the burning pain in the muscles of her upper arms and shoulders, flexing her stiff fingers as she balanced it across the canoe.

She saw it happening as if in slow motion. She lunged forward, one arm outstretched and the other holding onto the edge of the wildly rocking kayak. Just as her fingers touched the oar a current carried it away out of reach. Her centre of gravity lost, Zoe struggled to pull back, but just when it seemed inevitable she would be pitched into the grey swirling water she managed to recover, collapsing back with a sob of laughing relief into the canoe.

It hardly seemed possible that a couple of weeks ago she had decided that this stretch of the river, with its series of shallow waterfalls and half-submerged stone slabs where people sunbathed and children paddled in shallow pools, made for a really lovely afternoon stroll. Pretty, but not dramatic.

Today it did not lack drama. The river was wild white water, full of dark swirls and hidden obstacles. The boulders she strove to avoid were only just visible above the foaming white water. Zoe paddled with her hands but soon recognised it was hopeless. The kayak would never survive.

Feeling surprisingly calm in the face of impending disaster, Zoe was in the middle of telling herself she was overreacting when the kayak hit a submerged rock.

The jarring motion as it glanced off sent the flimsy craft rocking sideways. Thrown off balance, Zoe lurched sideways, throwing her body weight sharply to one side to right the canoe. For a moment it seemed to work, but it was hit by an extra-strong squall of wind and simply carried on going.

This time there was no reprieve and the immersion in the shockingly cold grey water took her breath. For a moment she panicked, flailing around blindly as she tried to free herself from the upturned canoe, hampered by clothes that dragged her downwards. When she did she surfaced almost immediately, choking as she gasped for air. Behind her the canoe was making its way upside down through the churning white water, before it vanished over the top of a weir.

That could have been me.

But it won't be. The twins would be all alone, they need me. Focusing on that one thought and not the cold seeping into her bones, she struck out strongly, aiming for the opposite bank, where she would be likely to see someone who could raise the emergency services. Zoe was a strong swimmer with no fear of the water, but even so the going was tough and her progress, hampered by her clothes, was torturously slow.

As she swam she was distantly aware of a sound above the echoing roar of the water and her own heartbeat but she didn't allow it to distract her. She couldn't stop. She had to keep going. Every second she wasted the twins could be… No, she wouldn't think like that. She needed to focus.

'Focus, Zoe,' she said to herself—but the water filled her open mouth and, choking, her head went under.

As she was lifted unceremoniously out of the water she continued to kick feebly, right up to the moment she was hauled over and left utterly disorientated in an inelegant heap in the bottom of what seemed to be a small motorboat.

She grunted as the boat swerved, sharply throwing her against a wooden seat. The locker underneath was open and a child's inflatable vest spilled out. Oh, God, the children were out there somewhere!

She began to cry great silent, gulping sobs that racked her entire body.

Once the boat was away from the immediate danger of hitting the rocks and in the relative safety of open water, Isandro cut back on the throttle and turned his attention to the sodden bundle of misery sitting in the bottom of the boat.

He experienced a gripping sensation in his chest almost as strong as the one he had felt when he had seen her head vanish under the grey water—though without the soul-destroying terror.

'What the hell did you think you were doing?' he blasted.

She recognised the voice but was convinced she was dreaming. Except in her dreams he hadn't sounded angry... Zoe dragged her hair back from her face. My God, it was him!

It was Isandro! Looking furious, very wet and not dressed for sailing!

'Isandro...how...?' She stopped. It didn't matter how he came to be here. 'No,' she croaked, grabbing at his leg and tugging. 'I've got to go back.'

'You want me to throw you back in the water? Do not tempt me,' he growled, seeing her vanish beneath the grey water again and feeling the visceral kick of fear in his gut again. He never wanted to relive the moment when he saw her go under.

'No, Isandro, you don't understand! I think the twins…'

Some of the anger died from his face as he placed his hands on her shoulders and dragged her up onto the wooden bench seat beside him. Shaking so hard that her teeth chattered, she transferred her desperate grip to his jacket. Frantic to communicate the urgency of the situation, she grabbed his lapels and pulled.

'The twins—'

'No, Zoe—'

'Listen, will you?'

He caught hold of her hands. 'The twins are with Alex, who is not, I admit, the most likely child-minder. In fact it is highly likely that he is even now teaching them to play poker. But they are safe.'

Zoe blinked as she shook her head, trying to clear the fog in her brain. Why couldn't she think straight?

'The twins are all right?' Without waiting for a reply, she pushed her head into his chest and began to cry in earnest.

His arms went out wide as he looked down at the head of tangled hair. His anger had vanished and he refused to recognise the feelings that had rushed in to fill the vacuum as tenderness. Her cries tore at him; finally the mewling sounds as she burrowed in deeper snapped his resistance and his arms closed around her. He lifted her body into the warmth of his.

'*Madre di Dios*, you're an imbecile, a raving… You make me want, you make me feel—' He stopped and thought, you make me feel…too much. Digging his fingers into her wet hair, he stroked her scalp and let her cry herself out.

He had stopped resisting the sexual desire he felt for her. Physical desire was normal, not complicated. It was something that he understood and accepted, not a weakness. It did not require that he surrender any control; it was not about trusting. He wanted her on his terms—he would have her on his terms. He would not fall into the trap of allowing emotions to cloud his judgement.

He was not his father.

Finally peeling herself away, Zoe straightened up, blinking like someone waking up.

'I'm...' She gulped and shook her head again as he removed his jacket and draped it around her shoulders.

'It's wet but better than nothing.'

The lining was still warm. 'Sorry,' she said, not meeting his eyes. She was too embarrassed by her total meltdown. Why did she always make a total fool of herself around him?

He kept one hand on her shoulder, the other on the tiller, guiding the boat towards the mooring.

'Sorry...I...I thought...' Her lips quivered as she struggled for composure. 'I thought they'd gone on the river...' She gave a frown, trying to remember the sequence of events as much for her own benefit as for his. 'We'd been to the craft fair in the park. When we started back it was late and I thought they were with me. I was running—they were going to clamp the car...' Wrong tense, she realised, they probably already had clamped the car. But having faced what she had thought was a real disaster, car clamping faded into insignificance.

She pushed the wet strands of hair from her eyes and pressed the heels of both hands to her temples before slowly turning her head to stare at him.

'What the hell made you go out on the water? Are you suicidal?'

'The twins—'

'And what would have happened to the twins if you

had drowned?' Her horrified little gasp felt like a knife sliding between his ribs, but Isandro didn't allow his expression to soften as Zoe went several shades whiter. The only colour in her face was her dramatic sapphire eyes and the blue discoloration around her lips.

'I was not going to drown,' she protested through chattering teeth.

Faced with this refusal to acknowledge, let alone show any remorse for, the total bloody selfishness of her reckless actions, Isandro was tempted to throw her back in the water.

'My mistake,' he gritted through clenched teeth. 'I can see now that you had the situation totally under control.'

Unable to tear her eyes off the nerve that was throbbing in his lean cheek, she shook her head. 'No, really, I'm a strong swimmer...obviously I'm grateful but...'

'But really you didn't need my help at all.' He gave a shrug and, cutting the engine, steered the gliding boat expertly between the moored vessels.

Before Zoe could respond he leapt out of the boat, landing lithely on the wooden pier where he proceeded to tie off the boat.

'I really am grateful, Isandro. It was really lucky you had a boat.'

'I don't have a boat.' A faint smile flickered across his face. 'Not here anyway.'

'But this?' The boat wobbled as she got to her feet. With a grimace Zoe sat down again abruptly. Her knees were still shaking and she had no desire to repeat her earlier immersion.

Considering the question, Isandro thought of Georgie's defence and smiled to himself. 'I borrowed it.'

'You stole it!' she cried, but then, not wanting to

come across as ungrateful again, she added, 'But I suppose it was an emergency.'

'What made you think they were heading for the
river?'

'Georgie wanted to go out in a canoe and I said no.
We really didn't have time...'

'You do not have to justify your decisions to me,
Zoe.'

'Georgie is...'

'Determined?'

Zoe acknowledged the dry suggestion with a shrug.
'She didn't fight it, which isn't like her. Saying no is
like a red rag to her. I should have known.' After a frac-
tional pause that was not lost on Isandro, she accepted
the hand he held out to her and rose unsteadily to her
feet. The boat swayed again and she lurched, making
an awkward leap as he tugged.

As she landed clumsily on the boarded walkway Zoe
heard a splash. Letting go of Isandro's hand, she twisted
around and saw the jacket that had been draped over
her shoulders floating on the water.

'Oh, God!' On an adrenaline high still, she moved
quickly without thinking and almost reached it.

An arm like a steel band around her waist hauled her
back from the edge.

'What the hell are you doing, woman? Do you have
some sort of death wish? I have to tell you once is my
limit when it comes to fishing suicidal maniacs out of
the drink.'

Zoe didn't struggle against the arms banding her.
She leaned back into his big, solid, hard body, allowing herself the luxury of feeling safe. She wasn't going
to drown and the twins were all right.

She was still shaking with the chill of the ice in her

veins but in the shelter of his arms she was protected from the wind. The feeling of security was an illusion but as illusions went this one felt good.

'Your lovely jacket.'

Isandro rested his chin on the top of her head, closed his eyes and shook his head… Jacket!

'I have others.' The woman was in need of professional help. He shifted his stance to ease the pressure on his groin and thought, *Dios*, she is not the only one!

CHAPTER SEVEN

HER LIPS TWITCHED faintly. 'The man who has everything.'

'You read the article.'

Two weeks earlier a Sunday paper had decided to dedicate half their glossy supplement to him. *The Man with the Midas Touch* was to his mind shockingly unoriginal and a perfect example of the dumbing-down of the press...ten pages that said nothing new.

He had everything? He supposed he did. But to Isandro his wealth represented not luxury or self-indulgence but the freedom to live his life just as he wanted. Did that make him selfish? Did it make him happy...? Was anyone happy?

He shook his head. *Dios*, this was not the time for a philosophical debate. This was definitely a time for action, decisive action, and the priority was warming up Zoe before she became hypothermic.

It did not take him long to weigh the options. Decision-making was, as the article author had suggested, Isandro's area of expertise.

'Chloe gave me her copy,' she admitted between chattering teeth. 'The entire village bought the paper. They were sold out. You're a local hero...for real now...'

'Even if you didn't need my help.'

Her lips twisted into a grimace. 'I really am grateful... Stop! You can't—!'

Isandro took no notice of her protests as he began to
stride up the path from the river.

'I can walk! Put me down...please put me down.'

He flashed her a look. 'You won't jump back in the
river?'

'Don't be stupid.'

'Seriously, though, you're chilled through. You need
to dry off and warm up.'

'I need to see the twins.'

'You think that's a good idea, looking this way?
You'll scare the life out of them,' he predicted. 'Which
in Georgie's case might not be such a bad thing. But
seeing you like that is likely to give Harry nightmares
for a month.' He arched a brow. 'What, no "you know
nothing about children, so butt out"?'

Zoe shook her head, biting her lower lip to stop it
quivering. He had summed up the twins pretty accu-
rately.

'You're right. It's me who knows nothing about
bringing up children,' she wailed.

A hissing sound of exasperation left his lips as he
hefted her a little higher with apparent ease. On another
occasion when she wasn't busy contemplating her failure at parenting, Zoe might have been impressed. She
was not exactly petite. 'I find it infinitely preferable
when you are defensive and rude. This self-flagellation
is boring.'

Finding herself unexpectedly placed on her feet, Zoe
waited a moment for her head to stop spinning before
she raised her swimming eyes to him, her quivering lips
tightening. 'Oh, I'm so sorry I bored you.'

He smiled. 'Better,' he approved. 'Now, come on.

What you need is a hot bath, a brandy—or maybe not brandy, you might kiss the concierge—and a change of clothes before you return to your niece and nephew.' Placing a hand on her elbow, he guided her past the selection of gleaming top-of-the-range cars parked in front of the hotel whose gardens went down to the river.

'Nice thought, but unless you have them in your pocket...' She tried a smile but her teeth were chattering too hard. Every squelchy footstep was uncomfortable. 'Where are you parked?'

'I'm not. Alex took the twins back to Ravenwood. I'll ring him, and he'll tell the twins we'll be back later.'

Belatedly Zoe realised his intention.

'You're kidding—no way!' She shook her head and shrugged off the guiding hand on her shoulder as she stared up at the recently restored art deco façade of the five-star hotel with a reputation that drew a lot of people to the area.

She'd often thought it would be nice to sample the food there—but not looking like this!

'Why would I be kidding?'

'You can't just walk in there looking like this.' She glanced at him and made the mental adjustment that while he could, she couldn't. Isandro's clothes might be sodden, but he had not been swimming, and even if he had, she acknowledged reluctantly, he would still have the presence to make any door open for him.

'Why not?'

'Well, I don't know what the dress code is but I'm pretty sure this isn't it.' She held her hands wide to reveal her sodden muddy clothes. 'They'll throw me out. They won't even let me walk across the hallowed threshold.' She took a step backwards, shaking her head in response to the gleam in his eyes. 'And before you suggest it, being carried won't change anything.'

Except possibly her pulse rate. She knew that later that night she was going to remember every little detail of being carried in his arms, which would have made her a disgrace to modern liberated womanhood had she not suspected that inside most modern independent women lurked a secret desire to be swept off her feet. And if a man like Isandro was doing the sweeping, she suspected that few would find the experience objectionable.

She couldn't help but wonder what it would have felt like if his motivation had not been totally practical—a scenario that would have required her not looking like a drowned rat and for him to not be her boss...

But this is the real world. And once more, as far as he's concerned, you've shown yourself to be a pain in the backside.

'I was not about to offer. The fact is you're not as light as you look, especially wet.' His grin widened in response to her indignant squeak. 'Who exactly do you think is going to stop us?'

Zoe, who felt oddly light-headed, didn't react to the question. 'Just take me home, Isandro.' She clutched her spinning head, suddenly feeling nauseous as frames of the past hour flashed before her eyes. 'I turned around and they weren't there, and I...'

Observing the blue discoloration of her beautiful lips, Isandro released a hissed imprecation from between clenched teeth before taking her chin firmly between his thumb and forefinger. He turned her face up to his. The problem was not so much her imminent collapse or her stubborn refusal to enter the hotel as his struggle to maintain the necessary level of objectivity.

'Look, adrenaline was the only thing that kept you on your feet, and it's crashed.' So had she.

'I do feel a bit...'

'You look a bit, too.' His glance drifted over the curve of her cheek, delineated by classic high cheekbones. Her perfect skin was marble pale, the only colour in her face was supplied by her eyes, which stood out as a flash of startling colour in a monochrome film.

'You didn't succeed in drowning yourself, so now you are inviting hypothermia.' The effort to conceal the concern her fragility evoked in him made Isandro's voice cold and flat. 'We need to warm you up, get you out of those wet clothes.'

The words had barely left his lips before a stream of images that Isandro could have done without flashed through his head. He was regaining his shattered control when a sly voice reminded him that skin-to-skin contact was a well-known treatment for hypothermia His control went out of the window!

Even a sub-zero body temperature was not going to save him from the spike of lust that hardened his already half-aroused body. *Madre di Dios*, he was turning into a sad adult version of some sex-starved teenager! For a man who prided himself on his self-control it was...not tolerable. The only thing that was going to restore him to sanity was spending a week in bed with Zoe Grace.

He exhaled. The first step to solving a problem was admitting it existed. This he had already done. The next step was to work out a strategy. He needed to treat this problem like any other and apply logic and cool objectivity. The problem was that where his housekeeper was concerned he struggled to think objectively, and as for logic—he'd just stolen a boat, for God's sake!

'I know what you're thinking,' Zoe said, looking at

him over the soggy tissue she had produced and was now sniffing loudly into.

The prosaic action was rather touching, but not touching enough to hold his attention when the competition was the heaving contours of her breasts under the thin layer of drenched cotton through which her peaked nipples were clearly outlined.

'I rather doubt that, *querida*.' His thoughts were pretty rampant.

'You think I'm not fit to look after a cat, let alone two children,' she wailed, in full self-pity mode.

He did not respond with any comforting denials, but glanced rather pointedly at his watch.

This callous behaviour drew a hiss of annoyance from between her chattering teeth. 'So sorry—am I keeping you?' she said, wondering why she had thought for a second that her problems would do anything but bore the pants off him.

Her eyes dropped, running the length of his long legs, then making the journey back once she had reached his now muddy boots. She could see that, for some women, getting his pants off by whatever method would be considered a good result but she... Who was she kidding? Even on the brink of what felt like imminent hypothermia she could not stop lusting after him.

'Not at all. Feel free to go ahead and beat yourself up,' he encouraged. Zoe tried to bear her teeth in a snarl but she was shaking too hard and she bit her lip instead, drawing a pinprick of blood and his disturbing dark stare. 'But do you mind if we continue this conversation indoors?'

Zoe glanced at the hotel entrance. The golden light shining through the doors looked warm and inviting... and she was very cold. She lifted a hand to the hair that was plastered to her skull. His was, too, but in his case the effect was not drowned rat.

'I can't.' It was an invitation for him to contradict her, and he accepted it.

'Can and will,' he said, catching hold of her hand. 'We need a room.' On so many levels they needed a room!

'You can't walk in and book a room for a few hours,' she said, pointing out the obvious. At least it seemed obvious to her.

'Why not? People do. Oh, I see.' He laughed. 'You're afraid your reputation will be ruined if you're seen going into a hotel room with a man.'

'Of course not. And nobody is going to think that you…me…we…unless you normally have to half drown a woman before she'll have sex with you.'

'Not so far.'

Before she could interpret the odd inflection in his voice he had tightened his grip and virtually dragged her up the shallow flight of steps.

The warmth inside the hotel foyer hit her like a wall. So did the stares. It seemed to Zoe that a thousand eyes followed their progress.

But, as he predicted, nobody attempted to stop them, though it would have taken a very brave person to approach Isandro, who had adopted what she privately called his 'to hell with the lot of you' expression. His antagonism was probably aimed at her. This couldn't have been the way he had intended to spend his day, but the people who cleared a path for him weren't to know that.

It was amazing, she reflected enviously, as at her side Isandro gave every appearance of being genuinely oblivious to the stares and hushed comments that followed their progress across the lobby. But then he was probably used to people staring. And who could blame them? she thought as she directed a covert sideways look through her lashes at his stern profile, dishevelled but beautiful.

Even as someone who had previously not been totally sold on the dark brooding aura, she was willing to admit he was a fantastically good-looking man, who didn't just have the perfect face and body but also the indefinable extra factor. Confidence, sheer arrogance— whatever it was, he had it, and being extremely damp with his clothes spattered with mud and badly in need of a shave did not lessen it. The liberal sprinkling of stubble on his jaw lent an extra layer of air of danger, and did not exactly diminish his appeal.

So who could blame people for staring? she thought, making a conscious effort to emulate some of his attitude. And promptly tripping over the sodden hem of her jeans. It would happen when one stared at a man and not where one was going!

The ripple of laughter at her near pratfall brought her chin up. Trotting now to keep up with Isandro, Zoe suddenly thought, To hell with this! and gave the person who had laughed an enquiring look, even managing to inject a little hauteur into it. The culprit looked away before she did.

Zoe smiled and looked ahead. No amount of shoulder hunching or wishful thinking was going to make her vanish so she might as well borrow some of Isandro's attitude, even if she couldn't carry it off with his style.

'May I help you, sir?' A man whose lapel badge identified him as the manager intercepted them when they were halfway across the lobby. He guided them towards the reception desk where the eager-to-please attentiveness continued.

The people behind the reception desk almost fell over themselves being helpful to the point of obsequiousness, but Isandro, who was firing off his list of requirements, didn't appear to notice. This was probably his life, she mused, giving impossible orders and having people fall over themselves to deliver.

After a few moments he turned to a shivering Zoe. He hadn't forgotten her after all. 'I'll be up presently. You go along.'

The manager reappeared holding a large blanket, which, on an approving nod from Isandro, he draped almost reverentially over Zoe's shoulders. 'Jeremy will show you the way, miss.'

Jeremy, neat in his uniform, nodded and motioned for her to precede him into the glass lift that he explained was for the exclusive use of the penthouse. Penthouse... Zoe almost laughed. She was well aware that if she hadn't been Isandro's satellite she wouldn't have got through the front door, let alone been given this VIP treatment.

In the second before the doors closed Isandro turned, zeroing in on her like radar. His smile flickered as he caught her eye and tipped his dark head.

As the door swished closed her heart was still beating fast. The moment, a mere nothing in reality, felt strangely intimate to Zoe, as if they were exchanging some private secret.

'I had a slight boating accident.' A half-smile flickered across her face as she realised that if Isandro had been there he would have been mystified and probably irritated by her need to explain herself to a hotel employee. Jeremy made a sympathetic noise but did not volunteer an opinion.

As soon as the door to the suite was closed, Zoe explored her palatial surroundings only as far as the bathroom that adjoined one of the bedrooms, conscious that she was leaving a trail of wet, muddy footprints.

The place was…well, wow! She had only seen hotel rooms like this in films. It felt like the set of an old movie, and she ought to be wearing a long slinky gown.

Instead she was wearing…ugh! She glanced down at her ruined clothes, her lip curling in distaste. As she peeled off the soggy garments she made an active choice not to look at herself in the mirror. It wasn't easy, as the room was full of them. Definitely a room for someone with no body issues, she thought, shedding her clothes with relief.

Free of her clothes, she did glance in passing at her reflection in a mirror. She saw long legs, a slightly rounded stomach… While she would have liked more inches up top and a bit more flesh to cover her prominent hipbones, Zoe was happy enough with her figure.

Would a man be so happy?

Her eyes half closed, her stomach muscles quivered faintly as she stroked a hand slowly down her flank. Would her first lover think her hips too narrow, or find her bottom too—she moved her hand over the curve and stopped. Her hand fell away. She was shocked— the man she saw in her mind as she imagined standing naked in front of her lover was Isandro!

Now that would be a tough audience!

The hollow-sounding laugh was not convincing and did not stop a wave of scalding shame heating her cold skin.

Refusing to dwell on the man who had now invaded,

not just her life, but her subconscious, too, she walked briskly away from the sodden pile of clothes—leaving a widening pool of water on the mosaic-tiled floor—and past the massive bath set on a raised pedestal, copper and big enough to swim in. She would normally have loved to try out this opulent fantasy tub but at that moment she did not feel much like swimming, so instead she decided on the more practical option: the massive shower behind a glass wall.

As she stood under the warm spray, liberally applying the luxury bath products supplied by the hotel, she focused her thoughts on safer subjects. Just how much did it cost to spend a night here? Perhaps Isandro would take the cost from her pay?

'No!' Fear and anger bubbling inside her, she picked up a sponge and began to apply it roughly to her skin. Why was it that the wretched man managed to infiltrate her every thought? When she finally stopped rubbing and dropped the sponge, her skin was glowing and tingling pink, and her mind was a blissful, exfoliated blank.

Picking up the shampoo, she lathered her hair for a long time after it was squeaky clean. She stood still like an alabaster statue, her eyes closed, her face lifted to the warm spray, thinking nothing.

The nothing vanished the moment she emerged from the shower and heard sounds of activity in the sitting room. Immediately tension slid down her spine.

'For goodness' sake, Zoe, get over yourself!' she told herself impatiently. 'You fancy him. Big deal! Half the planet fancies him so what makes you so special, other than the fact he thinks you're an incompetent idiot?' She sniffed and reached for one of the gowns hanging from a hook. 'And staff. He doesn't kiss staff even when they kiss him.' That mortifying memory was going to stay with her for a long time.

She wasn't even a colleague. She was the help.

She took a deep breath as she tightened the belt on her robe and flicked her wet hair back from her face.

As she entered the sitting room cautiously it was immediately clear there had been considerable activity in her absence. The table beside the open doors that led to the Juliet balcony had been laid with silver cutlery and fancily folded Irish linen napkins, and the antique candelabra in the middle was lit. It looked like a classic stage set for seduction... She could only assume that the staff had got the wrong idea.

She didn't immediately see Isandro, who had been sitting on a leather chesterfield in an alcove. She was alerted by the creak of leather before his throaty drawl.

'Feeling better?'

She flinched and spun around just as he got to his feet. Her skin had tingled when she'd ruthlessly scrubbed it, but now the tingle went deeper... I was better, but I'm not any more, she thought as she pasted on a polite smile.

'Yes, thank you. That smells good.' She nodded towards the domed covered serving dish set on the console table before looking at him—or, rather, past him.

'Clothes maketh the man' was not a phrase that applied to Isandro. He looked good in clothes, but he looked equally good, actually much better, without them...well, almost without them. He was wearing a robe similar to her own but on him the superior hotel-issue garment reached his thigh and revealed more of his dark hair-roughened skin than she was comfortable with.

'I almost came to look for you.'

It had taken all his willpower and the seemingly constant flow of waiters through the place not to follow the sound of the running water and his own instincts.

His own shower had been ice cold, which had given him a temporary partial relief from his agony, but the moment she'd walked into the room with a freshly scrubbed face and nothing more than an ankle on show he had been painfully aroused and unable to think about anything but throwing her on the bed. His desire had no subtlety; it was sheer primal hunger.

He wanted her so badly he could taste it.

'I only need rescuing once a day.' Her lips formed a smile but her eyes conspicuously avoided making contact with his. Isandro could feel her tension from where he stood. 'Did you contact Alex?' she asked, as businesslike as someone could be when bare-faced and barefoot. She ran her tongue across her dry lips. She didn't even have any lipstick to hide behind, though it was doubtful if a slash of cherry red would have made her feel more confident.

'Yes, he's got Rowena to come over and babysit.'

'Rowena.' Zoe gave a sigh of relief, losing some of her stiff formality as she smiled. 'Thank you.'

Isandro's eyes travelled up from her bare feet to the top of her wet head. The section in between was covered in a thick layer of fluffy white bathrobe, but the suggestion of curves, the thought of the soft skin it hid, sent his imagination into overdrive.

'What can I get you?' He walked over to the table and lifted a lid on one of the dishes.

You on a sandwich, she thought, but bit her lip. 'Thanks, but I can't eat. I should get back.' Before I make a total fool of myself.

'Why?' He looked irritated by her response. 'The twins are being well cared for. Or don't you think Rowena can cope?'

'It's not a matter of her coping.' Rowena was totally capable. The young woman's parents had been good friends of Dan and Laura, and the twins loved their daughter, who ran the local stables. 'I don't want to take advantage.'

Her sister and brother-in-law had had a lot of friends and it was good to know that in an emergency they were there. But it was important to her to stand on her own feet and not become reliant. Or infatuated, she thought, looking directly at him for the first time.

He arched a strongly delineated ebony brow. Everything about his face was strong. 'Have you ever said no when someone asks a favour? No, you haven't. But when they want to return the favour it becomes "taking advantage"?'

The mockery in his voice as he adopted a very shaky falsetto to mimic her brought a lump to Zoe's throat.

'I'm glad I give you something to laugh about.'

'I'm not laughing. I admire independence but not when it becomes bloody-minded stubbornness.' Sometimes he wondered when she slept, or if. His critical glance moved to the violet smudges beneath her spectacular eyes. She was struggling to fit into a job she was unsuited for, and struggling to be the perfect parent. It was admirable but impossible. Why couldn't the woman embrace her imperfections? He had!

The insight sent a stab of shock through Isandro. She roused feelings that he flatly refused to recognise as protective tenderness. He refused because he associated the emotions with weakness. It made him angry. *She* made him angry!

'What are you trying to prove, Zoe?' he asked, his voice hard.

'I'm not trying to prove anything!'

Glaring, her eyes slid down his body as he sat down and leaned back on the leather sofa. Stretching his long legs out, he folded one ankle across the other. The hair-roughened skin of his muscular calves looked very dark against the white of the hotel robes. She was wearing nothing underneath. Was he…?

Shivering, she stopped the speculation from progressing into dangerous territory and dragged her gaze back to his face.

'In that case take five minutes off from being a martyr and give us all a break.'

She sucked in a gulping breath, embracing the rush of anger as she clenched her fists. 'There's nobody here but you and me.'

'Exactly, and I won't tell if you fall off your perfect parent pedestal. Just you and me…what could be cosier?'

The question drew a gurgle from her throat. 'Oh, I don't know—how about hang gliding over an active volcano?'

And there was something combustible about him, even when he was still and silent like now, his long, lean body relaxed. She had the impression that he could explode into action at any moment.

He let out a low chuckle, his expression sobering as he added, 'Are you planning to put your life on hold for the next ten or fifteen years?'

'Fifteen years!' She snorted. 'I'm not thinking any farther ahead than next month's bills.' She found his anger inexplicable. 'I'm a single parent. My priority has to be the twins.'

'Single parents have been known to have sex.'

CHAPTER EIGHT

ZOE BLINKED, THE COLOUR flying to her cheeks as she lost any fragile illusion of composure. 'Since when were we talking about sex?'

'It's part of a healthy, well-balanced life. We're always talking about sex, even when we're talking about the weather. It's the subtext.'

She flushed and snapped in protest, 'I was drunk when that happened before.'

'You're not drunk now.' So there was zero reason for gentlemanly behaviour. 'And I'm not a teenager. I'm tired of the game.' And the frustration was killing him.

He had come up with a workable solution. Now all he had to do was sell it. Isandro did not doubt his ability to do so. That was what he was good at: selling ideas; producing packages that made everyone think they had a good deal.

Zoe had anticipated his anger. After all, from his point of view she was a grade A nuisance. But she had not imagined this level of simmering fury. Even while he had been yelling at her over capsizing the boat, there had been an underlying gentleness, almost a tenderness, in his manner.

Searching his lean, handsome face now Zoe could

see no trace of the tenderness. The gleam in his deep-set dark eyes was hard and calculating… She shivered.

'I don't play games,' she protested. 'And I happen to think that someone who changes his girlfriends like socks and never sees them during daylight hours is not qualified to preach to me on what constitutes a healthy, well-balanced life!'

Having said her piece, she sat down with a bump on the sofa opposite him, her cheeks burning. She drew the folds of the robe around her like a tent and pulled her knees up to her chest.

'Obviously, how you live your life is none of my business, but that goes both ways. I work for you, but that doesn't give you a right to criticise my lifestyle unless it impinges on my ability to do my work.'

'Pardon me for stepping over the line,' he drawled, tipping his head in mock apology. 'But I think that line has been blurred from day one with us.'

Eyes trained on the gaping neckline of her robe and the exposed curve of one smooth shoulder, he exhaled through flared nostrils, combating the stab of lust by focusing on the disruption this woman had caused in his life, and not the fact he wanted to touch her skin.

This situation was of his own making. He had broken a fundamental rule. He had allowed the lines to become blurred, and he needed a strict demarcation between his personal and professional lives.

Her eyes lowered. 'I know I made a bad first impression, but I hoped that by now you'd see that I really am capable of—'

'Drowning yourself?' An image of her vanishing under the water began to play on a loop in his head, the images accompanied by the dull bass soundtrack of his blood pumping in his ears.

She flashed him a reproachful look. 'No. Being a good housekeeper.'

He laughed, and it sounded cruel to Zoe, who sat hunched watching him. 'You're a terrible housekeeper.'

A part of her despised wanting to cry. She held the tears back by sniffing and concentrating on the part of her that wanted to throw something at him.

'I've made a few mistakes,' she conceded.

His brows hit his hairline. 'A few! You can't give the most basic instruction, you fall for any sob story and you invite people to take advantage of you.'

'I think more of people than you do. I trust them.'

'I know—that's why you're sacked.'

He hadn't intended to deliver the news quite so brutally, but a combination of need and frustration bypassed his subtlety circuits. And diplomacy did not come easy when you had a slow-motion nightmare playing on a loop in your head. He prided himself on his ability to apply cool logic to all situations, but for a moment back there on the water, even though he'd known the boat would get him to her quicker, he had been within a whisper of following his instincts and diving in.

If he had, who knew what the outcome might have been? She called herself a strong swimmer but he knew what he had seen. Though he actually was a strong swimmer, there remained a question mark—could he have reached her in time?

It was possible they might both have perished.

She stiffened as she shot to her feet, every muscle in her body clenched and defensive, refusing to acknowledge the cold fear in her belly. Clasping her hands together, she blew out her breath slowly and flicked back her wet hair.

'What did you say?' Her tone was conversational. She had obviously misheard him—nobody would be that brutal, that totally…totally vile.

'You're sacked.'

Desperation overcame her anger and she crumbled. 'I'm really trying—'

'Do not beg, Zoe. This is not open for discussion.'

She bit her lip.

'It doesn't matter how much you try. You're uniquely unsuited to the role of housekeeper. I think it'll be easier all around if we cut our losses rather than drag this out. You are not the sort of housekeeper I need.' You're the sort of sex I need.

Panic made her voice shrill as she came back, 'I could be. It's just I can't relax around you…' She caught his look and added quickly, 'Because you're my employer.'

Quite suddenly he was tired of this pretence. Sensual mouth compressed, his chiselled cheekbones jutting hard against his golden skin, he silenced her with a sharp jerk of his head as he rose to his feet. 'That situation has got nothing to do with the fact I pay your wages. A strong sexual connection makes all our encounters less than relaxing, especially when you work so hard trying to pretend it doesn't exist.'

Zoe turned her head, her mouth open to produce a strong rebuttal, her eyes connected with his glowing dark gaze. Her biggest fear had been him guessing the way she felt, and now he had. So what, she thought despairingly, was the point denying it?

'Don't you find it exhausting, Zoe?' he asked softly.

She stood there mutely staring at him. Inside she was dying of sheer mortification. This was her boss saying he knew she secretly lusted after him. What was she meant to say to that?

For a split second his resolve wavered. She looked so pale, so vulnerable. But it only wavered briefly. Another month like this one and he'd be a basket case.

'I can only assume you've had some problems in the past with female staff and…crushes, but I promise you're safe from me.'

He didn't want to be safe from her.

'Good to know, but you're still sacked.'

She flinched. The bastard had said it the way someone remarked on the weather. Somewhere deep inside her, rage stirred. 'Because I don't fancy you.'

'If that were true, there would be no problem.'

Her chest swelled as she flung him a look of withering contempt. 'Even if you were right I have my own rules, too. And the first one is that I never have sex with a man I don't respect. Believe you me, that rules you out, you contemptuous little snake!'

He gave a low throaty chuckle.

'Why didn't you just sack me on that first day?' That would have been bad but this was worse. Thinking her job was secure, she'd allowed herself to relax, she'd allowed herself to sit here thinking stupid ridiculous thoughts about him, imagining that they might even… Stupid…stupid…stupid! She was so angry with herself she wanted to scream. She took a deep breath and slung a look of loathing his way.

'I didn't sack you at that point because my company is in the middle of some sensitive negotiations which could mean a lot of…' He made a dismissive gesture with his hand. 'You are not interested in the whys, but the success of this deal will mean something in the region of a thousand jobs over a five-year period.'

'What's that got to do with me?'

'It's about protecting my company's brand. Any negative publicity would send the clients running for the hills, and the story of me sacking a woman because she used my property to host a charity fund-raiser would be the worst-possible PR.'

Trying to think beyond the static buzz in her head, a combination of anger and panic, she only really processed one word in two of what he was saying. 'I don't know what you're talking about.'

'Because you are an innocent.'

How long would her savings last…a month, two…? After that what was she going to do?

'I really hate you.' Her snarl was shaky but filled with venom and her eyes gleamed with loathing as she glared up at him. She grabbed at a side table, afraid that her shaking knees were about to give way. This body blow on top of the events of that afternoon had taken a physical as well as mental toll.

'Calm down. There's no need to react this way. It's not as though you enjoy the job.'

Calm down? What planet did this man live on?

'We can't all do jobs we enjoy. Some of us do jobs because we need to survive.' This job had been her plan A, and she didn't have a plan B. She wiped her brow as she felt the panic crowding in on her again.

'Will you stop acting as though you're a heroine in a Victorian melodrama and I'm the villain?'

She flashed him a look of sheer incredulity and shook her head. He made it sound as though she was overreacting. 'If the black hat fits…?'

With an exaggerated roll of his eyes he placed his hands on her shoulders, exerting enough pressure to force her back down onto the sofa. 'If you'd stop for a

minute and let me explain. I'm not throwing you out
anywhere. I'm suggesting that you move to the end of
the drive, that's all.'

'What are you talking about?'

'The gatehouse.' The solution had been staring him
in the face all along! Now that he had had his eureka
moment, he couldn't understand why he hadn't thought
about it earlier.

'The one you've just decorated?'

The building in question had not been included in
the initial refurbishment of the estate because there had
apparently been some planning dispute over a proposed
extension, but this had recently been resolved. Zoe had
not been involved with the renovation but the build-
ers had packed up and left a couple of weeks ago and
the team of decorators had literally finished the previous day.

'If I'm not working for you how can—?'

'I'm suggesting you and the children move into the
gatehouse, pay a nominal rent…'

'With what?' No job meant no money, which meant…
Oh, God, she couldn't think what it meant. She was no
longer in a position to sleep on a friend's couch until she
sorted things. The twins needed a home and stability—
they needed a guardian who didn't go around losing
her job!

I am such a loser.

Well, if she was a loser, he was a total bastard!

'I have a friend who has bought an art gallery. She
is looking for someone to front it. I have spoken to her
about you…'

Polly's astonished response when he had explained
that his unsuitable housekeeper's domestic situation

meant he couldn't simply let her go without providing some sort of safety net was still fresh in his mind.

'Since when did you worry about dismissing someone who wasn't up to the job, Isandro? And why are you going to so much trouble to help find the girl a job?'

She had accepted his explanation without question.

'So this is about avoiding bad PR. What a relief. For a moment there—' she laughed '—I thought you'd become a bleeding heart!'

'She is happy to offer you a trial,' Isandro told Zoe.

'What makes you think I'd be any less terrible at running an art gallery than I am running a house?' Zoe asked bitterly.

'You are artistic.'

'How would you know?'

'Had you not been accepted on a fine arts degree course before your sister and her husband died?'

In the middle of a miserable sniff, Zoe lifted her incredulous glance to his face. 'How did you know that?'

He shrugged and dropped his gaze. 'Tom might have mentioned it.'

'But why would your friend give me this job?'

'I asked her.'

'A permanent job?'

'Very few things in life are permanent, but there would be a very good severance package,' he told her smoothly. 'Enough for you to pay your way through art college as you planned and employ childcare in the meantime. I understand they run an excellent foundation fine arts course on an evening basis at the local college.'

'I don't understand. Why would this woman pay me a—' her nose wrinkled; what had he called it? '—severance package?'

'She wouldn't.'

Zoe shook her head as the confusion deepened.

'I would.'

'But I wouldn't be working for you.'

'Not as such,' he conceded. 'The point is, Zoe, the attraction is not one-sided. I want you in my bed and I am a man in a position to make my fantasies come true. You are my fantasy, Zoe.'

Things fell into place in her head with an almost audible clunk. She shot to her feet—no longer shaking, no longer terrified, just furious.

'Let me get this straight. This job you're talking about, it's as…your mistress?'

He shrugged. 'That's an old-fashioned term.'

She stuck out her chin, her blue eyes sparkling with wrathful contempt. 'I'm an old-fashioned girl.' He had no idea how old-fashioned. 'Though I suppose you think I should be flattered. Isn't it a bit of a risk, though? We've never even slept together. How would you know that I'd be…any good in the bedroom?'

'It takes two, and I think when a woman literally shakes with lust when I look at her I'm willing to take the risk on a sight-unseen basis—'

'My God!' she gasped. 'You really think I'm shallow enough to want to sleep with a man who is obviously deeply in love with himself. A man whose only redeeming feature as far as I can tell is a pretty face and a moderately all right body.'

Fingers crossed, because that was a lie. He had the body of an Adonis. She gave a derisive sniff and arched a brow before laughing.

'Yes, I do.' His sloe-dark eyes drifted over her lush sinuous curves shrouded beneath the robe, and his mouth grew dry at the thought of slipping the loose knot of the belt looped around her narrow waist.

It was an uphill struggle to act as though his slow, sexy smile was doing nothing to her. She knew that sex appeal wasn't just about looks, but the idea that she was any man's erotic fantasy—let alone a man like Isandro—was shocking. She swallowed and pressed both hands to her stomach, shamefully aware that the deep quivers that rippled low in her pelvis were not caused by shock. What he was suggesting was wrong on more levels than she could count, it went against every principle she held dear, yet she was excited… What does that say about me?

'Besides, we don't have to wait. This is the perfect opportunity to find out if it's as good as I think it will be.' The sweep of his hand took in the big bed piled with cushions, the open French door against which the light curtains fluttered in the breeze.

In the distance Zoe could hear a flock of geese landing on the water. She went hot, cold, then hot again.

'I'm not selling my body.'

'That's good, because I've never paid for sex.'

'What do you call what you're suggesting?'

'I'm suggesting we remove the barrier that is preventing us both doing what we want to. If you are no longer on my payroll we can be equal.'

'I'll never be equal to you. I'll always be superior!'

'Bravo!' he drawled.

Her lips tightened. 'Don't you dare patronise me! And why make up that stupid story about your friend?'

'That is not invented. It is real. I do have a friend who owns a gallery.'

Zoe felt a stab of something she didn't immediately recognise as jealousy. 'A female friend?'

Could you sound more jealous if you tried?

'Her name is Polly Warrender. She inherited a theatre from her husband.' Zoe had heard of the Warrender theatre, but then pretty much everyone had. 'When she diversified and bought into an art gallery she came to me for advice.'

She stifled a theatrical yawn, but the gesture unwittingly drew his eyes to the soft full curve of her rosy lips. 'So, let me guess, she listened to you and made a fortune,' she inserted with a roll of her eyes.

'Actually she ignored my advice and bought it and, yes, made a fortune.' He gave a faint smile. 'A smallish one.'

'So you were wrong?'

He reached out and tangled a wet curl around one long brown finger and drawled, 'You've discovered the chink in my infallible armour. Please do me a favour and keep it to yourself.'

As he released the curl his finger brushed her cheek. It barely made contact, but Zoe, who had been holding her breath, felt an electric tingle pass through her body all the way to her curling toes.

His voice was a soft attractive buzz. She could hear what he was saying, but over and above the words was a louder buzz—a combination of her own heartbeat and the thrum of the deep hunger that was coursing through her veins with each beat of her heart as she stared at the deep V of golden chest dark against the white towelling.

It took every ounce of her self-control to stop herself reaching out and touching him... She curled her hands into fists and tucked them behind her back.

'I put her onto the decommissioned church that was up for sale in town as a possible site for a new gallery. She has wanted to expand into this area for some time, so she owes me a favour. She is genuinely looking for someone to run it, and you have an art background... So it is perfectly feasible for you to live here and commute to do the foundation course.'

'And amuse you in bed.' He acknowledged her bitter addition with a tilt of his head. 'You have it all worked out.'

He gave a smile. 'The secret of success is taking control of events and not allowing them to control you.'

Yeah, you carry on telling yourself that, Isandro, if it makes you feel any better. The fact was he had felt out of control since the moment he had met this woman. From day one she had managed to turn his well-ordered life into chaos.

She shook her head. 'Don't you dare smile. I'm not listening to a word you're saying.'

He took the hands she had pressed to her ears and pressed them against his chest. Then holding her eyes with his, he brushed his lips across her cheek.

'You're not shouting, though,' he murmured against her mouth.

She wasn't. Zoe was barely breathing. Her body felt strange and tingly, as though it didn't belong to her. Her arms and legs felt heavy as though a great weight were dragging her down. Dizzy, she clutched at the towelling of his robe. Somehow it parted and her hands were flat on his skin, the warmth seeping into her cold fingers, the heavy thud of his heartbeat mingling with the frantic clamour of her riotous pulse.

Common sense told her to push him away.

'This isn't going to happen.' Why was she whispering? She should be shouting.

'If you say so, *querida*.' His big hand sank into her wet hair, cupping the back of her skull. His long fingers tangled in her hair while his thumb trailed tingling paths down her cheek. His breath was coming fast and hot against her neck.

Her knees gave out, but before she could slide to the floor his arms snaked around her waist. He was so close that his face was a dark blur. She could see the predatory glow of his beautiful eyes. Her own eyes burned but she couldn't blink, she couldn't look away, not until he tugged at the soft pink flesh of her lower lip, holding it between his teeth. Then her eyes squeezed tight closed as she released a soft sibilant sigh and opened her palms flat on his chest, pushing them under the thick fabric of the robe, up over his warm skin to his shoulders.

Still she didn't push. Like someone in a dream she clung, and still he didn't kiss her. The scent of his warm male body in her nostrils, she was desperate for the taste of him. The need consumed her utterly, so strong that it blotted every other thought from her mind. He radiated raw power, and it excited her unbearably, sent a primitive heat sweeping through her in waves crashing over her. She felt herself going under.

Need, primitive need, raw and all-consuming, blinding lust controlled his actions as he tilted her face up. *Dios*, but he had wanted to kiss her for… It felt like a lifetime.

His tongue slid between her parted lips and Zoe's brain closed down as instinct took over. Her moan was lost in the warm recesses of his mouth as her lips parted to deepen the sensual invasion.

She kissed him back, greedily drinking in the taste of him, wanting more…wanting everything. He hauled her body into him. His hands slipped down to her bottom as, cupping it, he lifted her off the ground. Without thinking, she wrapped her long legs tight around his waist as she framed his face between her hands, gave a throaty sigh and whispered, 'God, but you are so beautiful...the most beautiful man.'

With a deep groan that rose up in his throat he plundered Zoe's mouth, kissing her with barely controlled desperation, stealing the breath from her lungs, lighting a passion that flared into violent life. As she kissed him back with a wild and unrestrained hunger, satisfying the mutual need between them, everything else ceased to exist.

Her fingers dug into the muscles of his shoulders, her legs tightening around his waist as she fought to get closer to him, her strength fuelled by the primal desire to be joined with him...be one.

Joined with her that way still, he walked blindly towards the bed.

Zoe felt as if she were falling—and then she was really falling and he was falling on top of her. A pillow beneath her head, she barely noticed the weight of his body on top of her until he levered himself off.

Panting, her eyes as dark as midnight, she gave a small cry of protest, then she saw what he was doing. Kneeling over her, Isandro was shrugging off his robe.

'Oh, my God!'

He was long and lean, his skin gleaming like burnished gold. Not an ounce of excess flesh blurred the perfect lines of his powerful body. Every bone and sinew of him was perfect, like a bronzed statue. A rampantly, fully aroused bronzed statue.

She bit down hard on her full lower lip as heat washed her skin with a warm rosy flush. Her initial shock at the earthy image was replaced by a stomach-clenching, incapacitating, lustful longing that closed down every logic circuit in her brain.

His grin was fierce and his laughter strained as he husked, 'If you look at me like that, *querida*, this thing is going to be over before it has begun.'

'I want you,' she whispered, pulling herself up onto her knees. 'So badly...' She reached out and touched him, unable to believe her daring as she curled her fingers around the shaft of his erection. Silky smooth and rock hard, he pulsed hotly against her small hand. 'You feel—' her breasts quivered as she gave a fractured sigh and continued to stare, fascinated, at him '—incredible.'

A hiss left his lips as he caught her wrist.

'Too much,' he muttered, pressing her body back onto the bed before he joined her. Arranging his long lean length beside her, he kissed her, a kiss full of passion and promise that made words redundant. Lifting his head, he stroked her face and held her eyes as he reached for the tie on her robe.

The embarrassment she had anticipated did not materialise but the voluptuous pleasure did as he whispered fiercely, 'You are exquisite, flawless.'

His searing gaze swept upwards slowly, greedily drinking her in as it took in every detail from her narrow feet and ankles, the long elegant length of her legs, and over her belly. Then finally to her lovely, pertly pointed breasts.

His hand came to cover one perfect soft mound. Her skin was flawless. He could smell the perfume of the soap on her skin, and the faint but distinctive delicate, musky scent of her arousal made his vision mist red.

As he massaged the smooth skin, his touch firm but sensitive, running his thumb with slow deliberate strokes across the sensitised peaks, Zoe gasped and muttered his name. Her head thrashed wildly back and forth on the pillow. The pleasure was so intense—

beyond words, she clenched her hands into fists at her sides as she felt herself losing her struggle to stay in control.

Then his mouth was on her breasts, his hands on her body, touching her awakening senses. With a soft sigh of surrender, she stopped trying and gave herself up to the desire flowing like warm wine through her veins. She almost felt like laughing with the sense of release. Who knew that losing control, feeling enough trust to give it over to someone else, could feel like this?

She reached for him, her fingers tangling in his dark hair, holding him against her as she stroked the skin of his muscled shoulders. The raw power in him, the dramatic contrasts of his hard angularity and her own softness, her roundness, was more exciting than she could have dreamed possible.

Isandro lifted his head and smiled at her with his glorious eyes, a dark fierce smile filled with promise, then he kissed her belly, drawing a hoarse gasp from Zoe, and ran his tongue over the quivering skin, drawing a line that terminated just above the apex of her thighs.

At the first touch of his hands between her legs need exploded through her. She loosed a keening cry as her hips lifted off the bed. Her entire body ached and trembled with desire; her mouth opened but she had no words, just his name, which she said over and over. And when she stopped he lifted his head and said, 'Again, say it again.'

She did, and at the same time opened her legs in mute invitation, inviting skilful touch of his fingers over the slick, moist, swollen folds of her femininity, and the tight, sensitive nub they protected.

The first skin-to-skin contact was electric. Then, as her arched spine made contact with the bed and he

pressed down on top of her, it was totally, utterly blissful, a cocktail of intoxicating physical sensations that
made her senses spiral and spin. Bright lights exploded
behind her eyelids as she closed her eyes.

Her hips moved in a grinding motion as she rubbed
herself against his erection as it dug into her thigh, then
her soft belly. The pressure building inside her made
her thrash around, bite his neck as she dragged her fingers down his back, clutching at the firm contours of
his tight, muscular buttocks.

Unable to bear the erotic friction of his erection
against her any longer, she grabbed his hair, drawing his
face to hers, and kissing him hard, whispered, 'Please!'

With a savage smile he held her eyes as he drove
deep into her body. The breath left her in a shocked gasp
that was drowned out by his deep growl of pleasure.
Her heart racing, her eyes closed tight, she concentrated
on the intense pleasure of each slow, measured move-
ment of his hips as he moved inside her body. There
was layer after layer of sensations that she had never
imagined she could feel.

Each thrust built the erotic pleasure that she encouraged with each sinuous, sensuous grind of her hips
responding to age-old instincts she was delighted to
discover.

When the climax hit her, she was unprepared for the
strength of the expanding wave of pleasure and her eyes
flew wide with shock.

'Perfect, just go with it, my clever, beautiful…' His
eyes held her while she rode the wave. He waited until
she reached the vortex of the storm before he allowed
himself to find his own release and thrust one final
time into her.

When Zoe floated back to earth, she was curled up

in his arms, her head resting against his thudding heart, her sweat-slick limbs tangled with his.

'Well, I never saw that one coming. I remember hearing you say you did not approve of casual sex but I never equated that with… Was there a bad experience that put you off sex I should have known about?'

It seemed the only explanation for how a woman as sexy and passionate as Zoe Grace could be a virgin. And her surrender had been total; she had held nothing back. He had sensed the passion beneath the surface, but what he had released had startled and delighted him almost as much as the discovery she was a virgin.

'No bad experience, I just… I've moved around a lot and never got time to make any sort of lasting relationship. Not that this is lasting…obviously.' There was a short awkward pause. Dear God, it was a strange world when she was embarrassed to admit that, a secret romantic, she had always felt uneasy about casual sex.

'You must have had boyfriends.'

'Of course I have—I'm not a freak. I had boyfriends but they all seemed to suggest I was not very…good at that sort of stuff.' Her last date had culminated in a nasty little scene when the man who invited her to dinner had accused her of being a tease when she could not agree that the correct payment for a dinner was a make-out session in the back seat of a car.

He gave a throaty laugh of incredulity. 'I think you have been keeping the wrong company.'

She twisted in his arms and flipped onto her stomach, resting her chin on her elbows and affording him an excellent view of her breasts. 'And you're the right company?' she challenged.

He was definitely the right lover.

'It felt pretty right to me.'

'So what happens now?'

His wicked grin flashed. 'Give me five minutes.'

'I mean after this?' Had he really been serious about moving her and the twins into the gatehouse?

CHAPTER NINE

'I THOUGHT I had already made that clear.'

'But after?' Isandro was hot for her now, but Zoe did not anticipate the situation would last and when he lost interest, what then? 'When I am no longer flavour of the day?'

'That moment,' he purred, stroking the silky smooth skin of her forearm, 'feels like a long way off.'

'But it might not be.'

'Well, that is catered for. You will continue to live in the gatehouse for as long as it pleases you. It seems to me a win, win situation.'

He could say that but he wasn't on the brink of falling in love. Who was she kidding? Zoe thought bleakly. She was already in love and had been for the past weeks. She was going to be devastated when this was over, but she was going to be devastated anyway so why not have some weeks of delicious mind-blowing sex with this gorgeous man to remember and some financial security for the twins?

'All right, but no.' She twisted away from the hand that reached for her, knowing that once he touched her she wouldn't be able to think straight, let alone consider consequences. 'There have to be some rules.'

Isandro stared at her, taken aback—he made the rules.

'I don't want this to affect the twins. I don't want them to know about us. We have to be discreet. We know this is just sex but they are just...' Whichever way she looked, there were aspects to this arrangement that didn't feel right.

He tipped his head. 'That seems fair.' He tangled his fingers in her hair and kissed her mouth. 'Do not look so worried. We have weeks of pleasure ahead of us. You are not some little girl seeking the attention of men and mistaking it for love. This is an equal relationship of two people who know what they want.'

'What do you want?'

'You, *querida*, you in so many ways.'

She shivered. 'Many ways?'

His smile made her heart flip. 'Come here and let me show you.'

Zoe and the twins had been established in the gatehouse for six weeks. Her passion with Isandro had not flagged, and six weeks was new ground for him. Abiding by rules set by someone else was also new and on occasion frustrating.

There came a tapping on the window of his study—which had recently been knocked through to make room for the extra office equipment he needed since he had made the decision to do more work from home.

Isandro looked up from the computer screen.

When the red-headed figure at the window saw him she began to gesticulate wildly. A second later she vanished, and there was a clattering sound.

With a sigh Isandro levered himself up from his chair, stretching the kinks from his spine as he walked towards the window. Pulling up the sash, he leaned out. Georgina was lying beside an overturned crate she had presumably dragged over to the window and fallen off. She was picking herself up.

'What are you doing?'

'Looking for you, obviously.' Ever irrepressible, she dusted off the seat of her jeans.

'Did you hurt yourself?'

The kid treated the question with the scorn she appeared to think it deserved, shaking her head and looking offended by the question.

Like aunt, like niece, he thought.

'I would have gone to Chloe but they're not back until tomorrow. I can't wait to see Hannah again and she's walking with crutches, and there isn't really anyone else.'

So not first choice, or even second. 'I feel honoured.'

'If Zoe died, would we get put in a home?'

His half-sardonic smile snuffed like a candle caught in a chill draft and Isandro did suddenly feel as though a cold fist had plunged deep into his belly.

'Zoe is not going to die.'

'No...?' Her niece sounded scarily uncertain.

'What has happened to your aunt Zoe?' he asked, ruthlessly reining in his imagination and struggling to keep his tone light.

'She says she's fine but she doesn't look fine and she—'

He held up a hand. 'Wait there. I will be with you momentarily.'

Snatching up his jacket on the way out, he paused only to close his laptop before leaving the house. Outside Georgie was trotting around the side of the house to meet him when he emerged.

'Zoe sent you?'

She shook her head. 'She'll be mad with me,' she predicted gloomily.

'She doesn't need to know that you came to get me.'

Her eyes flew wide with shock. 'That would be lying!' Children were a minefield.

'Of course it would, and of course you should never lie…especially to your aunt.'

The child looked unconvinced as she climbed into the passenger seat of his car.

'Now tell me what is wrong.'

When they arrived at the lodge they entered through her open back door where Harry, his face scrunched in concentration, was standing on a kitchen chair trying to open a tin with an opener that looked like an antique. His small fingers looked perilously near the razor-sharp edges.

Conscious it might not be a good idea to startle him, Isandro walked across and, after a friendly pat on the shoulder, extricated the tin from his grip.

'Let me—there's a knack to this. There you go.' He glanced at the label. 'Chicken soup.'

'Mum always gave us chicken soup when we were sick. I thought I'd make Zoe some.'

'Good idea, but let's wait until we see if she wants to eat just now.'

'Until she stops throwing up, stupid,' his sister inserted critically.

'I'm not stupid.'

Isandro cleared his throat. 'How about if you two go?' Two expectant faces turned to him. 'Go to the shop and get me some…' He paused. 'Are you allowed to walk to the shop?'

They both shook their heads.

'Right, well…' *Madre di Dios*, give me a room of CEOs any day of the week.

'We could clean out your car. It was very messy. For money,' Georgie offered.

Her brother cast her a sideways warning look. 'For free.'

His sister sighed heavily.

'That would be very helpful.' His car had been valet cleaned the previous week. 'I will go and see how your aunt is feeling, but don't worry. It sounds like she has the flu bug that is doing the rounds.' He moved towards the hallway.

'Are you Zoe's boyfriend?'

Isandro might not be good with children but he did not fall into that trap. He paused and turned. His amused expression was not a direct denial but he hoped they took it as such. 'Is that why you came to get me? Because you think I am her boyfriend?'

'No, we came to get you because she was saying your name in the night. She woke us up and when we went in she was awake but really hot.'

'I told you it was just a nightmare,' Harry said.

A woman's nightmare…children certainly had a way of keeping a man's ego in check.

Isandro made his way to the bedroom at the front of the cottage. The door was ajar, and he pushed it open and found the curtains in the airy room pulled shut. The light filtering through the striped fabric illuminated the figure in the bed lying with one arm curled around her head.

He was used to feeling the tug of sexual attraction when he looked at her, used to feeling the electrical tingle when she was close. As he stared at her now, looking both vulnerable and utterly desirable—they were both there but there was something else in the mix, something he struggled to define as he stood nailed to the spot while something imploded in his skull.

Then she moved and shifted, groaning softly before she licked her lips as her eyelashes fluttered against her cheek. 'Harry.'

'Not Harry.'

The eyelashes parted to reveal blue blurry eyes. 'Oh, God,' she groaned. 'What are you doing here?'

He had had more enthusiastic welcomes. 'How are you feeling?'

She raised herself groggily up on one elbow, causing the nightdress she wore to slip over one shoulder. He felt a stab of inappropriate lust.

'Fine,' she croaked.

'I admire the stiff upper lip, naturally, but an honest answer would be more helpful.'

Zoe turned her head on the pillow and aimed a look of simmering dislike on him. He wanted to know what she felt like? Fine, she'd tell him.

'I feel like death warmed up. Happy?' She lowered herself with a groan onto the pillow. 'And I suppose I look that way, too.'

'Pretty bad,' he agreed, his mocking smile vanishing as her lips began to tremble. 'Are you crying?'

'Oh, well, so sorry I couldn't manage to put on my make-up for your benefit, but nobody asked you here.' Her brow furrowed. 'What are you doing here anyway?'

'Georgie came to get me.'

'Oh, God, she shouldn't have.'

'They are worried.'

Zoe clapped a hand to her aching head and groaned. 'I told them I'm fine. It's just a bug or something.'

'Symptom-wise, could you be a little more precise?'

'If I tell you will you go away? I have cymbals playing in my head, I ache all over and I feel sick...' She gave a him a narrow-eyed glare of 'Is that precise enough for you?'

'Very succinct. I am assuming our date tonight is off.'

Zoe didn't have the energy to prise her eyelids apart but she found the strength to correct him.

'We don't have a date. It's just sex. Do I know it's just sex? he asks me, like I'm a total idiot,' she mumbled. The comment he had made in the aftermath of the frantic love-making session they had fitted in while the children were having their riding lesson had been playing in her head all through the long interminable night.

'So how is our patient?'

This time Zoe's eyes didn't open as she resisted the temptation to declare she was nobody's patient.

'Doctor, who sent for you?' He had to have heard what she'd said. She comforted herself with the thought that doctors, like priests, couldn't blab about their patients. Presumably the Montero name, or possibly the cheque book, had made the man forget that GPs no longer made house calls at the weekend, she brooded, with a cynical sniff that became a cough.

Neither man answered her question.

'Beyond the general crankiness, she has a headache, joint pain and obviously a high temperature.' Isandro's glance slid once more to the figure lying on the bed. Her nightdress clung damply to her and the pinpoints of bright red colour stood out livid against the pallor of her skin. 'Nausea...have you been sick?'

Now they decided to acknowledge she was there. 'Mind your own damned business!'

The middle-aged medic laughed and suggested that Mr Montero might like to leave while he had a chat with the patient.

The doctor confirmed that Zoe had a dose of the bug doing the rounds and suggested she take an analgesic for her temperature, get plenty of rest and take lots of fluids.

'Which is what I was doing,' Zoe told Isandro.

'What can I get you?'

'Just go away and leave me alone.'

When the cranky invalid refused point-blank to be nursed or cosseted he did the next best thing—he offered to take the twins off her hands for the rest of the day.

An offer that did not strike him as odd until with the twins in tow he bumped into a school friend of Dana's in a hands-on science exhibition. Emma, who had her youngest in tow, was one of the few mutual friends that he had stayed in contact with after the divorce. Her parting shot of 'I'd really like to meet the woman who has domesticated you!' had stayed with him.

Ridiculous, of course—he hadn't changed in any fundamental way. He could walk away from this relationship at any time. He enjoyed the twins, they amused him…though they were exhausting.

Denial, Isandro, mocked the voice in his head.

The next day Zoe felt tired. Her head ached and things still hurt, but she was well enough to get up, which was just as well as she had promised to go the airport this morning to pick up Chloe, John and Hannah. She also needed to drop the kids off for their science field trip before—oh, God, just thinking about the day ahead made her headache worse.

'Get a wriggle on, you two!' she yelled, pulling open

the front door as Harry vanished to find his rucksack he had left 'somewhere.'

'What the hell do you think you are doing?'

Zoe reacted to the angry voice like a bullet zinging past her ear and spun around to face the tall figure who was striding up the path to the front door. He looked dauntingly angry, but Zoe, refusing to be daunted, pressed a hand to her throbbing head and returned belligerently, 'I might ask you the same thing. I thought you had a meeting in Paris today.'

'It was cancelled.' The lie came smoothly. Intercepting the direction of her gaze, he lifted the hand that held a large bouquet of flowers. 'The gardener heard you were unwell.'

It seemed unnecessary to Isandro to explain that he had told him. 'He says you prefer the flowers that have a scent to the hothouse roses...?'

'I do! How lovely of him,' she exclaimed, taking the fragrant ribbon-tied posy and lifting it to her nose. 'I must thank him.'

'I will pass on your message and you will go back to bed.'

Her chin went up at his dictatorial attitude. 'You can't just waltz in here and order me around. I'm fine and I have to pick up Chloe and co from the airport after I've taken the twins to—'

'Bed!' Isandro thundered just as the postman opened the garden gate.

'Nice morning,' the man said as he handed a pink-faced Zoe her letters.

'Well, thank you for that.' Zoe glared up at Isandro.

Georgie's voice cut across her. 'Isandro's here, Harry, he's taking us to school.'

Mortified, Zoe shook her head. The boundaries of

their relationship did blur on occasion but she was sure they would not stretch to the school run! 'No, no, he's not… Georgie, go—'

'Yes, I am. Go get in the car,' he said, directing this order to the twins, who ran out before Zoe could say a word.

'You're not!'

'I am.' Ignoring her squeal of furious protest, he snatched the car keys that were dangling from her fingers and put them in the pocket of his well-cut trousers. 'Now be a good girl and go back to bed.'

'Do not treat me like a child.' Even if I sound like one.

He looked impatient. 'You are clearly still unwell. You look terrible.' It was not his job to make her better, so why the hell had he taken it on himself to do so?

She gave a twisted smile. 'Thanks.' He must be right otherwise the comment would not have made her feel like crying.

'If you drag yourself out of bed unnecessarily you will only delay your recovery.'

In a perfect world another twenty-four hours would have been nice. 'So now you're a doctor.'

'You are a very bad patient.'

'I need to—'

'Has it not occurred to you that Chloe and her family will not thank you for infecting them with your flu bug?'

Zoe's face fell. 'I hadn't thought of that.'

Hands on her shoulders, he turned her around. 'So go back to bed, and for once in your life, woman, let someone else be in charge.' He broke off at the sound of a car horn. 'That is my car.'

He was being summoned by a pair of kids, and he was responding!

Zoe tried to remember the last time she had felt in charge and gave a small bitter laugh. 'This from the world's biggest control freak!' she muttered as the door closed.

By the time she reached her bed Zoe was too tired to undress. She fell on top of it fully dressed and fell into a deep sleep.

When she woke, the afternoon sun was shining through the window and she wasn't alone. She raised herself up on one elbow and gazed down at the man lying beside her. He too was fully dressed and sound asleep.

Or maybe not.

Isandro opened his heavy-lidded eyes and stretched a hand above his head; he had not slept the previous night but fortunately he survived well on catnaps.

He looked so gorgeous that it hurt; the pain was physical.

She was trailing her fingers lovingly down his cheek when it hit her. 'Chloe!' she yelped, glancing with horror at the time on the digital display of her alarm. 'I thought you were—'

She bit her lip—an assumption she should not have made. He had taken the twins to school because that had been pretty much a fait accompli, but the last thing Isandro wanted was involvement in her domestic life. He just wanted her in bed...for how long?

She pushed away this depressing thought.

'Relax, I have sent a car for them.' He gave a yawn. He was sure that nursing did not involve falling asleep beside your patient, but the last twenty-four hours had taught Isandro that he was not a natural nurse and when

Zoe had thrashed around restlessly and muttered his name in her sleep he had found himself unable not to respond. His physical closeness had seemed to soothe her.

'Their flight arrived on time and they are on their way home.'

'Thank you...I'm really sorry about being a nuisance...'

He reached and placed a hand behind her neck, his fingertips sending little flickers of electricity through her body as they pushed into her hairline.

'You are always a nuisance.' She turned his ordered life into total chaos and yet still he kept coming back for more...?

Zoe struggled to read his expression. 'The twins can be very—'

'I never do anything I do not want to do, *querida*.'

'You can't want to run the twins around and—'

He dragged her face down to his until their noses were touching. 'Right now I want—'

'Do you always get what you want?' she whispered against his warm lips... God, but he smelt incredible.

'I have that reputation.'

'What was that for?' she asked huskily when the long, languid kiss ended.

'Chloe sent her love.'

'Not like that, she didn't.'

His throaty laugh made her grin.

'You shouldn't be kissing me. I'm probably infectious.'

He stroked her cheek. 'I have an excellent immune system. I never get ill.'

You never get in love. She pushed the thought away. Why spoil what she had by wishing for something she never could have? It was hard sometimes.

'Thanks for this morning.'

He shrugged and levered himself into a sitting position before dragging both hands through his sexily ruffled dark hair.

'You should go. The twins will be home soon.' She swung her legs over the side of the bed, not seeing the flicker of annoyance that moved across his taut lean features. 'I really am feeling better now. I needed that sleep.'

After scanning her face, he nodded and got up from the bed. 'I have arranged for Rowena to pick up the twins after their field trip,' he said, rising with fluid grace to his feet. 'And there is something that Mrs Whittaker called a casserole in the fridge. Apparently all you have to do is heat it up.'

'That's so kind of her.'

'I'm flying to Paris in the morning.'

By the time he turned back at the door Zoe had wiped her face clean of the ludicrous disappointment she had felt at his casual disclosure. 'Oh, and Polly is not expecting you in work until Monday.'

As the door closed she picked up the phone. 'Polly— no, that's why I'm ringing. I'm fine—I'll be in work tomorrow.'

Even if it killed her it was too late not to fall in love with Isandro, but she was damned if she was going to let him micro-manage every aspect of her life. She had to make her own decisions, stay independent. He wasn't going to be around for ever.

CHAPTER TEN

INITIALLY IT HAD BEEN scary working in the gallery, but Zoe had soon gained more confidence and now she loved it. Especially since Polly had begun to give her responsibility, which she thrived on.

Today had been a good one. A buyer for an insurance firm had left having purchased several very expensive pastels by a new up-and-coming artist, and there was a spring in her step when Zoe finally locked up the gallery and fastened her jacket against the cold breeze blowing down the street. She was wondering if she'd make the early train when the loud honk of a car horn made her look up.

Pulled up beside the pavement, showing a selfish disregard for the parking restrictions, was a car she recognised. Her heart picked up tempo as she walked towards it, and as she reached it the window on the driver's side rolled down.

'What are you doing here?'

Isandro smiled. He hadn't actually known where he was heading until he had arrived just as she was emerging from the gallery. The sight of her slim, trim figure had, if not lifted his spirits, definitely alleviated the gloom.

'I'm heading home. Do you want a lift?'

The terse delivery made her look more closely at him, her brow furrowing as she studied his face. There was nothing specific, but she could tell that something was wrong.

'That would be good—my feet are killing me,' she admitted.

They had been driving along in total silence for ten minutes before she spoke. 'So what's wrong?'

He flashed her an impatient sideways glance. 'Nothing is wrong… What makes you think anything is wrong?'

'You haven't said a word.'

'Can't a man enjoy a little silence? Do we have to indulge in an endless stream of boring, meaningless drivel?'

She let out a long silent whistle. 'If you're going to speak to me in that tone you can drop me off.'

By way of reply he pressed his foot on the accelerator. 'Don't be so bloody touchy.'

'Me! So are you going to tell me what's wrong?' She gripped the door and closed her eyes as they approached a hairpin bend. 'Or are you going to drive us off the road?'

'I am perfectly in control of this car.'

Despite his reply she was relieved that he did perceptively slow his speed as the powerful car came out of the bend.

'I heard from my father today.' He compressed his sensual lips hard enough to rim them with white in a physical effort to stem the flow of information.

'That's nice.' Clearly it wasn't, and prodding gently was a dangerous strategy but she couldn't think of any other way to get him to open up. It was obvious to her he needed to even if he was too pig-headed to admit it.

Was there some problem between him and his father…? He had mentioned his mother once in past tense, and as he'd never said anything about his father she had always assumed that both his parents were dead.

'Nice!' he snarled.

Zoe's confusion and concern grew as her gaze travelled from his white-knuckled hands on the wheel to his taut profile.

'Sorry, is it bad news?' He couldn't accuse her of prying when he had introduced the subject…not that he wouldn't if it suited him, she thought with a wry smile.

'He's invited me to his wedding.' He elaborated, but as the additional information was in his native Spanish she was none the wiser.

'I suppose it's hard to see your father moving on. Has your mother been dead long?' Her blue eyes shone with sympathy as she looked at him through her lashes.

'Moving on!' His teeth came together with an audible grating sound. 'You think this is my problem?'

'It's only natural, especially if you were close to your mother—'

'My father moved on so fast the headstone was still being carved. My father—' He broke off, a nerve in his taut jaw clenching as he stared with white-faced intensity at the road ahead.

'There's a layby up ahead. Pull over, Isandro,' she said quietly.

'Why?'

She had wondered why he had chosen the minor road, a slightly longer route, in preference to the shorter journey on the motorway. Now she was glad; at least this road was almost empty.

'Because I don't particularly want to end up a road-traffic-accident statistic.' For a moment she thought he was going to ignore her, but to her intense relief at the last moment he swerved into the layby, sending up a shower of gravel.

He turned off the engine, and without a word got out of the car. Leaving the door wide open, he began to pace up and down on the grassy verge of the road.

Zoe didn't follow him. Isandro was a man who needed space, so she let him walk while he fought the devils that drove him. He couldn't not be elegant—the animal grace was an integral part of him, and even vibrating with anger he was riveting to watch.

This was a part of his personality he concealed behind a carefully contrived mask. This was the part of his personality that he liked to deny—the passion and fire—allowing it out only behind closed doors. She knew from experience that driving something underground didn't make it go away; it just consumed you.

Ignoring the fact she had fallen in love with him had not lessened her feelings. It had just meant that when it surfaced... She shivered and wrapped her arms protectively around herself, hugging tight. She wouldn't let it surface.

She stayed silent when he finally slid back into the car.

'What do you think?'

'About what, Isandro?'

'I was twenty-one when my mother died, and already married.'

Zoe had lost her own father when she was a baby and she had no memory of him. Her mother's death remained a strong and sad memory, even though at the end it had been a release.

'My father was a wreck. Then two months after she died, out of the blue he rang and told me he'd met a

wonderful woman who reminded him of my mother.'
His lips curled into a contemptuous smile. 'Turned out
the wonderful woman had a sweet daughter who he
planned to adopt. And yes, the likeness to my mother
was startling. It became obvious pretty quickly to everyone but him that she was a con artist. Friends, colleagues told him...'

'You told him?'

Isandro nodded. 'He told me I was jealous. When
they finally did a flit, he was one step away from bank-
ruptcy. He'd mortgaged my mother's home, sold off her
jewellery, and...' His chest heaved as he struggled to
contain his feelings.

'And now he's met someone else?'

'Apparently.'

'And he's invited you to the wedding?'

She got another nod.

'Do you really want to know what I think?'

'I asked, didn't I?' The belated realisation sent a
wave of shock through his body. One of the reasons
Dana had cited for the breakdown of their marriage
was the fact that, according to her, he never listened to
her, or asked her opinion.

*I need to be needed, Isandro, and you don't need
me—you don't need anyone.*

He had not disputed it, because it had been true...
It still was.

Zoe arched a delicate brow and wondered about the
odd expression on his face. 'That doesn't mean you
won't yell if I say something you don't want to hear.'

He pushed his dark head back into the leather head-
rest and gave a half-smile as he looked at her from under
the dark mesh of his preposterously long eyelashes.

'Since when has that stopped you?'

Zoe was the only woman who ever challenged him. She didn't go out of her way to say what he wanted to hear, and sometimes it seemed to him she took a perverse pleasure from winding him up.

'I think you should go to the wedding and wish your father well.'

He clenched his jaw and swore under his breath.

Zoe didn't let his response throw her. It was pretty much what she had anticipated. 'Well, not going isn't going to stop him. I know he screwed up once, but who doesn't?'

'He didn't just screw up, he—'

'He thought he was in love. That's not a crime.' Though Isandro's expression suggested he thought it should be. 'I'm sure he feels pretty stupid about what happened. Ashamed and embarrassed.'

'I suppose so.' Isandro rubbed his jaw. Had he ever really thought about how his father felt? Would a stronger man have shown more compassion?

He turned his brooding gaze on Zoe. Such uncomfortable thoughts had never come to him before.

'And I expect he knows you're still angry with him.'

'I'm not…' He caught her eyes once more and sighed, dragging a hand through his sable hair until it stood up in tufts around his bronzed face.

'All right, I am angry… How could he take the word of that woman and not his friends, people who he had known for years?'

'You, you mean?'

He shrugged and issued his response through clenched teeth. 'It is not important.'

Zoe felt her heart squeeze in her chest in sympathy. 'It must have been hurtful.'

Isandro looked from the blue eyes brimming with

sympathy to the hand that lay on his arm and thought, What the hell am I doing?

Regretting the outburst that had made him reveal so much of his feelings, and equating it with weakness, he slid his arm from under her hand. He was not a man who shared his problems. His cure for extreme frustration was mind-numbing laps of the pool, or a run that battered body and mind into numbness.

This time he had not sought the pool or donned his running shoes. He had… Why had instinct made him seek out Zoe?

'What was hurtful, as you put it,' he countered in a harsh voice, 'was being forced to put my own life on hold and pull in every favour I had owing in order to stop the firm going under and my father ending up in jail. It wasn't just his money the bitch got. He'd "borrowed" from clients' accounts.'

Zoe watched the shutters go back up, hearing the lack of emotion in his hard voice. She could have screamed in sheer frustration, but instead she put her hand back in her lap, her feelings see-sawing violently between empathy and a strong desire to shake him.

Did he imagine allowing her even a glimpse of the man beneath the mask gave her some sort of special power?

'Don't worry, Isandro, I'd already guessed you're actually human.' Their glances connected and Zoe saw the shock he was not quick enough to hide flicker in the second before his hooded eyelids lowered, leaving her looking at the gleam of his eyes through the mesh of his eyelashes. 'But I won't tell anyone. Your secret is safe with me,' she promised.

His lips tightened, but the faint flush along the angle

of his cheekbones suggested she had made her point. 'I am not in the mood for word games, Zoe.'

'Fine, is this straightforward enough? Your dad made a mistake once...all right, a big mistake,' she conceded in response to his snort. 'That doesn't mean there isn't an outside possibility he actually loves this woman.'

His lip curled contemptuously. 'My father believes in fairy tales.' While he despised the childlike credulity, there had been moments when Isandro almost envied his father.

'Isn't that a good thing? That the awful woman didn't win?' she said softly.

The suggestion caused Isandro to turn his head sharply to look at her, the compassion glowing in her eyes as much as the statement causing him to frown. A nerve jumped spasmodically in his lean cheek. A man was allowed some privacy, yet she continually ignored the 'keep off' signs and crossed the boundaries.

Didn't you invite her in when you offloaded your emotional garbage?

His frown deepened as he pushed away the question and barked, 'How do you figure that one out?'

Watching as she stuck out her chin to a belligerent angle, he felt his anger slipping away to be replaced with an emotion he was less comfortable putting a name to. The woman had more guts than anyone he had ever met.

'If your father had come out of the experience a cynic she would have won, but he hasn't. He hasn't become bitter, cynical and twisted.'

She saw the flicker of an emotion she could not name in his dark eyes before he turned his head away from her. The rain had begun to drum against the window.

'Are you saying I have?'

Instead of responding to the question, she voiced one

that had popped into her head during the conversation. 'Is that why your marriage failed?'

He turned to face her and instead, as she half expected, of telling her to mind her own business, shook his head and repeated the question.

'Is what why my marriage failed?'

Did he lay the blame for his failed marriage at his father's door? It would certainly go a long way to explain why, all these years later, he could not forgive and forget. Common sense told her this was a subject she shouldn't broach but a need to understand this man who had captured her heart was stronger. 'You were forced to concentrate your energy on saving your father and the firm and you didn't have time for your...' Her voice faltered as she stopped and gave a self-conscious shrug. 'It's none of my business. I just...'

'Want to pry and prod.'

Encouraged that he sounded amused, but not antagonistic, she lifted her gaze, studying his face as he replied.

'No, my marriage did not fail because I was busy rebuilding the company. Though I imagine it might have speeded up the process. Simply put, my marriage was never my priority. We married too young—we both wanted different things from life. Marriage requires compromise.' His dark eyes brushed her face. 'I do not do compromise.' He gave a sardonic smile, to which she had no response. 'The end was inevitable.'

Did this clinical analysis hide a broken heart Isandro could not admit to even to himself?

'I was not surprised when Dana left.' One side of his mobile mouth lifted in an ironic half-smile. 'Though I was not expecting her to leave with my best friend,' he conceded.

Unable to control her reaction, Zoe gasped.

Isandro placed a finger under her chin and lifted it. 'The open-mouth look is not so bad on you.' Head tilted a little to one side, he drew back slightly to look at her face, realising as he did so that nothing was a bad look on her.

His eyes darkened as he ran the pad of his thumb down her smooth, downy soft cheek. Inhaling the scent of her warm skin through flared nostrils, he felt the desire that was always close to the surface. Unable to resist the lush softness of her mouth, he bent his head, feeling her sigh as she opened her mouth to deepen the penetration of his tongue, winding her fingers into his hair, pulling him in close.

When he lifted his mouth they stayed that way, her nose pressed to the side of his, her fingers in his hair, their warm breaths mingling.

Reluctant to break physical contact, she slid her hands slowly down over his broad muscular shoulders before crossing them across her stomach in a protective hug. She was still shaking in response to the soul-stripping kiss, the barely leashed violence in his embrace; the simmering hunger still in his eyes made it hard for her to speak, let alone focus.

She felt his hand go to her breasts, cupping them through her clothes, as his other hand skimmed down the side of her face.

She was breathing hard now; her fingers went to his belt.

'If anyone comes…' she said thickly.

He pulled down his jeans and reached across to slide her skirt up her thighs, his fingers sliding up her silky warm skin under the hem of her panties.

'They won't.'

His hard, predatory expression made her shiver inside. Excited and aroused beyond reason or caution, she climbed onto his lap, facing him. His hands moved in a sweeping motion up and down her back and down her buttocks before coming to rest on her hips.

He wanted her so badly that he couldn't breathe; all he could think about was sinking into her. It was crazy and intense.

Zoe reached down to caress his shaft, waiting until he was groaning before she raised herself up and impaled herself on the hard, silky, hot length. Perfectly in tune, they moved together fast and hard in perfect harmony until they both came in a hot, violent flood.

Adjusting her clothes, aware that beside her Isandro was doing the same, she could hardly believe what she had just done. Anyone could have driven by and seen them, and she hadn't cared.

Her body still warm with the flush of desire, she turned to look at him.

'I'm sorry. I didn't know about... It must have been terrible for you.' Dana was a beautiful name. Had she been beautiful? Of course she'd been beautiful.

And he'd loved her... Zoe was shocked by the animosity she felt towards a woman she had never met. Had he been thinking about her while he made love just now?

It took him a few seconds to realise what she was talking about—his ex-wife! They had just made devastating love and she was talking about his ex. He didn't want to talk about Dana; he wanted to talk about where this was going. He wanted to talk about having Zoe in his bed nights.

'I was a hell of a husband. Basically I lived my own life and expected her to take it or leave it. In the end, she left it. I do not blame her. She was lonely and Carl was able to give her the things she wanted.' He held her blue eyes as he said, 'Some men are not meant for marriage.'

The warning was implicit. Wondering uneasily what she'd done to make him feel the need to spell out the obvious, she pulled her hands out from the warmth of his and laughed.

'I suppose there's still time to cancel the engagement notice I sent to the paper. Relax, Isandro, I'm not about to propose.'

And not even in her wildest dreams had she ever imagined Isandro doing so. She had accepted that what they had would never be deep and meaningful for him. What choice did she have? She was taking it one day at a time, enjoying the moments when they were together. Perhaps the knowledge that they would not last gave them a sweet bitterness, but she was determined not to waste a second.

Isandro leaned back in his own seat and turned his head to look at her. 'So you think I should go to my father's wedding?'

'Does it matter what I think?'

'Sometimes an objective view is good.'

Zoe laughed, the sound dredged from somewhere deep inside her bubbling from her lips. She couldn't help herself—objective where Isandro was concerned was something she could never be.

Biting her lip to stem the flow, she responded to his quizzical look with a shrug. 'I thought I was emotional and illogical?'

'You have the occasional lucid moment,' he threw back with a lazy grin.

'So will you go?'

'There is no point in burning my bridges.'

Zoe nodded and lowered her gaze. She had burnt her bridges some time ago. Would she regret it…? She shook her head; she didn't want to think about that now.

She glanced at her watch and was shocked to see how long they had been here. 'I need to pick up the twins. I promised Chloe's mum-in-law I'd pick them up at half past.' It was almost that time now. While she was being utterly selfish she would never let her own selfish desires come ahead of her duty to her sister's children.

'Calm down—it won't take long.'

It didn't. He delivered her to the cottage door only five minutes late. Zoe got out of the car. About to join her, Isandro paused and responded to the bleep of his mobile.

He scanned the screen and with a curse slid it back into his pocket. 'Are you all right getting home alone?'

'Of course.'

'I will see you…' He paused, as if unable to commit himself even to a minor thing like a time, and, nodding curtly, slammed the door and drove off.

CHAPTER ELEVEN

STRUGGLING TO PUSH all thoughts of Isandro from her head, Zoe tapped on the cottage door and walked inside the warm, homely, farmhouse-style kitchen. A second later the impossible was achieved: she wasn't thinking of Isandro.

'Oh, my God!' She dropped to her knees in front of the child seated at the table, her face creased in lines of anxiety as she touched the uninjured side of her nephew's face. 'Harry!'

'It's fine.'

Maud was on her feet, laying a hand on Zoe's shoulder.

'Seriously, it's a lot worse than it looks, dear.'

'How on earth…? Who did this? Has a doctor seen…?'

'The nurse at school cleaned the cut.' Georgie, who had come to stand beside her brother, provided the information to a stunned Zoe.

'But who did this to you, Harry? Why didn't the headmaster inform me?'

'Sit down, dear, you've had a shock.' Maud pushed Zoe down into a chair beside Harry and produced a cup of tea from somewhere. 'The head tried to ring you but you'd already left and your mobile was switched off.'

'He wants to see you tomorrow,' Harry muttered, licking his bruised and swollen lip.

'And I want to see him! I want to know the little thug who—your poor face…'

'It wasn't Adam, it was Harry. He just went for him.'

Zoe turned her head to look at Georgie. 'Harry fighting…?' She shook her head. The image of gentle, sweet Harry brawling was one she simply couldn't accept. Now, if it had been Georgie…

'He was. I saw it.'

'But, Harry, why?'

The little boy shook his head and looked away. It was Georgie who responded.

'It was the things Adam was saying about you and Isandro. I was telling him he was stupid but Harry came in just when Adam called you a bad name and Harry went for him… He was brilliant,' she enthused, turning an admiring look at her twin.

Digesting the information in shock, Zoe recovered enough to knock this on the head. 'It is never brilliant to fight,' she said numbly.

Oh, God, this was her fault!

Of this Zoe had no doubt. The child in question was the son of the attractive vet who had made a play for Isandro at Chloe's party. The woman had gone out of her way ever since to be unpleasant to Zoe, and she had no doubt the kid was only repeating what he had heard at home. Probably everyone was saying the same with various degrees of contempt.

How could she not have considered the possible fall-out for the twins when she had embarked on this affair? She had thought that by keeping the affair from them she was protecting them… Some protection, she thought, self-disgust bubbling like acid in her stomach.

She patted Harry's curly head. 'Don't worry, I'll make things right with the headmaster.'

'I told you not to tell, Georgie. Look, she's crying now.'

Zoe gave a watery smile and sniffed. 'No, I'm not crying. And I'm very, very cross with you.'

The kiss she then planted on Harry's head might have given mixed messages, but what mattered was putting this right. And she would. The sooner, the better. No gingerly easing off the plaster—it was a straight in there, hold your breath, grit your teeth and rip it off. The brutal approach might sting a bit at the time but why prolong the agony?

So the analogy was not perfect. No matter what spin she put on it, Zoe knew that this was going to hurt more than losing a few superficial layers of epidermis, but the important thing was not giving herself time for her resolve to weaken and waver.

That had been the theory anyway. But it was after eleven when the doorbell finally rang and by this time Zoe had gone through nail-biting apprehension and nervous pacing and come out the other side.

She let the doorbell ring a second time before she took a deep breath and headed for the hall. I'm totally calm, she told herself, serene even.

Her serenity lasted all the way up to the door and it swung inwards to reveal a tall, lean figure looking sleek and exclusive in a designer suit and, frankly, well out of her league. It hadn't been intended to last... They were a total mismatch outside the bedroom. She took a deep breath and pushed away thoughts of the bedroom and reminded herself all she was doing was hastening the inevitable.

So suck it up, Zoe, you're a grown-up, a parent...

running away or, even worse, running into his arms is not an option.

'Sorry I'm so late…' Drawn irresistibly to her body heat and softness, he began to lean forward, but was forced to draw back when she whisked away and began to walk towards the sitting room. His expression thoughtful, he watched her retreating back. It grew less thoughtful as his heavy-lidded eyes lingered on her rounded bottom. He shook his head to clear it. 'I hope the food isn't spoilt.'

'I didn't make any food.' Her spine stiff with tension, she walked ahead of him into the sitting room, trying desperately to remember her carefully prepared speech. It had vanished into the ether, or at least into some dark dead end of her stressed brain.

He had caught the negative vibes even before she avoided his embrace. Isandro's expression grew contemptuous as he asked himself what point exactly he had been making when he hadn't rung to say he'd be late.

It was simply another example of his increasingly pathetic attempts to pretend that this was all casual. Who was he kidding anyway?

Well, there, he'd admitted it, but this wasn't the time to rush on and make any dramatic declarations. Clearly if he wanted to keep Zoe in his bed and in his life he would have to bend some of his normal rules.

The painful acknowledgement had an aftertaste of relief to it… He felt a little of the tension in his shoulders release. Why on earth had that been so difficult? It wasn't as if he hadn't been bending the bloody rules to breaking point from the moment her blue eyes, sinuous curves and smart mouth appeared in his world.

Life was about to change, and he wasn't infatuated; he was…past infatuation.

Still unwilling to follow this insight through to its conclusion, he closed the door of the sitting room behind him. He should be opening doors. The contemplative furrow in his brow smoothed.

It was not a weakness to accept he wanted more from this relationship than sex, it was a weakness not to accept it.

He clapped a hand to his head. Will you listen to yourself, Isandro? the analytical portion of his brain mocked. This was exactly the reason he didn't go in for all that self-analysis crap. It could drive a man crazy and get him nowhere, especially when he'd not had a full night's sleep for how long…?

Before, he had never spent a full night with a woman out of his own choice. But now the roles were reversed and, back in his own bed, for some reason he just lay awake unable to sleep without her warmth in his arms.

Boyfriend… He tried the description on for size in his head. He'd never actually been anyone's boyfriend. The whole idea seemed…not him.

Her initial impression of intense weariness was more pronounced when he walked into the small living room. It was palpable. It took every ounce of her self-control to fight the compelling urge to rush to him.

He paused, appearing to sense her mood before he tilted his head towards the ceiling and said in a hushed voice, 'The children?'

'Are asleep.'

He expelled a sigh, silenced the narrative in his head and extended his arms. It did not cross his mind for one moment that she would not run into them. Zoe was more responsive to him than any other woman he had ever met. If his passion for her was unquenchable, so was hers for him.

She was infatuated.

She's in love.

Zoe stood, her feet glued to the spot, and shook her head. The effort caused beads of sweat to form on her upper lip, but she dabbed them with her tongue and shook her head.

He did not approach her, but instead closed the door behind him and leaned his broad shoulders against the wall. He looked very pale. His dark eyes were weirdly blank, they reminded her of someone in shock.

He cleared his throat. 'Problem?'

She laughed even though she felt like crying. That was so like Isandro, who never used two words when one would suffice. Then, gathering her determination in both hands, she nodded.

'This isn't working.'

He would appreciate brevity, she decided, stifling an irrational stab of guilt. It wasn't as if Isandro had invested any emotions in this relationship. It would be a mistake to imagine that he would feel as though he'd lost a limb if she vanished from his life.

The highly charged silence stretched and pulsed, then he laughed and broke the spell.

She cleared her throat. Either he was more all right with this than she had imagined or he was not taking her seriously. 'I'm not joking. I think we should agree to call it a day.'

He stopped laughing. 'You do?'

She nodded, then cleared her throat. She had seen granite walls more revealing than his expression. The only things moving were the muscles in his brown throat as they rippled under the surface of his bronzed skin. 'Yes.'

Isandro closed his eyes, fighting the urge to yell. The children were upstairs sleeping and he could not yell; he had to appear invisible.

Her insistence on maintaining the unrealistic illusion they were nothing but passing acquaintances had not seemed a big ask at the time. It had even seemed like a good idea. However, it had ceased to feel like a good idea some time ago.

There was a certain dark irony to the situation. He had always avoided having his name linked with a woman, and now he was with a woman who seemed ashamed to acknowledge they were sleeping together.

It should have been the ideal situation, but it wasn't.

The previous week he had driven past the school when she was picking up the twins. They had waved and Zoe had pretended not to see him. He had been contemplating leaping out of the car and hauling her into his arms and kissing her in front of the entire damned gossipy village whose opinion seemed to matter so much to her. It wasn't as if they didn't all know they were sleeping together anyway.

But he hadn't, because he wasn't a Neanderthal. Though lately he had seen there were certain advantages in following your baser instincts.

Obviously he did not want to set up house, but neither did he want to be treated like a dirty secret… It was demeaning for any man.

'You need a drink.'

Zoe felt panic as she watched him shrug off his jacket before walking across to the cupboard where she had put the half-drunk bottle of wine he had opened the previous evening.

'I don't drink, remember?' She took a deep breath, lowered her voice from the shrill, unattractive level it had risen to and reminded him, 'We agreed that when this didn't work we would simply call it a day. Look, I know it must be strange because you assumed— actually so did I—that it would be you who ended things.' She gave a sad smile. 'It's nothing personal,' she added earnestly.

He studied her face for any sign of irony but there was none. 'Well, I do want a drink,' he said, pouring the remnants of the bottle into a glass and swallowing the contents without tasting.

'So nothing personal, which of course makes all the difference,' he drawled, setting aside the glass with elaborate care while in his head he saw it smashing to a million pieces as he threw it into the fireplace.

'Please don't be like that,' she begged. 'This is hard.' She bit her trembling lip. She could not afford to lose her focus now, she could not afford to allow him to touch her…

'This is bloody ridiculous,' he contended, thrusting his balled fists into the pockets of his well-cut trousers and glaring at her.

Zoe recognised the cause of his belligerence but she was not in the mood to show much understanding for injured male pride. So maybe he had just been dumped for the first time in his life. There were any number of nubile women who would be gagging to massage his ego.

She, on the other hand, might never fall in love again. This man was her soulmate, and all he could do was sulk while her heart was damned well breaking.

Well, at least he should remember her, though for all the wrong reasons—as the woman who dared to dump him!

KIM LAWRENCE 175

'I know you said we could stay on here,' she said formally, 'but that wouldn't be right. I have made alternative arrangements.'

'You have what?' he roared as his smouldering temper sparked into full-blown conflagration. 'Since when is this not working?'

She kept her chin up, not easy when a man who appeared to be ten feet tall was towering over her like some sort of damned volcano. 'Since Harry came home with a black eye and a split lip after brawling with a boy who called me a cheap tart, among other things.'

Isandro took a step back, the air leaving his lungs in one audible, sizzling hiss.

CHAPTER TWELVE

'IS HE ALL RIGHT?'

Mingled with the protective outrage Isandro felt was a surge of pride that the boy had stood up for his aunt; he had protected her honour.

Which was more than he had done. The guilty knowledge that this situation was one of his making scratched away at Isandro's conscience like a nail on a blackboard.

No complications? He had known that was a total impossibility from day one. He had tried extremely hard to tell himself otherwise but he had known that this thing could get very complicated. He had taken refuge in technicalities—Zoe no longer worked for him; he never spent the entire night. He should have seen this coming. But he had wanted her...needed her with a hunger that was totally outside his experience. And in order to satisfy that hunger he had been prepared to break any and all rules.

She nodded, the concern now in his dark eyes making her tear up. 'He will be.'

She rubbed a stray tear with the back of her hand, and the gesture made Isandro's throat tighten.

'This is a small village and people gossip. It was

unrealistic of me not to expect this, and selfish of me not to consider the effect this sort of affair would have on the twins.'

'So you think that nobody in this village has sex outside marriage?'

The sarcasm in his voice brought a flush to her pale cheeks. 'That's not the point.'

'What are you going to do—take a vow of chastity until the twins leave home? No boyfriends? That is your idea of preparing them for the real world?'

'You're not my boyfriend. We don't have a relation-ship—we have sex.'

'Or do you need a ring on your finger? Is that what this is about?'

'Of course not. It's not sex outside marriage, it's sex with you!' she yelled before she remembered the sleep-ing children.

He did not respond to her announcement at all, though his feet-apart stance and stony, tight-lipped si-lence did not exactly convey happiness.

'I don't want to argue.' She gave a weary sigh and looked at him through her lashes, head tilted a little to one side. Seeing the familiar attitude, he felt his anger levels decrease.

'But it's true—you're not my boyfriend. And I didn't mean it to sound the way it did about sex with you, but it is true as well… How can I tell the children that sex within a loving, caring relationship can be a beautiful thing, when I'm having sex with you?' While it might be beautiful for her, she knew that for Isandro it was simply an act of physical release.

If ever she had come close to reading more into his exquisite tenderness and mind-blowing passion, she reminded herself of this: it was just sex for Isandro, for all that he did 'just sex' very well indeed.

He arched a sardonic brow. 'So you are only sleeping with me to pay for the rent.'

The suggestion brought a rosy tinge of anger to her pale cheeks. How dared he act like the injured party?

'Of course I'm not! I'd sleep with you if I had to crawl across a desert to get into your bed.' Her blue eyes held his, shining with passionate fervour, before she dropped her gaze, remembering a few crucial seconds late that she was ending a relationship, not declaring he was her drug of choice...legal but, oh, so addictive.

'But this isn't about what I want.' She inhaled and struggled to clear the haze of desire in her brain. The memory of Harry's bruised little face did the trick better than a bucket of cold water. She squared her slender shoulders and lifted her chin. 'It's what I need to do for the twins. I have to send out the right message and I know full well that even—'

His eyes held a complacent gleam as he added helpfully, 'You would crawl across a desert to sleep with me?'

As if he didn't already know that! Zoe slung him a cross look and sniffed. He wasn't making this any easier.

'A figure of speech,' she muttered, knowing it had been much more than that and hoping he didn't. 'We're really not discussing how great you are in bed.'

'Sex with you is worth the odd desert crossing, too.'

Even above the presence of his painful arousal, Isandro was conscious of a strange heaviness in his chest as he made a conscious effort to capture Zoe's eyes. She seemed determined to look anywhere but at him. The moment of success when he welded his sloe-black eyes on her bright burning blue… The heaviness in his chest bordered unbearable… Yet he felt strangely exhilarated. Was he having a heart attack?

Zoe licked her dry lips and struggled to think past the static buzz of electricity in the room.

'Thanks…' she said, not knowing what else to say, and not hearing the huskiness in her voice above the deafening clamour of her pounding pulses. 'Children can be very cruel.' She gave a loud sniff. 'So you see that I can't continue to live here to be your…mistress.'

'You are not my mistress.'

His offended hauteur in his attitude struck her as weird. 'I live here, and you own the place.'

'You pay rent.'

'A token amount. And the fact is you wouldn't have offered me this place if we hadn't been having sex.'

'I have never paid for sex.'

'We can play table tennis semantics all night, but it won't stop other people seeing me as a kept woman.'

'I don't give a damn what people think.'

'That's not a luxury I can afford, Isandro,' she said sadly. 'It stopped being the day I took on the twins. It's my job to be a good role model for them. Even if they didn't have to contend with the sort of teasing that happened today, what sort message am I sending?'

'Parents do have sex. That is the reality, and you cannot protect them from every hurt along the way. I will have a word with the headmaster.'

She stared at him. 'I can't believe you just said that!' she yelped, dropping into a chair.

'Neither can I,' he admitted honestly.

'You will not have any words with the headmaster.

You will not go near the school… I want the children
to know about adult relationships, know that sex should
happen within the confines of a loving relationship. Not
like…I may have…' Her eyes filled as she trawled her
vocabulary for a word that would cover what she had.

'You're overreacting,' he accused.

She thought of Harry's face and shook her head.
'No,' she said. 'I'm not.'

'You want the children to go to school here. Where
will you live? I know Polly well enough to know she's
probably paying you a pittance.' Polly would have
squeezed a stone dry if it put up her profit margins, and
Zoe was too self-deprecating to know her own value.

'I'm learning. She's paying me a fair wage and I've
already been looking for suitable accom—'

'Looking!' He pounced on the word like a circling
tiger looking for a weakness. 'So this thing with the
twins is just an excuse? It's not spontaneous. You were
already planning—'

She bit her lip. 'I wasn't planning—preparing.'

Sally at the shop had some holiday lets by the canal—
a row of terraced cottages that were empty now the season was over. She was willing to let Zoe have one until
she sorted herself something more permanent.

'You can't. I won't let you.'

'You can't stop me. It's my choice.'

'And you think it will be so easy, do you, to spend
your nights alone in your solitary single bed?'

She reacted to this deliberate cruelty with a display
of stubborn defiance. 'The cottage runs to a double.
And who says I'll be alone?'

He was out of his chair and beside her, hauling her
to her feet, before she had even finished speaking. His

warm breath brushed her cheek as he bent in close. 'Have you been preparing for that, too? Have you met someone?'

She closed her eyes, feeling faint, smelling the citrusy scent of the soap he used. Every instinct she possessed was telling her to sink into all his male hardness, but Zoe fought and from somewhere dredged up the strength to put her hands against his chest and push away.

'I thought your speciality was painless break-ups,' she panted as she drew her hair back from her face with a shaky hand. 'Or is that only when you're dictating the timing?'

He didn't respond to the accusation. He was watching her rub her arm where he caught hold of her. He swore and touched her hand lightly; her fingers immediately curled around his. 'Let me see…?'

Zoe shook her head and didn't let go of his finger. The thought of letting go permanently left a great aching hole in her chest.

Would it ever go away?

'It's nothing.'

'The thought of you with another man makes me…' Their eyes connected.

'How could you think there's another man, Isandro?'

'I didn't…I don't. I'm just…' He stopped, let go of her hand and raked his fingers through his hair. 'You can't go, Zoe.'

'Why can't I go?'

'I need you…I love you.' He blinked and looked like a man waking up from a dream. '*Dios*, of course I do. I love you!' he yelled.

She hitched a startled breath and stared up at him. 'Is this your idea of a joke?' she asked him shakily.

'Anything but, *querida*,' he retorted throatily.

'Are you saying this to get me into bed?'

His head reared back as though she had struck him. 'I suppose I deserve that for being so bloody stupid,' he admitted quietly. 'I have been a fool. I was so busy not being a loser like my father that I almost became a loser like me...the biggest loser in the world if I let you walk away from me.'

'You love me?' It still didn't seem real.

'Is that so hard to believe? I can barely stand to have you out of my sight for two seconds. The thought of losing you sent me into a blind panic. I just couldn't admit it, couldn't admit that my fate was no longer in my hands, but that I had put it in yours.' It had taken the prospect of losing her to make him wake up to himself and see what he strongly suspected everyone else already had.

Everyone but Zoe.

He captured her small hands and lifted them to his lips, looking deep into her eyes with an expression that brought tears of joy to them.

'I love you, Isandro.'

'I sort of guessed that.'

She gave a laugh. 'And I thought I was being so subtle.' He pulled her to him and kissed her, a hard, passionate kiss full of promise and love.

'Say it again, Isandro?' she begged huskily.

'I love you, *querida*.' The words that he had been afraid of now came easily; the problem now might be not saying them every second of the day.

'Shall we get married at the hall? Or would you prefer—?'

She drew back her eyes wide. 'Married?'

'Well, how else can I face this headmaster and sort things out for Harry? A boyfriend is not going to have the same pull as a fiancé.'

She blinked, unable to believe this was commitment-phobic Isandro talking. 'You'd do that? Take on the twins?'

'I think the question is more whether they will take me on.'

'Oh, I think they might be OK with it.'

'And you, my love—are you OK with it?'

She smiled and flew into his arms. 'So OK with it, Isandro, so very OK.'

Two months later they attended the wedding of Isandro's father, Raul, in Seville.

It was a lovely wedding, though not, to Zoe's way of thinking, a patch on her own the previous month.

It really pleased her to see Isandro and his father on such good terms. Their little family was growing and soon it would be even bigger.

She had kept the secret to herself two whole days and as the organist struck up the 'Wedding March' she could hold it in no longer. She leaned across and whispered in Isandro's ear.

He frowned at her and mouthed, 'What?'

She whispered again with the same result. Rolling her eyes, she leaned in and yelled, 'I'm pregnant!'

Of course, it coincided with the music stopping and her announcement echoed off the rafters of the church.

'Why do these things keep happening to me? What is wrong with my timing?'

Isandro, his eyes gleaming, bent towards her. 'Your timing is perfect and as far as I'm concerned you can shout it from the rafters every day… I want the world to know I'm the luckiest man alive.'

Zoe, who had never cried at a wedding before, cried at the second one in two months…tears of pure joy.

* * * * *

THE MAID'S
SPANISH SECRET

DANI COLLINS

For my editor, Laurie Johnson, and the wonderful team at Mills & Boon in London.

Romance novels taught me to chase my dreams, and writing for Mills & Boon Modern Romance was a lifelong goal.

Thirty books in, I'm still astonished and eternally grateful that you've made this dream come true for me.

Thank you.

PROLOGUE

RICO MONTERO ARRIVED at his brother's villa, two hours up the coast from Valencia, in seventy-three minutes. He'd been feeling cooped up in his penthouse, hungry for air. He had pulled his GTA Spano out of storage and tried to escape his own dark mood, not realizing the direction he took until he was pulled over for speeding.

Recognizing where he was, he told the officer he was on his way to see his brother—a means of name-dropping the entire family. The ploy had gotten him out of having his license suspended, but he still had to pay a fine.

Since he was literally in the neighborhood, he decided not to compound his crimes by lying. He rolled his way through Cesar's vineyard to the modern home sprawled against a hillside.

He told himself he didn't miss the vineyard he had owned with pride for nearly a decade—long before his brother had decided he had an interest in grapes and winemaking. Rico's fascination with the process had dried up along with his interest in life in general. Selling that property had been a clean break from a time he loathed to dwell upon.

It's been eighteen months, his mother had said over lunch yesterday. *Time to turn our attention to the future.*

She had said something similar three months ago and he had dodged it. This time, he sat there and took the bullet. *Of course. Who did you have in mind?*

He had left thinking, *Go ahead and find me another scheming, adulterous bride.* But he hadn't said it aloud. He had promised to carry that secret to his grave.

For what?

He swore and jammed the car into Park, then threw himself out of it, grimly aware he had completely failed to escape his dour mood.

"Rico!" His sister-in-law Sorcha opened the door before he had climbed the wide steps. She smiled with what looked like genuine pleasure and maybe a hint of relief.

"Mateo, look. Tío Rico has come to see you." She spoke to the bawling toddler on her hip. "That's a nice surprise, isn't it?"

She wasn't the flawlessly elegant beauty he was used to seeing on Cesar's arm, more of a welcoming home-maker. Her jeans and peasant-style top were designer brands, but she wore minimal makeup and her blond hair was tied into a simple ponytail. Her frown at her unhappy son was tender and empathetic, not the least frazzled by his tantrum.

The deeply unhappy Mateo pointed toward the back of the house. "*Ve*, Papi."

"He's overdue for his nap." Sorcha waved Rico in. "But he knows *someone* took *someone else* into the V-I-N-E-Y-A-R-D."

"You're speaking English and you still have to spell it out?" Rico experienced a glimmer of amusement.

"He's picking it up *so* fast. Oh!" She caught Mateo as he reached out to Rico, nearly launching himself from her arms.

Rico caught him easily while Sorcha stammered, "I'm sorry."

If Rico briefly winced in dismay, it was because of the look in Sorcha's eyes. Far too close to pity, it contained sincere regret that her son was prevailing on him for something she thought too big and painful to ask.

It wasn't. The favor he was doing for his former in-laws was a greater imposition, spiking far more deeply into a more complex knot of nerves. What Sorcha thought she knew about his marriage was the furthest thing from reality.

And what she read as pain and anger at fate was contempt and fury with himself for being a fool. He was steeped in bitterness, playing a role that was barely a version of the truth. A version that made a sensitive soul like Sorcha wear a poignant smile as she gazed on him holding his young nephew.

Mateo stopped crying, tears still on his cheeks.

"*Ve*, Papi?" he tried.

The tyke had been born mere weeks before Rico's ill-fated marriage. Mateo was sturdy and stubborn and full of the drive that all the Montero males possessed. This was why he was giving his mother such a hard time. He knew what he wanted and a nap wouldn't mollify him.

"We'll discuss it," he told the boy and glanced at Sorcha. "You should change," he advised, unable to bear much more of that agonized happiness in her eyes.

"Why—? Ugh." She noticed the spot where Mateo had rubbed his streaming face against her shoulder. "You're okay?" she asked with concern.

"For God's sake, Sorcha," he muttered through clenched teeth.

He regretted his short temper immediately and quickly reined in his patience. His secret sat in him like a cancer, but he couldn't let it provoke him into lashing out, certainly not at the nicest person in his family.

"I didn't mean to speak so sharply," he managed to say, gathering his composure as he brought his nephew to his shoulder. "We're fine."

"It's okay, Rico." She squeezed his arm. "I understand."

No. She didn't. But thankfully she disappeared, leaving him to have a man-to-man chat with Mateo, who hadn't forgotten a damned thing. He gave it one more try, pointing and asking for Cesar, who had taken his older brother Enrique to speak to winemakers and pet cellar cats and generally have a barrel of a good time by anyone's standards.

Mateo's eyes were droopy, his cheeks red, very much worn out from his tantrum.

"I know what you're going through," he told the boy. "Better than you can imagine."

Like Mateo, Rico was the younger brother to the future *duque*. He, too, occupied the unlit space beneath the long shadow of greatness cast by the heir. He, too, was expected to live an unblemished life so as not to tarnish the title he would never hold. Then there was the simple, fraternal rivalry of a brother being that few years older and moving into the next life stage. Envy was natural, not that Monteros were allowed to feel such things. Emotions were too much like pets, requiring regular feeding and liable to leave a mess on the floor.

Rico climbed the grand staircase to the bedroom that had been converted to a playroom for the boys, not dwelling on Cesar's stellar fulfillment of his duty with two bright and healthy children, a beautiful home and a stunning, warmhearted wife.

"There are some realities that are not worth crying about," he informed Mateo as they entered the room. "Your father told me that." It was one of Rico's earliest memories.

Cry all you want. They won't care. Cesar had spoken with the voice of experience after Rico had been denied something he'd desperately wanted that he could no longer recollect.

Cesar had come to reason with him, perhaps because he was tired of having his playmate sent into solitary confinement. Reason was a family skill valued far more highly than passion. Reason was keeping him silent and carrying on today, maintaining order rather than allowing the chaos that would reign if the truth came out.

Doesn't it make you mad that they won't even listen? Rico had asked Cesar that long-ago day.

Yes. Cesar had been very mature for a boy of six or seven. *But getting mad won't change anything. You might as well accept it and think about something else.*

Words Rico had learned to live by.

He was capable of basic compassion, however.

"I'll always listen if you need to get something off your chest," he told his nephew as he lowered them both into an armchair. "But sometimes there's nothing to be done. It's a hard fact of life, young man."

Mateo wound down to sniffling whimpers. He decided to explore Rico's empty chest pocket.

"Should we read a book?" Rico picked up the first picture book within reach. It was bilingual, with trains and dogs and bananas labeled in English and Spanish.

As he worked through the pages, he deliberately pitched his voice to an uninflected drone. The boy's head on his chest grew heavier and heavier.

"Thank you," Sorcha whispered when she peeked in.

Rico nodded and carried the sleeping boy to his crib. The nanny came in with the baby monitor.

Rico followed Sorcha down the stairs saying, "I'll go find Cesar. If Mateo wakes, don't tell him what a traitor I am."

"Actually, I was going to invite you for dinner later this week. There's something I want to talk to you about. Can we go into Cesar's office?" Her brow pleated with concern.

Rico bit back a sigh, trying to hold on to the temper that immediately began to slip. "If this is about me remarrying, Mother has passed along your concerns."

Your sister-in-law thinks it's too soon, his mother had said yesterday, not asking him how *he* felt. She had merely implied that in Sorcha's view, he was in a weakened state. His choice had been to confirm it or go along with his mother's insistence on finding him a new wife.

"This is something else," Sorcha murmured, closing the door and waving toward the sofa. "And my imagination could be running wild. I haven't said anything to Cesar."

She poured two glasses of the Irish whiskey she had turned Cesar on to drinking and brought one to where Rico stood.

"Really?" he drawled, wondering what she could possibly impart that would need to be absorbed with a bracing shot. He left the whiskey on the end table as they both sat.

"Please don't be angry with me. I know I was over-stepping, suggesting your mother hold off on pressing you to remarry, but I care about all of you." She sat with her elbows on her thighs, leaning forward, hands clasped. "You may not be the most demonstrative family, but you *are* family. I will never stay silent if I think one of you needs…" Her mouth tightened.

"Sorcha." He meticulously gathered his forbearance. "I'm fine." And, before he had to suffer another swimming gaze of tormented sympathy, he added, "If I were in your shoes, I would understand why you think I'm not, but honestly, you have to stop worrying about me."

"That's never going to happen," she said primly, which would have been endearing if he didn't find it so frustratingly intrusive. "And there may be other factors to consider." She sipped her drink and eyed him over it. Then sighed. "I feel like such a hypocrite."

He lifted his brows. "Why? What's going on?"

She frowned, set down her drink and picked up her phone, stared at it without turning it on. "Elsa, our nanny, showed me something that came up in her news feed."

"Something compromising?" Sorcha would have taken up the concern with Cesar unless— Oh, hell. Had something gotten out from the coroner's report? "Is this about Faustina?" His molars ground together on reflex.

"No! No, it's not about her at all." She touched her brow. "Elsa always comes with us when we have dinner at your mother's. She's acquainted with the maids there and follows some of them online."

At the word *maid* a premonition danced in his periphery. He refused to reach for the drink, though. It would be a tell. Instinctively, he knew he had to maintain impassivity. He couldn't tip his hand. Not before he knew exactly what was coming next.

"To be honest, I rarely check my social media accounts," he said with a disinterested brush of non-existent lint from his knee. "Especially since Faustina passed. It's very maudlin."

"I suppose it would be." Her expression grew pinched. She looked at the phone she held pressed between her palms. "But one way or another, I think you should be aware of this particular post."

Biting her lips together, she touched her thumb to the sensor and the screen woke. She flicked to bring up a photo and held it out to him.

"On first glance, Elsa thought it was Mateo dressed up as a girl. That's the only reason she took notice and showed me. She thought it was funny that it had given her a double take. I had to agree this particular photo offers a certain resemblance."

Rico flicked a look at the toddler. He'd never seen Mateo in a pink sailor's bib and hat, but the baby girl's grin was very similar, minus a few teeth, to the one he had coaxed out of his nephew before the boy's head had drooped against his chest.

"I actually keep my privacy settings locked down tight," Sorcha said. "I've heard photos can be stolen and wind up in ads without permission. I thought that's what had happened. Elsa assured me she never shares images of the boys with anyone but me or Cesar."

The Montero fortune had been built on the development of chemicals and special alloys. Rico had learned early that certain substances, innocuous on their own, could become explosive when in proximity to one another.

Sorcha was pouring statements into beakers before him. A maid. A baby that looked like other children in the family.

He wouldn't let those two pieces of information touch. Not yet.

"It's said we all have a double." His lifetime of suppressing emotion served him well. "It would seem you've found Mateo's."

"This is the only photo where she looks so much like him," Sorcha murmured, taking back her phone. "I looked up the account. Her mother is a photographer."

Photographer. One beaker began to tip into another.

"This is part of her portfolio for her home business. Her name is Poppy Harris. The mother, I mean. The baby is Lily."

His abdomen tightened to brace for a kick. A sizzle resounded in his ears. Adrenaline made him want to reach for his drink, but he only lifted his hand to scratch his cheek—while his mind conjured the forest of lilies that had surrounded them in his mother's solarium as he and Poppy had made love so impulsively.

"Do you…remember her?" Sorcha asked tentatively.

Skin scented like nectarines, lush corkscrews of curly red hair filling his hands as he consumed her crimson lips. He remembered the exact pitch of her joyful cries of release, the culmination of madness like he'd never known before or since.

And he remembered vividly the ticking of the clock on the mantel as he had sat in his mother's parlor the next morning, an itchy fire in his blood driving him mad. He'd been on the verge of going to look for her because he couldn't stop thinking about her.

Then Faustina had arrived, striking like dry lightning with sheepishly delivered news. Family obligation had crashed upon him afresh, pinning him under the weight of a wedding that had been called off, but now was back on. They would pretend the gap in the parade had never happened.

"Rico?" Sorcha prompted gently, dragging him back to the present. "I know this must be a shock." And there was that infernal compassion again.

He swore, tired to his *bones* of people thinking he was mourning a baby he had already known wasn't his. He was sorry for the loss of a life before it had had the chance to start. Of course he was. But he wasn't grieving with the infinite heartbreak of a parent losing a child. It hadn't been *his*.

And given Faustina's trickery, he was damned cynical about whether he had conceived *this* one.

"Why did you jump straight to suspecting she's mine?" he asked baldly.

Sorcha was slightly taken aback. "Well, I'm not going to suspect my own husband, am I?" Her tone warned that he had better not, either. Her chin came up a notch. "You were living in your parents' villa at the time. Frankly, your father doesn't seem particularly passionate about any woman, young or old. You, however, were briefly unengaged."

Rico had long suspected the success of his parents' marriage could be attributed to both of them being fairly asexual and lacking in passion for anything beyond cool reason and the advancement of family interests.

Sorcha's eyes grew big and soft and filled with that excruciating pity. "I'm not judging, Rico. *I know how these things happen.*"

"I bet you do." He regretted it immediately. It wasn't him. At least, it wasn't the man he was beneath the layer of caustic fury he couldn't seem to shed. Sorcha certainly didn't deserve this ugly side of him. She was kind and sensitive and everything the rest of them didn't know how to be.

She recoiled, rightly shocked that he would deliver such a belly blow. But she hadn't risen above the scandal of secretly delivering his brother's baby while Cesar had been engaged to someone else without possessing truckloads of resilience.

"I meant because my mother was my father's maid when she conceived *me*." Her voice was tight and strong, but there was such a wounded shadow in her gaze, he had to look away and reach for the drink she'd poured him.

He drained it, burning away the words that hovered on his tongue. Words he couldn't speak because he was trying to spare Faustina's parents some humiliation when they were already destroyed by the loss of their only child.

"I'll assume if you're lashing out, you believe it's possible that little girl is yours. How she came about is your business, Rico, but don't you *ever* accuse me of trapping Cesar into this marriage. I *left*, if you recall." She stood, hot temper well lit, but honed by her marriage to a Montero into icy severity. "And so did Poppy. Maybe ask yourself why, if you're such a prize, she doesn't want anything to do with you. *I* have an idea, if you can't figure it out for yourself."

She stalked to the door and swung it open, inviting him to leave using nothing more than a head held high and an expression of frosty contempt that prickled his conscience through the thick shields of indifference he had been bricking into place since Faustina had been found.

"I shouldn't have said that," Rico ground out, mind reeling so badly as he stood, his head swam. "I was shooting the messenger." With a missile launcher loaded with nuclear waste. "Tell Cesar what you've told me. I'll let him punch me in the face for what I said to you." He meant it.

She didn't thaw. Not one iota. "Deal with the message. I have a stake in the outcome, as do my husband and sons."

"Oh, I will," he promised. *"Immediately."*

CHAPTER ONE

POPPY HARRIS FILLED the freshly washed sippy cup with water only to have Lily ignore it and keep pointing at the shelf.

"You want a real cup, don't you?"

Two weeks ago, Lily's no-spill cup had gone missing from daycare. Poppy's grandmother, being old-school, thought cups with closed lids and straws were silly. Back in *her* day, babies learned to drink from a proper cup.

Since she was pinching pennies, Poppy hadn't bought a new one. She had spent days mopping dribbles instead, and she'd been *so* happy when the cup had reappeared today.

Unfortunately, Lily was a big girl now. She wanted an open cup. *Thanks, Gran.*

Poppy considered whether a meltdown right before dinner was worth the battle. She compromised by easing Lily's grip off her pant leg and then sat her gently onto her bottom, unable to resist running affectionate fingertips through Lily's fine red-gold curls. She handed her both the leakproof cup and an empty plastic tumbler. Hopefully that would keep her busy for a few minutes.

"I'm putting the biscuits in the oven, Gran," Poppy called as she did it.

She scooped a small portion of leek-and-potato soup from the slow cooker into a shallow bowl. She had started the soup when she raced home on her lunch break to check on her grandmother. Every day felt like a flat-out run, but she didn't complain. Things could be worse.

She set the bowl on the table so it would be cool enough for Lily to eat when they sat down.

"The fanciest car has just pulled in, Poppy," her grandmother said in her quavering voice. Her evening game shows were on, but she preferred to watch the comings and goings beyond their front room window. "Is he one of your models needing a head shot? He's *very* handsome."

"What?" Poppy's stomach dropped. It was completely instinctive and she made herself take a mental step back. There was no reason to believe it would be *him*.

Even so, she struggled to swallow a jagged lump that lodged in her suddenly arid throat. "Who—?"

The doorbell rang.

Poppy couldn't move. She didn't want to see. If it wasn't Rico, she would be irrationally disappointed. If it *was* him…

She looked to her daughter, instantly petrified that he was here to claim her. What would he say? How could she stop him? She couldn't.

It wasn't him, she told herself. It was one of those prophets in a three-piece suit who hand-delivered pamphlets about the world being on the brink of annihilation.

Her world was fine, she reassured herself, still staring at the sprite who comprised the lion's share of all that was important to her. Lily tipped her head back in an effort to drain water from an empty cup.

The bell rang again.

"Poppy?" her grandmother prompted, glancing her direction. "Will you answer?"

Mentally, Gran was sharp as a tack. Her vision and hearing never failed her. Osteoporosis, however, had impacted her mobility. Her bones were so fragile, Poppy had to be ever vigilant that Lily and her toys weren't underfoot. Her gran would break a hip or worse if she ever stumbled.

There were a lot of things about this living arrangement that made it less than ideal, but both she and Gran were maintaining the status quo, kidding themselves that Gramps was only down at the hardware store and would be back any minute.

"Of course." Poppy snapped out of her stasis and glanced over to be sure the gates on both doorways into the kitchen were closed. All the drawers and cupboards had locks except the one where the plastic dishes were kept. The mixing bowls were a favorite for being dragged out and nested, filled with toys and measuring cups, then dumped without ceremony.

"Keep an eye this way, Gran?" Poppy murmured as she stepped over the gate into the front room, then moved past her seated grandmother to the front door.

Her glance out the side window struck a dark brown bomber jacket over black jeans, but she knew that head, that back with the broad shoulders, that butt and long legs.

His arrival struck like a bus. Like a train that derailed her composure and rattled on for miles, piling one broken thought onto another.

OhGodohGodohGod... *Breathe.* All the way in, all the way out, she reminded herself. But she had always imagined that if this much money showed up on her doorstep, it would be with an oversize check and a television crew. *Not him.*

Rico pivoted from surveying her neighbor's fence and the working grain elevator against the fading Saskatchewan sky. His profile was knife sharp, carved of titanium and godlike. A hint of shadow was coming in on his jaw, just enough to bend his angelic looks into the fallen kind.

He knocked.

"Poppy—?" her grandmother prompted, tone perplexed by the way she was acting. Or failing to.

How? *How* could he know? Poppy had no doubt that he did. There was absolutely no other reason for this man to be this far off the beaten track. He sure as hell wasn't here to see *her.*

Blood searing with fight or flight, heart pounding, she opened the door.

The full force of his impact slammed through her. The hard angle of his chin, the stern cast of his mouth, his wide shoulders and long legs, and hands held in tense, almost fists.

His jaw hardened as he took her in through mirrored aviators. Their chrome finish was cold and steely. If he'd had a fresh haircut, it had been ruffled by the wind. His boots were alligator, his cologne nothing but crisp, snow-scented air and fuming suspicion.

Poppy lifted her chin and pretended her heart wasn't whirling like a Prairie tornado in her chest.

"Can I help you?" she asked, exactly as she would if he had been a complete stranger.

His hand went to the doorframe. His nostrils twitched as he leaned into the space. "Really?" he asked in a tone of lethal warning.

"Who is it, Poppy?" her grandmother asked.

He stiffened slightly, as though surprised she wasn't alone. Then his mouth curled with disparagement, waiting to see if she would lie.

Poppy swallowed, her entire body buzzing, but she held his gaze through those inscrutable glasses while she said in a strong voice, "Rico, Gran. The man I told you about. From Spain."

There, she silently conveyed. *What do you think of that?*

It wasn't wise to defy him. She knew that by the roil of threat in the pit of her stomach, but she had had to grow up damned fast in the last two years. She was not some naive traveler succumbing to a charmer who turned out to be a thief, or even the starry-eyed maid who had encouraged a philandering playboy to seduce her.

She was a grown woman who had learned how to face her problems head-on.

"Oh?" Gran's tone gave the whole game away in one murmur. There was concern beneath her curiosity. Knowledge. It was less a blithe, *isn't that nice that your friend turned up.* More an alarmed, *Why is he here?*

There was no hiding. None. Poppy might not be able to read this man's eyes, but she read his body language. He wasn't here to ask questions. He was here to confront.

Because he knew she'd had his baby.

Her eyes grew wet with panic, but through her shock, she reacted to seeing her lover, her first and only lover twenty months after they had conceived their daughter. She had thought her brief hour with him a moment of madness. A rush of sex hormones born of dented self-esteem and grand self-delusion.

Since then, her body had been taken over by their daughter. Poppy had been sure her sex drive had dried up and blown away on the Prairie winds. Or at least was firmly in hibernation.

As it turned out, her libido was alive and well. Heat flooded into her with the distant tingles of intimate, erotic memories. Of the cold press of his belt buckle trapped against her thigh, the dampness of perspiration in the hollow of his spine when she ran her hands beneath his open shirt to clutch at him with encouragement. She recalled exactly the way he had kissed the whisker burn on her chin so tenderly, with a growl of apology in his throat. The way he had cupped her breast with restraint, then licked and sucked at her nipple until she was writhing beneath him.

She could feel anew the sharp sensation of him possessing her, so intimate and satisfying, both glorious and ruinous all at once.

She blushed. Hard. Which made the blistering moment feel like hours. She was overflowing at the edges with mortifying awkwardness, searching her mind for something to say, a way to dissemble so he wouldn't know how far he'd thrown her.

"Invite him in, Poppy," her grandmother chided. "You're going to melt the driveway."

She meant because she was letting the heat out, but her words made Poppy blush harder. "Of course," she muttered, flustered. "Come in."

Explanations crowded her tongue as she backed up a step, but stammering them out wouldn't make a difference to a man like him. He might have seemed human and reachable for that stolen hour in his mother's solarium, but she'd realized afterward exactly how ruthless and single-minded he truly was. The passion she'd convinced herself was mutual and startlingly sweet had been a casual, effortless, promptly forgotten seduction on his part.

He'd mended fences with his fiancée the next morning—a woman Poppy knew for a fact he hadn't loved. He'd told Poppy that he'd only agreed to the marriage to gain the presidency of a company and hadn't seemed distressed in the least that the wedding had been called off.

Embarrassment at being such an easy conquest had her staring at his feet as she closed the door behind him. "Will you take off your boots, please?"

Her request gave him pause. In his mother's house, everyone wore shoes, especially guests. A single pair of their usual footwear cost more than Poppy had made in her four months of working in that house.

Rico toed off his boots and set them against the wall. Then he tucked his sunglasses into his chest pocket. His eyes were slate-gray with no spark of blue or flecks of hot green that had surrounded his huge pupils that day in the solarium.

After setting his cold, granite gaze against her until she was chilled through, he glanced past her, into the front room of the tiny bungalow her grandfather had built for his wife while working as a linesman for the hydro company. It was the home where Gramps had brought his bride the day they married. It was where they had brought home their only son and where they had raised their only grandchild.

Seeing him in it made Poppy both humble and defensive. It didn't compare to the grandiose villa he'd been raised in, but it was her home. Poppy wasn't ashamed of it, only struck by how he could so easily jeopardize all of this with a snap of his fingers. This house wasn't even hers. If he had come here to claim Lily, she had very few resources at her disposal. Maybe it would even be held against her that she didn't have much and he could offer so much more.

"Hello," he greeted her grandmother as she muted the television and set the remote aside.

"This is Rico Montero, Gran. My grandmother, Eleanor Harris."

"*The* Rico?"

"Yes."

Rico's brows went up a fraction, making Poppy squirm.

"It's nice to meet you. Finally." Gran started to rise.

Poppy stepped forward to help her, but Rico was quick to touch her grandmother's arm and say, "Please. There's no need to stand. It's a pleasure to meet you."

Oh, he knew how to use the warmth of his accented voice to slay a woman, young or old. Poppy almost fell for it herself, thinking he sounded reassuring when he was actually here to destroy their small, simple world.

Yet she had to go through the motions of civility. Pretend he was simply a guest who had dropped by.

Gran smiled up at him with glimmers of adoration. "I was getting up to give you privacy to talk. I imagine you'll want that."

"In that case, yes please. Allow me to help you." Rico moved to her side and supported her with gentle care.

Don't leave me alone with him, Poppy wanted to cry, but she slid Gran's walker in front of her. "Thank you, Gran."

"I'll listen to the radio in my room until you come for me." Her grandmother nodded and shuffled her way into the hall. "Remember the biscuits."

The biscuits. The least of her worries. Poppy couldn't smell them yet, but the timer would go off any second. She moved her body into the path toward the kitchen door, driven by mother-bear instincts.

"Why are you here?" Her voice quavered with the volume of emotions rocketing through her—shock and protectiveness and fear. Culpability and anger and other deeper yearnings she didn't want to acknowledge.

"I want to see her." He set his shoulders in a way that told her he wasn't going anywhere until he did.

Behind her, the sound of bowls coming out of the cupboard and being knocked around reassured her that Lily was perfectly fine without eyes on her.

A suffocating feeling sat on her chest and kept a vise around her throat. She wanted him to answer the rest of her question. What was he going to do about this discovery? She wasn't ready to face the answer.

Playing for time, she strangled out, "How did you find out?"

If they hadn't been standing so close, she might have missed the way his pupils dilated and his breath seemed to catch as though taking a blow. In the next second, the impression of shock was gone. A fierce, angry light of satisfaction gleamed in his eyes.

"Sorcha saw a photo you posted of a baby who looks like Mateo. I investigated."

Odd details from the last two weeks fell into place. She dropped her chin in outrage. "That new dad at the day care! I thought he was hitting on me, asking all those questions."

Rico's dark brows slammed together. "He came on to you?"

"He said he took Lily's cup by mistake, but it was an excuse to talk to me." Poppy was obviously still batting a thousand where her poor judgement of men was concerned.

"He took it for a DNA sample."

"That is just plain *wrong*," she said indignantly.

"I agree that I shouldn't have to resort to such measures to learn I have a child. *Why didn't you tell me?*" he asked through clenched teeth.

He had some right to the anger he poured over ice. She acknowledged that. But she wasn't a villain. Just a stupid girl who'd gotten herself in trouble by the wrong man and had made the best of a difficult situation.

"I didn't realize I was pregnant until you were married. By then, it was all over the gossip sites that Faustina was also expecting."

It shouldn't have been such a blow when she'd read

that. His wedding had been called off for a *day*. Loads of people had a moment of cold feet before they went through with the ceremony. She accepted she was collateral damage to that.

She had been feeling very down on herself by then, though. She ought to have known better than to let herself get carried away. She hadn't taken any precautions. She had been careless and foolish, believing him when he had told her that he and his fiancée hadn't been sleeping together.

The whole thing had made her feel so humiliatingly stupid. She had hoped never to have to face him or her gullibility ever again.

So much for that.

And facing him was so *hard*. *He* was so hard. A muscle was pulsing in his jaw, but the rest of him was like concrete. Pitiless and unmoved.

"Faustina died a year ago last September," he said in that gritty tone. "You've had ample opportunity to come forward."

As she recalled the terrible headlines she'd read with morbid anguish, her heart turned inside out with agony for him. She had nursed thoughts every day of telling him he had a child after all, but...

"I'm sorry for your loss." She truly was. No matter what he'd felt for his wife, losing his child must have been devastating.

His expression stiffened and he recoiled slightly at her words of condolence.

"My grandfather was quite ill," she continued huskily. "If you recall, that's why I came home. He passed just before Christmas. Gran needed me. There hasn't been a right time to shake things up."

His expression altered slightly as he absorbed that.

She imagined his sorrow to be so much more acute than hers. She mourned a man who had lived a full life and who had passed without pain or regret. They'd held a service that had been a true celebration of his long life.

While Rico's baby had been cheated of even starting its own.

Rico nodded acceptance of her excuse with only a pained flicker as acknowledgment of what must have been his very personal and intensely painful loss.

Had grief driven him here? Was he trying to replace his lost child with his living one? *No.* The thought of it agonized her. Lily wasn't some placeholder for another child. It cracked her heart in half that he might think she could be.

Before she could find words to address that fear, the timer beeped in the kitchen.

Lily had become very quiet, too, which was a sure sign of trouble. Poppy turned to glance around the doorframe. Lily sat with one finger poking at the tiny hole on a bowl's rim, where the bowl was meant to be hung on a nail.

Firm hands settled on her shoulders. Rico's untamed scent and the heat of his body surrounded her. He looked past her into the kitchen. At his daughter.

Poppy told herself not to look, but she couldn't help it. She was afraid he would be resentful that Lily had lived when his other baby hadn't. Even as she feared he was planning to steal her, she perversely would be more agonized if he rejected her. He had come all this way. That meant he felt something toward her, didn't it? On some level, he wanted her?

His expression was unreadable, face so closed and tense, her heart dropped into her shoes.

Love her, she wanted to beg. *Please.*

His breath sucked in with an audible hiss. He took in so much air, his chest swelled to brush against her back. His hands tightened on her shoulders.

At the subtle noise, Lily lifted her gorgeous gray eyes, so like her father's. A huge smile broke across her face.

"Mama." The bowls were forgotten and she crawled toward them, pulling herself up on the gate.

Lily's smile propelled Poppy through all her hard days. She was Poppy's world. Poppy's parents were distant, her grandfather gone, her grandmother... Well, Poppy didn't want to think about losing her even though she knew it was inevitable.

But she had this wee girl and she was everything.

"Hello, button." Poppy scooped up her daughter and kissed her cheek, never able to resist that soft, plump bite of sweet-smelling warmth. Then she brushed at Lily's hands because it didn't matter how many times she swept or vacuumed, Lily found the specks and dust bunnies in her eager exploration of her world.

This time when Poppy looked to Rico, she saw his reaction more clearly. He was trying to mask it with stoicism, but the intensity in his gaze ate up Lily's snowy skin and cupid's-bow mouth.

Her emotions seesawed again. She had needed this. Her heart had needed to see him accept his daughter, but he was a threat, too.

"This is Lily." Her name was tellingly sentimental, not the sort of romantic notion Poppy should have given in to, but since her own name was a flower, it had seemed right.

Poppy faltered, not ready to tell Lily this was Daddy.

Lily brought her fingers to her mouth and said, "Ee."

"Eat?" Poppy asked and slid her hand down from her throat. "You're hungry?"

Lily nodded.

"Sign language?" Rico asked, voice sharpening with concern. "Is she hearing impaired?"

"It's sign language for babies. They teach it at day care. She's trying to say words, but this works for now." Poppy stepped over the gate into the kitchen and snapped off the oven. "Do you, um…" She couldn't believe this was happening, but she wanted to put off the hard conversations as long as possible. "Will you join us for dinner?"

A brief pause, then, "You don't have to cook. I can order something in."

"From where?" Poppy chuckled dryly as she set Lily in her chair. "We have Chinese takeout and a pizza palace." *Not* his usual standard. "The soup is already made."

She tied on Lily's bib and set the bowl of cooled soup and a small flat spoon in front of her.

Lily grabbed the spoon and batted it into the thick soup.

"Renting the car was a challenge for my staff," he mentioned absently, frowning as Lily missed her mouth and smeared soup across her own cheek.

"Gran said you're driving something fancy," Poppy

recalled. She had forgotten to look, unable to see past the man to anything else.

"An Alfa Romeo, but it's a sedan."

With a car seat? Poppy almost bobbled the sheet of biscuits as she took them from the oven. "Are you, um, staying at the motel?"

He snorted. "No. My staff have taken a cottage an hour from here so I have a bed if I decide to stay."

Poppy tried to read his expression, but he was watching Lily, frowning with exasperation as Lily turned her head, open mouth looking for the end of the spoon.

In a decisive move, he removed his jacket and draped it over the back of a chair. Then he picked up the teaspoon beside Poppy's setting and turned the chair to face Lily. He sat and began helping her eat.

Poppy caught her breath, arrested by the sight of this dynamic man feeding their daughter. His strapping muscles strained the seams in his shirt, telling of his tension, but he calmly waited for Lily to try before he gently touched the tip of his teaspoon to her bottom lip. He let Lily lean into eating it before they both went after the next spoonful in the bowl.

Had she dreamed of this? *Was* she dreaming? It was such a sweet sight her ovaries locked fresh eggs into their chambers, preparing to launch and create another Lily or five. All she needed was one glance from him that contained something other than accusation or animosity.

"You said the timing was wrong."

It took her a moment to realize he was harking back to the day they'd conceived her. She could only stand there in chagrined silence while a coal of uncomfortable heat burned in her middle, spreading a blush upward, into her throat and cheeks and ending in a pressure behind her eyes.

He glanced at her. "When we—"

"I know what you mean," she cut him off, turning away to stack hot biscuits onto a plate, suffused in virginal discomfiture all over again. He'd noticed blood and asked if she had started her cycle. She'd been too embarrassed to tell him it was her first time. She was too embarrassed to say it now.

"I should have taken something after." She didn't tell him she had hung around in Spain an extra day, hoping he would come find her only to hear the wedding was back on.

That news had propelled her from the scene, consuming her with thoughts of what a pushover she'd been for a man on a brief furlough from his engagement. Contraception should have been top of mind, but…

"I was traveling, trying to make my flight." Poppy hugged herself, trying to keep the fissure in her chest from widening. She felt *so* exposed right now and couldn't meet his penetrating stare. "I honestly did think the timing was wrong. I didn't even realize I was pregnant until I was starting to show. I had next to no symptoms." There'd even been a bit of spotting. "I thought the few signs I did have were stress related. Gramps's health was deteriorating. By the time it was confirmed, you were married." She finally looked at him and let one hand come out, palm up, beseeching for understanding.

There was no softening in his starkly unforgiving expression.

"I didn't think you would—" She couldn't say aloud

that she had worried he wouldn't want his daughter. Not when he was feeding Lily with such care.

Helpless tears pressed behind her eyes.

He knew what she had almost said and sent her another flat stare of muted fury. "I want her, Poppy. That's why I'm here."

Her heart swerved in her chest. The pressure behind her eyes increased.

"Don't look so terrified." He returned his attention to Lily, who was waiting with an open mouth like a baby bird. "I'm not here to kidnap her."

"What, then?" She clung tight to her elbows, needing something to anchor her. Needing to know what was going to happen.

"Am I supposed to ignore her?"

"No." His question poked agonizing pins into the most sensitive spots on her soul. "But I was afraid you might," she admitted. "I thought it would be easier on both of us if you didn't know, rather than if you did, but didn't care."

Another wall-of-concrete stare, then a clearly pronounced, "I care." He scraped the spoon through the thick soup. "And not only because the maids in my mother's house are bound to recognize the resemblance the way Sorcha's nanny did and begin to talk. She's a Montero. She's entitled to the benefits that brings."

Now he stood directly on Poppy's pride.

"We don't *need* help, Rico. That's another reason I never told you. I didn't want you to think I was looking for a handout. We're fine."

"The day care with the nonexistent security is 'fine'? What happens when it's known her father is wealthy?

We take basic precautions, Poppy. You don't even have an alarm system. I didn't hear you click a lock when you opened the front door."

They lived in rural Canada. People worried about squirrels in the attic, not burglars in the bedroom.

"No one knows you're rich. Gran is the only person who even knows your name and I wasn't entirely forthcoming about…who you really are." Poppy gave a tendril of hair a distracted brush so it tucked behind her ear for all of five seconds. "Do you mind if I get her? She takes medication on a schedule and needs to eat beforehand. We try to stick to a routine."

"Of course." He lifted two fingers off the bowl he still held steady for Lily's jabs of her own spoon. "We'll discuss how we'll proceed after Lily is in bed."

CHAPTER TWO

POPPY OPENED THE GATE and set it aside, leaving Rico to continue feeding his daughter.

He had watched Sorcha and Cesar do this countless times with their sons. He'd always thought it a messy process best left to nannies, but discovered it was oddly satisfying. His older nephew, Enrique, had reached an age where he held conversations—some that were inadvertently amusing—but babies had always struck Rico as something that required a lot of intensive care without offering much in return.

Sorcha had pressed her sons onto him over the years, which had achieved her goal of provoking feelings of affection in him, but, like his parents, he viewed children as something between a duty and a social experiment. Even when he had briefly believed Faustina had been carrying his heir, the idea of being a father had only been that—an idea. Not a concept he had fully internalized or a role he understood how to fulfill effectively. Fatherhood hadn't been something he had viewed with anticipation the way other creative projects had inspired him.

But here he sat, watching eyes the same color as

his own track to the doorway where Poppy had disappeared. A wet finger pointed. "Mama."

"She'll be right back." He imagined Poppy would actually spend a few minutes talking to her grandmother in private.

Lily smiled before she leaned forward, mouth open.

Damn, she was beautiful. It wasn't bias, either. Or his fondness for the nephews she resembled. She had her mother's fresh snowy skin and red-gold lashes, healthy round cheeks and a chin that suggested she had his stubbornness along with his eyes.

A ridiculous swell of pride went through him even as he reminded himself that he didn't know conclusively that she was his. The DNA test off the cup had been a long shot and hadn't proved paternity either way.

Nevertheless, he'd been propelled as much by the absence of truth as he would have been by the presence of it. From the time Sorcha had revealed her suspicion, a ferocious fire had begun to burn in him, one stoked by yet another female keeping secrets from him. Huge, life-altering secrets.

He hadn't wanted to wait for more tests, or hire lawyers, or even pick up the phone and *ask*. He had needed to see for himself.

Who? a voice asked in the back of his head.

Both, he acknowledged darkly. He had needed to set eyes on the baby, whom he recognized on a deeply biological level, and on the woman who haunted his memories.

Poppy had seemed so guileless. So refreshingly honest and real.

He thought back to that day, searching for the moment where he'd been tricked into making a baby with a woman who had then kept her pregnancy a secret.

He remembered thinking his mother wouldn't appreciate him popping a bottle of the wedding champagne—even though she'd procured a hundred cases that had been superfluous because the wedding had been called off.

Rico had helped himself to his father's scotch in the billiards room instead. He had taken it through to the solarium, planning to bum a cigarette from the gardener. It was a weakness he had kicked years ago, but the craving still hit sometimes, when his life went sideways.

It was the end of the day, though. The sun-warmed room was packed to the gills with lilies brought in to replace the ones damaged by a late frost. The solarium was deserted and the worktable in the back held a dirty ashtray and a cigarette pack that was empty.

"Oh! I'm so sorry."

The woman spoke in English, sounding American, maybe. He turned to see the redheaded maid who'd been on the stairs an hour earlier, when Faustina had been throwing a tantrum that had included one of his mother's Wedgwoods, punctuating the end of their engagement. He would come to understand much later what sort of pressure Faustina had been under, but at the time, she'd been an unreasonable, clichéd diva of a bride by whom he'd been relieved to have been jilted.

And the interruption by the fresh-faced maid had been a welcome distraction.

Her name was Poppy. He knew that without looking at the embroidered tag on her uniform. She stared with wide doe eyes, the proverbial deer in headlights, startled to come upon him pilfering smokes as though he was thirteen again.

"I mean…um…*perdón*." She pivoted to go back the way she'd come.

"Wait. Do you have a cigarette?" he asked in English.

"Me? No." She swung back around. "Do I look like a smoker?"

Her horror at resembling such a thing amused him.

"Do I?" he drawled. "What do we look like? The patriarchy?"

"I don't know." She chuckled and blushed slightly, her clear skin glowing pink beneath the gold of filtered sunlight, like late afternoon on untouched ski slopes. "I, um, didn't know you smoked." She swallowed and linked her hands shyly before her.

Ah. She'd been watching him, too, had she?

His mother's staff had been off-limits since his brother's first kiss with a maid before Rico had even had a shot at one. He didn't usually notice one from another, but Poppy had snagged his attention with her vibrant red hair. Curls were springing free of the bundle she'd scraped it into, teasing him with fantasies of releasing the rest and digging his hands into the kinky mass.

The rest of her was cute as hell, too, if a bit skinny and young. Maybe it was her lack of makeup. That mouth, unpainted, but with a plump bottom lip and a playful top was all woman. Her brows were so light, they were almost blond, her chin pert, her eyes a gentle yet very direct dark ale-brown.

No, he reminded himself. He was engaged.

Actually, he absorbed with a profound sense of liberation, he wasn't. Faustina had firmly and unequivocally ended their engagement, despite his mother's best efforts to talk her back on board.

His mother had retired with a wet compress and a migraine tablet. He had come in here because he couldn't go home. His house was being renovated for the bride who was now refusing to share her life with him. Driving all the way to his brother's house to get blind drunk had felt like an unnecessary delay.

"I don't smoke." He dropped the empty pack and picked up his drink. "I rebelled for a year or so when I was a teen, but it seemed like a good excuse to talk with Ernesto about football and other inconsequential topics." He was sick to death of jabbering about weddings and duty and the expected impact on the family fortune.

Her shoulders softened and her red-gold brows angled with sympathy. "I'm really sorry." She sounded adorably sincere. "I'll, um, give you privacy to…"

"Wallow in heartbreak? Unnecessary." Faustina's outburst had been the sum total of passion their marriage was likely to have borne. "I don't want to chase you away if you're on your break."

"No, I'm done. I know we're not supposed to cut through here to get to the change rooms over the garage, but I was hoping to catch Ernesto myself. He gives me a lift sometimes."

"Are you American?" he asked.

Her strawberry blond lashes flickered in surprise, her expression growing shy. Aware.

An answering awareness teased through him, waking the wolf inside him. That starved beast had been locked inside a cave the last six months, but unexpectedly found himself free of the heavy chain he'd placed around his own neck. The sun was in his eyes, the wind was ruffling his fur and he was picking up the scent of a willing female. He was itching to romp and tumble and mate.

"Canada." She cleared her throat. "Saskatchewan. A little town with nothing but canola fields and clouds." She shook her head. "You wouldn't have heard of it."

"How did you wind up here?"

"I'd tell you, but I'd bore you to death." Despite her words, a pretty smile played around her mouth and a soft blush of pleasure glowed under her skin.

"I came out here to smoke. Clearly I have a death wish."

After a small chuckle, she cautioned, "Okay, but stop me if you feel light-headed."

Definitely not bored, he thought with a private smile. She wasn't merely a first cigarette years after quitting, either. To be sure he was drawing in this lighthearted flirting with avid greed, but he found himself enjoying her wit. He was genuinely intrigued by her.

"I saved up to trek around Europe with a friend, but she broke her ankle on the second day and flew home." She folded her arms, protective or defensive, maybe. "I tagged along with some students from a hostel coming here, but a few days after we arrived, one of them stole everything I had." She slapped a what-can-you-do? smile on it, but the tension around her eyes and mouth told him she was still upset.

He frowned. "Did you go to the police?"

"It was my fault." She flinched with self-recrimination. "I gave him my card to get some cash for me one morning. He must have made a copy or something.

Three days later he'd syphoned all of my savings and was gone. I had my passport, a bag of raisins and my hairbrush. Losing my camera gutted me the most. It was a gift and my memory card was still in it, not that I'd had the chance to fill it. It was a huge bummer." She summed up with philosophical lightness.

"You're a photographer?"

"Not anymore," she asserted with disgust, then shrugged it off. "At least I had prepaid for a week at the hostel. I asked around and got on with a temp agency. I was brought in to help clean the pool house and guest cottage. Darna liked my work and asked me to stay on full-time in the big house. I've been saving for a ticket home ever since."

"How much do you need?" He reached into his pocket.

"Oh, no!" She halted him, horrified. "I have enough. I just worked it out with Darna that today was my last day. She thought she would need me through the rest of June for—" She halted, wincing as she realized who she was talking to.

Rico let the awkwardness hang in the air, not to punish, but because he was finding her candor so refreshing.

"It seemed like the wedding was going to be really beautiful." She sounded apologetic. "I'm sorry it didn't work out."

He wasn't. That was the naked truth, but he deflected by saying, "I've heard that Canadians apologize a lot. I didn't believe it."

"We do. Sorry." She winked on that one.

Was she sorry?

Rico came back to the tap of a dirty spoon against the back of his knuckles.

Poppy had been twenty-two, disillusioned after being shortchanged on chasing her dreams, yet willing to come home to fulfill family obligations. He had understood that pressure and had confided his own reasons for going along with family expectations.

That affinity had led to a kiss and his feet had somehow carried her to the sheet-draped furniture hidden amongst the jungle of fragrant lilies.

Since learning about Lily, he'd been convinced Poppy had somehow tricked him the way Faustina had, for her own nefarious ends.

That suspicion wasn't playing as strongly now that he was here. Her home was unpretentious, dated and showing signs of age, but neat and well cared for. Her bond with her grandmother and daughter seemed genuine and from the reports he'd commissioned, she was this side of financially solvent. She didn't even have a speeding ticket on her record.

He'd picked up two on his way here, but that was beside the point.

In the past, he had seen what he wanted to see. He couldn't allow himself to be so credulous again.

He made himself take a cool moment to watch Lily's concentrated effort to touch the end of her spoon into the soup and bring the taste to her mouth. She grinned as she succeeded, spoon caught between her tiny white teeth.

He had no proof, but he was convinced she was his. He *had* to claim her.

As for Poppy, he was still absorbing the impact she

continued to have on him. He still reacted physically to her. One look at her in jeans and a loose pullover and his mouth had started to water. No makeup, hair gathered into a messy knot of kinks on her head, wariness like a halo around her, yet he'd had to restrain himself from reaching for her. Not to grab or take possession, but simply to *touch*. Fill his hands with the textures of her.

Was her skin as smooth and soft as his erotic dreams replayed? Would her nipples tighten if he licked then blew lightly again? Did her voice still break in orgasm and would that sound once again send pleasurable shivers down his back?

That chemistry was a weakness, one that warned him to keep his guard up, but it didn't deter him from his plan one iota.

In fact, it stoked a fire of anticipation deep in the pit of his belly.

Poppy's tension remained through dinner, even though Rico went on a charm offensive against her grandmother, breaking out levels even Poppy hadn't realized he possessed, asking after her health and offering condolences over Gramps.

"I'm very sorry to hear you lost him. I remember Poppy saying he wasn't well, just before she left Spain."

Poppy released a subtle snort, suspecting he only recalled that detail because she had reminded him of it an hour ago.

He frowned with affront. "I asked you why you weren't using the money you'd saved to see more of Europe. You said your grandparents needed help moving into a care facility."

For one second, she saw glints of blue and green in his irises, telling her he remembered *everything* about that day.

A spike of tingling heat drove sharp as a lance through her. She crossed her legs, bumping her foot against his shin in the process and sending a reverberation of deeper awareness through her whole body.

"We were talking about moving," Gran said, forcing Rico to break their eye contact. "I couldn't look after Bill myself, but having Poppy here bought us an extra year in our home." Gran squeezed her hand over Poppy's, the strength in her grip heart-wrenchingly faint. "He would have faded all the faster if we'd been forced to leave this house. I'll always be grateful to her for giving us that. I don't know what I would have done if she hadn't been here in the months since he's been gone, either. She's been our special blessing her whole life."

"Gran." Poppy teared up. She knew darned well she'd been more of a burden.

"And Lily is ever so precious, too." Gran smiled at the baby. "But it's time."

"Time?" Poppy repeated with muted alarm.

"I'll call your aunt Sheila in the morning," she said of her sister, patting Poppy's hand before she removed her touch. "I'm on the top of the list at that facility near her apartment. I'm sure I can stay with her until a room opens up."

"Gran, *no*."

"Poppy. We both know I shouldn't have been here this winter, making more work for you on top of looking after the baby. You were shoveling the drive on your one day off to get me to the doctor's office. I have no business near that ice by the front steps, either. You're penning up Lily, worrying I'll trip over her. *I'm* worried. No, I don't want to hold you back from the life you ought to be leading."

"This *is* the life I want to lead." Poppy's chin began to crinkle the way Lily's did when she was coming down with a cold and Poppy had to leave her at day care.

"Oh, is your fancy man moving in with us, then?" Gran asked.

"I see where Poppy gets her spark." A faint smile touched Rico's lips. "Poppy and I have details to work out, but you're right that my life is in Spain. I'm here to marry her and take Poppy and Lily home with me."

After a brief, illogical spike of elation, Poppy's heart fell with that bombshell news. Her mind exploded. He wasn't wrenching their daughter from her arms, but she wasn't relieved in the least. She immediately knew this wasn't about her. He'd married for coldly practical reasons the first time. He might dazzle her grandmother with kindness and charisma, but it was a dispassionate move to get what he wanted by the quickest, most efficient means. She shouldn't be shocked at all by his goal or his methods.

"*My* life is here with Gran," Poppy insisted shakily. "She needs me nearby, even if she moves into assisted care."

"Poppy." The fragility of her grandmother's hand draped over hers again. "What I need is to know that when I'm gone, you're settled with someone who will take care of you and Lily. That person ought to be her father." She patted lightly, saying with quiet power, "I know what this would have meant to you."

If her own father had shown up to take her home, Gran meant. The hot pressure behind her eyes increased.

Even so, there was a part of Poppy that simply heard it as her grandmother wishing Poppy would cease to be a burden upon her.

A spiked ball lodged behind Poppy's breastbone, one she couldn't swallow away. It was so sharp it made tears sting her eyes.

"It's obvious Poppy won't be comfortable unless you're comfortable, Eleanor. Give us a chance to finish our talk. Then you and I will discuss your options. I'm sure we can find solutions that satisfy all of us."

Poppy wanted to shout a giant, scoffing, *Ha!* She rose to clear the table.

CHAPTER THREE

POPPY BATHED LILY and put her to bed, not giving her daughter the attention she deserved because her mind was still whirling with Rico showing up and demanding more than his daughter. *Marriage.*

Had she spun that fantasy in her girlish mind? Yes. Even before she slept with him. She had been fascinated by him for weeks, acutely aware of him whether he was making a dry comment or sipping a glass of orange juice. He'd seemed aloof, but in a laid-back way. When she had overheard Faustina going full Bridezilla, shattering a vase and screaming that their wedding was off, Rico had only said in a calm voice, "Let me have the bottom of that. I'll have to replace it."

Deep down, she'd been thrilled that Faustina had ended things. Happy for him.

In the solarium, he'd been that charming man she'd seen tonight at dinner, the one who expressed so much interest in others, it was easy to miss that he gave away very little about himself.

He had told her enough that day, however. Enough that she had been fooled into thinking he liked her. That there was a spark of...*something.*

She'd been wrong. This was the real man. He was severe and intimidating, not raising his voice because he didn't have to. His wishes, delivered in that implacable tone, were sheer power. She instinctively knew there was no shifting him on the course he had decided.

He didn't want her, though. She was merely an obstacle he was overcoming as expediently as possible. Her grandmother would see this marriage as a move toward security, but Poppy refused to trust his offer so easily. What if he got her over there and promptly divorced her? Took her to court for custody? There was no way she could survive without Lily.

Lily settled and Poppy went to the front room. Rico had finished the calls he'd been making and was chatting with her grandmother.

Having him in her home made her squirm. It was her private space where she revealed her true self in faded, toothless photos on the wall next to some of her earliest photography efforts. She and Gran had been working their way through a box of paperback romances that Poppy had picked up at a garage sale and Poppy's latest passionate cover was splayed open on the coffee table.

On the mantel stood Poppy's framed employee of the month certificate. Her boss at the bus depot had given it to her as a joke. Aside from him, she was the only employee and she was part-time. Gran had had her first good laugh in ages when Poppy had brought it home. Then they'd wept because Gramps would have enjoyed it, too.

Beside the certificate stood a generic birthday card from last month signed, *Love, Mom*. It was the only message besides the preprinted poem.

Rico was seeing far too much of *her* in this space. Maybe gathering ammunition for why his daughter couldn't stay here. A man so low on sentiment wouldn't recognize the comfort in the worn furniture and the value of memory-infused walls.

"The weatherman said it's a good night for stargazing," Gran was telling Rico while nodding at the television. "You might even see the northern lights."

"It's freezing outside," Poppy protested. "Literally." Spring might be a few days away on the calendar, but there was still thick frost on her windshield every morning.

"Bundle up." Gran dismissed Poppy's argument with the hardy practicality of a woman who'd lived on the prairies her whole life. "Your grandfather and I always came to agreement walking around Fisher's Pond. I have the phone right here." She touched the table where the cordless phone lived. "I'll call if Lily wakes and fusses."

Poppy glanced at Rico, hoping he would say it was late and he would come back tomorrow.

"I left my gloves in the car. I'll collect them on my way."

She bit back a huff and layered up, pulling on boots, mittens and a toque before tramping into what was actually a fairly mild night, considering the sky was clear and there was still snow on the ground.

The moon turned the world a bluish daylight and her footsteps crunched after Rico as they started away from the car. He wound a red scarf around his neck as they walked.

"Before today, I had only flown over prairies, never driven through them." His breath clouded as he spoke.

"Were you fighting to stay awake?"

"No, but it's very relaxing. Gives you time and space to think."

She didn't ask him what he'd been thinking about, just took him past the last house on their street, then along the path in the snow toward the depression that was Fisher's Pond.

It was a busy place midwinter. Neighborhood children played hockey every chance they got, but signs were posted now that the ice was thinning and no longer safe. The makeshift benches and lights were gone leaving only the trampled ring around the pond that was popular with dog walkers in summer. Tonight, they had the place to themselves.

"I haven't seen the Milky Way like that, either," he said, nodding at the seam of stars ripped open across the sky. "Not clear and massive like that."

"Rico, I can't go to Spain with you."

"I can hire a live-in care aid." His tone became very businesslike. "Or support her in any facility she chooses. You can be back here within a day if concerns arise. Do not use your grandmother as an excuse to keep my daughter from me."

Wow. She rubbed her mitten against her cold nose, trying to keep the tip of it from growing numb.

"She's not an excuse. She's my family."

He absorbed that, then asked, "Where are your parents? Why has it fallen on you to look after your grandparents?"

"I wanted to." She hugged herself. "They've always been good to me. Even when I came home pregnant."

Especially then. Buying the assisted-living unit

would have required selling the house, leaving Poppy without anywhere to live. It had been everyone's wish that they stay together in that house while Gramps was so sick, but Gran was right. They couldn't sustain this. Poppy had been mentally preparing herself for spending the summer clearing out the house. That didn't mean she was ready to move with her daughter around the globe, though.

"Did your parents pass away? Have you always lived with them?"

"I have, but my parents are alive. Divorced. Dad works in the oil patch." She tried not to sound as forlorn as she had always felt when talking about her parents. "He shows up every few months for a week or so, sleeps on the couch and does some repairs. He used to give Gran money sometimes, for taking care of me. I think he gambles most of what he makes. It's one of those things no one in the family talks about, but money has always been an issue with him."

"Thus the divorce?"

"I'm sure that was part of it. Mom had her own issues." She turned from the cleared patch that faced the pond and started on the path around it.

She hated that she had to reveal her deepest shame, but he ought to know it, so he would understand her reasons for refusing to marry him.

"They were really young when they had me. Mom was only nineteen. Not ready for the responsibility of being a parent. My dad brought her here to live with his parents then left to work far away. Mom stuck around until I was two, then she started moving around, living the life she thought she was entitled to, I guess."

"Partying? Drugs?"

"Freedom, mostly." Poppy understood now how overwhelming parenting was, but *she* hadn't dropped her daughter like a hot potato just because it was hard. "She didn't want to be a mom. She wanted to 'explore her potential.'" Poppy air-quoted the phrase. "She tried modeling in Toronto and worked as a flight attendant out of Montreal. She was a music promoter in Halifax, went to Vancouver to work on a cruise ship. Followed a man to India for a year then came back and opened a yoga studio in California. That's how she met her current husband, teaching one of his ex-wives to downward dog. He's a movie producer. They have two kids."

Two sulky, spoiled children who complained about the meals Poppy's mother cooked for them and the music lessons and soccer practices she drove them to.

Poppy tried not to hate them. They were family, but they were also entitled little brats.

"You never lived with her?" Rico asked behind her.

"By the time she was settled, I was starting high school. Bringing me across the border even for a visit was more bureaucracy than she wanted to face. She still hasn't seen Lily except over the tablet. I think she wishes I had never been born. Not in a spiteful way, but she would rather pretend her youthful mistake had never happened."

The path became streaked by the shadows of a copse of trees. She plodded into it, trying not to be depressed by her parents' neglect when they'd left her with such amazing grandparents.

"What I'm hearing is that you wish both of your parents had taken steps to bring you to live with them."

"Is that what you're hearing?" She stopped and turned, thinking her grandparents had been onto something because there was safety in the darkness, where her vulnerability wasn't painted in neon letters across her face. "Because I've come to realize they did me a favor, leaving me with people who tucked me in and told me they loved me every night."

She had surprised him by turning to confront him. He had pulled up, but stood really close. His face was striped by ivory and cobalt.

"Have you told them? Your parents?" she asked.

"I told them she was likely mine, even though the DNA results were inconclusive. I said—"

"What?" Poppy's elbows went stiff as she punched the air by her thighs. "Why did you even *come* here if you didn't *know*?"

"Because I had to know," he said tightly, "Your guilty expression when you opened the door was all the proof I needed."

She was such a dope, confirming his suspicions before he even *knew*. How did he disarm her so easily again and again?

"What was their reaction?" she asked, focusing on her deeper concerns. The *duque* and *duquesa* had struck Poppy as being aliens in human skin, assimilating on earth well enough not to be detected, but incapable of relating to normal people or showing genuine emotion.

"They asked to be kept informed."

"I see. And is your mother still on the hunt for the next Señora Montero?"

"How the hell do you know that?"

"I'm capable of reading a headline."

"Elevate your browsing choices. Gossip sites are garbage. If you wanted to know what I was doing with my life, you should have called *me*."

"I'm more interested in how your mother is going to react to Lily."

"She'll accept a fait accompli. She's done it before."

When Cesar's indiscretion with Sorcha had resulted in Enrique. But as far as Poppy could tell, Rico's father had barely noticed he had a grandson while his mother had given Enrique tight smiles and offered unsolicited suggestions on how he could be improved. *He looks due for a haircut, Sorcha.*

So Poppy snorted her disbelief. "I've seen what her type of 'acceptance' looks like and it's colder than an arctic vortex."

"Be careful, Poppy."

"That wasn't a cheap shot. I'm saying Lily is far too important to me to set her up to be the subject of criticism and disapproval for the rest of her life. If they're going to treat her like a stain on the family name, I won't take her anywhere near them."

He probably thought she should be grateful he was planning to let her accompany him and her daughter, but he only said, "They're not demonstrative people. There will be no welcome embrace from either of them. Reconcile yourself to that right now. They do, however, bring other strengths to the table. We Monteros look after our own."

"My stepfather can put her in movies if she decides she wants wealth and fame."

"Wealth is not fortune, fame is not standing," he stated pithily. "What sort of future are you planning for her? You'll date, perhaps introduce her to a few contenders and, one day, when you're convinced you're in love, you'll allow another man to raise *my* child without any of the genuine advantages to which she's entitled? In ignorance of her family and the attached opportunities overseas? No. I won't let you deny her what's rightfully hers."

"It's not up to you. And don't say it like that! 'When I'm *convinced* I'm in love.' *I love Lily.* Try to tell me that feeling is a figment of my imagination." She would knock him through the ice. "Do *you* plan to love her? Because, given what I saw of your upbringing, you were never shown how."

A profound silence crashed over them.

"Just as you were never taught to hold your temper in favor of a civil conversation?" Oh, he sounded lethal. The cold in the air began to penetrate her clothes.

"Answer the question," she insisted. "My love for Lily took root the day I learned I was pregnant." It had grown so expansive her body couldn't contain the force of it. It quivered in her voice as she continued. "I won't set her up to yearn for something from you that will never happen. I've been there and it is far too painful a thing to wish onto my child. *You know it is.*"

She had pushed herself right out onto the ledge of getting way too personal. She knew she had, but that was how much her daughter meant to her.

The umbrage radiating off him should have flash-melted the snow and razed the trees, illuminating the skies in an explosion of light.

Even so, she nudged even further by warning through her teeth, "Don't shove your way into her life unless you intend to be there every single moment, in every possible way she might need you to be."

His hands jammed into his pockets and his profile was slashed with shadows.

"You—" Something made him bite off whatever he had been about to say. He made a sucking noise through clenched teeth, as though enduring the removal of a bullet or something equally wounding. "My brother's sons are not unhappy. He had my same upbringing. He's managed to become quite attached. I would expect to form that sort of connection with my own child."

She was glad for the dark then, because sudden, pitying tears froze to her lashes. His words were such a careful admission that he was fine with not being loved as a child, but would find a way to extend his heart to his daughter.

For that reason alone, for the opportunity to gift him with his child's unconditional love, she knew she would have to allow him into Lily's life.

"Even so…" She folded her arms and squished handfuls of her quilted sleeves with her woolen mittens. She had had a front-row seat to the way his parents' marriage worked and it was…*sad*. They spoke without warmth to each other, as if they were inquiring about a telephone bill minus the anxiety that they might struggle to pay. "What kind of marriage would that be as an example for her?"

"A calm and rational one?" he suggested.

"I don't want rational! I want what my grandparents had." She waved wildly in the direction of the house where she had witnessed deep, abiding love, every single day. "I want pet names for each other and a love that endures through a lifetime."

"You want me to call you red?"

"Don't make fun of me. Or them," she warned. "Gran stayed in that drafty house an extra year for Gramps, because she knew it would break his heart to leave it. Now she can't stand to sleep in it without him there beside her."

"And you want that?" He sounded askance.

"It beats being married to a stranger. Occupying a mausoleum of a house while pursuing separate lives."

"My parents' marriage is an alliance based on shared values. That's not a bad thing if you agree on those values beforehand."

"Speaking from experience, are you?"

Another harsh silence descended. This time she regretted her words. His pregnant wife had died. He might not have loved Faustina, but it must be a very raw wound.

Recalling that, her suspicions of his motives arose again. Maybe he would come to care for Lily, but why was he here now? What did he *really* want?

"Rico… You understand that one baby cannot replace another, don't you?" She knew she had to tread softly on that one, but couldn't hold that apprehension inside her. "If that's why you're here, then no." It broke her heart to deny Lily her father, but, "I won't let you do that to Lily."

He stiffened and she braced herself for his scathing reaction, but it wasn't at all what she expected.

"Faustina's baby wasn't *mine*."

CHAPTER FOUR

THE WORDS WERE supposed to stay inside his head, but they resounded across the crisp air. Through the trees and off the sky. They made icicles drop like knives and stab into the frozen snow.

From a long way away, he heard Poppy say a hollow and breathless, "What?" Her thin, strained voice was no louder than his own had been, but rang like a gong in his ears.

He pinched the bridge of his nose, the leather of his gloves cold. All of him was encased in the dry ice of Canadian winter while his blood pumped in thick lumps through his arteries. His chest tightened and his shoulders ached.

"I shouldn't have said that. We should get back." He glanced the way they'd come, but it was shorter if she would only keep moving ahead on the path.

Thankfully, he couldn't see a soul. They were the only pair of fools out here stumbling through the dark. He waved for her to proceed.

"Rico." Her mitted hand came onto his forearm. "Is that true?"

The quaver in her voice matched the conscience

still wobbling like a dropped coin in the pit of his stomach.

"Forget I said it. I mean it, Poppy."

"I can't." She didn't let him brush away her grip on his sleeve. "*It matters.* Tell me."

"If I tell you…" He shifted so he cupped her elbow, holding her before him. "It stays between us. *Forever.* Do you understand?"

He had already said too much, but she was the mother of his child. His *actual* child. He had only tentatively absorbed that knowledge, only enough to know that one way or another he would bring them both back to Spain with him. Marriage was the quickest, most practical means of doing that. Therefore, she deserved to know the truth about his first marriage. As his wife, he expected her to protect his secrets as closely as he would guard hers.

And, damn it, he felt as though he'd been holding his breath for a thousand years. He couldn't contain it one minute longer.

"Her parents found her," he said, overcome with pity for them, despite his bitterness at Faustina's lies. The colossal waste of life couldn't be denied. The unborn baby might not have been his, but he was a decent enough human being to feel sadness and regret that it had been as much a victim as its parents.

"Where?" Poppy asked with dread.

"The garage. It wasn't deliberate. They'd packed bags, had train tickets. She was with her parents' chauffeur, naked in the back seat. They must have made love, perhaps started the car to warm it, then fallen asleep. They never woke up. Carbon monoxide poisoning."

"Oh, my God." She covered her mouth. "That's *horrible*."

"Yes. Her parents were devastated. Still are. They didn't know about the affair. They begged me to keep it under wraps."

"So you've been letting everyone think— How do you know the baby wasn't yours?"

"I had the coroner run tests."

"You told me that day you two weren't sleeping together." She twitched in his grip.

He released her. His palm felt cold, even inside his glove. He was solid ice, all the way to his core, still playing what-ifs in his head.

"Do you think *she* knew it wasn't yours?" she asked tentatively.

"Of course she knew," he spat with the contempt he felt for himself as much as for Faustina. "I had already begun to suspect. As soon as they found her, I knew what she had done. We *weren't* sleeping together. We made love *once* during our engagement. Faustina insisted. Said she wanted to be sure we'd be a good fit. After that, there were excuses. Headaches. Finally she said we should wait until the ceremony, to make our wedding night more exciting."

He hadn't argued. The first experience had barely moved him, certainly hadn't rocked his world the way another very memorable experience had. He skimmed his gaze over Poppy's face, so ghostly in the moonlight.

He'd told himself things would improve with Faustina once they got to know one another. He hadn't realized yet that it was possible to fall into immersive pleasure so profound he could be transported from the world around him. So much so that he made love with a woman he barely knew in the near-public solarium and had thought about her every day since.

He ran his gloved hand over his face. The seam in his palm scraped his skin, allowing him to focus on the rest of the ugly story.

"I believe she learned she was pregnant and slept with me so she could pass the baby off as mine."

"When?"

He knew what she was asking. "A few weeks before she broke things off with me on the day you and I were together."

Poppy rubbed her arm where he'd held her elbow.

"I've since learned that when she left my parents' house, she went straight to her own and told them she had called off the wedding. Her father threatened to disinherit her. They're very faithful and strict, demanded she abide by the agreement. They would have fired the driver if they'd had any inkling of her reason. Maybe even sued him for damages or destroyed him in some other way. Faustina's choice was to live destitute with her lover or crawl back to me."

It was the only explanation for how a stable, well-bred, otherwise honest woman could have behaved in such an underhanded way.

"A week before they died, she used her settlement from our marriage to close on a small house in the north of Spain, near his relatives. That's where they were headed."

"That's so…sad."

"Sad and sordid and I torture myself every day wondering if she would be alive if I'd refused to marry her that next morning."

"Why did you agree? The presidency?" Her voice panged in a way that grated against his conscience. The opportunity to run Faustina's father's company, proving himself in his own arena away from Cesar's shadow, had been the carrot that drew him into the engagement, but it wouldn't have enticed him to go through with the wedding the second time.

"She said she'd just found out she was pregnant, that it was the reason she'd been so emotional the day before. She said the baby was from that *one time*—when I used a condom, by the way. I should have suspected she was lying, but…" Here were the what-ifs. What if he had asked more questions, balked, told her he'd slept with the maid? That he'd *liked* it.

He hadn't done any of that. He'd done his duty by his family. He had done what was expected because, "I thought the baby was *mine*."

"When did you start to suspect it wasn't?"

"The wedding night. She didn't want to have sex. Said the pregnancy was turning her off." Rico had been nursing his own regrets and hadn't pressed her. "She was very moody. Conflicted, obviously. And putting her ducks in a row to leave me. We never did sleep together again. Things grew strained as I realized she was keeping something from me. I put off a confrontation, but it was coming. Then I got the call from her father."

"I'm so sorry, Rico. It's truly awful that you've had to carry this."

"I don't want your pity, Poppy." He curled his hands

into fists, straining the seams in his gloves. "I want your silence. I expect it. Not even Cesar knows and we don't keep much from one another. But I swore to her parents I'd keep it quiet."

"What about the company?"

"Her father asked me to stay on as President. He's sickened that she tricked me. I could weather the scandal if the truth came out, but it would destroy them. Despite Faustina's behavior, they're good people. I don't want to hurt them any more than they have been."

"I'll never say a word," she promised.

He nodded, believing her because they were in this together now.

"You understand why I told you? If she had been honest and up front about her situation, I would have helped her, maybe even raised that baby if she had asked me to. I wouldn't have punished the child for her failings." His anger returned, making his nostrils sting. "But I don't appreciate that you have also kept secrets from me, Poppy."

He heard her breath catch as though he'd struck her.

"I will *not* ignore my actual blood. I want *my* daughter."

She took a step back, but he caught her arm, keeping her close and tilting his head to peer through the shadows straight into her eyes.

"You *will* come to Spain. You *will* marry me and we will make this work."

Poppy might have knocked his hand away if she hadn't needed his touch to steady her; his words were that impactful.

"That's a big leap," she managed shakily. "I won't keep you from knowing her, Rico. I see why Lily being yours has extra significance for you." Her heart was aching under the weight of what he'd revealed and she had only just heard it. It had been festering in him for nearly two years. "But you and I barely know each other."

"We know each other," he scoffed gently. "I just told you something I haven't told *anyone*."

And she had shared her heartache over her parents' neglect.

A similar thing had happened that day in the solarium. Their conversation had somehow become deeply personal. Her crush on him had been instant and she'd never meant it to become obvious to him, but for weeks she had longed to talk to him in a meaningful way. She had wanted to find out who he was beneath his shell of gorgeous looks, easy manners and unsmudged armor.

She recalled telling him about that liar of a backpacker who had stolen everything she had, then asked why he had agreed to an arranged marriage.

Why compete with a business rival if a marriage can turn them into a partner? Faustina's very upstanding family would never connect themselves so intimately to any but the most exemplary politician, which polishes my father's already stellar reputation in the upper house of Parliament. Faustina gains the social standing of marrying into a titled family. My mother gets the heiress and the wedding event she envisioned for my brother.

It had seemed so laughably factual. She had asked him what he stood to gain and he'd mentioned running a company he would control, allowing him to pursue ambitions away from working for his brother.

A rational part of her brain had warned her that she deserved someone better than a man bouncing off a broken engagement, but her pride had needed the focused attention of someone so much grander than she was. She had thought the camera thief had genuinely liked her, but he'd been flattering her to blind her. Rico hadn't wanted anything from her except *her*. If he was rebounding after his own rejection, that was okay. It was one more detail that made them equals.

And when their kisses had escalated with passion, she hadn't wanted to stop. His lovemaking had been exactly what she had needed in that moment. Much as she believed she would only marry for love, she had known a soul-mate connection was an elusive thing. Expecting the full package of love and pleasure and a lifelong commitment for her first time wasn't realistic.

It had been enough to have infatuation and a man who ought to be firmly out of her reach, but who brought her entire body to life by simply watching the release of a button on her dress, then lifting his gaze to check in with her as his finger traced a caress against her skin.

She put a halt to recalling the rest or she'd succumb to him all over again without so much as a single protest.

"This is the second time we've spoken," she pointed out, inwardly shaking at how profound their encounters had been. "We made love *once*."

"With spectacular results." His gloved hand took hold of her chin. "I'm not just talking about Lily."

She was so glad he couldn't see her blush, but her helplessness was on full display in her strained voice. "That was… You were relieved you weren't marrying," she accused. "Coming off a dry spell with the first woman you happened across."

"I noticed you before that."

They were close enough that the fog of their breath was mingling.

"I wouldn't have kissed you if you hadn't made a point of telling me you'd finished your last shift and were no longer an employee," he reminded. "The attraction was mutual."

"I didn't make a *point* of it." Maybe she had. He had asked if she wanted to leave and had moved aside, giving her plenty of space to walk past him to the change rooms where she'd been headed when she had bumped into him. She had stayed, eager to keep talking to him. Basking in the glory of being noticed by him.

"Do you ever think about that day?" he asked.

Constantly. She wouldn't admit it, though.

"Hmm?" he prompted, lowering his head. He stopped before he kissed her.

She let her eyes flutter closed and parted her lips in invitation.

He only grazed his mouth against hers, provoking a buzzing sensation in her lips.

She put out a hand, but the knit of her mitten only found the smooth leather of his jacket, too slippery to hold on to.

While he kept up that frustratingly light tickle. His hand shifted to cup the side of her neck, the rough seam on his thumb grazing the tender skin in her throat.

"Do you?" He refused to give her what she wanted until she answered.

Her skin grew too tight for the anticipation that swelled within her. Beneath the layers of her thick jacket, her breasts grew heavy. Her thighs ceased to feel the cold through the denim of her jeans.

"Yes," she admitting on a throb of longing.

He made a noise of satisfaction and stepped so his feet were outside her own. His hot mouth sealed across her lips.

A sob of delight broke in her throat as his hard lips raked across hers, making real all the erotic fantasies she'd replayed in the long nights since leaving Spain. Her arms went up around his neck and he swept her closer still. So close she could hardly breathe.

She didn't care. The thick layers of their coats were a frustration, one that seemed to hold them off from one another. She wanted them *gone*. Wanted passion to take her over the way it had that day, blanking out the world around her with levels of excitement and pleasure she hadn't known existed.

His kiss deepened with greed, as though he couldn't get enough of her, either. She opened fully to him, licked into his mouth and felt his arms tighten around her in response. She ran her hand up past his scarf, pressed the back of his head, urging him to kiss her harder and harder still. She wanted him to mark her. Savage her.

Because he already had.

This passion between them was as destructive as it was glorious. She needed to remember that. Otherwise, she would succumb and wind up far out of her depth again.

As though he recognized the risk as well, he dragged his head up and sucked in a breath, but he didn't let her go.

Panting, she blinked her eyes open. His face was in darkness with a kaleidoscope of colors haloed behind him.

"Look." She seized the distraction to pull herself out of his arms. She wasn't even sure if what she was seeing was real or the leftover fireworks he had so easily set off behind her eyelids.

She staggered slightly as she led him out of the trees. The expanse of sky was bigger than a thousand movie screens above them and the stars had faded behind glowing swirls. Shimmering bands of pink and purple and red danced within the curtains of green. Every few seconds a spear of color shot toward the earth in knife-like streaks. The jabs of color felt so tangible and close, she expected to be struck by one.

"This is beautiful." Rico drew her back against his chest and folded his arms across her collarbone and stomach.

She was still weak from their kiss. She leaned into the wall he made, wondering if he could feel the thump of her still unsteady heart through their winter layers.

"One of my first memories is coming out here with my grandfather," she confided softly. "I asked when my mother was coming back and he brought me out here. I thought he was going to tell me she had died. He said he didn't know if she was coming back, but then he pointed to the sky. I asked what it was and he said he didn't know that, either. That there would always be things in this world we're left to wonder about."

"Gas particles from the sun collide with the earth's atmosphere," Rico informed her.

"Don't ruin it." She nudged her elbow back into his ribs. "It's *magic*. I've taken a million photographs of them, but none capture how amazing this really is. How small it makes you feel."

"I've never seen it like this." His chin touched the top of her head.

"Me, neither." This was the most glorious display she'd ever witnessed and she didn't care that she didn't have her camera. She would never forget sharing this with him: the timbre of his voice vibrating through her jacket, the heat of his breath against her earlobe where it poked from beneath her toque, the weight of his arm across her and the way all those colors glowed inside her even as they danced before her unblinking eyes.

She hesitated then confessed softly, "Gramps brought me out here when I was pregnant, too. I wanted to keep Lily, but I didn't know how I would manage it. It felt too much of an imposition to stay with them. He was upset that he wouldn't be around to look after me and Gran. We had a little cry then saw these lights. He said it was a reminder that even dark nights offer beautiful moments and said that's what Lily would be for all of us if I stayed with them."

Rico's arm tightened across her chest. His voice was low and sincere. "I'm sorry I didn't meet him."

Her chest ached. "I think that's him right now."

A startled pause, then, "I don't believe in things like that, Poppy."

"It's okay." She touched the arm that continued to hold her close. "I do."

"If I did—" His lips pressed to her ear through the knit of her toque. "I think we both know what he's saying."

Her throat grew tight. *Marry Rico*.

He drew back slightly so he could reach into his jacket. When he brought his hand around in front of her, he held a small box. He stayed behind her as he pried up the lid so she stood in the circle of his arms as he offered her the ring.

The band could have been silver or yellow or rose. The diamond caught glints of colored light, blinding her.

Had he really come all this way, not knowing for sure if Lily was his, but brought a ring just in case?

She let him pick up her left hand and tug at the mitten. She took the discarded mitt with her free hand. As though under a spell, she turned to face him.

She tried to think of reasons to persuade him this was wrong or stupid or doomed to fail. Marrying him was all of those things.

But she wanted to marry him. Her compulsion to know him remained. Beneath the anger and armor of indifference was a man who wanted to know his daughter. That meant everything to her.

As the aurora borealis continued to crash silently over them, full of mystical power and spirit voices, she told herself that Gramps wouldn't steer her wrong. He wouldn't tell her to marry Rico if this would ruin her life. He was telling her to say goodbye to her home and family and begin building her new one.

The cool ring caught slightly on her knuckle, then it was on her finger, heavy as the promise it symbolized.

Rico's mouth came down to hers again with magnificent heat, burning away her bleak doubts and fears, filling her with hope and possibility.

CHAPTER FIVE

You should have told me sooner. I would have made arrangements. Someone from the family should have been there.

RICO READ THE TEXT from Pia and swore, then dropped the phone onto the custom recliner beside the one he occupied.

Across from him, buckled into her own, Poppy looked up from distracting Lily with a book. Lily was making noises of dismay at being strapped into her car seat while the view beyond the windows turned to clouds.

"What's wrong?" Poppy asked him.

"A text from my sister, scolding me about the wedding."

"She's upset?" Poppy's expression dimmed.

"That I didn't invite her. I pointed out there hasn't been time."

It hadn't occurred to him Pia would want to come. His parents had urged him to wait for the DNA results and expressed consternation that he hadn't. Cesar's reaction to his impending nuptials had been a curt text.

Sorcha told me. Congratulations.

Rico had given up at that point and focused on the tasks at hand.

Poppy's gran had been moved to her sister's apartment, where she would occupy a guest room for a few days. Rico had had to push to make it happen, but he had arranged to have her personal items moved into a nearby, private seniors' complex that was so well-appointed, Eleanor had asked him if he'd won a lottery.

Poppy had been anxious about the entire process until she'd spoken with the extremely personable, on-staff doctor who had already been in touch with her grandmother's specialist. A nutritionist had made note of her grandmother's dislike of cumin. Her sensitivity to certain detergents had been conveyed to the housekeeping staff. Eleanor had looked in on the pool where physical therapy sessions were held and checked out the lively games room, approving the entire complex with a delighted nod.

Poppy's father had pointed out that the location in Regina would be easier for him to visit, too. He typically spent half a day driving after his flight landed. Rico had even hired a caretaker to look after the house until decisions had been made on whether to keep it in the family.

The last task had been a brief civil service at the courthouse. Poppy's father had given her away and her grandmother had wept happy tears. They had eaten brunch at an upscale café then climbed aboard his private jet.

Another text rang through, but he ignored it.

"Tell her I didn't even have my mother there," Poppy said.

"I explained why I was keeping it private."

"That wasn't a complaint," she said stiffly, making him aware of how tersely he'd spoken. "I didn't *want* my mother there." She picked up the book Lily dropped, mouth pinched.

Poppy had said she would inform her mother after Rico issued the press release. He'd had enough to juggle in the moment that he hadn't questioned her. Now he did.

"Why not?" Had she been afraid she wouldn't show up? Her mother sounded even less emotionally accessible than his own. At least La Reina Montero maintained appearances.

"I was afraid she wouldn't keep her mouth shut," Poppy muttered crossly. "I agree with you that it's kinder to let your parents inform Faustina's parents and give them a few days to prepare their own statement."

Loathe as he was to bring Faustina into this marriage on any level, he appreciated Poppy's understanding. Having a child Lily's age wouldn't reflect well on his fidelity, narrow window of a called-off wedding notwithstanding. This news would come as a shock to many, including Faustina's parents.

"I didn't mean to speak sharply. I don't usually make mistakes and they've been piling up lately."

For the most part, Rico was a meticulous planner. He had always been taught success was a matter of research and preparation. That lesson had played out as true more often than not and he had heeded its wisdom—right up until he had impulsively made love with his mother's maid.

He had promptly fallen back in line with the precisely orchestrated pageant his first wedding had been, only to discover his wife's betrayal. As resentful as he still was of that, he had to face the fact that if he had refused to marry Faustina when she had come back that next morning, she might be alive and happily ensconced with her lover and child. He wouldn't have the presidency that had seemed like such a delectable consolation prize, but he would have had the first year of Lily's life. Poppy bore some responsibility for his missing that, but so did he.

He had believed his tryst with Poppy was all the bucking of expectations he had needed before settling into the life laid out for him. Even after Sorcha had dropped this earth-shattering news on him, he had attempted to defuse it with surgical care, ordering an investigation and telling no one.

Then the test had come back inconclusive and he had come out of his skin. Mere days later, he had a wife and child. His parents thought he was behaving recklessly and a rational part of him wondered if they were right. He was relying on instinct without concrete evidence or other facts to back it up.

He caught Poppy's affronted glare and heard his own words.

"I wasn't suggesting this marriage is a mistake. But it will cause a tragic death to be splashed across the gossip sites again. *You* will be cast as the Other Woman."

She would be labeled an opportunist and a gold digger. Given her shock at his arrival, he couldn't accuse her of that, but others would.

"I'll look like a faithless husband and a deadbeat father. I'm not proud of any of that. Scandals are not my MO. I'm disgusted with myself for creating this situation."

"And what about Lily? Are you sorry you created her?" The fiery challenge in her expression was quickly schooled as the flight attendant approached to ask after their comfort.

Lily lifted her arms at the woman and pitifully begged, "Oof?"

"She thinks that means up," Poppy explained with a stiff smile. "I guess I was making that noise whenever I lifted her and didn't notice. Button, you have to stay in your seat. I'll apologize now for how miserable she's going to become."

Rico preferred a happy baby over one who was screaming, same as anyone. The baby in question, however, was his. He hadn't fully unpacked that knowledge and very tentatively felt around in the dank spaces within him, looking for the regret Poppy had accused him of feeling toward Lily.

"Our flight should be very smooth until we're over the Atlantic," the attendant said. "She could walk around if you want to let her work out some energy."

"She doesn't walk yet."

"There isn't much she can get into," Rico pointed out, still searching through the bitterness that encased him for resentment that was wrongly aimed at an innocent child. "All the drawers have catches so they won't open midflight."

Poppy peered at the floors. They were as spotless as they ought to be, given the salaries he paid his flight crews.

"You really wouldn't mind?" Poppy asked the attendant.

"Of course not." The attendant was bemused by the question and disappeared to fetch the coffee he requested.

Poppy heard his snort and shot him a frown as she unstrapped Lily. "Why am I funny?"

"This is my plane. If my daughter wants to pilot it through loop-de-loops, it's the crew's job to make it happen." That much he *was* sure of.

Poppy released a small oof of exertion as she pulled Lily out of her seat and stood her on the floor, next to her knee. Then she reached into the toy bag and handed Lily a giraffe. She tossed the half-dozen other toys onto the empty seat next to Rico.

Lily reached for the bag, needing to peek inside to see if more would appear.

"It's empty. They're all there," Poppy told her, pointing.

Lily dropped the giraffe, let go of Poppy's knee and took three toddling steps, completely unassisted.

Poppy gasped and reached out to catch her, but Lily slapped her dimpled hand onto Rico's knee. Her fingers closed like kitten claws into the fabric of his trousers as she steadied herself. Then she cruised around his leg and began examining the array of toys.

Poppy clapped her hand over her open mouth. Her eyes brimmed with excited tears. "Did you see that?" She dropped her hand, but emotion husked her voice.

"Those weren't her *first* steps." It couldn't be. There'd been no fanfare. No announcement over the PA that it was about to happen. It had occurred naturally, as if she'd been doing it all along.

Poppy nodded like a bobblehead doll on the dash of a derby car.

"They were. Just like that. Baby is gone and she's a toddler." She wiped her damp eyes. "I shouldn't be so silly about it. Gran kept saying it would happen any day."

Lily had found his phone amid the stuffed toys and plastic keys. He started to take it from her, but a fierce swell of pride moved his hand to her hair. He faltered briefly then grazed his palm lightly over her fine red hair, downy as a duckling.

She was such a tiny, perfect little human. Recognizing how vulnerable she was made his heart clench in a strange panic. An urge to protect rose in him, but he already knew he wouldn't be sufficient to the task. Not forever. Things would happen beyond his control. Then what? He had instinctively shied from this depth of responsibility, but here it was, thrust upon him, heavy and unavoidable, yet oddly welcome.

How could he not want to shield such a precious young life? How could he ever blame her for existing?

"You don't have to impress me, you know," he told Lily, rueful that he was so button-bursting proud of three little steps.

Lily grinned and held up his phone.

"Thank you," he said politely and pocketed the item, offering a teething ring in exchange. He shifted his attention to Poppy.

"We both could have handled many things better," he told her, clearing his voice to steady it while he mentally allowed the cloak of fatherhood to settle more comfortably over his shoulders. "But I will never, ever regard Lily as a mistake."

Rico gently transferred Lily into a blue crib that likely belonged to Mateo. Rico had said this darkened penthouse in Madrid was used by any member of the family who happened to have business in the capital.

Poppy carefully tucked blankets around her overtired little girl. The first half of the flight had gone well. Everyone had caught a few hours of sleep, but Lily had begun fussing when turbulence forced her to be strapped back into her seat. By the time she had cried herself out and begun to nod off, they were descending and her ears were popping, upsetting her all over again.

"I think she's down for the count," Poppy said with relief as they stepped out of the room.

Rico clicked on the baby monitor and brought it with them into the lounge where he turned on a few lamps. He moved with casual confidence, hardly a wrinkle in his clothes, his eyes heavy-lidded and inscrutable.

"Are you hungry?"

"No. I feel like all I did was eat on the flight." She crossed her arms and hunched her shoulders, hyperaware that they were alone for the first time since they'd stood under the stars that first night.

They were also married.

She had heard him tell the driver to leave their luggage in *his* room, but there was a conversation they needed to have before they shared it. She hadn't figured out yet how to broach it. She wished she could be blasé and sophisticated, but she felt callow and fearful of his reaction. Would he laugh? Look at her with disappointment?

"I…um…wouldn't mind a shower," she murmured, more for a chance to be alone and clear her head.

"Do you want company?" His voice lowered, growing thick with sensual invitation.

Her stomach took a rollercoaster dip and swirl while a wave of heat pushed out from her center, leaving her fingers and toes, nipples and scalp all tingling.

She wanted to laugh at how easily he segued into addressing the elephant, but some of her trepidation must have shown. His expression tightened.

"We don't have to if you're tired."

"It's not that," she murmured, more wired than tired, still trying to come to terms with everything that had happened in such a whirlwind. Drawing a breath of courage, she said, "I'm not sure what you expect."

A brief pulse of surprise, then he said stiffly, "I expect this marriage to include a sexual relationship. I'll never force it, though. And I would normally say a woman doesn't need an excuse for turning me down, but given Faustina's reasons, I'd like to understand yours."

"I'm not turning you down," she said with a small, nervous smile that wouldn't stick. "I expected we'd have sex. When I took Lily for her blood test the other day, I left her with the nurse so I could get an IUD." Sometimes her hair gifted her with the clichéd fiery blushes and now was one of those times. The entire room should have turned bordello red, she glowed so hotly with the admission that she had premeditated having sex with him.

He frowned. "You don't want more children?"

"Not right away." Her cheeks hurt, they were scorched so deeply. "This is a lot to get used to, don't you think? Without bringing a newborn into the mix?"

He tipped his head slightly, acknowledging the point, but a hint of suspicion glinted in his narrowed eyes. Perhaps he saw the rest of the logic that had propelled her decision—a new baby would make it more difficult for her to leave if she had to.

"I want this marriage to work," she assured him. "But there are things…" Her voice failed her. She cleared her throat. "Things we should discuss before…"

"Health concerns?"

"You mean disease? No! I'm perfectly fine. Are you—?"

"Completely fine," he clipped out. "I was asking if there were complications with delivering Lily that affected you?"

"No. Just the usual leftover imperfections of stretch marks and… Well, you can see I'm still carrying a bit of baby weight. Lily weaned herself three months ago and apparently these aren't going away." She waved at the chest that remained a cup size bigger than prepregnancy.

"I assure you I don't consider any of those things 'imperfections.' Particularly the added curves. Is that the source of your hesitation? You're self-conscious? We can keep the lights off if it will make you more comfortable. I'd prefer it, too. Otherwise my scar from my appendix surgery might turn you off."

"Why would— Oh. All right, I get your point." She rolled her eyes.

He paced closer, which made her freeze in place, skin growing tight with anticipation while nervous butterflies filled her torso, swirling around in every direction.

He touched her chin, coaxing her to meet his gaze with her own. "We've done this before," he reminded her.

"About that…" She clasped his flat wrist and squeezed her eyes shut. "That's the only time I've had sex. Ever."

She felt the flex in his wrist and the slight increase of pressure in his grip on her chin.

"Open your eyes," he commanded, voice seeming to resonate from the depths of his chest.

She did, meeting his gaze with chagrin. She wasn't ashamed of being a virgin so much as feeling guilty for having misled him that day.

All she could see were his eyes, iridescent almost. Like granite that revealed flecks of precious gems when wet, glints of blue and green in the gray surrounding a giant black pool. His pupils were huge. Atavistic.

Yet skeptical.

"*Ever*," she reiterated helplessly.

Rico couldn't think of another time he'd been utterly speechless. Not that his mind had the capacity to filter any moments other than the one she was referring to. The shyness of her hands squeezing him through his pants and fumbling with his belt.

Enthusiasm counted for more than expertise when it came to lovemaking. If he'd given any thought to her

lack of finesse, he had likely imagined she was as overcome as he was. He couldn't say his own performance
had been particularly adept, given the stolen nature of
their tryst.

He remembered clearly that moment afterward,
though, when his lingering pleasure had dimmed because he had feared he had hurt her.

Is your cycle starting?

I guess. Sorry. She'd been mortified.

Don't apologize. At least we're safe from—

He'd been appalled at forgetting the condom. He
never forgot.

"I don't like lies," he warned her now, lips numb.
This news was melting his face off his skull.

"I'm being honest." She winced as though she was
squirming inside. "I want to sleep with you, but I don't
want you to be..." She swallowed. Her voice remained
strained. "Disappointed. *I* don't want to be disappointed."

The word wafted over him, so far from what he
might be feeling as to be incomprehensible. Then his
ego absorbed the hit.

"Were *you* disappointed that day?"

"No." She withdrew from him a few steps and
crossed her arms.

But she had nothing to compare it to. Her lack of experience began to penetrate. Belated concern struck.
They'd been quite passionate. "Did I hurt you?"

"No. I mean, a little, but not..." She looked to the
ceiling as though seeking deliverance. "I was fine with
the discomfort. There were compensations," she added
with a small groan of embarrassed irony.

"You felt pleasure?" He had to know. "You weren't faking your enjoyment, were you? Did you climax? Because I thought you did, but—"

"Are we really doing a forensic audit on it?" she cried, face so red it should have been accompanied by five alarms.

"I need to know, Poppy." It was imperative.

"I didn't fake anything! Okay? Quit asking such personal questions."

"How is this too personal? We were both there and I'm making sure we were both *there*. My pride is every bit as delicate as any man's. When it comes to the bedroom, if you're not satisfied, I'm not satisfied. I will make you that promise right now."

She ducked her eyes into her hand. "Thanks. And I'd love to make the same promise, but *I don't know what I'm doing.*"

"You don't have to be defensive about it. I'm glad you told me. And your number of past lovers is far less important to me than how many you have *now*." Obviously. "Shall we agree we'll keep it to one?"

She peered at him over her hand, admonishing, but also earnest as she promised, "Of course I'll be monogamous."

"Thank you. So will I." But he was still having trouble believing she had shelved all her passion once she'd discovered it. "There really hasn't been anyone since me?"

"Who would I sleep with, pregnant out to here?" She set her hand in the air beyond her navel. "I was looking after my grandparents and a newborn. Babies make you want to have a date with your pillow and no one else, trust me."

She looked too uncomfortable to be telling him anything but the truth.

It was starting to impact him that the most profound sexual experience of his life had been with a virgin. He wasn't sentimental, but there was something endearing in knowing he was her only lover.

"Why me?" he asked gently. "Why that day?"

"Because I was feeling like my whole trip had been a bust and I wanted one decent memory to take home with me."

"I was a *souvenir*?"

"I was just a notch on your belt, wasn't I?" she shot back.

His heart lurched and he had to look away, thinking of the way he had obsessed about her ever since. He had tried to relegate her to a notch. Instead, she'd been another persistent what-if.

"It's fine that you were only taking what I offered," she said, hugging herself. "I didn't care that you had all the experience and seduced me. I wanted you to. But now you're only having sex with me because we're married and you're stuck with me. That would be fine if I felt like I was bringing something to the table, but I don't have any sexual confidence because I've only done it *one time*." Her brow furrowed.

Aside from the chaste kiss after the ceremony, he hadn't touched her since their kiss under the stars, but he'd been acutely aware of her every minute since she had opened her door to him. His ears were attuned to each inflection in her voice—the chuckling remarks she exchanged with her grandmother, the loving tone she used when speaking to Lily. He had studied the fit of her jeans, drunk in the scent of her hair, enjoyed the smooth warmth of her hand if their fingers happened to touch. He had noted the way her lips closed over a fork and the little frown that appeared between her brows if she was growing stubborn.

He had spent every night lying awake, recalling their passionate union until he was so filled with ardor, he ached.

He couldn't believe she didn't know that.

But he had taken pains to keep his reaction hidden so as not to let her undermine him with what he perceived as a weakness. He hadn't wanted to admit that he had obsessed about her from the first moment he'd seen her dusting his mother's furniture.

"You have a lot to compare to and I don't want to start our marriage by falling short of your expectations." She offered a dejected smile. "That's why we're standing here instead of in the shower."

CHAPTER SIX

POPPY FELT LIKE a head case and was trying not to apologize for it. Women were allowed to have reservations. To feel conflicted. She might want sex, but she didn't want empty sex. Not this time. Not when she had tried that the first time and discovered she wasn't capable of keeping her emotions out of the experience.

But Rico was her husband and the father of her child and their kisses had reassured her that their lovemaking would be as pleasurable as it had been the first time.

Maybe she was expecting too much.

Was that what he was thinking behind that enigmatic expression? A muscle was pulsing in his jaw as though he was trying to crack nuts with his teeth.

"I haven't been with anyone else, either," he finally said.

"Oh, please." Disappointment in him descended like a curtain while her heart latched a little too hard on to that outrageous statement. "It's been nearly two years!" He could have his pick of supermodels. He'd gotten the maid with a wink and a smile, hadn't he?

"I already told you that I slept with Faustina *once*. Weeks before you." He opened his eyes to scowl with affront at her distrust. "I didn't cheat on her, and given the way my marriage ended, I haven't been feeling very amorous."

She found that believable, actually.

"Until very recently," he added pointedly, pretty much flinging sexual awareness at her and leaving her coated in it. "All of which could impact *my* performance. You're not the only one with high stakes here."

"Oh, I'm sure we're on exactly the same level of nerves," she muttered sarcastically.

He relaxed slightly, eyeing her. "Do you think about it?"

"What? Sex?" The whole world tilted like a magnifying glass. One moment certain things had loomed large, now all of that went out of focus while a bright ray of heat singed into her bones. "With you, or…?"

"Anyone. But sure, me."

She was *not* going to admit that she thought about him *all the time*. "I can't believe you're asking me these things."

"This is exactly the sort of conversation a husband and wife should be able to have."

"Do *you*?" she challenged.

"Think about you? Of course. I've often recalled our lovemaking and imagined doing things with you that we didn't have time to enjoy."

He was admitting to fantasizing about her. And he wasn't flinching in the least. He was staring right into her eyes and making *her* think of things she wished they'd done.

His brow went up in a light challenge.

She swallowed, hot all over.

"I imagine you're in the shower with me. For instance," he provided in a drawl that somehow pulled all her nerve endings tight. "If you're looking for a seductive move, I guarantee you an invitation to join you will always pique my interest."

She narrowed her eyes. "I don't appreciate you making fun of me."

"I'm not joking," he assured her, but amusement lurked around his mouth.

"Fine," she said with annoyance. "Let's move this to the shower, then."

"Poppy."

His voice caught like a hook in her heart, pulling her around without even touching her before she could hurry down the hall.

She caught her breath. If he said he didn't want to, she might lose her nerve and never find it again.

"What?" she demanded when he waited until she quit spinning her gaze around the room in avoidance and made herself look at him.

"This isn't a test." His voice grew grave. Tense. "If you're not ready, say so."

"I said I want to!" She waved in the direction she'd been headed.

He came toward her, brows raised in a mild scold. "You're nervous. Maybe instead of barreling into the shower, we should slow down."

"I want the awkwardness over with," she admitted, bordering on petulant.

He gently peeled her hands off her elbows and held them in a loose grip. "But if I'd been in less of a hurry last time, I might have noticed you were new to this. *I* want to be sure you're with me every step. Why don't we start with a kiss?"

"Really?" She rolled her eyes toward the ceiling. "Fine. If that's what you want."

"Humor me." He stepped in and stole a single kiss, one of those deliberately light ones that made desire soak through her like gasoline.

She shifted lightly on her feet, instantly restless, but not in a hurry to go anywhere. "You could try that again."

He did, lingering. Taking his time finding the right fit, playing with levels of pressure.

While she shyly returned his kiss, her whole body became sensitized to everything around them. The lamplight chasing them toward the hall, the scent of faint cologne against his cheek and the slight rustle of their clothing as they stopped holding hands and reached to touch. Her hand came to rest on the fabric of his shirt, curling into a fist that crushed the fine linen while her mouth moved with tremulous passion beneath his, encouraging him.

That bashful invitation seemed to test his control. He growled and deepened the kiss. His hands found her waist and drew her fully against him.

All the memories she had convinced herself were fantasy were becoming real. He was here. She was in his arms, in his home. This was her new life. It was too much. A small cry sounded in her throat.

He lifted his head. Both of them tried to steady their breath.

She suddenly remembered him saying, *You deserve better than the lowlife who took your camera.*

She had known she did, but she hadn't believed she deserved him. Not for more than a brief hour. At the time, she had countered, *She didn't deserve you, either. I hope you find someone better.* She had wanted him to see *her* as an option. To *want* her.

Did he? She could tell he was affected by their kiss, but he was pulling himself back under control as she watched.

This was the true source of her apprehension. That she would lose herself to his touch again and whatever grip or autonomy she had over her life would slip away. After their first time, even before she had learned she was pregnant, she had known her life would never be the same. Every other man would be compared to him and fall short.

After tonight, he would know he could do this to her. He could break down her barriers without effort, own her body and soul. Her eyes began to sting at her defenselessness.

His hands moved soothingly across her lower back. His eyes had gone more blue than gray and were shot with sparks of green, hot as the center of a flame. As he slowly drew her in again, he made a noise that was a question.

She settled gladly against him. Melted into him.

If she had had the strength of mind, of willpower, she might have balked. But she wanted this. She craved his touch like she'd been sucked into quicksand and suddenly found the vine that would pull her free.

He lowered his head and took another thorough

taste of her, long and lazy and luscious. The stab of his tongue acted like alcohol, shooting pleasurable trickles of heat through her veins. She grew loose of limb and warm and weak. She moaned softly and curled her arms around his neck, encouraging him.

He settled into a passionate kiss, not aggressive, but full of confidence. Unhurried and possessive. Seductive.

She quit thinking about whether she was being reckless or not skilled enough. She let herself sink into the play of his mouth across hers and simply feel. Feel the hardness of him with her whole body as she rose on her tiptoes. Feel the silk of his hair with her fingers and the faint abrasion of chin stubble as he twisted his head and swept his tongue across hers.

She immersed herself in the feel of *him*. The sweep of his hands across her back and down to her hips, the iron thighs holding steady as she leaned into him. The erotic hardness of his erection pressing into her abdomen, telling her she was affecting him.

The knowledge he was aroused sent arrows of answering lust deep into her belly. Lower. Each bolt was tipped with flame, burning her hotter as their kisses went on until she was melting and dripping with anticipation. Making pleading noises without conscious awareness of it.

The scoop of his hands under her backside surprised her, but her legs locked around his waist as he lifted her. She found herself nose to nose with him.

"Hold on." He looked as though he commanded armies, his face a mask of sharp angles as he carried her down the hall.

She clung across his shoulders, and buried her face

in the masculine scents against his neck. She nuzzled his throat and lightly bit his earlobe, smiling when she made all the muscles in his body flex in reaction.

His hands tightened against her backside and she chuckled with feminine power, thrilling, then falling—

She gasped and let go to put out her hands, but he caught her with strong arms across her back, bending with her, coming with her and covering her as she landed gently on the mattress.

Barely any light had followed them into the room. They'd forgotten the baby monitor, but Lily was across the hall. Poppy would hear her—but dearly hoped she wouldn't.

She glanced toward the en suite.

"We'll get there," he murmured of the shower, propping himself over her on one elbow. "This is nice for now." His legs were tangled with hers, his hips heavy on hers. With his free hand, he popped the first button on her top. *"Sí?"*

She smiled shyly, not sure what she was supposed to agree to. He could undress her if he wanted to, but this was the furthest thing from "nice." It was exhilarating and dangerous and consuming. It was everything she wanted.

And there was something awfully sweet about a man who wanted to seduce her when she was already there.

"You have to answer, *cariño*." His fingers came up to comb tendrils of hair away from her face.

"Sí," she whispered.

"Perfecto." He stroked the backs of two fingers down her throat and finished opening her shirt, revealing her breasts in her demicups.

She tried to open his shirt, but, like the first time, had none of his skill. His buttons were small and tight. Impossible. He brought his hand up and brushed hers away then swept his hand in a sharp yank that tore off buttons and ripped holes.

She gasped. "You didn't have to do that!"

"I did," he assured her, catching her hand and bringing it to his hot chest. "I've waited a long time for your touch."

His words sent her heart into a spin. She greedily brushed aside the gaping edges of his shirt and claimed his taut skin. The texture of his chest hair played against her palms and his breath sucked in when she skimmed the heels of her hands across the tight points of his nipples.

He said something in Spanish that she didn't have the wherewithal to translate, but his hand slid across her waist, making her realize he had finished releasing her buttons and now took his time exploring all the flesh he had bared. He made a circle against her quivering belly, stroked his thumb across the bumps of her ribcage, then traced the zigzag stitching on the bottom of her bra.

She should have bought something better. Her underclothes were boring beige, purchased from a big box store. He didn't seem to mind. He drew circles on the soft cups. There was no padding. She felt his touch almost as if she was naked. Her nipples stood up against the thin fabric, waiting for more. Begging for it.

Time stood still. His smile of pleasure was almost cruel as he teased her. She didn't realize she was furtively raking her thumbs across his nipples until his fierce gaze came up to hers and he said in a low growl, "Two can play that game, *preciosa*."

With a casual flick of the front closure, her bra released and he brushed the cup aside. His nostrils flared as he took a moment to admire her blush-pink areoles and the turgid nipples atop them. Then he dipped his head, catching her nipple in his hot, damp mouth, devouring her.

She bit back a cry and arched, barely able to withstand the burn and rush of blood that made the tips unbearably tight and sensitive before he began to pull and tease and scrape with his teeth.

She bit her lip and thrust her fingers into his hair, but he didn't let up. He continued his delicious torture until she writhed against him, hips lifting in ancient signals of willingness.

He rose to kiss her mouth, drowning her in pure sensuality before he moved to her other breast, keeping his hand on the first, circling his thumb on the wet, taut button in a way that sent currents of desire straight through her. She grew wet with yearning. She was both embarrassed and becoming desperate, alternately trying to squeeze her thighs together and open them with invitation.

His legs were pinning hers, though, keeping her beneath him in a sensual vice where she couldn't escape the pleasure he was bestowing on her. She finally clasped the sides of his head and dragged his mouth up to hers again. She pushed her tongue between his lips, flagrant and uninhibited.

Take me, she begged with her kiss.

He groaned, shifted. Got his hand between them and

released her jeans. He made another sound of deep satisfaction as he pushed his hand into her open fly, covering heat and damp cotton. His touch was wickedly skilled, rocking as he eased his touch deeper into the notch of her thighs, until she was lifting into the pressure of his palm, streaks of glorious pleasure arcing through her back. Only then did he slide a finger beneath the placket to brush her skin, leave her pulsing, then returning to soothe. Incite.

"I thought it was my imagination, the way you reacted like this," he said against her throat, deepening his caress in a way that was exquisitely satisfying, yet a profound tease.

"Rico." Growing mindless, she ran her hands over his chest and sides beneath his open shirt and across his back, arching to feel more of his naked skin with her bare breasts.

"Show me you weren't faking. Show me I can make it happen for you."

His trapped hand was making her wild. She moved with his touch, unable to resist the lure of the pleasure he offered. His mouth went back to her breasts and that was it. Seconds later she fell off the edge of the earth, but went soaring into the ether.

As cries of culmination escaped her parted lips, he lifted his head and covered her mouth, kissing her with rapacious hunger that she returned with greed.

She gave up trying to open his belt and tried to worm her hands under it.

He was speaking Spanish again, swearing maybe. His hand caught her chin and he licked into her mouth as if he couldn't get enough of her. Then he made a pained noise as he lifted enough to jerk his own belt open and release his pants.

They moved in unison, pulling away to yank and divest and kick their pants off their legs. Naked, they rolled back into one another, near frantic.

This was how it had been that other time. There was no stopping this force. It was stronger than both of them.

And knowing he was as helpless to it as she was made it okay.

As he settled himself over her, however, she felt his tension. The care he took as he settled his hips low between her thighs and braced his weight on his elbows. She could feel his exertion of will over himself and by extension, her.

His whole body shook with the effort, but there was clarity behind the passion that glazed his eyes.

"Rico." She closed her eyes against that betrayal, wanting him to fall back into the miasma with her. She slid her touch between them, seeking the shape of him. So taut and smooth, damp on the tip, tight at the base.

His breathing grew ragged, telling her she was lacerating his control.

"Poppy." His voice reverberated from somewhere in his chest, ringing inside hers. "Open your eyes."

She didn't want him to read how anguished she was. How her soul was right there, seeking his as her body yearned for the impalement of his flesh. It was too much.

"Let me see you."

She opened her eyes and time slowed.

"Take me into you," he commanded, biting at her chin, using his powerful thighs to spread hers apart.

She guided the tip of him against her folds, parting, distantly thinking she ought to be more self-conscious, but she was only joyful. She was *aching*. She needed this slick motion of him against her sensitive button of nerves. She hummed with pleasure, growing wetter. Needier. She gloried in the pressure as he slowly forged into her, so hot as to burn her slick, welcoming flesh.

And sweet. Oh, the sweet, sweet easing of the ache as he invaded. The breadth of him was exactly as she remembered it. There was even a moment of distress when she thought he was more than her body could accept. Her fear eased within the next heartbeat as he settled and pulsed within her.

They were both quaking.

She thought he might have asked her if she was all right, but she only pulled him into a kiss. This moment was utterly perfect. She never wanted it to end.

But after a few drugging kisses, he began to move and she remembered now that pleasure was music on a scale, some notes sharper than others, but every single one a necessary part of the beautiful whole.

There was the smoothness of his skin across his shoulders, the power in them so delicious against the stroke of her palms. There was the friction of his waist against her inner thighs as her legs instinctively rose to hug him. The stretch of tendons at her inner thighs somehow added to the sweet tension that gripped her.

There was his mouth, dragging new, glorious sensations against her throat and jaw, then sucking her earlobe and making her scalp tighten before he kissed her, letting her taste the blatant sexuality in him. There was the silk of his hair grazing her cheek when he sucked a love bite against her neck. The moans they released were the chorus to their dance and the colors behind her closed eyes were matched only by the erotic sensations streaking through her whole body as he thrust and withdrew.

The sensations where they joined were particularly acute. No friction or tenderness, just shivering waves of joy that began lapping closer together, coiling tension within her until the intensity became unbearable.

"Rico." She writhed beneath him, fingernails digging into his buttocks, aching for more of him. Harder. *Deeper.*

"Only me." He held her face between his hands. Possessive, no question, but she thought she tasted wonder in the graze of his lips across hers. A strange reverence that sent quivers of joy through her whole being.

"Only you," she agreed. But she didn't think she could stand this level of tension. Trembles of arousal shivered over her, alarming in their intensity. "It's too much."

"Bear it," he said with a savage flash of his teeth. "Feel what we do to each other."

He moved in heavier strokes, her slippery heat gripping him instinctually, making the friction all the more acute and glorious. She gasped in breathless need as the universe opened with infinite possibility. Her hips rose to meet his and his shoulders shuddered with tension as he held back. Waited for her. Waited.

His eyes were black, his cheeks flushed. They were both coated in perspiration. She wanted to tear the flesh from his bones, she was at such a screaming pitch of arousal.

Then she tightened convulsively in the first notes of release. His control cracked. He moved faster, the bed squeaking beneath them. She didn't care about anything but the purposeful thrusting that was driving her so close to the edge she was ready to scream with agony. Anticipation. Craven demand for satisfaction. Her thighs clamped around his waist and her arms clung to his shoulders. She was ready to beg.

He made a feral noise and pushed his hand under her tailbone, tilted her hips and struck a fresh spear of sensation through her, throwing her soaring off the cliff, her climax so profound she opened her mouth in a soundless scream, gripped in the paroxysm of complete ecstasy.

While his own body clenched and shuddered over her. Within her. His eruption became an intimate complement to her own, extending her pulses of pleasure so they simply held each other tight, letting the convulsions, the clenches and twitches and fading pulses of aftershock wash over them again and again.

CHAPTER SEVEN

POPPY WOKE DAZED and tender and alone. She sat up, looking for the baby monitor without finding it. It was daylight. The clock said 9:10 a.m.

She looked at the pillow, but even though both of their suitcases were still standing near the foot of the bed, his pillow was undented.

After making love, they had dozed, caught their breath, then made love again. She had a vague recollection of him leaving after that. She hadn't been able to move or even ask where he was going, but apparently he hadn't come back.

Which put a hollow ache in her chest.

Waking alone felt like a terrible start to their marriage. She had thought his passion meant he wanted her. After soaring through the heavens most of the night, she was juddering back to earth, landing hard as she realized he might want her physically, but that was all.

She put on yesterday's clothes and scowled at her pale face in the mirror. Her hair stuck out like shocks of lightning and she couldn't even get a brush through it. She wanted to check on Lily before she showered, though. She grabbed the mass together in a fat ponytail and walked out in search.

A glance into the room where Lily had slept showed the single bed had also been slept in. Her heart panged at the evidence he hadn't had insomnia. He'd preferred to sleep apart from her. Were they to have a marriage like his parents? One based on "shared values"?

They shared two things—a child and passion. It might be enough to build on, but relationships were a two-way street. If he was going to put literal walls between them, they didn't stand a chance.

Telling herself this was only Day One and she needed to give this time, she continued to the lounge.

She found Rico on the sofa, reading his tablet and nursing a coffee. Lily was on a blanket nearby, working her way through a box of unfamiliar toys. She gave a scolding cry when Poppy appeared and held up her arms, demanding a cuddle where she rested her head on Poppy's shoulder while Poppy rubbed her back. Lily was a resilient little thing, but they both needed the reassurance of a hug after facing all these recent changes.

"Why didn't you wake me when she got up?" She hid behind their daughter, mouth muffled against Lily's hair while she kept her lashes lowered, too nervous of what she might see in his eyes to meet his gaze.

"I wanted to let you sleep." His voice rasped across her nerve endings, waking her to sensual memory without any effort at all. Maybe it was the words, the suggestion that he had worn her out—which he had.

"She's had toast and banana," he added. "The housekeeper is making us a proper breakfast. It should be ready shortly."

"I could have cooked."

"We pay her to do it."

Lily pointed at the toys and Poppy set her down to continue playing.

"Thank you." Poppy hugged herself. "I'm not used to anyone getting up with her. Gran could keep an eye on her if my back was turned, but Lily was getting too heavy and fast for her to do much else."

"A potential nanny is meeting us in Valencia. You can look forward to sleeping in every day, if you want to."

"I can look after my own daughter." Especially if she wasn't working. That part was bothering her. Her income had been piecemeal with a small, but reliable paycheck from working part-time at the bus depot and occasional top-ups with school portraits and the odd headshot or boudoir shoot. Now she was reliant on Rico. It was way too much like being a burden. Again.

"There will be many occasions when you'll have to be at my side without her. You'll want the consistency of a regular caregiver."

"What do you mean, 'many'?" She finally looked at him, but he only raised his brows in mild surprise.

"Do you need a paper bag to breathe into? Why are you looking so shocked?"

"Because I thought you would go to work and maybe I'd find a job around your hours and we would eat dinner together, watch TV and go to bed like normal people."

He sipped his coffee. As he set it aside, he revealed a mouth curled into a mocking smile.

"This is my normal. Whether you work is entirely

your choice. I know many power couples in which both spouses hold down high-profile positions."

Maybe not the bus depot, then.

"I also know many women, including my mother and Sorcha, who make a career of running a household, planning charity fund-raisers and attending events in support of their husbands."

"How charmingly old-fashioned." She meant antiquated and patriarchal.

The deepening of his smirk told her he knew perfectly what she was saying.

"As I say, my normal. If you do intend to work, we'll definitely need a nanny. At least that much is settled."

Poppy wanted to stamp her foot in frustration. She couldn't go after him about doing his share on the child-care front, though. Not when he'd gotten up with Lily on his first morning with her, letting Poppy sleep in.

"I've booked a stylist to come by in an hour or so." His gaze went to her bare, unpolished toes and came back to her electrocuted hair.

Her hand went to the seam in her distressed jeans. "Why?"

"I'm introducing you and Lily to my parents this evening."

"I've met them," she reminded with an urge to laugh, because it was such a gross overstatement. She had stood behind Darna on three occasions without garnering even a glance as Darna had nodded understanding of the duquesa's orders. Rico's father had once held out a dirty glass as she walked by, not even looking at her, let alone thanking her for taking it.

"The press release will go out while we're there. I

expect a few photographers will gather at the gate. You need to look the part."

"Paparazzi are going to want photos of *me*? Really?" She crossed one foot over the other and hugged herself. "How are your parents going to react to that?"

"By presenting a united front. That's why we're having dinner there."

"*Presenting* a united front," she repeated. "That tells me how sincerely they'll welcome me at their dining table, doesn't it? And then what?" She thought of all the gossip sites where she'd seen pictures of him with Faustina, then snapshots of his grim expression as he put her in the ground. "Rico, I can't do this," she realized with sudden panic. "I'm not prepared. You know I'm not."

"That's why I've called a stylist. You'll be fine."

To her horror, tears of frustration and yes, fear, pressed into her eyes, but the housekeeper came in and invited them to sit down to the breakfast she had prepared.

Poppy had to suck up her misgivings and let her new life unfold.

"You look beautiful," Rico said sincerely. "If you could drop the wide-eyed terror, you'd be flawless."

His attempt to lighten Poppy's mood fell flat.

Her stylist had understood perfectly the effect Rico wanted and had spent a good portion of the day achieving it.

Poppy wore a bronze slip with a lace overlay embroidered with copper roses. It was simple and feminine, sophisticated yet held a decidedly innocent flair. Her hair had been meticulously coaxed into tamer waves then gathered into a "casual" chignon suitable for a low-key dinner with family. Her makeup was all natural tones and her heels were a conservative height.

By the time he'd offered the jewelry he'd bought her, she'd looked like a dog that had been at the groomers so long she'd lost her will to live.

Now the fresh-faced nanny, who couldn't be more than a year over Poppy's age, suggested carrying Lily into the villa so their daughter wouldn't stain or snag Poppy's dress.

Rico agreed and Poppy shot him a glance of betrayal then fell into step beside him, mouth pouted.

Her angry dismay plucked at his conscience like a sour note on a string. He kept telling himself that she had already seen the workings of his family from an insider's perspective. None of this should be a surprise to her. And this was how it *was*. He couldn't pretend their life would be anything different. That would be a lie.

Even so, he sensed she'd put up a wall between them and it rankled. Which was hypocritical on his part because he'd taken steps to withdraw from her last night, after their lovemaking had left him in ruins.

What should have been a sensual celebration of a convenient marriage had become a conflagration that had turned him inside out. He had been right back to that interminable family dinner after his encounter with Poppy two years ago. Cesar and Sorcha had turned up—an engagement Rico had completely failed to recall had been scheduled. They'd eaten in polite silence while his mother had stiffly come to terms with Rico's wedding being off. She had already been floating the names of alternatives and a timeline for courtship.

Rico had sat on the pin of a land mine, wanting to rise from the table and go after Poppy. He hadn't seen a way in which he could even sustain an affair with her, though. As he'd eaten what might have been sawdust, facts had been reiterated about his father's prospects in the next election. The importance of certain alliances had been regurgitated.

Rico wasn't so shallow as to value money and appearances and power over all other things, but he understood how possessing those things allowed him and his family to live as comfortably as they did. All the actions he took were about them, never only himself.

So, even though his engagement had been broken, even though he was sexually infatuated with his mother's maid, another bride would be slotted into place very quickly. The show must go on.

There had been some relief in living up to those expectations, too. As earth-shattering as his encounter with Poppy had been, he had instinctively recognized how dangerous that sort of passion was. How easily exposure to a woman who provoked such a deep response within him could dismantle him. Turn him against the best interests of his family and even impact him at a deeper level. A place even more vulnerable than the injuries of bruised ego and broken trust that his first wife had inflicted on him.

That premonition was playing out. His daughter had been the excuse, but the lure of Poppy had drawn him halfway around the world. He hadn't waited for tests to prove they should marry. He had accomplished it with haste and dragged her back here as quickly as he could.

Last night had proved to him they were still a volatile combination. Afterward, he'd felt so disarmed, so *satisfied* with having blown up his own life, he had had to leave her to put himself back together.

If Lily hadn't awakened a few hours later, he might very well have succumbed to temptation and crawled into bed with Poppy again.

He couldn't let her have that kind of power over him. That was what he kept telling himself. He had to keep control of himself or there would only be more scandal and disruption.

But he loathed that stiff look on her face.

It was too much like the ones on his parents' faces as they entered the small parlor where Faustina had once thrown down a vase like a gauntlet.

He ground his teeth, wishing at least Pia was here, chronically shy and uncomfortable as she might be. His sister was off studying snails or some other mollusk in the Galápagos Islands, however. Cesar had taken Sorcha and the boys to visit Sorcha's family in Ireland. There was nothing to soften this hard, flat evening for Poppy.

"My father, Javiero Montero y Salazar, Excelentísimo Senor Grandeza de España, and my mother, La Reina, the Duque and Duquesa of Castellón. You both remember Poppy." He wasn't trying to be facetious, but it came out that way.

His mother smiled faintly. "Welcome back."

Poppy was so pale he reached for her hand. It was ice-cold.

She delicately removed it from his hold and gave Lily's dress a small tug and drew the girl's finger from her mouth, smiling with tender pride. "This is Lily."

His parents both took a brief look at their grand-daughter and nodded as if to say, *Yes, that is a baby.*

"A room has been prepared upstairs," Rico's mother said to the nanny, dismissing her and Lily in a blink.

The light in Poppy's eyes dimmed. It struck Rico like a kick in the gut.

This is who they *are*, he wanted to tell her. There was no use wishing for anything different, but he could still hear the thread of hurt and rejection in her tone as she had told him about her parents never coming back for her.

He wanted to take her hand again, reassure her, but at his mother's invitation, she lowered to perch on an antique wing chair, hands folded demurely in her lap.

Champagne was brought in; congratulations were offered. Poppy's hand shook and he neatly slid a coaster under her glass before she set it on the end table.

His mother very tellingly said, "I imagine you're still settling in. We'll move into the dining room right away so the baby can have an early night."

This evening would *not* be a drawn-out affair. The rush was a slight, but Rico didn't want to subject Poppy to their company any longer than necessary so he didn't take issue with it.

The first course arrived and Poppy tried offering a friendly smile at the butler. It was countered with an impassive look that made her cheerful expression fall away. She blinked a few times.

The staff would talk to her when his parents weren't around, he wanted to tell her. This was how they were expected to act with guests and she shouldn't take it as a rejection.

His father cleared his throat.

Poppy glanced at him with apprehension. Rico briefly held his own breath, but his father only asked Rico about the progress he'd made on some alloy research.

Annoyed, Rico was forced to turn his attention to answering him, which left his mother to make conversation with Poppy.

"I'm told you enjoy photography, Poppy. How did your interest come about?"

Poppy shot him a look, but he hadn't provided that tidbit. This was also who his mother was. She would ferret out any item suitable for small talk that would avoid addressing more sensitive horrors like the fact Rico had messed with the maid, had an illegitimate child and brought them into the villa as "family."

Poppy spoke with nervous brevity. "When I was ten, my grandfather asked me to help him clean the basement. We came across his father's equipment. My great-grandfather was a freelance photographer for newspapers."

"What type of newspapers?" his mother asked sharply.

"Mother." Rico quit listening to his father and gave the women his full attention.

"The national ones," Poppy replied warily, sensing disapproval. "Sports, mostly. The odd royal visit or other big event. I was intrigued so my grandfather closed in a space and showed me how the development process worked."

"You should have shown me." Rico was ridiculously pleased to hear she shared the same spark of curiosity that had drawn him into chemical engineering.

"I haven't used it in years. We quickly realized the cost of chemicals and paper wasn't sustainable. I switched to digital photography."

"Metol or hydroquinone," Rico's father said in one of his stark interjections, as though he'd retrieved a file from the dusty basement of his own mind. "Sodium carbonate and sodium sulfite for proper pH and delay of oxidation. Thiosulfate to fix it. None are particularly expensive, but there's no market for the premixed solutions. We got out of it years ago."

"Only niche artists are using them, I imagine," Poppy murmured.

"Speaking of art," his mother said with an adept pivot from boring science. "I'm attending an opening in Paris next month. I imagine you'll be decorating a house very soon. What sort of pieces might you be looking for?"

Poppy looked as though a bus was bearing down on her.

"It's early days, Mother," Rico cut in. "We'll talk more about that another time."

At this point he was only looking as far as getting through this evening.

The meal passed in a blur of racking her brains for the names of Canadian politicians who might have said something brilliant or stupid lately and trying to look as if she knew how to eat quail in gazpacho. Poppy was infinitely relieved when they left and went to Rico's Valencian penthouse.

This wasn't a family property. It was his own home, purchased after Faustina had died. It was luxurious and in a prime location with a pool and a view, but it was a surprisingly generic space, tastefully decorated in masculine tones yet completely without any stamp of his personality.

She dismissed the nanny, put Lily to bed herself, then moved into the bedroom to kick off her heels and sigh with exhaustion.

Rico came in with a nightcap for each of them.

She immediately grew nervous. It had been a long, trying day, one that had started out with a rebuff when she'd woken alone. That sense of foreboding had grown worse as his stylist had spent hours turning her into some kind of show pony.

She suspected she had disappointed anyway. As he set down his own drink and loosened his tie, she had a sick, about-to-be-fired feeling in her stomach, much like the one she'd had when she'd lost her first babysitting job after accidentally letting the hamster out of its cage.

"Well?" she prompted, trying to face the coming judgment head-on.

"I thought it went well."

She strangled on a laugh. "Are you kidding? I've never spent a more horrendous two hours and twenty-three minutes in my life."

"You were there, then." He shrugged out of his jacket.

"Don't make jokes, Rico." She stared at him, but he wasn't laughing. Uncertain, she asked, "Was that really a normal dinner for you? The way it's been your whole life?" She had thought her own mother awful for calling in lame efforts at nurturing with insincere apologies from afar. His parents had displayed zero remorse as they had openly dismissed his newfound daughter.

"Don't be ridiculous," he said with scathing sarcasm. "I didn't sit at that table until I was twelve. Children are invited to the dining room when they know how to eat quietly and speak only when spoken to."

She thought of the way Lily squealed and slapped her tray and wore more food than she ate. But even Gran with her old-fashioned ideals about child-rearing had always insisted that dinner was a time for the whole family to come together.

"Why are they *like* that?"

He stripped his tie and threw it away with a sigh. "My father is a scientific genius. He only speaks logic and rational debate. Emotion has no effect on him. It's one of the reasons he makes a genuinely good politician. He reads and considers policy on its own merit, not worrying about his popularity or future prospects. Mother was born with a title, but no money. She had to marry it and prove she was worth the investment. Having brought herself up this far, she refuses to backslide. And, after thirty-five years of my father's lack of sentiment, she's abandoned any herself."

"That sounds so empty. Is she happy?"

"They set out with specific goals and achieved them. They are content, which is the standard to which we've been taught to aspire."

She searched his expression. "And you're *content* with that?"

"Why wouldn't I be? My life is extremely comfortable." He peeled off his shirt, revealing his gorgeous chest and tight abs.

She swallowed and turned away, annoyed with herself for reacting so promptly to the sight of him.

"Is that why you agreed to an arranged marriage the first time? To maintain the status quo?"

"Yes. I was expected to do my part in preserving the life we all enjoy." His voice was suddenly right behind her, surprising her into lifting her gaze to the mirror.

He lightly smoothed his hand across her shoulders, grazing an absent caress against her nape as he ensured no tendrils of hair would catch as he unzipped her.

"How angry are they that Lily and I ruined everything?" She braced herself as she held his gaze. "Be honest. I need to know."

"They don't get angry." He sounded mild, but she thought she caught a flicker of something in his stoic expression.

"What about you? You were angry when you showed up at my door."

"And I wound up telling you something I had sworn to take to my grave. Heightened emotions don't help any situation."

"What does that mean?" With a niggling premonition, she began unpinning her hair, not wanting to remove the gaping dress and be naked when she was beginning to feel defenseless. "I want to fit in, Rico. I want to be a team player and know what to say about decor and houses and all those different people she was talking about. But along with not being prepared to live at this level of wealth, I'm wired for emotion. Don't expect me never to get angry. Or to stop feeling."

His cheek ticked and she could hear the thoughts behind that stiff mask. *Don't expect me to start.*

Which made her angry. Furious that she'd spent every minute since he'd shown up on her doorstep having her emotions bombarded until they were right there, under the thin surface of her skin, tender and raw, while he had somehow used tonight's endurance event of a dinner to shore up his shields so he was more withdrawn than ever.

"That's what you want, though, isn't it?" she realized, appalled to see her shimmering nascent hopes for deeper intimacy disappearing faster than she could conjure them. "You want me to learn not to care. To feel nothing. Certainly I shouldn't aspire to happiness, should I?"

"Happiness is achieved by keeping your expectations realistic. That's a proven fact."

It was such a cynical thing to say, it physically hurt her to hear it.

"What about desire?" In a small stab at getting through to him, she let the dress fall off her arms. She stepped out of it before tossing it onto the foot of the bed. "Do you want me to quit feeling *that*?"

"That's physical." He let his gaze rake slowly down her pale form from shoulder to thighs, jaw hardening along with his voice. "And you're starting a fight for no reason."

"I'm sorry you feel that way," she said facetiously. "I'm going to shower. Would you like to join me? Yesterday it was one of your many fantasies, but maybe you *feel* different today."

His eye ticked and she knew he was sorry he had ever told her that. Did she feel guilty for using it? Not one bit.

She slid her panties down and left them on the floor.

It was a bold move, one far beyond her experience level. If he left her to shower alone, she would probably drown herself in there, but she desperately wanted to prove to both of them that she had some kind of effect on him. Some means of reaching through that armor of his.

She moved into the bathroom and stepped into the marble-tiled stall, bigger than the porch on Gran's bungalow.

He came into the bathroom as the steam began to gather around her. He dimmed the light so the gilded space became golden and moody and he stripped off his pants.

She watched him, reacting with an internal clench when she saw he was aroused.

When he came into the shower, she lost some of her moxie and turned her face into the rain of warm water from the sunflower head above her.

His cool hands settled on her hips and his thumbs dug lightly into the tops of her butt cheeks. "You have a gorgeous ass."

"Even with the dimples?" Her heartbeat was unsteady.

"Especially with." He took hold of the wet mass of her hair, holding her head tipped back while he scraped his teeth against the side of her neck. "I will always accept this invitation, Poppy. But you had better know what you're inviting."

She gasped. The sensations he was causing were cataclysmic. All her senses came alive. He settled his cool body against her back, his chest hair lightly brushing before the warm water sealed them together. His hard shaft pressed into the small of her back and her buttocks tightened in excited reaction. Her breasts grew heavy, her loins tingled. The humid air became too heavy to breathe and her bones melted like wax in the sun.

Blindly she shot a hand out to the slick wall and wound up leaning both hands there while her hips instinctively tipped with invitation.

"What are you trying to prove?" he growled, slapping one hand beside her own on the wall.

Nothing. She was reacting, pure and simple.

He briefly covered her like any male mounting his mate and his teeth sank lightly against her nape again. His free hand splayed across her abdomen, then roamed her wet skin to cup her breast.

In a sudden move, he pulled her upright and spun her so the world tilted around her. She found the hard tiles against her shoulders. His knees nudged between hers and his thighs pinned hers. He bracketed her head between his forearms and touched his nose to hers before he claimed the kiss she was starving for.

He held nothing back, wet mouth sliding across hers with carnal greed, slaking her thirst after this arid day. She flowered. She opened and ran with dewy nectar. She unfurled her arms around him and twined them across his back, lifted her knee up to his hip and invited him into her center. Rocked and tried to make him lose control the way she continued to abandon hers.

"Let's talk about your fantasies, hmm?" His hands caught her wrists and pinned them beside her head while his tongue slithered down her neck and licked into the hollow at the base of her throat. "What do you want?"

He drew back slightly and gazed down on her with unabashed hunger.

"Rico." She turned her wrist in his grasp and shifted with self-consciousness. Her nipples stood up with blatant, stinging arousal. She brought her foot back down to the floor, but his feet were still between hers.

"Did you ever touch yourself and imagine it was me?" He dropped one hand and drew his fingertip through her swollen folds, looking down again as he languidly caressed her. "Did you want to *feel* my hand here?"

She was immediately disoriented, glad for the hard wall at her back as she rose into his touch and draped her arm across his shoulders, seeking balance.

"Tell me," he commanded between kisses. "Tell me or I'll stop."

"Yes," she gasped.

He rewarded her by bending to suck one nipple, then the other, driving further spikes of pleasure into that place he continued to tease. A keening noise sounded and she realized it was her, unable to express her agonizing climb of desire in any other way.

Now he was on his knees, licking at her. Splaying her and gently probing and circling and driving her to the brink of madness. She realized distantly that she had her hands fisted in his wet hair, that she had completely abandoned herself to him. To the exquisite pleasure he relentlessly inflicted upon her. Within moments, cries of ecstasy tore from her throat, filling the steamy, hollow chamber.

He ran his mouth all over her thighs and stomach, soft bites that claimed his right to do so as she stood there weakly, heart palpitating, breath still splintered.

He stood and snapped the water off, staring at her while she leaned helpless and overwhelmed. Outdone.

Meeting his gaze was like looking into the sun, painful in its intensity. Painful in how blind and exposed she felt, but she couldn't look away. Couldn't pretend he hadn't peeled her down to her core until she was utterly at his mercy.

While he remained visibly aroused, but in complete control.

"The way we make each other feel is a hell of a lot more than many couples have. Recognize that. Be satisfied with it."

She wasn't and never would be.

But when he held out a hand, she let him balance her as she stepped out onto the mat. He dried her off and took her to his bed, where he satisfied her again and again and again.

CHAPTER EIGHT

RICO WOKE IN the guest bed he'd been using all week and listened, thinking Lily must be stirring. He ought to be sleeping more heavily considering the quantity and quality of sex he was enjoying, but his radar remained alert to the other occupants of his penthouse.

He listened, thought he must be imagining things, started to drift off then heard the burble of a video chat being connected. The volume lowered.

He rose, already wearing boxers in case he had to go to Lily. His door was cracked and it swung open silently, allowing him to hear Poppy's hushed voice reassuring her grandmother.

"No, everything's fine. I couldn't sleep and thought this would be a good chance to chat without a baby crawling all over me. How are you settling in?"

"Same as I told you yesterday," her grandmother said wryly. "You're the one with the gadabout life. What have you been up to?"

He stood and listened to Poppy relay that the nanny had taken Lily for a walk today while she had pored over properties with a real estate agent. He'd been going in to work each day, but taking her out at night. She mentioned this evening's cocktail party where he had introduced her to some of his top executives and their wives.

She made it sound as though she had had the time of her life when she'd actually been petrified and miserable, not that she'd been obvious about it. He knew how she behaved when she was comfortable, though. She laughed with Lily and traded wry remarks with her grandmother.

That woman was making fewer and fewer appearances when she was with him, however, which was beginning to niggle at him. He glimpsed her when they made love. She held nothing back in bed, but tonight she had disappeared quickly after they had wrung untold pleasure from each other. She had rolled away and her voice had pulled him from his postcoital doze.

"Will you check on Lily as you go?"

"Of course." He had told himself he was glad she'd kept him from falling asleep beside her. His will to leave her each night grew fainter and fainter, but staying seemed the even weaker action. He wasn't Lily, needing his cuddle bear clutched in his arm in order to drift off.

He wasn't sure what he had expected from this marriage. When contemplating his first to Faustina, he had anticipated following his parents' example. Like his siblings, he had been raised to keep his emotions firmly within a four-point-five and a four-point-seven. Not a sociopath, but only a few scant notches above one. He had never been a man of grand passions anyway and had been comfortable with the idea of a businesslike partnership with his spouse.

That certainly hadn't worked out. Given the betrayal

and drama he'd suffered at Faustina's hands, he had wanted this marriage to conform to that original ideal.

It didn't. Poppy didn't. He kept telling himself she would get used to this life, but seeing her natural exuberance dim by the day was eating at him. He didn't know what to do about it, though. This was their reality.

"Dinner will be served soon. I have to start making my way or it will be cold by the time I arrive," Eleanor said with a papery chuckle.

"Okay. I love you. I miss you." She ended the call, but didn't rise.

He was growing cold standing there, but didn't go back to bed. He could see her shoulders over the back of the sofa. They rose slightly as she sighed deeply. Her breath caught with a jag. She sniffed.

A terrible swoop of alarm unbalanced him. The embarrassed moment of walking in on something personal struck, yet he couldn't turn away and leave her to it.

As her shoulders began to shake and she ducked her head into her hands, beginning to weep in earnest, a rush of something indefinable came over him. A sharp, shimmering, deeply uncomfortable *ache* gripped him. It was so excruciating, it made him want to close himself in the guest room and wait for it to pass.

But he couldn't turn his back on her while she was like that. A far stronger compulsion pushed him down the hall toward her.

"Poppy." Her name scratched behind his breastbone. At some level he understood he was responsible for this misery she was exhibiting. He had some scattered thoughts of all that he was providing her, but he knew she didn't care about those things. She was a complex, emotional creature and it struck him how completely ill-equipped he was to handle that.

She lifted a face tracked with silver and made an anguished noise, clearly mortified that he was seeing her this way. Again he thought to give her privacy, but he couldn't let her suffer alone. This was his fault. That much he understood and it weighed very heavily on him.

"Come." He gathered her up, the silk of her pajamas cool against his naked chest.

"I don't want to make love, Rico. I want to go *h-home*." The break in her voice rent another hole in him.

"Shh." He carried her to the bed where he'd left her a few hours before and crawled in with her to warm both of them. He told himself that was what this was, even though the feel of her against him had the effect of pressing a cut together. It didn't fix it, but it eased some of the pain. Slowed the bleeding and calmed the distress. "It's okay," he murmured.

"No, it's not." Her words were angry, despairing sobs. "I'm so homesick I hurt all the time. At least the last time I was stuck here, I made friends, but no one will talk to me."

"Who's refusing to speak to you?" he asked with sharp concern.

"*Everyone.* The staff. They only ask me if I want something, never joke or make me feel like they like me. They're only being polite because you pay them to be."

"That's not true." He suddenly glimpsed how isolated she must be in her new position and cursed himself for not recognizing it would be so acute.

"I have nothing in common with *your* friends. They

talk too fast for me to even understand them. You're Lily's father and I want her to know you, Rico. I know I have to stay here for her sake, but why does the nanny get to take her for a walk while I have to go to stupid parties? I hate it here. I hate it so much."

"Shh," he soothed, closing his hand around the tight fist on his chest and kissing her hard knuckles. "This is going to be an adjustment for all of us."

"How is this an adjustment for *you*? You're completely unaffected! I can't do this, Rico. I *can't*."

His neck was wet and her hair stuck to the tear tracks, keeping that fissure in him stinging. He rubbed her back, trying to calm her while her desolation shredded his ability to remain detached.

There are some realities that are not worth crying about, he had told Mateo a few weeks ago. He'd been taught to believe no one would care, but he *did* care. Not the generic regard of one human for another, but a deeper, more frightening feeling he didn't know how to process.

Everything in him warned that he should distance himself, but he couldn't ignore her pain.

He knew what he had to do. It would cost him, but he would do it. This anguish of hers was more than he could bear.

Poppy woke from the dense fog of a deep sleep to hear Rico's morning voice rasping on the baby monitor.

"We'll let Mama sleep this morning."

The transmission clicked off, but as Poppy rolled onto her back and straightened her limbs, she discovered the warm patch beside her on the bed.

He had stayed the night? She was chagrined that he'd caught her in the middle of a pity party, but she hadn't been able to hold it in any longer. She had tried, honestly tried not to care about all of those things.

She did care, though. She was lonely and out of her depth. Her only friend was the daughter she had to share with a nanny who adored her, but whom Poppy was growing to resent by the day.

She threw her arm over her eyes, trying not to spiral back into melancholy. They had appointments to view properties today, she recalled. She could hardly wait to have a bigger house to get lost in, and more staff to treat her like some kind of visiting foreign official.

A few hours later, she was beside Rico as he drove a shiny new SUV up the coast. Poppy had understood the property agent would be driving them to view potential homes, but she didn't complain. It felt nice to be just the three of them for a change.

"You should have told me to bring my camera," she murmured, quite sure she would have a kink in her neck from swiveling her attention between the sunny coastal beaches and the craggy hillocks interspersed with picturesque ancient villages. "I'm used to staring at wheat and sunflower fields on long drives."

"Think about what sort of space you want for your studio as we look at potential homes. I'm sure a darkroom could be built into just about any corner of a house, but give some thought to how that will fit with our day-to-day living."

"A darkroom! I told you, that's expensive." She wouldn't mind a studio, though.

"As it turns out, I happen to have money. If that's

where your interest lies, pursue it." He turned into a private road that lacked a for sale sign and wound through a vineyard.

"There's no money in photography." Not the sort his level of society expected a woman to make if she was going to pursue a career over homemaking.

"I don't expect you to make money. Do it for yourself. Be an artist."

"You're going to be my patron? Don't pander to me just because I acted like Lily last night." She spoke to the window to hide her embarrassment.

"I'm not. I want you to be happy."

That swung her around because no, he didn't. He had specifically told her to settle.

He might have recalled that conversation, too. His expression grew stiff as he braked and threw the vehicle into Park.

Poppy glanced around. "I don't see the agent."

"It's not for sale. This is Cesar and Sorcha's home."

"Why didn't you tell me we were meeting them today?" She glanced down at the pantsuit she'd put on hoping to look the part of a rich man's wife viewing villas as if she knew what such a man needed.

"You look perfect." He stepped out. "They don't know we're coming so they'll be equally casual."

"Why don't they know we're coming?" she asked as he came around while she was opening the back door to get Lily.

"You're supposed to wait for me to come around and open your door for you," he chided.

"I know how to open my own car door. I also know how to look after my own daughter." She brushed him

away from trying to reach in, then grunted as she released Lily and took her weight, dragging her out.
"What I don't know is how I'm supposed to behave
when you drop me on relatives who don't know I'm
coming."

Lily squinted as Poppy drew her from the car and
buried her face in Poppy's neck.

"I'll keep her," Poppy murmured as Rico tried to take
her. It was pathetic to hide behind her daughter, but she
needed Lily's sturdy warmth to bolster her.

A maid let them in and the view took her breath as
they moved from the foyer to a front room where huge
picture windows overlooked the Mediterranean.

"Tío!" A young boy of about four ran in wearing red
trunks and nothing else.

Rico picked him up. "You remember Enrique? Cesar's eldest?" he asked Poppy.

"You've grown," she murmured. *"Bon dia,"* she
added in the small amount of Valencian dialect she
knew the family used among themselves.

"Say hello to Poppy and Lily," Rico prompted him.

"Hola. ¿Cómo estás?" Enrique asked with a confidence beyond his years.

Rico gave Enrique's backside a pat. "You're wet.
How are you swimming? It's too early in the year."

"I got in to here." Enrique touched his belly button.

"And now you're eating your lunch," Cesar said,
strolling in wearing crisp linen pants and a shirt he
was buttoning. He nodded to send Enrique back outside.

This was the most relaxed Poppy had ever seen
Cesar, but he still projected a chilly formality not unlike

the duque and duquesa. In fact, he greeted his brother with a look that bordered on hostile.

"You've lost your drop-in privileges with my family." It was a very civil, *Get the hell out*.

Because of her and Lily? Because they were a stain on the family name?

With a muted noise of distress, Poppy closed her arms protectively around Lily and looked to the door.

Rico glanced at her with concern then scowled at his brother. "Now you've gone and hurt *my* wife's feelings."

Cesar frowned at her. His gaze dropped to Lily and his frown eased.

"Whose feelings?" Sorcha came up behind her husband. She was blond and effortlessly beautiful in a summer dress with a forget-me-not print. Daywear diamonds sparkled in her ears.

"Poppy." Her surprise warmed into a welcoming smile that sent the first trickles of relief through Poppy's defensively stiff limbs. "And here's Lily." Sorcha came right up to them and gave Lily's elbow a tickle. She tilted her head to meet the gaze Lily shyly kept tucked into Poppy's neck.

"Will you come see me? Let me introduce you to your cousins?" Sorcha held out her hands. "They'll share their lunch with you. Are you hungry?"

Lily went to her. Who could resist the promise of food and the warm lilt of an Irish accent?

"Thank you, darling. That's quite a compliment." Sorcha cuddled her close, then glanced at Rico. Her tone dropped to permafrost. "*You* can wait in the car."

"I deserve that," Rico said with tense sincerity. "I regret the hurt I caused you. I wouldn't interrupt your weekend, but Poppy needs you, Sorcha. Will you help her? If not for me, then for her sake and Lily's? Please? I know how you feel about family."

"That's below the belt!" Sorcha tucked her chin, looked as though she wanted to punish him further, then gave a little sigh. "Since you've brought me this *very* precious gift—" She snuggled Lily more securely onto her hip. "I will forgive you. *This one time.*" She smiled at Poppy without reserve. "And of course I'll help you any way I can. I would have called you later this week." Another dark look toward Rico. "I didn't want to wait until our gala next month. I'm so glad you're here. Come join us."

"What did you do?" Poppy hissed at Rico as he fell into step beside her.

"Said something that doesn't bear repeating." To her surprise, he took her hand and wove their fingers together, giving her a little squeeze. "But Sorcha knows what you're up against. Let her be your guide."

It struck her that this had been hard for him. She doubted it was in his nature to ask for help any more than it was in hers. He and Cesar were obviously on rocky ground, but he had invaded their family time for her sake.

"Please tell Chef we're four adults and three children for lunch now," Sorcha said easily to the hovering butler.

"Champagne," Cesar added, holding Sorcha's chair as she lowered with Lily and kept her in her lap. "Boys, this is your cousin, Lily. Can you say hello and welcome her and Auntie Poppy to the family?"

Enrique began to giggle. He pointed his fork at Cesar. "That's Papi."

Poppy smiled. "Maybe you'll have to call this one Tío Mama now." She thumbed toward Rico as he helped her with her own chair.

Enrique nearly tumbled out of his, laughing at the absurdity as he repeated, "Tío Mama."

Poppy bit her lip with remorse, suspecting she'd released a genie that wouldn't go easily back into its bottle. She called on one of Gramps's favorite tricks for getting through to a child who had a case of the sillies. She leaned over and spoke very softly so Enrique would have to quiet to hear her.

"My grandfather used to tell me it was okay to tease your family with a funny name when you were alone, but you have to remember to be respectful when you're with others. Will you be able to do that?"

Enrique nodded and clamped his smile over his fork, eyes full of mischief as he looked at Rico.

"Sorry," Poppy mouthed as she caught Sorcha's amused glance. "You have a very beautiful home," she added, glancing at the placid pool and the profusion of spring blooms surrounding it.

"Thank you. We're extremely happy here." Sorcha looked to her husband for confirmation, but her smile reflected more than happiness. Even two years ago it had been obvious to Poppy these two were deeply in love.

While Rico wore his customarily circumspect expression.

"I want one of those," Cesar informed Sorcha with smoky warning, nodding at Lily where she sat contentedly in Sorcha's lap, fist clenched around a spear of juicy peach.

"Let's keep this one." Sorcha pressed her smile to the top of Lily's head. "She's exactly what we've been thinking of."

"We should probably try making our own before we resort to stealing."

"Picky, picky. But if you insist, I'll have my people talk to your people. Schedule a one-on-one for further discussion."

"Really?" Rico drawled of the flirty banter. "In front of the children?"

"They've walked in on worse," Cesar muttered, rising as the butler arrived with the champagne. "Learn to lock doors," he advised while Sorcha looked to the sky.

The lunch passed with easy chatter and the wiping of sticky fingers.

"I'm so glad Rico brought you today," Sorcha said later, after a travel cot had been found for Lily and she'd been put down for her afternoon nap while the men took the boys into the vineyard. Sorcha sobered. "I'm very glad he went looking for you. Are you angry with me?"

"For telling him? No." Poppy crossed her arms. "I'd been thinking about doing it. Things were complicated at home so I put it off, but it's all worked out." For Gran and Lily. Her? Not so much.

"I'm sorry for interfering. I know how hard that decision can be, but I couldn't let him miss out on Lily. He shut right down after Faustina. My heart broke clean in half for him. I'm so happy to see the way he's taken to her."

Poppy nodded dumbly, shielding her gaze with a glance toward the floor so Sorcha couldn't read the bigger story in her eyes.

"He wants to be a good father. I was afraid of... Well, nothing, I guess," Poppy admitted ruefully. When it came to Rico's feelings for Lily, she had every confidence their bond would only continue to grow.

"But?" Sorcha prompted.

"It's hard." Her throat thickened and she felt tears pressing behind her eyes. "This is all really hard. Rico and I don't have what you and Cesar did. The years of familiarity and caring."

Sorcha choked on a laugh. "Do I make it look like it was easy for us to get where we are? That is quite a compliment and good on me for selling that image, but no. I assure you that what we have was achieved through blood, sweat and tears. Years of loving my boss, if you want the truth. Which is how and why Enrique came about," she added dryly. "But like the rest of his family, Cesar had kicked his heart under the sofa and forgotten about it. So there will definitely be some heavy lifting required to find Rico's. I'm sorry to tell you that." Sorcha sobered. "But I think it's understandable, given what he's been through."

Sorcha thought she knew what Rico had been through, but he wasn't nursing a broken heart over a lost baby. That was what made this so hard. This wasn't a matter of mending his heart. Or finding it. It was a matter of him wanting to give it to her. And he didn't.

But she only nodded again, protecting the secret Rico had entrusted to her.

"It will all be worth it, Poppy. I promise you," Sorcha said with a squeeze of her arm. "In the meantime, you have me. I'm happy to help you navigate this new world. When I was in your position, I needed help, too.

One of these days we'll go shopping with my friend Octavia. She really does know how to make all of this look easy. For now, let's go to my closet. I'll show you what is absolutely essential. Try not to faint."

Poppy could feel Rico's heart slowing to lazy slams beneath her breast. Her sweating body was splayed bonelessly across him. She knew she ought to move, but he stroked his hand down her spine and traced a circle on her lower back, making her shiver. She clenched around him in a final aftershock of ecstasy.

He turned his head, brushing his lips against her temple in what she took as a signal to move. As she started to pry herself off him, however, his arms closed more firmly around her.

"You can stay right here all night," he murmured lazily.

"Don't you want to go to the guest room?"

His arms dropped way from her. She rolled off him.

"Do you want me to?" All the indolent warmth disappeared from his tone.

"No." Her voice was barely audible. "But why are you staying? Because you feel sorry for me?"

"No. Why would you think that?"

"You slept with me last night because I was crying."

"I came to bed with you because you were crying. I stayed because I wanted to."

"You didn't want to those other nights?"

A sigh.

"Rico, I keep telling you I've never done this before. This might be how you normally conduct a sexual relationship, but it's not the way I thought marriage was supposed to be."

He bit off a laugh. "This isn't normal. That is the problem, Poppy." He sighed and repeated more somberly, "That is the problem."

Even she, with her limited experience, understood that their passion was exceptional. She had climaxed three times before he'd clasped hard hands to her hips and bucked beneath her, releasing with a jagged cry. She imagined she would have fingerprint bruises under her skin and perversely enjoyed having such an erotic reminder linger for days.

Sex was the easy part. Talking to him, catching him alone and digging up the courage to speak her mind and face difficult answers was the hard part. But she made herself do it.

"Is that why you haven't wanted to sleep with me? Too much sex? Am I being too demanding?"

He blew out a breath that was amused yet exasperated. "No. Although I fear for our lives on a nightly basis."

"Please don't make jokes, Rico. I need to understand. You're the one who said I should keep my expectations realistic. Tell me what realistic looks like because I don't *know*."

"I don't know, either," he admitted after a moment. "That's why I'm not processing this any better than you are. I thought our first time was an anomaly. It wasn't. It's shocking to me how powerfully we affect each other. It doesn't matter that you just spent an hour wringing me out. I want you again. *This isn't normal*."

"I don't like it, either! I hate that you can snap your fingers and I fall onto my back."

He threw his arm over his eyes and released a ragged, self-deprecating laugh. "I'm the one who was on his back tonight, *corazón.* In case you hadn't noticed."

"It's not very comforting to hear that when you're clearly annoyed by it. Why does it bother you so much that we react this strongly?"

Another silence where she thought he might ignore her question. Finally he admitted, "Passion is dangerous. You know that Cesar was in a car crash some years ago?"

"I only know what's online about it."

"Mmm. Well, it happened after he slept with Sorcha. Directly after. I'd always been aware he had a physical infatuation with her. He didn't give in to base urges any more than I ever thought I would, but that day he did. And he decided the passion they shared was worth blowing up his life for. Mother was pushing him toward an arranged marriage. He went to Diega and told her he wouldn't be asking her to marry him. We don't know if he was overwrought or what, but he skidded off the road after he left her and nearly died."

Part of her panged with empathy. For all his habitual detachment and his recent disagreement with Cesar, Rico was as close to his brother as he was capable of being with anyone. It must have been a terribly worrisome time for him.

But what she also heard was that he really did think the passion between them posed a mortal danger—which equally told her he would hold her at arm's length because of it.

"It's not like I'm doing this on purpose, you know." She rolled away. "I'm a victim, too."

"I know." He followed her, dragging her into the spoon of his body. His voice tickled hotly through her hair. "I'm realizing that uncontrollable passion isn't only a crazed act in a quiet solarium. It's a hunger that refuses to be ignored. I'm not a dependent person, Poppy. I don't like being unable to suppress a craving that isn't a *need*. But I don't see the sense in hurting you, making your assimilation here more difficult because I'm displeased with myself."

It was hardly a declaration of love, but he didn't want to hurt her. It was something. She relaxed deeper into the bend of his body.

"You *are* trying to kill me," he accused, aroused flesh pressed to her backside.

She rolled to face him, stretching against him in a full-body caress.

"Maybe this is our normal."

"Maybe it is. Let's hope we survive it."

Over the next few weeks, Poppy tried to think of this new life as something she could do, rather than something that was being done *to* her. It helped to take the wheel, even if she wasn't sure where she was going. She began reviewing the week's menu with the housekeeper and making additions to the shopping list. She toured several properties and told Rico why she felt some of them wouldn't suit—one had a distinct perfume in the air from the fertilized fields next door, another had rooms that were very closed off from one another.

Rico was dead set on getting a vineyard again and

wanted a pool. Poppy mentioned she'd prefer to be close to Sorcha and Lily's new cousins, to which he said, "Of course. That's the area I'd prefer as well."

She even sat down with the nanny and cleared the air. Poppy admitted this was all new to her and she sometimes felt threatened. Ingrid confessed to feeling she wasn't working hard enough and that's why she kept stepping up, trying to take Lily off her hands. By the time they finished their coffee and cake, they'd worked out the fine points of a long-term contract, both of them relaxed and smiling.

Rico continued dragging her to dinners and networking events, but they went more smoothly after she began taking Sorcha's advice and asking the other wives for recommendations on things like shoe boutiques and hair stylists. Their responses went in one ear and out the other, but at least they seemed to warm to her.

"Let me know when you need an interior designer," one said at one point.

"We have to find a house first. That's proving a challenge," Poppy admitted with genuine frustration.

Twenty minutes of sharing her wish list later, the woman offered a lead on a property that was farther up the coast from Cesar's villa. It wasn't officially on the market, but rumor had it the family needed the money and would accept the right offer.

Rico made a few discreet inquiries and they viewed it the next day.

"I asked Mother if she knew anything about it. She said to be careful when we open the closets," Rico told her as they stepped from the car.

"Skeletons?" Poppy asked, but her smile wasn't only

amusement. Despite the clear signs of age and neglect, a covetous joy rang through her as she took in the stone house, instantly falling in love with the tiled roof and cobbled walkway and darling gated courtyard where she imagined Lily safely playing for hours.

Arches down the side formed a breezeway that wrapped around both levels then overlooked the pool—which needed repair and filling—but it offered a view of the Med that rivaled Cesar and Sorcha's.

Inside, the rooms were desperate for updating. Rico went a step further and said, "This floor plan should be completely reconfigured."

"When are they moving out?" she asked, looking at the furniture draped in sheets.

"They've already taken what they want. We would buy it as is. Mother will know which collectors to call to get rid of most of this."

The scope of the project was enormous, but Poppy was strangely undaunted. In fact, as she discovered a spiral staircase, she excitedly scooted up it. The small rooftop patio looked in every direction for miles and doubled as a sheltered place for intimate dining, utterly charming her.

"We could build out this direction," Rico said, firmly holding on to Lily as he leaned to see off the side. "Perhaps put a guest cottage at the edge of the orange grove."

There were other fruit trees along with a flower garden and a plot off the kitchen for a small vegetable garden, something Poppy's grandparents had always had when she'd been young. It became too much for all of them in later years, but the idea of Lily eating fresh strawberries gave Poppy such a sense of nostalgia and homecoming, she had to swallow a cry of excitement.

"Everything is pollinated by the bee hives in the lower corner," Rico informed her, referring to some notes on his phone. "Apparently we would have our own honey."

Poppy blinked. "Why do I love the idea of keeping bees?"

"I don't know, but I'm intrigued, too."

As they walked out a lower door to view the hives, Rico nodded meaningfully at an exterior door. "Wine cellar."

She knew what he was driving at and shook her head, not wanting to get her hopes up. It was too perfect already. "You'd need it for wine, wouldn't you?"

They entered a big, dim room filled with nearly empty racks. While he glanced at the labels on the handful of bottles left behind, she explored the rear of the cellar, discovering a narrow, windowless room with a low ceiling. A few shelves held empty glass canning jars, suggesting it was a root cellar. A bare bulb was the only light.

Poppy was overwhelmed by what seemed like her birthday, Christmas and every other wish-making day come true. She began arranging her future darkroom. The tubs would go there, the enlarger there. She might cry, she wanted this so badly.

"Am I wrong or is this everything we want?" Rico was carrying Lily and followed Poppy into the narrow room.

This was everything she could ever wish for herself

and her daughter. The only thing she could want after this was her husband's heart.

Her own took an unsteady tumble as she realized how deeply she was yearning for that when every other part of their marriage was slotting into place.

Then he slid his free arm around Poppy and scooped her in for a quick kiss, sending her emotions spinning in another direction.

"Well done."

"We haven't seen the bees yet," she pointed out, wobbling between delirious happiness and intense longing. She worried often that his feelings toward her were still very superficial, but if he was willing to give her this— not just the castle above it, but the space to explore the creativity inside her—surely that meant he cared for her on a deeper level?

"By all means, let's go see the bees," Rico said magnanimously, oblivious to her conflict. "If there are birds to go with them, I'm sold."

"Your daddy thinks he's funny," she told Lily, trying to hide her insecurities.

"Da." Lily poked him in the cheek.

"Dada, yes." He caught her hand in his big one and kissed the point of her tiny finger. "You're as smart as your mama, aren't you?" He kissed Poppy again. "Yes?"

She shakily nodded.

Rico called to make an offer before they left. A week later, Poppy added meetings with interior designers and landscape contractors to her already busy weeks.

Even with those small successes, she was hideously nervous when she finished dressing for the Montero gala. It was an annual event, one that Sorcha and Rico's mother hosted on alternate years. Sorcha had told her what she had spent on her own gown and said, "Match it. This is your debut as a Montero." Then she had sent her favorite designer to the penthouse to consult with Poppy.

Poppy turned in the mirror, feeling like the biggest fraud in the world. Who was that woman? Had she gone too demure? The gown had a high neck and cap sleeves, but the fitted bodice accentuated her curves. The top was a very dramatic gold satin with a floral pattern in carmine and saffron and chestnut. The skirt was an A-line in crimson silk that moved like pouring paint, graceful and luxurious, following her in a small train even after she put on five-inch heels.

Her final touch was an art deco bracelet the stylist had recommended. Poppy, neophyte that she was, hadn't realized the stones were genuine sapphires and topaz and the gold twenty-four karat until the woman had looked up from her phone with excitement.

"Your husband signed off on it. He *does* want to make a statement, doesn't he?"

Poppy had smiled wanly, head swimming at what she'd accidentally bought.

She felt light-headed now as she walked out to the lounge, wondering what he would make of all of this, especially her hair. It had been straightened to within an inch of its life, then a slip of gold ribbon woven through a waterfall braid around her crown.

Rico paused with his drink halfway to his mouth.

She wrinkled her nose and took a slow turn, corkscrewing the skirt around her. *Super sophisticated,*

Poppy. Don't try that again. She gave it a small ruffle to straighten it then stood tall, facing him again.

He hadn't moved.

"What's wrong?" She started searching for the flaw.

"Absolutely nothing." He set aside his drink and came to her, lifted the hand with the bracelet. "You look stunning."

"Really? Thank you. You look really nice, too." A tuxedo, for heaven's sake. She covered her racing heart. "Are we solving an international crime this evening?"

Someone was definitely targeting his heart. Rico almost said it, but it was too close to the truth.

She looked up at him and he read the sensual awareness that was always there between them, ready to be stoked into flame. There was a glow from deeper within her, too. One that was wide and bright and hot, like the sun about to rise behind the mountains and pierce through him.

It was beautiful, making him catch his breath in a strange anticipation, but he made himself break eye contact and move them out the door.

He was still trying to find the middle ground between providing Poppy the supportive attention she craved and maintaining some sort of governance over himself. He recalled chiding his brother once for having affection for Sorcha. *You don't want to admit you have a weakness where she's concerned.*

It was a weakness. Not only of character. It was a vulnerability that could be exploited so he steeled himself against allowing his affections to run too deep.

Even so, he found himself eager to show her off.

He'd never been one of those men who wore a woman like a badge of virility, but apparently, he was capable of being that guy.

The pride swelling his chest and straining the buttons of his pleated shirt wasn't really about how Poppy made *him* look, though. Hell yes, he stood taller when he escorted her into the marquise behind Cesar's villa. But he stuck close to her not to be seen with her, or even to protect her—which he would in a heartbeat if anyone stepped out of line.

No, he was enjoying watching the way her confidence was blossoming. He couldn't change his world to make it easier for her to fit into it, but seeing her grow more comfortable with these trappings pleased him. *Eased* him.

She smiled and greeted couples she had already met and calmly ignored the occasional sideways glance from people still digesting the gossip that Rico Montero had married the mother of his love child.

She even showed less anxiety when they caught up with his parents, exchanging air kisses with his mother and speaking with genuine enthusiasm about the new house. She had clearly been studying at Sorcha's knee because she then asked his mother, "Would you have time next week to review the floor plan with me? Sorcha assures me I'll need the space for entertaining, but I don't want the front room to feel like a barn."

"Email my assistant. I'm sure she can find an hour for you."

It sounded like a slight, but the fact his mother was willing to make time for her was a glowing compliment.

"You're building a darkroom," Rico's father said.

"Yes." Poppy faltered briefly with surprise, then tried her newfound strategy on him. "I wondered if you could advise me on where best to source the chemicals?"

"Your husband can do that."

Rico bit back a sigh. He held Poppy's elbow cradled in his palm and lightly caressed her inner arm while saying, "It's not always clear whether my father is genuinely interested or merely being polite." *Be polite*, he transmitted with a hard look into his father's profile.

"Rico," his mother murmured, her own stern expression reminding him they were all aware of his father's limitations. And they were in *public*.

"I am interested." Rico's father frowned, being misinterpreted. "Keep me apprised of your progress," he ordered Poppy. "I'd like to observe the process when you're up to full function. La Reina, I've seen people we ought to speak to."

"Of course." They melted into the crowd.

"Wow," Poppy said as they moved away. She slapped a bright smile on her face, but he saw through to the woman who felt ground into the dust.

"This is why the house you found us is so perfect." He stroked her bare arms. "It's even farther away from them than this one."

Her hurt faded and her mouth twitched. "That's not nice."

"No. And you don't realize it, but he was being as nice as he gets. His asking to observe you is quite the commendation."

"Really?" She dipped her chin, skeptical.

"Mmm-hmm. If I cared about scoring points with my parents, I would be high-fiving you right now."

"We could dance instead," Poppy suggested. "What's wrong?"

"Nothing." Except he'd just recalled the steps he was taking that, as far as scoring points with his parents went, would wipe him to below zero in their books. He would owe future favors. *That* was the cost of giving in to base feelings like passion and infatuation.

So he wouldn't.

"Let's dance," he murmured and drew her onto the floor.

CHAPTER NINE

POPPY WAS FALLING for Rico. Really falling. This wasn't the secret crush of a maid for a man who hadn't even noticed her. It wasn't the sexual infatuation of a woman whose husband left her weak with satisfaction every night. It wasn't even the tender affinity of shared love for their daughter, although what she was feeling had its roots in all of those things.

This was the kind of regard her grandparents had felt for each other. She knew because she began doing the sorts of little things for Rico that they used to do for one another. If he tried a particular brandy while they were out, and liked it, she asked the housekeeper to order some in. When discussing the decor of his home office in the new house, she had the designer track down a signed print of his favorite racecar driver, now retired but still revered.

And when she had an appointment to spend the morning looking at photography equipment, she impulsively called Rico's assistant and asked if her husband had plans for lunch. He was pronounced available so she booked herself as his date and made a reservation, dropping in to surprise him.

His PA, a handsome man about her age whom she was meeting in person for the first time, rose to greet her. He looked startled. Alarmed. Maybe even appalled.

"Senora Montero. You're early." He smoothed his expression to a warm and welcoming smile. "I'm Anton. So good to meet you. Why don't I show you around while Senor Montero finishes his meeting?"

Poppy might be a country girl at heart, but she knew a slick city hustle when she was the victim of one. She balked, heart going into free fall. All her optimistic belief that she and Rico were making progress in their marriage disintegrated. One dread-filled question escaped her.

"Who is he with?"

Before Anton could spit out a suitable prevarication, the door to Rico's office cracked. He came out with an older couple. Everyone wore somber expressions.

Rico's face tightened with regret when he saw her. Anton offered a pinched smile of apology. He moved quickly to the closet where the older woman's light coat had been hung.

The older couple both stiffened, clearly recognizing her while Poppy's brain scrambled and somehow made the connection that they must be Faustina's parents.

The brief anguish she had suffered mildewed into horror. Rico wasn't meeting some Other Woman. *She* was that reviled creature.

How did one act in such a profoundly uncomfortable moment? What should she say? All she could conjure was the truth.

"I wanted to surprise you," she admitted to Rico,

voice thick with apology. "I didn't realize you would be tied up." She thought she might be sick.

Rico introduced her to the Cabreras. Neither put out their hand to shake so Poppy kept her own clutched over her purse, nodding and managing a small smile that wasn't returned.

"The woman you 'dated very briefly when your engagement was interrupted,'" Faustina's mother said with a dead look in her eye.

"I'm very sorry," Poppy choked, reminding herself that they had lost their only child and would hurt forever because of it.

"I'm sure you are," Senora Cabrera said bitterly. "Despite gaining all the prestige and wealth my daughter brought to this marriage. What do *you* bring except cheap notoriety and a bastard conceived in adultery?"

Poppy gasped and stumbled slightly as Rico scooped her close, pressing her to stand more behind him than beside him.

"The hypocrisy is mine. Don't take your anger out on Poppy." His tone was so dark and dangerous, she curled a fist into the fabric of his jacket in a useless effort to restrain him, fearing he would physically attack them. "Leave innocent babies out of this altogether."

A profound silence, then Senora Cabrera sniffed with affront. Her husband clenched his teeth so hard, Poppy could have sworn she heard them crunching like hard candy behind the flat line of his lips.

"I've given you some options," Rico continued in a marginally more civilized voice. "Let me know how you'd like to proceed."

"Options," Senor Cabrera spat. "None that are worth

accepting. This is hell," he told Rico forcefully. "You have sent us to hell, Rico. I hope you're happy."

The older man whirled and jerked his head at his wife. She hurried after him. Anton trotted to catch up and escort them to the elevator while Rico swore quietly and viciously as he strode back into his office.

Poppy followed on apprehensive feet, quietly closing the door and pressing her back against it. She watched him pour a drink.

"I am *so* sorry. Anton didn't tell me they would be here or I wouldn't have come. I asked him not to tell you I was dropping in. This is all my fault."

"I knew you were coming." He threw back a full shot. "I thought we would be finished an hour ago. It went long—you were early. Bad timing." He poured a second. "Do you want one?"

"It was that bad?" She wondered how many he'd had before talking to the older couple. Maybe she ought to make some espresso with that machine behind the bar.

"It was difficult." He poured two glasses and brought them to the low table where melting ice water and full cups of coffee sat next to untouched plates of biscotti. He set the fresh glasses into the mix and threw himself into an armchair.

She lowered herself to the sofa, briefly taking in the classic decor of the office with its bookshelves and antique desk. A younger version of Senor Cabrera looked down in judgment from a frame on the wall. She felt utterly helpless. Deserving of blame, yet Rico wasn't casting any, just slouching there, brooding.

"What sort of options did you give them?" She hated

to ask, sensing by their animosity his suggestions hadn't been well received.

"I told them I was stepping down."

"From being president?" A jolt went through her. It was the last thing she had expected. "Why?"

"I have to." He frowned as if it was obvious. "I had my parents prepare them for it when they informed them about you and Lily. I've stayed to keep things on an even keel, but today I gave them the alternatives for transitioning me out of the chair."

She could only blink, remembering what he had told her in the solarium the day Faustina had broken his engagement. Poppy hadn't meant to pry, but she had admitted to not understanding the appeal of an arranged marriage. She had been compelled to ask what he would have gained.

I was to become president of Faustina's father's chemical research firm. Cesar and I work very well together, but this would have given me a playground for my personal projects and ambitions. My chance to shine in my own spotlight.

He'd been self-deprecating, but she had sensed a real desire in him to prove something, if only to himself. She completely understood that. It was akin to what drove her interest in photography.

"What will you do?" she asked now.

"Go back to working under Cesar. There's always room for me there."

But it wasn't what he wanted. "You married Faustina so you could move out from his shadow. You have your own ambitions."

"I'll find another way to pursue them." He flicked his hand, dismissing that desire.

"But—" She frowned. "What happens with this company? Do they become your competitors again?"

"One option is to leave this enterprise under Cesar's direction. Another would be for us to sell this back to them at a discounted price. They'd be gaining a much more lucrative business than when I took over." He muttered into his glass. "So I think that's what they'll choose."

"How much would it impact you if they do? Financially, I mean?" Her blood was congealing in her veins. They'd just bought a house. Not a cute bungalow in a small prairie town that a union wage could pay off in twenty years, but a mansion with acres of grapes and the sort of view that cost more than the house. Her palms were sweating. "Why didn't you tell me this was happening?"

"Because it doesn't affect you. The sting in the pocketbook will be short-lived, some legal fees and a return of some stocks and other holdings. I'll have to restructure my personal portfolio, but our family has weathered worse. Things will balance out."

She could only sit there with a knot of culpability in her middle.

"Rico, I hate that I brought nothing to this marriage. I didn't know I was going to *cost* you. Not like this." Her eyes grew hot and she braced her elbows on her knees to cover her eyes with her palms. "I've been spending like a drunken sailor. I just ordered equipment for— I'll call them. Cancel it." She looked for her purse.

"Poppy." He leaned forward and caught her wrist.

"Don't take this the wrong way, but a few thousand euros on photography equipment isn't going to make a dent in what's about to change hands. Cesar and I have discussed how to finance this. You and I are perfectly fine."

"But this is my fault! Now he's going to hate me, too. Sorcha will stop being my friend. I'm sorry, Rico. I'm so sorry I slept with you and ruined everything."

Her words hit his ears in a crash, like the avalanche of rocks off a cliff that continued roaring and tumbling long after the first crack of thunder, leaving a whiff of acrid dust in the air.

They came on top of words spoken by Señora Cabrera that had made him see red. *A bastard conceived in adultery.*

That was not what Lily was. Their attack against Poppy had been equally blood boiling and now *Poppy* was expressing regret over their daughter's conception?

"Don't you *dare* say that."

Maybe it was the alcohol hitting his system, maybe it was the pent-up tension from his meeting releasing in a snap. Maybe it was simply that he was confronted with Poppy's emotions so often, he was beginning to tap into his own, but rather than suppress his anger, he let himself feel it. It raged through him because her words *hurt*.

"I told you I will never regard Lily as a mistake and don't you ever do it, either." He threw himself to his feet, trying to pace away from the burn of scorn that chased him. "I would give up every last penny I possess so long as I can have her in my life."

Damn, that admission made him uncomfortable. He

shot her a look and saw her sit back, hand over her chest, tears in her eyes. She was biting her lips together, chin crinkling.

Was he scaring her? He swore and pushed a hand into his hair, clenching hard enough to feel the pain of it, trying to grapple himself back under control.

"Thank you, Rico," she said in a voice that scraped. "I hope you know that's all I've ever wanted for her. Parents who love her. Not all of this." She flicked a hand around the room.

"I do know that." He swallowed a lump from his throat, but it remained lodged sideways in his chest. He felt pried open and stood there fighting the sensation.

"But I'm starting to see that you and your family support a lot more people than just me and Lily. It shouldn't be such a revelation to me. When I needed a job, your mother gave me one and I was grateful. Now I can see that this lifestyle you're protecting has value to more people than just you. That's why it's upsetting to me that I'm undermining it. I think I'd feel better about it if you'd at least yell at me."

"I'm not going to yell at you." Was he angry? Yes. About many things, but none that mattered as much as his daughter. "My career ambitions and the bearing our marriage has had on them are insignificant next to what I've gained through this marriage. *You brought our child.* There's nothing else you could have brought that comes close to how important she is to me."

There was a flash of something like yearning in her eyes before she screened them with her lashes. She reached to pluck a tissue from the box and pressed it under each eye.

"It means a lot that you would say that. I struggle with exactly what they said. Every day." Her mouth pulled down at the corners. "Feeling like I snuck in through a side door, using my daughter as a ticket. I feel like such an imposter." She sniffed.

"Stop feeling that way," he ordered, coming over to sit beside her, facing her. "It's a terrible thing to say, but I can't imagine Faustina showing our baby the same sort of love that you show Lily. I'm lucky my child has you as her mother."

Her eyes grew even bigger and swam with even more tears. Her mouth trembled in earnest.

"Please don't cry. You're making me feel like a jerk."

"You're being the opposite of a jerk. That's why I'm crying."

She had worn her hair in a low ponytail today and half of it was coming loose around her face. He wound a tendril around his finger, thinking of how often he saw her wince and pry Lily's fist from the mass, never scolding her for it.

How could anyone resist this mass, though? He dipped his head to rub the ribbon of silk against his lips. Watched her gaze drop to his mouth and tried not to get distracted.

"There's something I've been wanting to ask you," Rico began.

Her gaze flashed upward, brimming with inquisitive light. "Yes?"

Unnatural, fearful hope filled him even as he second-guessed what was on his tongue. He couldn't believe these words were forming inside him. Not as the next strategic move in the building of the Montero empire, either. Not in reaction to what outsiders said about their marriage. No, this was something that had been bubbling in him from the earliest days of their marriage, something he didn't want to examine too closely because it occupied such a deep cavern inside him.

"Rico?" she prompted.

"With the house almost ready, I keep thinking we should talk about filling more of those rooms."

Her pupils threatened to swallow her face. "Another baby?"

"I know you wanted to wait." He let go of her hair and covered the hand that went limp against his thigh. He pressed his lips together, bracing himself for rebuff. "If you're not ready, we can table it, but I wanted to mention it. My relationship with Pia and Cesar—we're not as close as some, but I value them. I realize many things contribute to the distance between you and your half-siblings, but the age gap is a factor. That's why I thought sooner than later would benefit Lily."

He heard his upbringing in the logic of his argument and recognized it as the defense tactic it was. If he kept his feelings firmly out of the discussion, there was no chance they would get trampled on.

Poppy blinked and a fresh tear hit her cheek, diamond bright. "Are you being serious? You want to make a baby with me *on purpose*?"

The magnitude wasn't lost on him. Marriages could be undone. Property could be split. The entanglement of a child—*children*, if he had any say in it—was a far bigger and more permanent commitment.

"I do."

* * *

"You didn't tell me there's such a thing as a babymoon," Rico said a month later as they toured the empty rooms of their villa, inspecting freshly painted walls, window treatments and light fixtures. Furniture delivery would start next week.

"You'd have seen one by now if you had ever changed a diaper," she teased. "Instead of handing Lily off to the nanny."

Rico's mouth twitched, but he only drew her onto the private balcony off their master bedroom. It made her feel like the queen of the world to stand there looking so far out on the Mediterranean she was sure she glimpsed the cowboy boot of Italy.

"Besides, we're not there yet."

After a visit to the doctor a couple of weeks ago, they were officially "trying." Today, Rico had asked the designer about setting up a nursery *when the time comes*. The woman had cheerfully promised a quick turnaround on redecorating the room of their choice. "Most couples take a babymoon for a few weeks so we aren't disrupting their daily life," the woman had added, then had to explain to Rico what it was.

"We never even had a honeymoon," he pointed out now.

"There's been a lot going on. A lot for Lily to adjust to. I wouldn't want to leave her even now, when we're about to move into this house and change everything again."

"We could take her with us."

"I think that's called a family vacation, not a honeymoon."

"You're full of cheek today, aren't you?" He gave one of her lower ones a friendly squeeze. "We could take the nanny so we get our alone time. Really put our back into the honeymoon effort. See if we can't earn ourselves a babymoon."

She chuckled. "So romantic." But she kissed him under his chin, ridiculously in love when he was playful like this—

Oh. There it was. The acknowledgment she'd been avoiding. Because if she admitted to herself that she was fully head over heels, she had to face that he wasn't.

"Romance is not my strong point, but sound logic is."

He gathered her so her arms were folded against his chest, fingertips grazing his open collar, but his words echoed through the hollow spaces growing wider in her chest.

"The transition is almost finished with the Cabreras," he continued. "Cesar has some projects he wants me to take the lead on in a couple of months. I won't have much downtime once I'm knee-deep. This is our window for a getaway. Let's take it."

"If you want to," she murmured, thinking she ought to feel happy. Excited. But she only felt sad. She felt the way she had as a child, wishing her mother and father wanted her. It shouldn't have mattered. She'd been loved by her grandparents.

But she'd still felt the absence of it from people she thought *should* love her.

And she felt it again now.

"What's wrong?"

"Nothing," she lied, conjuring a smile. "Where…? Um…where would you want to go?"

"I don't know. Somewhere that Lily would enjoy and you could play with your new camera. Maybe we could tie in a visit to your grandmother at the end. I know you're missing her."

"You wouldn't mind?"

"Of course not. I wish she would agree to come live with us here. You know you can visit her anytime. I'll come with you as often as I can."

"Thank you." A tiny spark of hope returned. Whenever he doted on her, she thought maybe he *was* coming to love her. Tentative light crept through her. "Okay. Let's do it."

Two weeks later, they were riding elephants through the rainforests of Thailand.

"This is not camping," she told him when they arrived at the hidden grotto where sleep pods were suspended in the trees. "Camping is digging a trench around your tent in a downpour at midnight so you don't drown in your sleep."

"I think this is 'glamping,'" the nanny murmured in an aside as the pod she would share with Lily was pointed out to her. "And *thank you.*"

They dined on rare mushrooms and wild boar, coconut curry soup and tropical fruit with cashews. When they fell asleep, replete from lovemaking, the wind rocked their pod and the frogs crooned a lullaby. They woke to strange birdcalls and the excited trumpet of a baby elephant as it trampled into a mud pool.

Poppy caught some of the elephant's antics with her new toy, a Leica M6. She switched out to her new digital camera to catch some shots of Lily to send to Gran then held her as she fed the baby elephant, chuckling as Lily squealed in delight.

A click made her look up and she found Rico capturing them on his phone.

"New screen saver," he said as he tucked it away.

Poppy flushed with pleasure, in absolute heaven. She began to think she really was living happily-ever-after, cherished by her husband, making a family with him. Her life couldn't be more ideal.

Then, as they came off their last day in the forest to stay a few days at a luxury beach resort on the coast, she discovered that, for all their success the first time, they weren't so lucky this time. She wasn't one-and-done pregnant.

It wasn't even the light spotting that had fooled her with Lily. She had a backache and a heavier than normal case of the blues.

Plenty of women didn't conceive right away. There was no reason she should take it this hard. She knew that in her head, but her heart was lying there in two jagged pieces anyway.

Rico came into the bedroom of their suite as she was coming out of the bathroom.

"I sent the nanny to the beach with Lily. We—" He took off his sunglasses and frowned. "What's wrong?"

He wore a T-shirt and shorts better than any man she'd ever met. The shirt clung to his sculpted shoulders and chest and his legs were tanned and muscled. One of her favorite things in the world was the scrape of his fine hair when she ran the inside of her thigh against his iron-hard ones.

Everything about him was perfect.

And she wasn't. She hadn't even gotten this right.

"It's not working. I'm not pregnant."

"Oh." He was visibly taken aback. "You're sure?"

She bit back a tense, *Of course I'm sure*, and only said, "Yes." She turned her back and threw sunscreen and a few other things into a beach bag.

"But it only took once last time."

"I know that." She drew a patience-gathering breath. "I don't know why it didn't happen." She blinked, fighting tears. "But it didn't and there's nothing I can do about it."

"Poppy." He touched her arm. "It's fine. We're having fun trying, right? Next time."

She didn't want him to be disappointed. That would make her feel worse. But it didn't help to hear him brush it off, either. She dug through her bag, unable to remember if she'd thrown her book in there.

"You go. I'll catch up."

"Poppy. Come on. Don't be upset. This isn't a test that we have to pass or fail."

"Not for you it isn't. For me? Yes it is. Every single day! Either I bring value to this marriage or I'm just a hanger-on."

"I have *never* meant to make you feel like that."

"I feel like that because that's what I *am*." The rope handle of her bag began to cut into her shoulder. She threw the whole works onto the floor, standing outside herself and knowing this was toddler-level behavior, but there was poison sitting deep inside her. The kind that had to come out before it turned her completely septic. "At least when I was looking after my grandparents, I was *contributing*. You don't need me to look after Lily. The nanny does most of the work."

"You *love* Lily. I told you that's all—"

"Yes! I love her. That's what I bring. The ability to give you babies and love them. Except now there's no baby." She flung out a hand.

"We've just started trying! Look." He attempted to take her by the shoulders, but she brushed him off and backed away. "Poppy. I don't know much about this process, but I do know it takes some couples a while. There is no need to be this upset."

"I *want* to be upset!" She hated how backed into a corner she felt. She pushed past him and strode to the middle of the room only to spin around and confront. "But I'm not allowed to be upset, am I? There's no such thing as emotion in your world, is there? I'm supposed to fit into a tiny little box labeled Wife and Mother." She made a square with her hands. "And uphold the family image, except I'll never be able to do that because I'm forever going to be a blotch."

"Calm down," he ordered.

She flung out a hand in a silent, *There it is*.

He heard it, too, and sighed. He gave her a stern look. "You're not a blotch. We've been over all of this. You contribute. I don't know why you struggle to believe that."

"Because I've been a burden my entire life, Rico. My grandparents were planning to do things in their retirement. Take bus tours and travel and *see* things. Instead, they were stuck raising me."

"It didn't sound to me like that was how your grandmother felt."

"That's still how it *was*. That's how I wound up working in your mother's house. I couldn't bear the thought of asking them for money when they'd supported me all those years. Then I came home and bam. Pregnant. Back to being a parasite. Gramps didn't want to sell that house because he was afraid I would go broke paying day care and rent. I was supposed to pay Gran back after all those years she took care of me, but now you're supporting her. *And* me. That feels *great*."

"You are not a parasite. Eleanor is my daughter's great-grandmother. I *want* to look after her. And you."

"See, that's it." She lifted a helpless hand. "Right there. You don't want to look after *me*." She pressed her hand to the fissure in her chest where all her emotions were bleeding out and making a mess on the floor. "You want to look after Lily's mother. Exactly the way they took in their son's daughter for his sake. You don't want *me*, Rico."

"You're upset. Taking things to heart that don't require this much angst."

Her heart was the problem. That much he had right. It felt like her heart was beating outside her chest.

"Do you love me?" she asked, already knowing the answer. "Do you think you're ever going to love me?"

Her question gave him pause. The fact a watchful expression came across his face as he searched for a response that was kind yet truthful was all the answer she needed.

"Because I love you," she admitted, feeling no sense of relief as the words left barbs in her throat. Her lips were so wobbly, her speech was almost slurred. "I love you so much I ache inside, all the time. I want so badly to be enough for you—"

"You are," he cut in gruffly.

"Well, you're not enough for me!" The statement burst out of her, breaking something open in her. Between them. All the delicate filaments that had connected them turned to dust, leaving him pallid. Leaving her throat arid and the rest of her blistered with self-hatred as she threw herself on the pyre, adding, "This isn't enough."

His breath hissed in.

"At least my grandparents loved me, despite the fact I'd been dumped on them. But I waited my whole childhood for my parents to want me. To love me. I can't live like that again, Rico. I can't take up space in your home because your children need a mother. I need more. And what breaks my heart is knowing that you're capable of it. You love Lily. I know you do. But you don't love me and you won't and *that's not fair*."

He let her go.

He shouldn't have let her walk out, but he didn't know what to say. He knew what she wanted to hear him say, but those words had never passed his lips.

From his earliest recollection of hearing the phrase, when he realized other children said those words to their parents, he had instinctively understood it wasn't a sentiment his own parents would want to hear from him. They weren't a family who said such a thing. They weren't supposed to feel it. Or *want* to feel it.

So he let her walk out and close the door with a polite click that sounded like the slam of a vault, locking him out of something precious he had only glimpsed for a second.

Which seemed to empty him of his very soul.

He looked around, recalling dimly that he'd thought to enjoy an afternoon delight before joining their daughter on the beach for sand castles and splashing in the waves.

Not pregnant. He had to admit that had struck harder than he would have expected. It left a hole in his chest that he couldn't identify well enough to plug. He knew how to manage his expectations. He'd spent his entire life keeping his low, so as not to suffer disappointment or loss. Despite that, he was capable of both. He wanted to go after Poppy and ask again, *Are you sure?*

She was sure. The bleak look in her eyes had kicked him in the gut. He wasn't ready to face that again. That despair had nearly had him telling her they didn't have to try again ever, not if a lack of conception was going to hit her so hard it broke something in her.

He wanted a baby, though. The compulsion to build on what they had was beyond voracious. How could Poppy not realize she was an integral part of this new sense of family he was only beginning to understand?

Family wasn't what he'd been taught—loyalty and rising to responsibility, sharing a common history and acting for the good of the whole. That was part of it, but family was also a smiling kiss greeting him when he walked in the door. It was a trusting head on his shoulder and decisions made together. It was a sense that he could relax. That he would be judged less harshly by those closest to him. His mistakes would be forgiven.

Forgive me, he thought despairingly.

And heard her say again, *You're not enough for me.*

He was still trying to find his breath after that one. He knew how it felt to be accepted on condition, better than she realized. The gold standard for approval in his childhood had been a mastery over his emotions. Tears were weakness, passion vulgar. He should only go after things that made sense, that benefited the family, not what he *wanted*.

Do you love me?

He didn't know how. That was the bitter truth.

He would give Poppy nearly anything she asked for, but he refused to say words to her that weren't sincere. How the hell would he know one way or the other if what he felt was love, though? He hadn't had any exposure to that elusive emotion, not until his brother had gone off the rails with Sorcha, causing his parents to shrink in horror, further reinforcing to Rico that deep emotions prompted destructive madness.

Love had *killed* Faustina, for God's sake.

He hated himself for hurting Poppy, though. For failing her. The sick ache sat inside him as he went out and looked for her. She wasn't on a lounger under the cabana with the nanny, watching Lily play in a shaded pocket of sand.

He moved to stand near them, scanning for Poppy, figuring she would turn up here eventually.

It took him a moment to locate her, walking in the wet sand where waves washed ashore and retreated. Was she crying? She looked so desolate on that empty stretch so far from the cheerful crowd of the resort beach.

She wasn't a burden. It killed him that her parents had

let her grow up feeling anything less than precious. She brought light into darkness, laughter into sober rooms.

She had brought him Lily—literally life. He glanced at his daughter. She was batting down each of the castles the nanny made for her. The most enormous well-being filled him whenever he was anywhere near this little sprite. Poppy shone like the sun when she was with Lily, clearly the happiest she could possibly be.

That was why he wanted another baby. He didn't know how to express what he felt for Poppy except to physically make another of these joy factories. With her. He wanted her to have more love. The best of himself, packaged new and flawless, without the jagged edges and rusted wheels. Clean, perfect, unconditional love.

From him.

He swallowed, hands in fists as he absorbed that he may not know how to love, how to express it, but it was inside him. He would die for Lily and if Poppy was hurting, he was hurting.

He couldn't bear that. Not for one more minute.

He looked for her again, intent on going after her.

She had wandered even farther down the beach, past the flags and signage that warned of—

He began jogging after her, to call her back.

Long before he got there, the sea reached with frothy arms that gathered around her legs and dragged her in. One second she was there, the next she was gone.

"Poppy!" he hollered at the top of his lungs and sprinted down the beach.

One moment she was wading along, waves breaking on her shins. Without warning, the water swirled higher.

It dragged with incredible strength against her thighs, eroding the sand from beneath her feet at the same time. The dual force knocked her off-balance and she fell, splooshing under.

It shocked her out of her morose tears, but she knew how to swim. She mostly felt like an idiot, tumbling like a drunk into the surf. As she sputtered to the surface, she glanced around, hoping no one had witnessed her clumsiness.

As she tried to get her feet under her, however, she couldn't find the bottom. She was in far deeper water than she ought to be. As she gave a little dog paddle to get back toward the beach, she realized she was being sucked away from it. Fast.

Panic struck in a rush of adrenaline. She willed herself not to give in to it. This was a rip current. She only knew one thing about them and that was to swim sideways out of it.

She tried, but the beach was disappearing quickly, making her heart beat even quicker. Her swimsuit wrap was dragging and tangling on her arms. When she tried to call out for help, she caught a mouthful of salt water and was so far away, no one would hear her anyway.

Terrified, she flipped onto her back, floating and kicking, trying to get her bearings while she wrestled herself free of the wrap and caught her breath.

Think, think, think.

Oh, dear God. She popped straight and the people were just the size of ants. Had anyone even noticed she'd been swept out? She looked for a boat. Were there sharks? *Don't panic.*

She was beyond where the waves were breaking.

This was where surfers would usually gather, sitting on their boards as they watched the hump of waves, picking and choosing which to ride into shore.

She didn't know how to bodysurf, though. It was all she could do to keep her head up as the waves picked her up and rolled toward the beach without her.

Treading water, she saw nothing, only what looked like a very long swim to shore. She thought she might be on the far side of the current that had carried her out. A crosscurrent was drifting her farther toward the headland, away from where she'd left Lily on the beach.

Lily. She tried not to cry. Lily was safe, she reminded herself.

This was such a stupid mess to be in. She had picked a fight with Rico then walked away to sulk. Why? What did she have to complain about? He treated her like a queen. No one she knew took tropical vacations and rode elephants and slept in five-star oceanfront villas with butler service to the beach.

I'm sorry, baby, she said silently as she began to crawl her arms over her head, aiming for the headland that was a lot farther than she'd ever swum in her life. A few laps in a pool were her limit. Just enough to get her safety badge when she was ten. *I'm sorry, Rico. Please, Gramps, if you can hear me, I need help.*

Rico absconded with a Jet Ski, scaring an adolescent boy into giving it up with whatever expression was on his face. The only words he'd had in him had been a grated, "My wife."

Her coral wrap had been his beacon as he raced to the family with the Jet Skis. Now it was gone.

He ran the Jet Ski along the edge of the riptide, gaze trying to penetrate the cloudy water, searching for a glint of color, of red hair, terrified he'd find her in it and terrified he wouldn't.

He sped out to where the head of the current mushroomed beyond the surf zone, dissipating in a final cloud of sand pulled from the beach. Still nothing.

Dimly he noted two surfers and a lifeguard from the resort joining his search, zigzagging through the surf.

He had to find her. *Had to.*

In a burst of speed, he started down the far side of the rip and had to fight the Jet Ski to get back toward the current. Another one, not as strong, ran parallel to the beach. He realized she might have been drawn toward the headland. It was a huge stretch of water to get there.

Despair began to sink its claws into him.

Bill, help us out, he silently begged her grandfather's spirit.

A glint above the water caught his attention. A drone?

He looked toward the beach and saw the operator waving him toward the headland.

Using the drone as a beacon, he gunned the Jet Ski that direction, searched the chop of waves. *Please, please, please.*

A slender arm slowly came out of the water. It windmilled in a tired backstroke, slapping wearily on re-entry.

Swearing, he raced toward her. The resignation in her eyes as she spotted him told him how close she'd been to giving up. He got near enough she put a hand on the machine, but he had to turn it off and get in the water with her to get her onto it, she was that weak.

She sat in front of him, trembling and coughing, breaths panting and heart hammering through her back into his own slamming in his chest. She hunched weakly while he reached to start the Jet Ski again. He shifted her slightly so he could hold on to her and steered it back to shore.

He was shaking. Barely processing anything other than that he had to get them to dry land.

"I'm sorry," she said when he got to the small dock where the startled family had gathered with damned near every living soul in Thailand.

The crowd gave them a round of applause. The nanny stood with Lily on her hip, eyes wide with horror at the barely averted catastrophe.

"Oh, Lily," Poppy sobbed, and hugged her daughter, but Lily squirmed at her mother's wet embrace.

A lifeguard came to check on Poppy.

"Have a hot shower. You'll be in shock. Lie down and stay warm. Drink lots of water to flush the seawater you drank."

Rico nodded and took her into their villa, bringing her straight into the shower and starting it, peeling off their wet clothes as they stood under the spray.

"I'm so sorry," she said, feeling like she was drowning all over again as the fresh water poured like rain upon them.

He dragged at the tie on her bikini top only to tighten the knot. He turned her and she felt his fingers between her shoulder blades, picking impatiently at the knot.

"I wasn't paying attention. It was stupid. I'm really sorry. Please don't think I did that on purpose. I was upset, but I wouldn't leave Lily. I know she needs me."

"I need you!" he shouted, making her jump.

She turned around and backed into the tiles, catching the loosened top so she clutched the soggy, hanging cups against her cold breasts.

"You scared the hell out of me. I thought—" His face spasmed and she saw drops on his cheeks that might have been from the shower, but might have been something else. "What would I do without you, Poppy?"

He cupped her face and the incendiary light in his eyes was both fury and something else. Something that made her hold her breath as he tenderly pressed his thumbs to the corners of her mouth.

"I wanted to go looking for you the day after the solarium. Do you know that? I didn't know where to start. Ask the staff? It was too revealing. Try to catch you at the hostel? The airport? You hadn't told me the name of the town where you lived, but I imagined I could find out. I didn't want to wait that long or travel that far, though. Not if I could catch you before you left."

He was talking in a voice so thick and heavy with anguish it made her ache.

"It was an irrational impulse, Poppy. We don't have those in this family. I couldn't admit to *myself* how attracted I was. I couldn't let anyone else see it, not even you. I had to live up to my responsibilities. After Cesar, *I* had to show some sense. It was better to let you go. *But I didn't want to.*"

Her mouth trembled. "Then Faustina took away any choice you might have."

"Yes." He moved his hands to lift the bathing suit cups off her chest and high enough to pull the tie free from behind her neck.

Her hair fell in wet tendrils onto her shoulders. He drew her back under the spray, took a squirt of fragrant body wash in his palm and turned her to rub the warm lather over her back and shoulders, working heat into her tired, still trembling muscles.

"Everything in my world went gray. Through the wedding, into my marriage and after she was gone. I didn't care about anything. I had achieved maximum indifference." His hands dug their soapy massage into her muscles, strong and reassuring. "Then Sorcha told me you might have had my baby. I tried to approach the situation rationally. I did. But the test came back inconclusive and I got on the plane. I had to see you. I had to know."

"What if Lily hadn't been yours?"

He turned her. A faint smile touched his mouth. "Can you imagine? There I was spitting fire and fury and you might have said she was Ernesto's."

"The seventy-year-old gardener? Yes, he's always been my type."

He turned her to settle her back against his chest. He ran his firm palms across her upper chest and down her arms, not trying to arouse, but the warmth tingling through her held flickers of the desire that always kindled when they were close.

"I have a feeling it wouldn't have mattered if she wasn't mine." His voice was a grave rumble in his chest. A somber vow against her ear. "I can't see myself turning around and going home just because I happened to be wrong. One way or another, you were meant to be here in my life. I was meant to be Lily's father."

She swallowed, astonished. Shaken. Questioning whether this man of logic really believed in fate.

"You're talking like your bohemian wife who thinks her grandfather can talk to her through the stars."

His hand slowed and his chin rested against her hair. "You think I didn't ask him for help? Did you see the drone above you?"

"No. But that would be a tourist, not Gramps."

"It was in the sky, Poppy. I was begging him for some sign of you."

He turned her to face him.

Her arms twined themselves around his neck because they knew that was where they belonged. Lather lingered to provide a sensual friction between their torsos.

"I love you." He stared deeply into her eyes as he spoke, allowing her to see all the way to the depths of his soul. To the truth of his statement. "I'm sorry it took something like this for me to say it. To *feel* it. In my defense, it was there—I just didn't know what it was."

She tried to hold it together, but her emotions were still all over the place. Her mouth trembled and tears leaked to join the water hitting her cheeks. "I love you, too." Her voice quavered. "I shouldn't have said you weren't enough. I was upset."

"I know." His gaze grew pained. "Maybe instead of 'trying,' we'll just see. Hmm? I don't want you to think our marriage hinges on whether we have another baby. I love *you*."

"Okay. But I really do want your baby." The yearning and disappointment was still there, but as she let her head rest on his shoulder, the hollowness eased. The darkness was dispelled by the light of his love.

"Me, too." He pressed his wet lips to her crown. "And when the time is right, I'm sure we'll have one."

Weeks later, Rico crowded her to scan the strips of negatives with her.

"I want the one I took of you in front of the waterfall," he said.

Poppy never minded the touch of his body against hers, but, "You're here to tell me how your father will behave. Act like him and pick something he might like."

His parents were coming for an early dinner, their first visit to the finished house. Sorcha and Cesar had plans elsewhere so it would be only the four of them. They would show them the beehives and the wine cellar and, at the explicit request of the duque, Poppy would demonstrate her darkroom.

"The waterfall is a good shot," Rico said, not backing off one hairbreadth. "The ripples in your hair mirrored the path of the water. I've wanted to see it since I took it."

It was poorly framed and crooked, but she could fix that.

Actually, it was a decent shot, she decided, once the negative was in the enlarger. It was perfectly focused and the light was quite pretty, dappling through the jungle leaves. It was taken from behind her. She sat up to her waist in the water, looking toward the waterfall. She had been wearing her bikini and the strings were hidden by the fall of her hair so she looked like a naked nymph spied in her natural habitat.

"I am not showing this one to your father."

She had already run test strips from this batch so she set her timer and switched the overhead light to red. Then she set the paper for exposure.

"How long do we have?" His hands settled on her waist.

"Not long enough." The timer went off and she chuckled at the noise of disappointment that escaped him.

She moved the paper into the developer bath and gently rocked until the second timer pinged. She moved the paper to the fixing bath, explaining as she went.

"This last one is water, to wash off the chemicals." She left the image in the final bath.

"See? It's great," he said.

"It is," she agreed, washing her hands and drying them. "*Now* ask me how much time we have."

"Enough?"

"It shouldn't stay in there more than thirty minutes." She closed one eye and wrinkled her nose. "But we shouldn't stay in *here* more than thirty minutes or we won't have time to get ready for our guests."

"I can work with that."

"I know you can," she purred throatily and held up her arms.

He ambled close, crowded her against the counter beside the sink then lifted her to sit upon it. "Have I told you lately how much I love you?"

Every day. She cradled his hard jaw in soft hands, grazing her lips against the stubble coming in because he hadn't yet shaved. "Have I told you lately that you make all of my dreams come true?"

Maybe not all. They were still "seeing," not "trying,"
but their love was tender and new. They were protecting it with gentle words and putting no pressure on it
with expectations they couldn't control.

"I want to," he said, hands slowing as he ran them
over her back and up to pull the thick elastic from her
hair. "I want you to be happy."

"I am. So happy I don't know how to contain it all."
She skimmed her fingers down to his shirt buttons,
good at this now. She smiled as she spread the white
shirt. It glowed pink in the red light. She slid light fingers across the pattern of hair flat against thick muscle
and drew a circle around his dark nipples.

"Me, too," he said, skimming the strap of her sun-
dress down her shoulder and setting kisses along the
tendon at the base of her neck. "I didn't know happiness
like this was possible. That it was as simple as opening my heart, loving and allowing myself to be loved.
You humble me, being brave enough to teach me that."

This was supposed to be a playful quickie, but his
words and the tenderness in his touch were turning it
into something far more profound.

"This is what I wanted the day we made love the
first time. I wanted to know the man you didn't show
to anyone else. Thank you for trusting yourself to me."
She held his head in her hands, gazed on the handsome
face that she read so easily these days. She pressed her
mouth to his.

He took over, gently ravaging in a way that was hungry and passionate and reverent. She responded the way
she always did, helplessly and without reserve. She
trusted herself to him, too, and it was worth that risk.

Their intimacy went beyond the right to open his belt or slide a hand beneath her skirt. His touch was possessive and greedy, but caring and knowing. Hers wasn't hesitant or daring, but confident and welcomed with a growl of appreciation.

He slowed and gazed into her eyes, not because he sensed she needed it, but because, like her, he sensed the magnitude of the moment wrapping around them. Their love would grow over time, but it was real and fixed and imprinted into their souls now. Irrevocable. Unshakable.

They moved in concert, sliding free of the rest of their clothes, losing her panties to a dark corner, drawing close again and *there*. He filled her in a smooth joining that set hot tears of joy to dampen her lashes.

"I love you," she whispered, clinging her arms and legs around him. "I love when we're like this. This is everything."

"Mi amor," he murmured. "You're my heart. My life. Be mine, always."

They moved in the muted struggle of soul mates trying to break the limits of the physical world and become one. For a time, as they moved with synchronicity, mouths sealed and hands chasing shivers across each other's skin, they were nearly there. The rapture held them in a world where only the other existed, where the culmination was a small death to be eluded before the ecstasy of heaven swallowed them whole. Golden light bathed them as they held that delicious shudder of simultaneous orgasm.

Slowly it faded and they drifted back to the earthly world. Poppy came back to awareness of the hard surface where her backside was balanced, the leather of Rico's belt chafing her inner thigh. One bared breast was pressed to his damp chest, his heart still knocking against the swell. His breathing was as unsteady as hers, his arms folded tightly across her back, securing her in her precarious position. She nuzzled her nose in his neck and licked lightly at the salty taste near his Adam's apple.

Within her, he pulsed a final time. She clenched in response.

"I may have a small fetish for the scent of vinegar and sulfur for the rest of my life," he teased, nuzzling her hair. "That was incredible."

She suspected they might have a small something else after this, but she didn't say it. It was only a feeling. An instinct. A premonition she didn't want to jinx.

It proved true a few weeks later.

"Really?" Rico demanded with cautious joy. "It's absolutely confirmed? Because—"

"I know," she assured him, understanding why he was being so careful about getting attached to the idea. She had been wary to believe it, too, despite missing a cycle and having a home test show positive. "But the doctor said yes. I'm pregnant."

He said something under his breath that might have been a curse or a murmur of thanks to a higher power. When he drew her into his embrace, she discovered he was shaking. She felt his chest swell as he consciously took a slow, regulated breath and let it out.

"You're happy?" she guessed, grinning ear to ear, eyes wet as she twined her arms around his waist.

"I want to tell the whole world."

"Most people don't tell anyone until after twelve weeks."

"Can I tell Lily?"

That cracked her up. "Sure. Go ahead."

After a frown of concentration, Lily grabbed a doll by the hair and offered it to Poppy. "Baby."

"Pretty much how I expect my mother to react," Rico drawled. "But at least you and I know what an important occasion this is. Where should we go on our babymoon?"

"I was thinking exotic Saskatchewan?"

"To see your Gran? Excellent idea. But first, come here." He drew her into his lap and kissed her. "I love you."

"I love you, too."

They kissed again and might have let it get a lot steamier, but Lily stuck an arm into the cuddle and said, "Me."

"Yes, I love you, too. Come on." Rico scooped her onto Poppy's lap and kissed the top of his daughter's head. "I don't know where we'll put the new baby, but we'll find room."

EPILOGUE

One year later...

POPPY WATCHED RICO carefully set their infant son in her grandmother's welcoming arms while Poppy's heart swelled so big, she thought it would burst.

"Sé gentil," Lily cautioned her great-grandmother with wide eyes.

"English, button," Rico reminded her, skimming his hand over the rippling red-gold waves. He called Lily button and angel and he called Poppy flash and treasure and keeper of my heart.

"Be gentle," Lily repeated in the near whisper they'd been coaching her to use when her little brother was sleeping. She was two and a half and talking a blue streak in two different languages, sneaking in a little Valencian and the Swiss nanny's French here and there.

"I will be very gentle, my darling," Gran said with a beaming smile and damp eyes. "Will you stand here beside my chair while your mama takes our picture?"

Rico stepped out of the frame, waited while Poppy snapped, then took the camera so she would have a few of her with her grandmother and the children. She didn't let herself wonder how many more chances she would get for photos like this, only embraced that she still had the opportunity today.

"He's beautiful," Gran said, tracing her aged fingertip across the sleep-clenched fist of Guillermo, named for her husband, William. "And heavy," she added ruefully.

"He is," Poppy agreed, gathering up Memo, as Lily was already calling him. Poppy kissed his warm, plump cheek. "Two kilos more than Brenna—that's Sorcha and Cesar's little girl. She's only a couple of weeks younger."

"Brenna is, is, is—" Lily hurried to interject with important information, but hit a wall with her vocabulary.

"Your cousin, sweetheart."

"My cousin," she informed Gran.

"You're very lucky, aren't you? To have a little brother and cousins, too."

"Mateo is bossy."

"Mateo might express similar opinions about his cousin," Rico said with dry amusement, waving Poppy to sit on one end of Gran's small sofa. He took the other and patted his knee for Lily to come into his lap.

Lily relaxed into his chest, head tilted to blink adoringly at her daddy. "Can I see Mateo?"

"In a few days. We're visiting Gran and then we're going camping. Remember?" Poppy said.

"And buy Mateo a toy," Lily recalled.

"That's right. Before we go home, we'll buy toys for him and Enrique."

"And Brenna?"

"And Brenna," Poppy agreed.

"You were so homesick when you first went to Spain. Now look how happy you are." Eleanor reached out her hand to Rico. He took it in his own. "Thank you for making her smile like this."

"Thank *you*." He secured Lily on his lap as he leaned across to kiss Gran's pale knuckles. "We still have a room in Spain for you," he told her for the millionth time. "It's very warm there."

"I'm too old for migrating around the world like a sea turtle," she dismissed with a wave of her hand. "I have my sister and my friends here. But you're sweet to keep asking."

They stayed through the dinner hour so Gran could show off her great-grandchildren and handsome grandson-in-law.

"Poppy is becoming famous for her photography," Gran made a point of announcing over dessert. "There was a bidding war at the auction."

"It was for charity," Poppy said, blushing and downplaying it. "Rico's brother was being nice, topping each bid."

"Don't be modest. That's not what happened at all," Rico chided. "Cesar was incensed that people kept trying to outbid him. My sister-in-law wanted it and he wanted her to have it."

"It was so silly," Poppy said, still blushing. "I could have printed her another."

"They wanted the only one and now they have it," Rico said. The negative had been signed and mounted into the frame. "Poppy has an agent and is filling out her portfolio. We expect she'll have her first show next year. We're heading north in the morning, hoping to catch the aurora borealis."

The whole table said, "Ooh."

The next night, they were ensconced in a resort that billed itself as one of the best places for viewing the northern lights. Their children were abed, the nanny reading a book by the fire and Poppy and Rico were tramping through the trees to a lake that reflected the stars and the sky.

The world was still and monochromatic under the moonlight, the air crisp with the coming fall. They stood holding hands a long moment, absorbing the silence.

"Well, Gramps," Poppy murmured. "We haven't heard from you in ages. Care to say hello?"

Nothing.

"I vote we pass the time by necking," Rico said.

"I always have time for that," Poppy agreed, going into his arms.

His lips were almost touching hers when she sensed something and opened her eyes. She began to laugh.

"There he is."

Rico looked above them and couldn't dismiss the appearance with science. Like love, it was inexplicable, beautiful magic.

* * * * *

MILLS & BOON

THE HEART OF ROMANCE

A ROMANCE FOR EVERY READER

MODERN

Prepare to be swept off your feet by sophisticated, sexy and seductive heroes, in some of the world's most glamourous and romantic locations, where power and passion collide.

HISTORICAL

Escape with historical heroes from time gone by. Whether your passion is for wicked Regency Rakes, muscled Vikings or rugged Highlanders, await the romance of the past.

MEDICAL

Set your pulse racing with dedicated, delectable doctors in the high-pressure world of medicine, where emotions run high and passion, comfort and love are the best medicine.

True Love

Celebrate true love with tender stories of heartfelt romance, from the rush of falling in love to the joy a new baby can bring, and a focus on the emotional heart of a relationship.

Desire

Indulge in secrets and scandal, intense drama and plenty of sizzling hot action with powerful and passionate heroes who have it all: wealth, status, good looks…everything but the right woman.

HEROES

Experience all the excitement of a gripping thriller, with an intense romance at its heart. Resourceful, true-to-life women and strong, fearless men face danger and desire - a killer combination!

To see which titles are coming soon, please visit

millsandboon.co.uk/nextmonth

JOIN US ON SOCIAL MEDIA!

Stay up to date with our latest releases, author news and gossip, special offers and discounts, and all the behind-the-scenes action from Mills & Boon...

 @millsandboon

 @millsandboonuk

 facebook.com/millsandboon

 @millsandboonuk

It might just be true love...

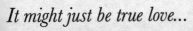

GET YOUR ROMANCE FIX!

Get the latest romance news, exclusive author interviews, story extracts and much more!

blog.millsandboon.co.uk

MILLS & BOON
MODERN

Power and Passion

Prepare to be swept off your feet by sophisticated, sexy and seductive heroes, in some of the world's most glamourous and romantic locations, where power and passion collide.

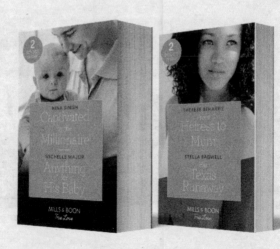